# Sons of Isaac
## Roberta Kells Dorr

MOODY PUBLISHERS

CHICAGO

Edited by Barbara A. Lilland
Interior design: Ragont Design
Cover design: Brand Navigation, LLC
Cover image: © istockphotos LP: Desert scene / CRSHELARE; Sky / Lorado;
                                   Mom & Boys / marcelmooij; Texture / spxchrome;
                                   Isaac / Yuri-Arcurs;

Library of Congress Cataloging-in-Publication Data

Dorr, Roberta Kells.
The sons of isaac / Roberta Kells Dorr.
    pages cm
 Summary: "You will live the grand story of the descendants of Abraham in this capstone of the Roberta Kells Dorr biblical fiction series. This work is a new, previously unpublished title, of Abraham's descendants featuring Isaac's sons, Jacob and Esau, told with the same critical eye and careful study Dorr is known for. In it, faith keeps Abraham from accepting the king's daughter as a wife for Isaac, but fear almost keeps Rebekah from leaving her home to become Isaac's spouse. When God tells Rebekah that she will bear Isaac twin sons and the youngest will serve the older, Jacob is skeptical. But that revelation will mark the lives of Jacob and Esau and influence generations to come. This tale of family love, greed, jealousy, hope, manipulation, stubbornness, idol worship, famine, and faith in the one God, Elohim, is taken from the pages of biblical history but sounds like a headline from today's magazines. It ends much like it begins, when Jacob blesses two of his grandsons, Manasseh and Ephraim, saying that the younger will become greater than the older, a theme that is seen throughout The Sons of Isaac. "-- Provided by publisher.
 ISBN 978-0-8024-0959-1 (pbk.)
 1. Bible. Old Testament--History of Biblical events--Fiction. I. Title.
 PS3554.O694S77 2014
 813'.54--dc23
                      2013049009

We hope you enjoy this book from River North Fiction by Moody Publishers. Our goal is to provide high-quality, thought-provoking books and products that connect truth to your real needs and challenges. For more information on other books and products written and produced from a biblical perspective, go to www.moodypublishers.com or write to:

River North Fiction
Imprint of Moody Publishers
820 N. LaSalle Boulevard
Chicago, IL 60610


1 3 5 7 9 10 8 6 4 2

*Printed in the United States of America*

Old Nahor shuffled out of his room and squinted up at the sky that appeared as a bright, blue patch above the walled courtyard. "It's a good day for a wedding," he muttered. Then slowly with many yawns and a few hiccups, he made his way to the water jar, lifted the lid, and peered down. He could see nothing and so impulsively pulled back his sleeve and thrust his arm into the jar.

"Grandfather, what are you doing?"

Nahor groaned as he pulled his arm out of the jar and turned to face his laughing granddaughter. "There's no water. They've used it all."

"Of course, we've been cleaning and cooking. Have you forgotten? Laban is bringing his new bride home today."

"Who could forget?" Nahor muttered as he pulled down his sleeve. "So her family's rich. Truth is he's getting nothing but an ugly, bucktoothed she goat of a woman."

"Grandfather," she said with a giggle, looking around guiltily. "If Laban heard you . . ." She lifted the heavy jar of water from her head and leaned it carefully against the wall. "I'll help you over to the bench and then get whatever you want."

She took his arm gently. He held back, grimaced, and looked at her. "My son named you wrong. You're not a noose around his neck. I never understood." His old voice cracked with emotion as he shook his head in bewilderment. Reluctantly he let her lead him over to the shaded area beneath the grape arbor.

She helped him ease onto the bench where he usually spent the day. "Father says he called me Rebekah, or noose," she said, "because I was pretty enough to catch a rich husband."

"Of course, of course, he's always thinking of ways to get rich."

"That's just how he thinks," she said. She noticed that in the effort he had lost one of his slippers. Snatching it up, she quickly knelt and helped him work his foot into it.

"Now sit here," she said, "and I'll bring you some fresh water."

When she came back with a dipper overflowing with the clear, cool water, he was still muttering to himself about the name his son, Bethuel, had given his beautiful granddaughter.

"Grandfather, don't worry. I'm his favorite and that's all that really matters."

"Favorite? Then why are dark secrets and bargains made with the clay gods under the stairs?" His eyes grew wild and he wiped his brow with a trembling hand.

For a moment Rebekah was afraid he was about to have another of his fainting fits. "Dark secrets and bargains?" she repeated as she tucked a throw of soft woven material around his shoulders.

He leaned toward her, cupping his hand around his mouth as he whispered, "They've greased the old goat-man's bald head and made big promises if he finds a rich husband for you."

Rebekah squatted beside him. She could hardly believe what she was hearing. "They've refused all the young men who've asked for me."

"Of course, of course, they're greedy. They want riches, gold, favors. And the old clay goat-man is to get it for them."

Rebekah stood up. She knew Nahor had strange dreams and delusions at times. "Maybe you dreamed it," she said.

"Go look, see for yourself." He pointed in the direction of the stairs and then leaned back against the stone wall, exhausted, and closed his eyes. He would doze and forget, but Rebekah was disturbed. She knew her father, Bethuel, and her brother, Laban, put great store by the gods of clay and stone made by old Terah, her great-grandfather, before he left Ur. The god with the greatest powers was the one they called the old goat-man. He was a moon god and could control any situation for a price.

She started toward the pigeon houses fastened to the far wall but stopped when she came to the stairs that led to the roof. She stared at the crude, bolted door that opened to the space below the stairs. Behind this door were shelves on which sat the family gods. Except for the small fertility gods the women were allowed to have, all the gods were kept here. This was a forbidden area for the women. They were not allowed to even look on the gods. Bethuel and Laban carried out the secret rituals at night when everyone else was asleep.

"Go look and see," her grandfather had said. The idea would never have occurred to her, but now she felt she had to know. She had to find out.

With trembling hands she slid the heavy bolt to one side and pulled the great wooden door out toward her. For a moment she was blinded by clouds of incense with their sickeningly sweet smell. She recognized the odor. It was Bethuel's most valuable incense; he had given five sheep for one little jar of it. She waved the smoke away and to her horror saw that her grandfather had been right . . . the old goat-god's bald head was glistening with freshly applied sacred oil.

"Rebekah, what are you doing!" Her mother's voice vibrated with shock and horror. She had come to the edge of the roof and was leaning over the parapet.

Rebekah jumped back, letting the door slam shut.

"It's true. What Grandfather said is true," she stammered.

"What are you talking about?" her mother asked as she came hurrying down the narrow, uneven stairs.

With one swift movement Rebekah pushed the bolt into place and stood with her back to the door. "They've made a bargain with the old goat-man. He's to find a rich husband for me."

"And what's so bad about that?" Her mother stood with her hands on her hips, a puzzled expression on her face.

"All they care about is their own gain and high position. I want something better than that."

"What's better than a rich husband? Laban understands these things. He's even marrying an ugly wife for the gain it will bring him."

"It's his choice. She may not be beautiful but he can have other wives. I can have only one husband."

Her mother brushed past her, muttering, "Your father has burned his prize incense, poured out his most expensive oil. He wants the very best for you and for the family."

Rebekah said no more, but that night she sought out her beloved nurse, Deborah, in the vine-covered shelter on the roof. She told her everything and was comforted when the older woman held her in her arms. "It may not be so bad," she said. "For your family it isn't just the old goat-man god under the stairs but all the gods, even the Elohim of your uncle Abraham."

"They always seem to be at odds with each other," Rebekah said. "Who can we trust? Who is the strongest?"

Deborah drew back and looked at her for a long moment before answering. "All the gods are greedy," she said. "They want gifts and make hard bargains. Your father and your brother are trusting the old goat-man. We'll see what comes of it."

Rebekah adjusted her headpiece and brushed back the coins that fell from it down each side of her face. They made a pleasant tinkling sound as she laughed. She bent over and hugged her nurse. "Then I'll ask the Elohim of my uncle Abraham to find me a husband, and we will see who wins."

* * *

Rebekah had never seen her uncle Abraham or her aunt Sarah. They had left the family long before she was born. She had heard very little of them, and what she had heard was usually carried on in whispers. Even this talk stopped when any of the children appeared. She had finally learned that Abraham and Sarah had no children. (News had reached them of a son born to them in their old age, but that was taken to be a rumor, as it was clearly impossible.) This seemed very strange since her grandfather, Nahor, the brother of Abraham, had eight sons by his wife Milcah and five by his concubine Reumah. Most of these sons were gone on trading trips or out herding their father's sheep.

Rebekah and her brother, Laban, were the children of Bethuel, the youngest son of Nahor and Milcah. They still lived in the home of their grandparents, a large, sprawling house with several courtyards, large kitchens, and adequate space for quite a few animals when it was necessary to bring them inside.

On this particular day Laban was spending the afternoon with the men of his family at the public baths. His bride, Barida, had taken over the same facility with her maidens that very morning. The village of Haran had only one such nicety, which had to be shared. Three days of the week women and children took over the steamy, dark rooms with their warm stone floors and tepid pools, but the other days belonged to the men. If there was a wedding, as was the case on this day, the bride and the women of her family and friends had the morning and the groom with his male family members and friends the afternoon. The people of Haran considered themselves fortunate that the river Balikah flowed nearby and they had plenty of water for bathing and irrigation.

That night Laban and the men of his family would go to escort Barida to his home. The agreement had already been signed and Laban was excited.

Though he had been warned by his mother and his sister of Barida's snaggle-toothed ugliness, he was pleased beyond reason to be marrying into the family of Nazzim.

Nazzim always had the best of everything. His house was of the same mud brick as the rest of the villagers, but it had many rooms and the courtyard was large and shaded. He owned the local caravansary and shop where travelers and men from the village could sit and talk while drinking his fine barley beer or eating roast lamb that turned endlessly on a spit over the fire.

Nazzim was old now. Though his face was creased like a crumpled sheet and his thin lips sucked in over toothless jaws, his eyes were hard as agates and missed nothing. There was now no hint that in his younger days he had been a lusty, handsome man. Numerous stories were told of his questionable exploits right in their village and in the countryside beyond.

It was said that if he saw a woman he wanted, he would go to any lengths and pay any price to get her for his harem. Things had changed now, and it was whispered that he had outlived all of his favorites and had even sent some of the younger women back to their families in disgrace. "They were totally useless," he complained. "None of them were entertaining and any dish they prepared was uneatable."

* * *

As Laban sat getting the last fine shaping of his beard by one of the slaves, he heard a commotion in the outer room. The men with Laban fell silent as they listened. Voices could be heard, muffled and indistinct, rising and falling as though in some urgency. Then there was silence but for the soft padding of bare feet on wet stones.

A young man appeared in the doorway. He stopped and peered around the room until his eyes grew accustomed to the dark. When he spotted Laban, he came quickly and knelt before him. "My lord," he said. "My master, Nazzim, waits outside. He wishes to see you alone."

Laban was immediately alarmed, though he struggled to look unconcerned. He had visions of the old man calling the whole arrangement off, even taking his daughter back to give her to a more likely prospect. "Show him in," he said nervously. He waved for the members of his family to leave him alone.

The young man disappeared and again came the sound of voices in the outer room and then a shuffling, slow, dragging sound accented by the solid thumping made by a staff. Laban's anxiety became acute as he realized how important this meeting must be for Nazzim. The old man had trouble walking and rarely left his own courtyard. What could possibly be so important that he would come to the public bath to seek out the bridegroom of his daughter?

By the time the old man stood in the dim half-light of the doorway, Laban was dabbing the sweat from his brow. He rose and came to kiss the old man's hand as was the custom, then led him to one of the benches that surrounded the wall. "I'm most honored," he stammered as he puzzled over the strange affair.

Nazzim thumped his staff on the hard stone floor and shouted an unintelligible order that brought two young men carrying cushions and a tray with brass goblets filled with his famous date wine. He jabbed the staff at the bench, indicating where he wanted the cushions and the armrests. Then with great difficulty he sat and again ordered the cushions to be adjusted and the armrests to be put in place. When he was comfortable and the young men had helped him pull his feet up so he could sit cross-legged on the bench, he signaled for Laban to come sit beside him.

Laban hurried to accommodate him while the two young men held the tray of drinks for both of them. With this completed, Nazzim motioned for them to wait just outside the door; then he turned to Laban. "This is a good day for our families," the old man said, looking with sharp, piercing eyes at Laban.

"You greatly honor me," Laban said as he tried to find some clue as to Nazzim's purpose in coming.

"May this day be blessed by all the gods," Nazzim continued.

"May I bring happiness to your family," Laban said as he became more relaxed.

"May my daughter be fruitful in your house."

Nazzim obviously had not come to call off the wedding. Laban became more confident that he had come to ask some favor that could not wait. The sense of relief was so great that he was inclined to grant any favor the old man might ask.

The two sat in silence sipping the date wine and testing the atmosphere for any hostility. Finally with guarded words, Laban spoke, "What can I do to show my gratitude for the privilege of marrying your daughter?"

Nazzim stroked his beard and smiled. Laban had obviously said the right thing.

"Since you have broached the subject . . ." He hesitated and looked at Laban as though needing encouragement.

"What subject, my lord?" Laban asked, leaning forward with eager anticipation.

"Why, the subject of marriage," old Nazzim said as he chuckled and then coughed with the exertion.

"Marriage?" Laban said, puzzled. Did the old man have wedding counsel for him at this late hour?

"Yes, marriage. I have decided to marry again."

Laban choked and coughed in surprise. Then collecting himself, he asked, "May I ask who is to receive this great honor?"

Again Nazzim laughed. "Of course, that's why I've come to you. I am an old man but rich. I can give great favor to those I choose." As he said this he leaned over and tapped Laban on the arm. He didn't smile but instead grimaced and nodded with a knowing look.

Laban was more puzzled than ever. He couldn't imagine what he might have to do with Nazzim's getting married. If the old scoundrel wanted help, he would give it gladly. He quickly sifted through the possible meanings and could think of nothing. "You are very generous," he said at last. "I'll do anything I can to help you find the happiness you seek."

Nazzim sucked in his breath and worked his lips back and forth over his toothless gums; a cunning look came on his face. Laban had seen this look before when he was about to make a clever bargain. "Then it is settled."

Laban squirmed uneasily. "Everything is settled but to find who the lucky woman is."

"Of course, of course, I can't expect you to presume so much. How could you possibly guess? Quite simply, it's your sister."

"My sister!" Laban could not keep the surprise from his voice.

"Yes, I believe her name is Rebekah. Strange name. They say she is a beauty and yet is not lazy." Nazzim's small eyes settled on Laban as if waiting for some expression of his pleasure.

Laban squirmed uncomfortably. He smiled a forced, stiff smile and stared at Nazzim. The man was as old as Haran and more feeble. He smelled of musty grain, garlic, and rotting flesh. Rebekah would never go along with such an arrangement if she could help it. It would be very difficult to persuade her. However, he could see many advantages.

9

It was almost as though the old goat-god beneath the stairs had answered their prayers in record time. Someone rich, they had asked, and who in all the area was as rich as Nazzim? If Rebekah married the old man, he began to think, what wealth they would control. With his marriage to the daughter and her marriage to the old father, they would soon be in charge of everything the old man owned.

There had always been a problem when marriage to Rebekah was discussed with other young men and their families. They all expected, even insisted, that any young woman they would consider must first participate in the secret fertility rites at the temple of the goddess. Above all else they wanted a bride who would produce children, and such rites were deemed an absolute necessity. The family of Terah had always managed to cleverly evade these demands by marrying their women within the family. However, with Rebekah there were no young men available within the family.

Now Laban looked closely at Nazzim. He had sons and daughters by his many wives and there was a slight chance he would not feel so strongly about the fertility rites. If he really wanted Rebekah, it was possible he would not insist on the offensive rituals.

Laban felt he must somehow manage this. What did it matter that he was old and repulsive? He was so feeble he was not likely to last a year. "I am honored, greatly honored," Laban stammered as he smiled.

"There is one thing you must do for me first," Nazzim said. "The fertility rites in the temple are not necessary, but it is important that I see her before we draw up the final agreement."

Laban was elated. The old man must have heard from his daughter about the problem of the fertility rites, and he was willing to marry Rebekah without that requirement. He smiled and then quickly frowned. To grant the old man's request to see Rebekah would be very difficult to manage. "Rebekah is sometimes out with my father's sheep and you could . . ." he began hesitantly.

"No, no, no, I am too old to go running about after a pretty shepherdess. It must be something less troubling, something easier."

"You could just happen to be riding by the well at the time the women go out to fill their jars."

Here Nazzim was even more emphatic. He shook his head and muttered a few well-chosen curses. "My son, until now you have been extremely clever. I have been impressed with your understanding of difficult situations."

"If you must see her . . ." Laban dared not show his impatience, but he was getting more and more frustrated.

"To be wise, my son, you must learn to study the facts. The facts will always lead to the solution."

"The facts?"

"Exactly. If you had said, 'Nazzim has hurried here today. There must be some urgency about his request.' Then if you followed with what day it is and what is going to happen this evening . . . you would find an easy solution."

Laban looked at Nazzim and listened closely to what he said, but even then he did not at first understand. "This day is my wedding day," Laban began. "I will come with the men of my family to get Barida and take her to my house." When he said this it began to dawn on him just what Nazzim had in mind.

"Yes, yes," Nazzim broke in impatiently. "It is not usually done . . . but a man of my distinction can make his own rules. If I decide that I, along with the men of my house, wish to escort my daughter to her new home, who would dare criticize?"

"And I am to manage to have my sister where you can see her."

Nazzim beamed. "You are indeed as clever as I had at first thought. Be assured, you will be richly rewarded whether I decide to marry her or not." With that he assumed it was as good as agreed upon. He handed Laban his walking stick to hold for him while he clapped loudly three times for the young men who were waiting for him. They helped him to his feet, gathered up the mats and cushions, and within minutes Laban heard the soft, shuffling sound, the tapping of the walking stick, and Nazzim's heavy breathing.

Then all was quiet.

When the men of his family returned, Laban ignored their questions about Nazzim's visit. He needed time to ponder the strange turn of events. He wanted no discussions on the subject. He was determined to see that no one gave his sister even a hint of his plans until all the arrangements were made and it was too late for them to be changed.

When he reached home he saw that everything was in order for the celebration. "Go to the roof and sit," the women advised. "We don't want you in our way until you are to bring the bride." He had time only to warn them of Nazzim's coming, and then he got out of their way.

Laban headed for the stairs and then turned around and came back. He opened the big door under the stairs and sprinkled more of the precious incense in the dish in front of the old goat-god.

"See Laban," one of Rebekah's maids whispered. "He wants things to go well with his bride tonight."

Laban heard her and laughed to himself. "Not for myself, old goat-man, but may my sister find favor in the eyes of Nazzim."

## 2

*W*hen evening came the men of Nahor's family made final preparations for the short ride through the city of Haran to the house of Nazzim. The dancers and drummers arrived, torches were lit, and last touches were given to the trappings of the donkeys that were to carry Laban and his entourage. Laban was obviously nervous. He shouted orders, made hasty decisions and then canceled them, paced back and forth until old Nahor cautioned that he would wear out the tiles of the court.

When at last the moon rose over the courtyard, Laban announced that it was time to leave. He glanced quickly in the direction of the small room under the stairs and noted with satisfaction that a thin trail of sweet incense was oozing out around the door. The old goat-man should be well pleased with his work.

As he rode out the gate he stopped to anoint the clay plaque dedicated to the moon god, Sin. Sin was the god of the people here in Haran, and Laban believed in acknowledging all the gods. He was determined to leave nothing to chance. He was sure that with these gods favoring him he would at last have the good luck and riches he so desperately wanted.

As he rode along the dark, cobbled streets lit only by moonlight and their own flaring torches, people appeared in the lighted windows above him. Some even leaned over their parapets to shout raucous advice and good wishes, which could hardly be heard over the drumming and singing of the wedding party.

However, as he neared Nazzim's house one old woman leaned far out of her upper window and shouted, "There goes the handsome Laban to marry Nazzim's ugly daughter."

Laban looked up quickly to see who dared to shout such a thing, but the woman had disappeared and the shutters had been quickly pulled together with a bang. He glanced around to see if anyone else had heard what the woman said and then determined that they were more interested in the dancing, jigging step they fashioned to the steady beat of the drums.

It was the words, however, that continued to beat in Laban's head. He wanted to be envied not pitied. If the old women shouted such rubbish, then it was certain that the people of Haran were whispering the same thing behind his back. If they felt that he was so mismatched, what would they think when they heard that Rebekah, who had turned away many suitors, was going to marry old Nazzim? He could feel the blood rising hotly and knew his face was red with frustration.

At last they turned from the narrow lane out into a wide cobbled area. Facing them was an impressive doorway opening to the courtyard of Nazzim's house. Palm branches festooned the opening and torches flickered and flamed. The sweet odor of incense filled the air. From inside the courtyard the cry went up, "The bridegroom comes, the bridegroom comes." Immediately torches appeared along the wall and the cry sounded from every corner of the inner court, across the roof, and down into the servants' quarters. Cymbals crashed and women gave the yodeling joy cry that signaled a wedding procession.

Framed in the gate were dancers and jugglers. Behind them could be seen the bridal party with the bride covered from head to toe in a glittering garment fashioned of imported material decorated with pearls and rare medallions. On her head she wore a queenly crown of cleverly fashioned flowers and gold leaves, and from it hung a bridal veil so thick her features were completely hidden. Laban did not see all of this at first glance, but as they led his tawny donkey in to stand beside her white mule, he noticed every detail.

The torches glinted on the elaborate crown and flickered over the costly gown and elegant trappings of her mule. Only her hands were visible, and they were well shaped and smooth. It was obvious they had been spared from the hard work of most women. He noticed with satisfaction that they were jeweled and decorated with a careful tracery of vines and flowers done in black kohl. If there was anything ugly about his bride, it was carefully hidden under the heavy veil, and for the advantage he was gaining, he could manage to live with that.

She sat with her head held high and had not looked in his direction. Most brides feigned shyness. It was the custom. A shy bride had to be approached like a skittish mule. Every man in Haran knew how to deal with such a situation, but if she were so unafraid and bold as to not be crying and downcast, it bode no good. Laban felt a bit unnerved by the prospect of encountering not only an ugly woman but one who dared look a man in the face as though she were his equal.

With a shrug he dismissed the bad omens and looked beyond her to see Nazzim sitting on a gray mule dressed in his most festive attire. Nazzim had obviously been watching him and now slightly raised his hand in recognition and greeting. A surge of well-being reassured Laban that all would be well. Even the marriage of Nazzim to his sister would be for the best. It was an opportunity that could not be missed and certainly Rebekah would understand.

With a nod of his head and a slight tap of his riding prod to the mule's flank, Laban led the procession out the gate and down the dark lanes that led to his own home, the house of Nahor.

The pleasant odor of meat turning on spits filled the air. Barley cakes were ready to serve hot off the rounded ovens, while big woven trays of fat figs, dried raisins, and nuts of every variety sat waiting to be served.

The women had prepared a raised seat with carpets and cushions for the bride and groom, and beside the bride's seat, a place of special honor for her father, Nazzim.

When the bridal party arrived, Laban's father, Bethuel, met them at the gate and led the bride and her father to the places prepared for them. Laban followed and was surprised to see that when his bride was helped down from her mule, she was as tall as her brothers. She still held her head in the proud, arrogant way he had first noticed. She paused for a moment, lifted the top veil slightly, and took a quick look at her surroundings. This was not something most brides would have dared to do. Once more Laban felt a twinge of concern lest she be more than he could easily manage.

There was some stir when the bridal pair came to be seated. Nazzim insisted on sitting between his daughter and Laban. "How else can you point out your sister?" he whispered.

Laban looked around the courtyard. At first Rebekah seemed to be missing. Then he spotted her squatting beside his grandfather. She had brought him some choice pieces of roast meat on a rounded loaf of bread and was helping him as he ate. "See," Laban said, nodding in the direction of his grandfather's favorite seat next to the wall, "she has gotten some food for the old man."

Nazzim leaned forward and squinted. "Is she always that helpful?" he asked.

"Yes, I suppose so," Laban answered.

Nazzim clutched his arm and spoke in a low, urgent tone, "Get her to come here. I must have a closer look."

Laban was irritated at the old man's insistence, but he didn't dare show his true feelings. Instead he called for one of the servants and ordered him to go bring his sister to serve the bride.

They watched the man go elbowing through the crowd and then talk and gesture toward the dais. Rebekah smiled and nodded, then hurried off. Laban watched her go and almost felt a twinge of pity for her that he hadn't felt before. *She has no idea that with her nice ways and pleasant smile she is sealing her fate. He will pay any price to get her and there will be no way for her to escape.*

When she came back with a tray of the most succulent roast and fattest figs, she first offered his bride the food. Laban noticed it was rejected. Rebekah was not at all upset. Instead she turned to Nazzim and said with her most enticing smile, "I'm sure you must be almost faint with hunger."

"Hunger, yes, yes." He took a bone with some meat on it and began to chew at it, while all the time he was looking at her and mumbling unintelligible grunts of approval. Laban could see the confusion on her face. He glanced quickly at Nazzim and saw that his greedy eyes were traveling over her in much the same way as he would examine a sheep he was going to buy.

Laban had seen enough. He wanted to go through with the deal, and he realized if he watched a second more, he would be calling it off. He dismissed her with a nod and watched her go back to where the women were serving the trays of dried fruit.

Nazzim finished the meat and threw the bone on the floor, then wiped his mouth and fingers on his sleeve. "As fine a young woman as I've seen," he said, turning to Laban. "You can ask your price and I'll pay it."

"You must give me time," Laban said as he thought of the difficulties he would face.

"Don't take too long. I'm an impatient man where pretty women are concerned," Nazzim said.

The remark momentarily sickened Laban, but he quickly squelched the feeling and smiled. "Before the new moon I'll bring you the good news."

With that Nazzim motioned for his men, gave Laban a long, meaningful look, and then followed them out to where his mule was waiting. He had not said a word to his daughter and she had not spoken to him. She appeared silent and unmoving like a graven image. Laban moved over to sit beside her and the crowd of well-wishers shouted and clapped.

Laban would have liked to prolong the time in the courtyard, but he felt so awkward sitting beside this silent, proud woman that he was ready to bring the whole thing to a swift conclusion. To be alone with her was to face the whole bargain squarely, and then he would know just what he had to deal with.

He stood and nodded to the relatives and friends. He noted that they whispered in amazement that he was so obviously anxious to be alone with his bride. At this signal, Rebekah and her mother with the serving girls from Nazzim's house came to lead the bride into the bridal chamber.

Laban glanced at his bride and noted that as she stood she was still holding her head high with the same arrogant air about her. "She is not one to submit to anyone for any reason," he conjectured.

The men led Laban to the side room where he waited for a signal from his mother that the bride was ready for him. As the time passed he became more and more nervous, and the men laughed at him and gave him bits of advice. "First, you must get the veil off so you can look at her face," one of them joked.

"Remember if it isn't to your liking you can send her back to her father before any damage is done," one of the others whispered.

Laban didn't answer. No matter what she looked like, he was going to keep her. Nazzim was rich beyond belief, and with Rebekah married to him they would have control of all the wealth of Haran.

To his surprise it was Rebekah who came to get him. When he stepped outside the door, she whispered, "Your bride insists that she will not take off her veil until daylight. Even though we have made the bed and helped her in, she will not take off the veil."

Laban shrugged. "That may be just as well. Who knows what secrets are hidden by that veil."

\* \* \*

As it turned out Laban was pleasantly surprised. His veiled bride was bold and passionate, with none of the giggling shyness brides were rumored to hide behind. This woman was confident and shamelessly aggressive. Laban even found himself imagining that she was ravishingly beautiful. Since there was no oil lamp and the moon did not shine into the high window of the room, he saw nothing until morning.

When the day dawned Laban woke first and took several moments to figure out where he was and what had happened. He turned and saw his bride, still hidden by the veil, and it all came back to him. Carefully he touched the gold coins that held the veil in place. Immediately Barida was awake. She sat up slowly and then tossing her head she spoke in a slow, deliberate manner, "If you find I am not to your liking, will you send me back?"

"No," Laban answered after a slight hesitation, "I have no intention of sending you back. What made you think I might send you back?"

"I've been told that I am not beautiful. Most men want a woman to be beautiful."

"Who told you that?"

"My father will not have a woman unless she is beautiful."

Laban was quiet for a few minutes while he thought about what he should do and what he should say. He remembered that his first impression of this woman was of someone who was willful and arrogant. He must not give her the satisfaction of knowing that she pleased him in any way. Let her worry a bit about her status. Finally he said, "With me beauty isn't everything. There are other things that matter even more." He didn't tell her what they were.

"Now," he said, "it's time to see the bride." She lifted her head slowly and turned toward him but made no move to unfasten the coins that held the veil. Awkwardly he fumbled with the fasteners and slowly the veil dropped. He had expected her to look away but instead she faced him still with the proud lift to her jaw. She was indeed very plain. She had small eyes pinched into a permanent squint, a large nose like her father's, and her mouth was small and pouting. "For my purposes you will do very well," he said at last.

He never mentioned his disappointment to anyone, and he consoled himself in his choice by reminding himself that his sister, Rebekah, would face a far more difficult proposition. Old Nazzim was lusty and ugly and he could not imagine Rebekah having a moment's happiness. *It will all be worthwhile. He will not require the special fertility rites at the temple, and once the marriage takes place we will be well on our way to controlling the old man's fortune.*

✳ ✳ ✳

Laban wasted no time before telling Rebekah and his father what he had in mind. It was two days later in the afternoon while the others were taking a noonday nap that he broached the subject. "My sister," he began, "my father and I have prayed and given choice gifts to the old goat-man under the stairs. We all know that he has unusual powers."

Here he stopped and looked at Bethuel, hoping he would go on and tell Rebekah about Nazzim. Bethuel said nothing and finally Rebekah asked, "I know you have burned the costly incense and anointed the old god's head, and I have even been told you did all this so he would find a rich husband for me. Is that true?"

Both Laban and Bethuel were taken aback. Neither knew what to say. Finally Laban nodded. "It's true. We asked for a rich husband."

"And?" Rebekah said.

Again Laban and Bethuel looked at each other. Neither wanted to be the one to break the news to her. Finally Laban spoke. "The old goat-man has answered wonderfully. It is the rich Nazzim himself that has asked for your hand."

"Nazzim?" Rebekah puzzled for a moment over the name. "Certainly not the old man that came with Barida?" she said finally.

"Yes, yes," Bethuel said. "He is old and very ugly but he is rich. He could give you everything."

"That's what we asked the old goat-man for . . . a rich husband," Laban said.

"Rich husbands come with some disadvantages," Bethuel hastened to add.

"He is old. You won't be bothered with him for long," Laban said, seeing the look of disgust on Rebekah's face. He desperately wanted her to agree without any unpleasantness.

"Well," she said finally after recovering from her initial shock, "you can go tell the old goat-man I have other plans." She looked at them with complete confidence as though she knew something they didn't.

"What other plans?" they almost shouted.

"Well, when I heard of your dealings with the old goat-man, I went and talked to my old nurse, Deborah. She reminded me of the God of Abraham, Elohim, and I have asked Him to find me a husband."

Bethuel and Laban were speechless for a moment. They couldn't imagine such foolishness. "The God of Abraham," Laban finally said. "He can't be seen; you can't deal with Him."

"Why not?" she asked with a saucy toss of her head.

"Well, you can't bargain with Him," Bethuel said.

"You can't even threaten Him," Laban said.

"We can take the old goat-man out and beat him if he disappoints us, but Abraham's God can't be touched," Bethuel added.

"Where would Abraham's God ever find anyone richer than Nazzim and someone who would not require the fertility rites?" Laban felt they were certainly winning and she would have to agree.

Rebekah was standing with her back to the courtyard wall. Behind her spread a huge grapevine with shiny leaves and ripe fruit. Carefully she pulled off a cluster of grapes and looked at them. It gave her a moment to think. "If by the time of the new moon," she said finally, "Abraham's God has not brought me a better and richer husband, I promise to marry old Nazzim."

Bethuel and Laban looked at each other and smiled. They felt they had won and with so little trouble. "Then you agree to marry Nazzim?" Laban said, wanting to pin her down.

"Only if the God of Abraham fails to send me a better and richer husband," she repeated.

Laban could hardly believe it had been so simple. He smiled again. "The God of Abraham has undoubtedly gone off into the desert with him, and it is the god Sin and the goat-man that rule here. I have no fear that Elohim will hear you or that He will answer and send you a rich husband. This is all just foolishness." He began to feel a bit sorry for her, seeing how trusting she was and how sure she was that the God of Abraham could help her. "To marry Nazzim may seem hard to you, but you won't regret it, I promise you. The old man will be dead in a year and then you can marry anyone you please."

With that Laban and Bethuel went out the gate and left her standing by the grape arbor. "Oh God of my uncle Abraham," she prayed, "You see how they are thinking. If You don't hear me and help me, the old goat-man will win and I will have to marry that horrible old man." There was no answer but she was excited. If the God of Abraham did accomplish this impossible thing, how splendid it would be. She sat down on the bench where Nahor usually sat and enjoyed a few of the dark red grapes.

Would Elohim act in time? Or would she be stuck with the distasteful, ugly old man?

# 3

*A*t this same time, down in the Negev just outside the small town of Gerar, Nahor's brother Abraham sat alone outside his tent mulling over a recurring concern. It had been three years since Abraham's beloved wife, Sarah, had died. As she lay dying he promised her that he would move with all haste and diligence to find their son Isaac a wife. However, after all this time, he had found no one.

Since Isaac was to have the birthright and the blessing, he must marry someone suitable. It couldn't just be one of the local women who believed in omens, charms, and idols. It must be someone like Sarah who understood why they lived apart from the cities and worshiped the creator God. So far he had found no one, but he had consoled himself with the thought that in time Elohim would guide him to the right person.

The irony in the situation was that while he had not found a proper bride for his son, he had taken a concubine for himself. Her name was Keturah and she was from one of the desert tribes friendly to Abraham.

Now as he sat alone, mulling over the past, he found himself remembering all that had taken place since Sarah's death, all that led up to his taking Keturah as his concubine.

It had been one full year after Sarah's death and he had been still groping through abysmal depths of despair. He had taken no interest in his food, friends, or the usually joyful festivals and celebrations. He no longer spent any time in his town house in Gerar, nor did he visit his flocks and shepherds. Worst of all, Sarah's tent remained empty and lifeless as a constant reminder of his loss.

He remembered vividly the evening when all this had changed. It had been just at dusk before the evening star shone in the sky or the moon had risen above the distant palms. His old friend and chief steward, Eleazar, came to him with a suggestion. "The time of grieving is long past," he said. "It's time you picked up the pieces of your life and returned to us. We miss you, old friend. More than that, we're in great need of your good judgment."

Abraham answered, "The world holds no luster for me now. All things seem dull. I care for nothing. This is no easy sickness. No special herbs can cure it and no prayers can add days to my life or bring back the past. It's all gone."

Eleazar did not answer but, instead, idly poked at the small fire in front of them until the thorn branches crackled and snapped and burned more brightly. At just the right moment he reached out and carefully added a pinch of precious incense taken from the leather pouch at his belt. Then he leaned back and waited. Almost immediately a pleasant odor, reminiscent of weddings and happy times, rose from the fire.

Abraham smiled remembering. "And what is the occasion," he asked, "that you are burning such costly incense?"

"Perhaps you have forgotten," Eleazar said, "your good friend who visits you from the wilderness of Paran has hinted that he has a marriageable daughter."

"Have I ever seen her?" Abraham asked, thinking he was suggesting someone for Isaac.

"Perhaps. When she was very small she used to come with her mother, and they would visit Sarah while you talked with your friend."

"Yes, yes I remember," Abraham said. "Such a special little person. When she would get bored with the women and their conversation, I would see her peeping around the qatah dividing my tent, and I would invite her to come sit with her father and me. She would always come quickly and seat herself on a cushion beside us and listen quietly to our discussions. Then she became too old for such things and I didn't see her anymore."

"She's no longer a little girl," Eleazar said. "In fact she is quite a lovely young woman. Not beautiful like Sarah but quite charming."

"You have seen her then?" Abraham asked.

"Yes, she is here with her father. He says he knows you cannot forget your wife, Sarah, but it is time you at least took a concubine. He has brought you his daughter."

"He has brought his daughter for me?" Abraham's eyebrows rose just in the remembering.

"She's too old for Isaac, though she's still of a childbearing age. To take her as a concubine, as her father suggests, would not be so strange. It's often been the custom for a young woman to marry or become the concubine of an older man. It's always been a way of easing the hardship of old age."

Abraham shook his head sadly. "I'm not only old but my best years are over. I've little to give someone like Keturah."

Eleazar laughed. "It's not that you are old; the problem is that you are bored and lonely. Keturah is just the medicine you need."

*  *  *

So in just such a simple, natural way, it came about that Abraham agreed to take Keturah as a concubine. To marry her would have suggested that she was taking Sarah's place, and to move her into Sarah's tent was unthinkable. Abraham had realized that this would be too difficult for Isaac. However, she was given a tent of her own, and within the fortnight Keturah was with child.

Abraham thought it would be difficult for Isaac to accept this new relationship. To his surprise he found that at first Isaac seemed unconcerned about the marriage. He was merely happy to see his father moving among his men as in the past and tending to the affairs of business that had been neglected.

However, a fortnight later Abraham noticed that Isaac seemed to have become disturbed and even moody. He voiced his feelings to no one, but spent a great deal of time wandering out among the rocks and barren places of the desert. He had realized that when this child was born, it could take his place and receive the blessing and the birthright. His father had sent Ishmael away for his sake, but would he also send away any son that Keturah might have?

These thoughts drummed in his head and caused him almost physical pain. He had longed for his father to regain his interest in life, but he had not imagined it would come about in this way. Worse still, he felt guilty for thinking such things.

When the child was born Isaac witnessed with alarm the great feast given in his honor. They had named the child Zimran, meaning celebrated, saying that Abraham was indeed blessed with a concubine who could give him many sons like Zimran.

In the days that followed, Isaac became more and more withdrawn and lonely. Finally, he tried to put aside all such gloomy thoughts by spending more time in his father's house in Gerar and visiting the king's palace. Here he was always welcome. The old king had many wives and a dozen daughters. The young women, like the Egyptians, found it no disgrace to sit with young men and enjoy simple board games like Jackals and Hounds or to play haunting love songs on their decorated lyres.

All of this seemed innocent and to the lonely young man a wonderful distraction. One of the king's daughters was especially attracted to him. Her name was Anatah, suggesting that she was a devotee of the goddess Anat.

Now two years had passed since Abraham had taken Keturah as his concubine and a situation had developed that brought everything to a sudden climax.

It had started with what seemed another harmless visit to the palace in Gerar. Keturah and her handmaidens had been invited to the palace and they needed an escort. It was not thought wise for Keturah to go alone or even with her maidens, since Sarah, on a similar visit, had been forcefully detained and almost married to the king. It was finally decided that Isaac should accompany her so there would be no danger of the same thing happening again.

They went with gifts and serving women and were welcomed with a great show of affection and excitement. There were one or two young princes but many more princesses. It was evident that they had planned an elaborate party. They had taken over the king's royal porch and had ordered a rich feast, even hiring some dancers from the market.

The palace was designed after an Egyptian prince's house. It had formal gardens, a pool with lily pads and frogs, an orchard, and pavilions for the king's slaves and concubines. There was a wall around the grounds and a guard house at the gate. The king of Gerar always explained to visitors that his city was the very gateway to Egypt from the north. Actually during the long history of the city, it had often belonged to Egypt as one of its outposts.

Inside the walls of the palace were the atmosphere, fragrance, and even music of Egypt. Whatever was new in Egypt would be copied in Gerar within the month. The princesses wore the same style clothes and had their hair done by designers from Egypt. Their eyes were outlined in dusky kohl and their hands and feet were softened by lotions and unguents from the bazaars on the Nile. Their guests were travelers from the great cities of Carchemish and Damascus in the north, while from the south, they came from all the cities of the Nile. Only Abraham and his family among the local inhabitants were considered as equals and friends.

Now as the guests found seats on cushions and carpets spread out around the porch, the drumming began and was blended with the high falsetto of one of the singers. One by one, the dancers from the market got up and danced; with slapping feet and swiveling hips, they kept time to the music. A juggler joked and toyed with a handful of walnuts while one of the servants went around passing out small cakes.

"This is boring," Anatah whispered to Isaac. "Let's go to the bench by the pond and play a new game that everyone's playing in Egypt." Isaac was charmed by her attention and readily followed her out into one of the private gardens.

Once settled on a bench she opened out a parchment game board and they both bent over it, trying to decide how the game was played. Every now and then when Anatah wanted to get his attention, she would reach out and touch his hand. Ordinarily this would have seemed very forward, but now in this garden, Isaac thought it was most exciting. He noticed the way her lashes framed her dark eyes and especially the way she tossed her head and half closed her eyes when she laughed at something he had said. Her lips were soft and the way she spoke his name was most provocative.

He felt a strange urge to reach out and hold her hand and perhaps to even kiss her. A certain irresistible feeling drew him to her. To make it even more intriguing, he noticed that she seemed to be feeling the same thing. He briefly wondered what the custom was in this Canaanite palace. Would his touching her hand or kissing her be considered an accepted dalliance, a shameful thing, or an invitation to marriage? *How delightful to be forced to marry someone as lovely as Anatah.*

Soon they no longer even pretended to be playing the game. He was alert to every movement she made and more than that to the scent of tuberoses that floated from her hair and her garments. Her laughter was like sistrum all jangling together, and her smile more brilliant than moonshine on water. He forgot where he was and, most of all, who he was.

When she reached out and took his hand firmly in hers and insisted that she could tell his destiny by reading the lines on his hand, he was so overcome with emotion he hardly heard a word she said. Only the word *lovers* penetrated and strangely moved him. Without waiting for his response, she jumped up, and pulling him to his feet, said, "Come, we must go and pledge ourselves to each other so no one can come between us."

She led him around the edge of the small pond, then pulled some bushes aside to reveal a niche in the stone wall. In the niche was a clay figure. Slowly Isaac realized this was an image of the local earth goddess. The statue had the body of a naked woman with small pointed breasts and a frighteningly ugly head. She had a large nose but there was no mouth and the eyes were slitted and strange. Around her feet curled a snake.

Isaac drew back. He was jolted by the terrible reality of the thing. Anatah was lovely and beautiful, but this image was ugly and he could not imagine what the image could have to do with them.

Anatah laughed. "Don't be afraid. This is my goddess and she will see that we have whatever we desire."

"But she is only clay," Isaac stammered.

"Of course she is clay, but inside the clay is a being of such power that she can grant any wish."

Isaac was astounded. His father had told him about idols but he had said they were lifeless clay or stone and had no power at all. "How," he asked, "can she do this?"

Anatah grew serious. "So it is a jinn but it can grant wishes."

"The jinn are evil spirits," Isaac said, drawing back.

Anatah tossed her head and laughed. "This jinn is good and will grant whatever I ask of it," she said.

With that she flung her arms around Isaac and kissed him, then pulling back she said in a low chanting voice, "This is the man, oh my goddess, that I must have. Grant me my wish and let no one come between us."

For a moment she had a strange look about her eyes and then she released him. "Now you can go," she said in her normal voice. "Your stepmother is probably looking for you. Remember we have pledged in the presence of the great earth goddess and such pledges are binding."

\* \* \*

All the way back to camp Isaac was silent. He rode as in a dream, but it was a disturbing dream. One minute the lovely, desirable Anatah with her tempting lips and seductive glances appeared before him and the next he was remembering the ugly idol in the garden and the ritual he had witnessed and even been a part of.

He found that something strange had happened to him. He wanted

Anatah with a terrible urgency like wanting water when out in the desert and the water skins were empty. To add to his torment Anatah had whispered just before he mounted his mule ready to leave, "Now that we are pledged to each other, I can give myself to you whenever you come."

What would his father say to such things? He feared to tell him and yet he had never held anything back from his father. He must tell him. But instead of being excited and joyful, he dreaded the encounter.

Abraham noticed as the men sat around the campfire that night that Isaac was silent and looked disturbed. Something had happened to his son and it could well have to do with the trip to Gerar. It was always in the cities that evil occurred. Even when he had drawn himself and his family away from them, they still intruded with their evil.

When the others were leaving, Abraham drew Isaac aside and invited him to come sit with him for a time. The two walked back in silence to Abraham's tent, where an oil lamp had been left burning. This was always a favorite time of day for Isaac. Even as a small boy he had loved the evening. To sit just inside his father's tent with the flaps up so they could see the stars was a special treat. They seemed so close, almost alive in the black curtain of the sky.

His father was always talking about the stars. Coming from Ur he knew many interesting facts about them; more than that, he always mentioned the promise. The strange promise from Elohim that his descendants could be numbered as the stars.

Eventually the moon would rise over the jagged mountains to the east, changing familiar objects into mysterious and fanciful shapes. The soft glow of the hanging oil lamp cast long shadows on the sides of the tent and across the ground coverings. It was a magical time, a time for talking and confiding, and the two had shared many such times ever since Isaac could remember. Since it was his habit to never hold anything back from his father, he now struggled to find words to tell him of the strange happenings in Gerar.

"There is a lovely young princess in Gerar," he said finally.

"And, this princess, is she a good match for you?" Abraham asked.

"Oh yes, she loves me and has even made arrangements to give herself to me."

Abraham's eyebrows shot up and his eyes narrowed. His fingers pulled at the fringe on his shawl as he struggled to form a statement or word a question. "So," he said finally, "she plans to give herself to you. Does her father approve?"

"Well, she has the approval of the goddess she worships."

For a moment there was silence. Abraham leaned forward and opened his mouth but no words came. He stared at Isaac as though really seeing him for the first time. He had assumed so much. It had never occurred to him this child of the promise could be tempted by someone who worshiped idols.

Of course it was evident he was no longer a child. In fact he was almost forty years old and might have been married long before this if his mother had lived.

"My son," Abraham said at last, "I have been remiss in that I have not sought out a wife for you as Sarah insisted before she died. Other sons of mine like Ishmael can marry as they please, but you are different. You are the child of promise and those who come from you will inherit the blessing."

Isaac's face clouded as he struggled to put his thoughts into words. "But is a woman of that much importance?" he asked finally.

Abraham understood. Often, even among his own people, it was thought that since the man ruled the family, his wife was of little importance. She was simply a means of bringing children into the world and taking care of them until they could care for themselves. He pondered this as he struggled to find words to express his own thoughts.

"My son," he said, "all my life, starting in my old home in Ur, I have studied the stars and it is evident that there is a pattern in things, a plan behind all that we see. It is the pattern put there by Elohim, and when we fit into that pattern, things go well for us. A father and mother both guide their children and teach them the ways of Elohim. That is His plan."

"But this princess, she's not just beautiful, she's everything I could want in a wife. I would be so happy with her."

Abraham frowned. He had not imagined that it had gone so far. Something must be done quickly, but what he didn't know. This was going to be very difficult. He realized once more that as much as he might wish for a proper wife for Isaac, he knew no one who met the requirements. He wondered what Sarah would have done. Surely she would have known how to find the ideal bride for her beloved son.

"Isaac," he said, "it's late and such important decisions need much thought and prayer. We must not decide this quickly." The two sat for a while longer, discussing a hunting trip into the desert and then Isaac said good night and left for his own tent.

Abraham watched him go with an aching heart. He could see that Isaac was drawn to this woman who was so wrong for him. He saw only the glittering attraction and had no idea of the price he would pay if he married her. *Marriage,* he thought, *is the union of two people who will bring children into the world, and so the world is changed for better or for worse with every new generation. Good children are the reward of wise marriages.*

Abraham sat by the fire for a long time thinking about all that had been said, but most of all he pondered the problem of where he would find the right wife for his son.

Later that night he was unable to sleep. He rose quietly and paced back and forth, trying to piece together some solution to the problem. He bitterly regretted that he had let so much time pass since Sarah's death without finding a wife for Isaac. Certainly a Canaanite princess who worshiped idols was in no way a proper bride for this son who was to have the blessing of Elohim as well as that of Abraham, and would claim the birthright.

Early the next morning he sent for Keturah. Abraham thought that she might have some solution to the problem. Keturah wished she could say something that would relieve his anxiety.

"It's difficult for the lad," she said after reviewing the events of the visit to the palace. "There's no one in our camp who would be really suitable for Isaac."

"It's all the more complicated than it may have seemed at first," Abraham confided. "He says he has found the woman who can make him happy. Her name is Anatah."

"I saw Anatah. She is a proud beauty with a saucy manner that could be quite flattering to any young man she was attracted to."

Abraham groaned. "Where can we ever find a wife for him who is acceptable and who can make him forget someone like that?"

"He'll want to go back," she said, "and what will you say to that?"

"He must not go back. She has told him that since they have pledged themselves in front of the goddess, she will give herself to him even without her father's permission."

Keturah drew back and covered her mouth as though to stifle an expression of shocked disbelief. "In front of one of their images? He told you this?"

Abraham was silent. He felt embarrassment and shame that he hadn't paid more attention to training his son in their beliefs. "It's my fault. I assumed too much. He was the promised son. When I had to take him up on

Moriah to sacrifice him, he trusted me and Elohim."

"As I heard it from Sarah," Keturah said, "he trusted you and you trusted Elohim. That is different. He loves you and will do anything you ask . . . but he knows very little of Elohim."

"How can this be? All my life I have tried to do the will of Elohim. How can my son not know Him?"

* * *

Before the morning star blazed in the eastern sky, Abraham knew what he must do. First of all it was evident that he must send back to his own people in Haran to find a bride. A traveling merchant had brought word of Nahor's family, saying, "By his wife, Milcah, he has eight sons and by his concubine, Reumah, he has four sons." No mention was made of daughters, but undoubtedly there were girls in the family too.

It was true that many of his people still worshiped idols, but they did not engage in the hurtful, evil practices of the Canaanites or the Amorites. To indulge in human sacrifice or to offer young children to the fertility gods was not something his family had ever taken part in. Furthermore they were of the family of the old patriarch, Noah. They had descended from his son Shem, and it was Shem who had Noah's special blessing.

No matter how hard it would be to carry out such a plan, it was the only choice he had. To give his son to one of those who did not have Noah's blessing would be to somehow cheat him of what was due him. A blessing given by a man of God's own choosing, such as Noah, was not lost or dissipated in one or two generations. It would carry down the years, bringing blessing to thousands of children yet unborn.

He wondered if he himself should go back to Haran to choose the bride. Then he thought better of it. He was no longer agile enough to travel so far. It would be better to send someone he could trust. Someone who knew just what was wanted and would be most sensitive to the bidding of Elohim. Immediately one man came to mind, Eleazar, his chief steward. He had never failed in any trust. He was also a man who listened to and knew the voice of Elohim and would not move without such guidance.

He had no doubt that Eleazar would agree to go, but far more difficult would be the persuasion of Isaac. He had trusted his father when they had climbed Mount Moriah, but would he trust his father and Elohim when it meant giving up the princess who had already captured his heart?

He hoped it wasn't too late to find a bride for him who would blot out the memory of the princess of Gerar. This too he must put in the hands of Elohim. Only the creator God could know who was right for Isaac and lead them to her.

It was time to find such a bride.

*A*fter a sleepless night spent in prayer, Abraham walked out into the desert and sat down under an acacia tree to watch the sun come up. He felt as though a great burden had lifted. He didn't know how it would happen, but he felt his prayers had been heard and an answer was on the way.

He walked back to camp with high expectations. As he neared the first tent, a young boy ran to meet him with the news that a messenger had come from the king of Gerar and that he was needed right away.

It was as the boy had said; the messenger carried a written parchment that was fastened with the king's own seal. When Abraham arrived, the messenger stepped forward, broke the seal with a flourish, and read the formal message. To everyone's surprise it announced the coming of the king's steward. The king's steward dealt only with the most serious business of the king's realm and they wondered why he would be coming to visit them.

Immediately after the message was read, the young man snapped the scroll back together and dropped it into the leather case. With military precision he turned and shouted at the few retainers who had come with him. In minutes they were back on their mules headed toward Gerar in a cloud of dust.

As soon as the dust cleared there was much speculation as to what the steward's business might involve. At first it was suggested that it probably concerned the wells and herding grounds that had become crowded. Only Eleazar suggested that it might have to do with the king's daughter.

"Perhaps we should call Isaac and determine just what happened during his visit to the palace," Eleazar said. "If the king believes that Isaac has chosen his daughter, this could be serious enough and important enough for the king's steward to be sent to negotiate the terms."

Abraham was horrified. "It's impossible. My son can never marry a Canaanite. He's the son of promise, the one to receive the blessing and the birthright."

"But don't you see," said Eleazar, "if the king thinks his daughter wants to marry Isaac and they have reason to believe he has agreed to some relationship, it will be very difficult to back out. They will be greatly offended."

"And," said Abraham, tugging at his beard and wiping his brow, "if we are to live in peace with them, we must not offend them."

"There is no offense greater than to spurn a king's offer of his daughter."

Both men sat silently contemplating the possibility of such a disaster. The more they thought about it, the more likely it seemed that the king was sending his chief steward on some such mission. "He wouldn't send his chief steward to discuss the water rights or the grazing difficulties, and a mere boy could deliver an invitation to a feast," Abraham said.

"Do you intend to ask Isaac to be with us when we receive the steward?" Eleazar asked.

"He'll not be here. He's ridden out with my men to Hebron to buy some special rams in the market."

"That's good," Eleazar said, looking relieved. "We must deal with this first and then we can talk to Isaac. It will be better that way."

"If the marriage of the king's daughter is the business to be discussed, it will not come out well, no matter what we say or do. I'm afraid the lad's heart will be broken and the king will be looking for vengeance."

"It may not be that bad," Eleazar said, hoping to cheer his old friend.

"I know exactly how bad it will be. I've dealt with such matters before, and I've always tried to get out of the difficulty by telling half-truths."

"And," said Eleazar, leaning forward with interest, "what will you do this time?"

"I intend to tell the truth. I have only Elohim to help me, and it's hard for Him to help a man who tells half-truths."

Eleazar toyed with the fringe on his robe and struggled to think of something encouraging to say, but in his heart he knew this situation could be both dangerous and hurtful to all of them.

News of the expected guests had reached the women, and while the men had been talking the women had been making preparations. It was a rare honor for the king's chief steward to visit, and under other situations they would have had several days to prepare. Now they rushed around in a great flurry of activity.

Some were making sweet date cakes and others arranged dried figs and choice fat raisins on leaf-covered straw mats. They sent one of the young servants out to milk several goats and another to draw water at the well. Still others spread special floor coverings of fresh woven reeds in the main reception area of Abraham's tent.

Just as everything was ready, one of the young goatherds ran in to say there was a cloud of dust on the horizon in the direction of the city of Gerar. Immediately Abraham rose and went to the door of his tent. He still wore the garments of Ur and spoke with the accent of Mesopotamia. He called for his fringed cloak of fine linen and his girdle of polished brass. A young aide anointed his beard with rose water and fastened his sandals on his feet.

The king's chief steward arrived with all the pomp of his royal position. He had fifty retainers, forty of which were soldiers carrying shields and spears, five carrying banners, three drummers, and two trumpeters running before his chariot. Abraham sent Eleazar out to escort the steward and the king's scribe to his tent while the retainers waited at attention in the hot afternoon sun.

When the steward was finally seated, they exchanged extensive greetings. The weather was discussed, arriving caravans noted, and finally the news of Egypt digested. As always, this gave time for each man to size up the situation.

Abraham was pleased to see that the steward drank the grape wine leisurely and lingered over the honey cakes. All this took place before the steward was even ready to begin edging toward the business he had come to discuss.

"My friend," he said as he slowly ran his finger around the edge of the brass goblet, "you have found exceptional favor in the eyes of the king."

Abraham nodded and waited with growing apprehension to hear what had brought this all about.

"The king has observed that you manage your business well."

"He is kind to say such things."

"He has even heard that you speak five languages."

"I was a merchant for some years, and one must learn many languages in such a business."

"It seems that at one time you were a special friend of the pharaoh of Egypt. Is that true?"

"Yes, yes, that is true." He could tell by the man's hesitation and sly look that he wanted to ask about Sarah's experience with the pharaoh but didn't dare for fear of offending him.

"You have a fine son," he said slowly as he gave Abraham a penetrating look. "I have seen him at times in Gerar. I suppose he will marry a princess

34

from Egypt." Though Abraham knew it was the custom for any messenger to edge up cautiously onto the main subject of his visit, still this bantering made him uneasy. He was especially uncomfortable as the subject of marriage and his son was brought up. The steward was obviously closing in.

"No, there are no plans for my son to marry an Egyptian princess."

"Do you have plans for him to marry within your family, or perhaps the daughter of a friend?"

"We are making such plans concerning my family." Abraham felt trapped. He could see clearly where things were going and he had no way of stopping them.

The steward didn't seem to hear the hint. "Well, if he is not yet betrothed to anyone, my news will certainly find a ready welcome." Slowly and deliberately, the steward wiped his hands on the scented towel held for him by one of the young servants, waved aside the tray holding the date cakes, and turned to face Abraham. "My lord," he said, "you will be delighted to hear the king has found that his daughter Anatah favors the young Isaac. She has had many suitors but now insists she wants only your son." He leaned back among the cushions and smiled. He was relaxed and confident as he waited to get some reaction from Abraham.

"I'm aware of the mutual attraction that exists between the princess and my son," Abraham said slowly and deliberately as he struggled to find words that would not offend the king's messenger but would put an end to the matter.

Thinking that Abraham was waiting for more information, the steward continued, "There are only a few very minor conditions that must be agreed to first."

"Minor conditions?" Abraham said, frowning.

"Yes, they are very minor but important to the king."

"And . . ." Abraham said as he struggled to remain calm.

"Any king would require the same." He took the scroll from the scribe and unrolled it. "You will see the first is simply that his daughter and her husband must remain in the city of Gerar. It is quite obvious that the young man must become a part of the royal household. He must worship our gods and would be expected to pledge himself to defend the king at all times. If these simple conditions can be agreed upon, it will bind your two families closer together and make these young people very happy."

Abraham's worst fears had come to pass. He dared not offend the king's steward, and yet the conditions were impossible. How could Isaac, the son of promise, marry a foreign princess? Furthermore it was unthinkable that he become a part of the worship and the family of the king. "I am greatly honored," he said. "The king's daughter is a great prize. To be a part of the king's household is also a very great honor."

The steward smiled. "Then it is all very simple. I've brought the king's scribe with me, and the agreement that must be signed. It can all be done very easily."

The scribe's aides had quickly placed the small stand in front of Abraham with the reeds all laid out ready for the signing.

Abraham was appalled. He saw that there was going to be no easy way out of the dilemma. He must do something that was entirely contrary to his very nature; he must be strong and resolute even if it offended the king. "My friend," he said, "as much as I admire the king, this marriage can never take place."

The steward was shocked. "What do you mean? This is a great honor for you and your family. How can it be refused?"

"I am well aware of the honor. I wish it were possible to accept, but I must be honest, this marriage can never take place."

There was a moment of stunned silence and then the scribe backed off with a look of scorn. He snapped the scroll back into its case, gathered up the reeds and the stand, and then retreated to the waiting retainers. The steward stood to his feet. "The princess is very desirable," he said as his mouth twisted into a sneer. "She has other suitors who will be glad to hear that your son no longer stands in their way."

"I have no doubt this is true," Abraham said, standing. "It's not that the princess is not desirable or that the king's offer is not generous. It's because of our faith and commitment to the creator God we call Elohim. He is the one who governs our lives and makes such an agreement impossible."

It was obvious the steward did not understand. He motioned for his chariot and then turned back to Abraham. "You must realize that we also worship the creator God. It's just that we worship the other gods too."

"Ah yes," Abraham said, "I remember. When the old king took my wife into his harem, it was the creator God who warned him in a dream."

For a few moments the steward stood and thought about all that had been said. Then turning to Abraham with a stern, forbidding look, he said, "It would be better for you to leave this god if He spoils such opportunities. That is what most of us do."

As the chariot of the king's steward disappeared in a cloud of dust and his retainers followed with their half-running march, Abraham sank back among the cushions and mopped his brow. "Eleazar," he said at last, "I hope I never have to do a harder thing."

Eleazar sat down beside him, obviously very thoughtful. When he spoke it was with foreboding. "You still have an even harder thing before you. I know you well, and to tell Isaac the news will be most difficult." Abraham did not answer but Eleazar noticed that his face turned pale and his eyes registered the pain that he felt.

*  *  *

Isaac found his father still sitting where the king's steward had left him. Eleazar was beside him and the half-eaten trays of dried fruit and sweet cakes were stacked over on the side. Abraham stood and Isaac came and kissed his hand and embraced him. "My father," he said, "I'm sorry to have caused you so much trouble."

"I wish there could have been some other choice," Abraham said.

"The goatherder Zeb came and told me everything," Isaac said. "I wish I had been here. Perhaps then things would have been different."

"I know how disappointed you are. We must understand that to the king his terms were not difficult. They were to be expected."

"How will I ever find a bride? Most fathers will have terms that would not be pleasing to Elohim."

"Ah, my son, that is where we have failed. We should have asked Elohim to find the right bride for you."

Isaac sat down where his father had motioned. He was obviously puzzled. He didn't understand how such a thing could be done.

"I have been thinking," Abraham said, "and I have already talked to Eleazar. We both feel the right bride will be found among our own people in Haran."

"But that is very far away," Isaac said.

Abraham didn't answer. The silence was broken only by the sound of dried thistles snapping in the fire and the lonesome cooing of a pair of doves in the nearby hedge.

"As you know," he said finally, "I have another son, a firstborn son, and I may have many more sons, but you are the son of promise. You will inherit both the blessing and the birthright, and those that come from you will in turn inherit the promise and the blessing. This is a great privilege and a great responsibility. You cannot marry a Canaanite or an Egyptian as Ishmael did. You are the chosen one, the son of the promise, and there are choices you cannot make."

"And do we know there is going to be someone in Haran for me?" Isaac asked.

"No, we only know that some time ago, before your mother's death, a merchant brought news that Nahor had a large family. Certainly any woman who is of age will be promised to someone, but there may be a young woman who hasn't been spoken for. We must also realize that even if she is unmarried, she may not agree to travel so far to marry someone she doesn't know. We are trusting Elohim to lead us."

There was a long moment of silence and then Isaac asked, "So what do we do now?"

"It takes a wise man to observe and choose quality. Eleazar is such a man. He is also a man who listens closely for guidance from Elohim just as I do. He will choose the very best for you."

"I suppose this is one of those times when you will remind us that God will provide." He said it with respect but there was a bit of an edge to his voice.

Abraham didn't see his face or respond to the tone of his voice. Instead he was simply pleased. He had not known whether Isaac would remember the words Elohim had given him the day he left for Mount Moriah, thinking he must sacrifice his son.

"It's true, my son," he said, "and what our God gives is always the very best."

There was again silence as each thought of all this might mean to them. "Well," Isaac said finally, "I suppose the choice I would have made seems very foolish to you, but you have not seen Anatah."

Abraham was already planning the venture and he did not hear the lack of enthusiasm in his son's voice. "Within the week Eleazar will leave for Haran," he said. "It will take that long to prepare the camels and arrange for gifts for my family and the young maiden."

Isaac found it hard to be excited about the venture. He had many questions that no one seemed to be answering. *What father would willingly let his daughter travel so far from home, and what young woman would agree to go with a complete stranger? Also, if she is very attractive, she will already be promised to someone.* Though he did not express his reservations, he was not satisfied that Eleazar would be able to choose the right bride for him.

Finally he gleaned some comfort from a conversation he chanced to overhear between his father and Eleazar. "The Lord God of heaven," Abraham said, "which took me from my father's house; which swear unto me saying, 'unto your seed will I give this land,' He will send an angel before you. The angel will guide you to the right one and will have prepared her heart to come with you."

How strange this was. Elohim, the Creator of the whole earth and sky and creatures and fish and fowl, cared enough about him to actually send an angel to guide Eleazar. He was immediately curious to know what sort of woman this would be. What woman would the angel lead Eleazar to, and how would he know it was the right one?

✳ ✳ ✳

Later that night Abraham made another difficult decision. It would be impossible under the circumstances for them to spend so much time in the city of Gerar and to continue such close ties with the king. They must move again, and this time farther into the Negev, where they would not be expected to participate in the life of any of the cities. "We will move to the region of the well at La-hai-roi," he said aloud.

The name had been given the well after Hagar had met the angel there. "The well of the living God who sees me," it had been called. It was on the way to Shur and in the midst of a desert region where they would encounter only merchants and travelers going to and from Egypt. *As soon as Eleazar leaves I will send to have the house in Gerar closed and give the order to move our camp. This will help Isaac forget the princess and will keep any new bride from being influenced by the temptations of the city.*

✳ ✳ ✳

In the palace in Gerar, Anatah was furious with her father and the clay goddess. She felt they had both failed her. Isaac had wanted her as much as she had wanted him. What had gone wrong? She was too proud to show her disappointment before her father and his court, but she was not too proud to confront the goddess who had cruelly tricked her.

She made her way to the small garden near the quiet pool just at moonrise when the court of the women was quiet and everyone was supposed to be asleep. A mist hung in the air; the leaves of the small trees were already wet with the evening dew. Just as she reached the niche where the goddess stood, she broke off a branch from the olive tree nearby. With a few swift movements, she soundly thrashed the stone figure. "That will show you," she whispered. "You have totally failed me and I won't forget it."

She was so angry she wanted to do something that would hurt the cool, silent goddess that seemed to sit unmoved by her pain. "I hate you," she said. "You have no shame. It's because of their God they call Elohim that Isaac won't marry me. Doesn't that burn your ears?"

She stood gazing at the image and it infuriated her that it seemed so calm and confident. She had trusted it so completely. It had never occurred to her that it could fail her.

She sat down on the bench beside the pool and tried to think. *Perhaps the clay goddess may not have totally failed. Where will the family of Isaac ever find another bride for him? He can't marry any of the shepherd folk and his father has been at a loss to find a bride for him all these years. Why would they think that now it will be any different?* She smiled. "The goddess may win yet. I may not have lost him if there is no one else available." With that she went to the image and twisted the olive branch into a crown around her head. "Forgive me, oh wise one," she said. "You may yet have other means to bring about my desire."

With that assurance, she went to bed and slept soundly. Isaac must surely be hers soon.

## 5

*I*t took fifteen days for Eleazar to prepare the camels, round up the supplies, and consult on the best route to take for the journey. During this time Abraham was restless and thoughtful. He remembered vividly how his brother had acted the last time he had seen him. Nahor had been totally against his leaving Haran, had accused him of breaking up the family, deserting his father's grave, and making it impossible for their family to continue in their lucrative trading enterprises. Abraham wondered if he had changed. More to the point, would he let anyone from his family go off with a stranger to marry the son of this brother who had so disappointed him?

He paced back and forth, keeping within the bounds of the tent's deep shadow as he pondered the intricacies of the situation. This was the strange part of the whole thing. He was making all these plans and sending his steward on this long journey and he had no real assurance there was a suitable maiden available. He had only the nudging feeling when he prayed that this was what he should do.

*I must send the ring with the family emblem on it so my brother will know Eleazar comes at my bidding,* he thought as he turned the ring on his finger and pondered the difficulties. For a brief moment he considered sending Isaac so they could see the fine lad and be more sure to approve a marriage.

"No, I must not do that," he muttered. "Nahor has always been crafty and it would be just like him to keep him there. He'd let him marry one of their young maidens but would insist on his staying and working for him. No," he concluded, "the lad stays here."

Next Abraham began to fear that Nahor might convince Eleazar to take a bride from the local women. He was totally capable of hiding any relatives and offering some other young woman instead. He would not easily be willing to part with anyone from his own family. Abraham wondered how he could keep Eleazar from falling for such a ruse.

If he insisted that Eleazar take a strong oath to propose marriage only to someone from the family of old Terah, this should work. Oaths were respected in every country and among all people.

There were many ways of making an oath binding, but an oath taken on the honor of one's ancestors and one's descendants was the most binding. To place the hand under the thigh invoked both groups as witnesses and guardians. It was just this sort of oath Abraham had in mind.

Just as he was mulling over these problems, Eleazar appeared around the side of the tent. "My lord," he said, "the camels are being groomed for the trip, and early tomorrow morning we will load them and start out for Haran."

"Come sit with me," Abraham said. "There is much to be discussed."

"Yes," Eleazar said as he went into the tent and sat down in the place Abraham had indicated. "I hope my journey to Haran is successful. It has occurred to me that even if I find the girl and she meets all our requirements, she may not agree to come with me. Should I offer to bring Isaac to Haran?"

"No," Abraham said quickly. "If she will not come, you are free from any responsibility, but do not consent to take my son to Haran."

Now to make the agreement binding, Abraham called witnesses and Eleazar put his hand under Abraham's thigh and swore to abide by all Abraham's instructions.

* * *

The next morning, long before dawn, Eleazar assembled his entourage. He took ten camels loaded with provisions for the trip and with presents for Abraham's family in Haran. The journey had been carefully planned. The first goal was to reach the wells at Beersheba before the heat of the day, and then the next evening travel on to Hebron. From there they would discuss with other travelers whether to go down to Jericho or travel up the central ridge to the fords of the Jordan.

Many routes led to Damascus and they must determine which were the safest and best for them. From Damascus to Haran they must again gather information from fellow travelers. It was a long and tiresome journey but comparatively safe since most of the area was under Egyptian control.

Before they left, Abraham appeared out of the shadows of his tent leaning on Isaac's arm. "I must speak a final blessing on your journey," he said.

At that Eleazar gathered the camel drivers, guards, and general servants to come and stand before Abraham. It was like many other mornings but strangely different. The moon had not set and the east was still dark beyond the jagged mountains of the wilderness of Zin. The brook Besor with its narrow band of oleanders and reeds was dank and mysterious with the rising mist. The nesting birds and small animals that lived along its banks were not yet awake.

It was a magical time and they were all caught up in the romantic purpose of their journey. This time it was not for trade or adventure but to find a young woman and bring her back as a bride for Abraham's handsome son. None of them knew if such a woman existed. After all their effort and struggle, the journey could prove futile. To any thoughtful man it would seem foolishness. The dream of the old man who stood before them spurred them on. To him it was all-important and so they must go and do their best.

Abraham must have sensed some of their doubts because he again reminded them, "The Lord God of heaven, which took me from my father's house and from the land of my kindred, and which spoke to me saying, 'unto your seed I will give this land'; He shall send His angel before you and you shall take a wife for my son from there." The steady look in his eyes and the firm assurance in his voice gave them confidence. However, their ultimate comfort during difficulties on the road would come from his reminder that an angel would go before them to prepare the way.

At the last moment, just as Eleazar was ready to mount and give the word for the caravan to move out along the path, Isaac motioned for him to wait. From his leather girdle he took a small box of intricate design. "When you find the maiden it would please me for you to give her these. They were my mother's most prized possessions."

He opened the box and showed Eleazar the earrings of pure beaten gold and two bracelets of ten shekels weight. "You will have other jewels to give her and other more costly ornaments, but this is more precious because it is all that I have of real value from my mother."

Isaac was confused and unsure of his true feelings. He simply knew that this would have pleased his mother and he determined, for her sake, to go along with the plans peacefully.

Abraham wept in the darkness of the predawn mist and was comforted. He knew by the gift that Isaac too was beginning to trust the dream. Perhaps, in time, he would also stop yearning for the princess of Gerar.

They stood together and watched as the camels moved out and away onto the road that led up the valley to Beersheba.

* * *

As Eleazar traveled, he thought about the young woman he was to choose. What sort of woman must she be, and how would he recognize her? At first he thought that surely he must choose the most beautiful maiden. She would be competing for Isaac's heart with the princess of Gerar. He pictured himself looking over any women who might be in Nahor's family and then choosing the most attractive one.

However as he rode along he found his whole concept changing. Physical beauty did not last. He had seen young girls who were astonishingly beautiful who soon after the marriage became frumpish and coarse. Then again he had seen women who were quite plain blossom into women of real beauty.

How could one possibly tell what a woman would become? How would Elohim judge the right woman for Abraham's son? He thought of Isaac's attraction to Anatah's beauty. He knew nothing about her disposition or character. It was obvious that this was not the way to choose a partner for life.

He pondered over the various traits that were important. She should be honest and kind; one almost took these for granted. Beyond that, he began to see that if a woman was always complaining and unhappy, a husband would soon tire of her, and if she was selfish, it would color all her relationships.

His final conclusion was that a generous, happy woman would make the best choice. One would not tire of her and he had noted that generous people were usually happy. Sorting out the women of Haran might be very difficult. He would have to take it one step at a time and depend on Elohim to guide him.

* * *

The caravan traveled at night when it was cooler, and finally arrived in sight of the town of Haran just at daybreak. Eleazar knew the women of the village would soon be going to the well to draw water, and so he found the well and camped there. He could observe them and perhaps get some clue as to what sort of women he would find in Haran. Surely the women who came for water at this hour would not be the lazy, unpleasant ones.

He stopped near the well and directed his camels with their drivers to rest in the shade of a large almond tree. It was the time of year that the tart, green outer shell of the almond was especially good, and since the tree was out in the open and unprotected, they felt sure it was public property. Eleazar plucked a handful of green almonds and then sat on the low stone wall beside the well.

He could see that the water was reached by six stone steps that were uneven and worn from constant use. The morning sun cast a warm glow on the smooth stones of the wall and glinted from the leaves of the caper plants that grew out of the cracks. Off to one side was a stone trough, and Eleazar surmised that this well was also used for watering the flocks.

Looking up the road toward the village, he could see one lone figure hurrying along with the jar on her shoulder tipped at a jaunty angle, signifying she was a maiden, unmarried. Behind her, just leaving the gate, were other young women and children, and then a few older women with jars standing upright, which signified their married state. They were coming at a more leisurely pace.

Eleazar felt his pulse quicken. How would he approach this first young woman? How would he find out what he needed to know? He stood up and prayed. "Oh Lord God of my master Abraham, here I stand by the well of water where the daughters of the men of this city are coming to draw water. Let it come to pass that the young maiden to whom I ask a drink of water will not only give me to drink but will say that she will give my camels to drink also."

Before he finished praying, the young maiden he had first noticed came to the steps of the well. He caught a glimpse of her face as she lifted the clay jar from her shoulder and was startled by her dark beauty. The wind had blown her mantle off and her hair bounced and curled about her flushed face. She stooped and lowered the jar into the water, then stood up holding it out from her while it dripped. He saw her more clearly now and realized what he had taken for great beauty was more simply the joy and animation that shone in her face. There was a healthy vitality about her, and he found himself hoping with all his being that she would measure up to his strange test.

Quickly he approached her. "Would you mind giving me a drink from your water jar?"

She turned around and seemed to notice him for the first time. She smiled and tossing back her hair mounted the steps until she stood beside him. "Drink, my lord," she said as she lowered the jar on one hand and clasped the neck with the other. The water was fresh and cool and he drank from his cupped hands until he was satisfied.

"I'll draw water for your camels also," she said as she turned and emptied the jar into the trough. Without another word, she hurried back to the well and drew water and filled the trough again and again until all the camels had finished drinking.

Eleazar was astounded. He had asked that he be guided to the right woman by just such a test, and yet he could not believe what he was seeing. To give him water was easy, but to give water to his camels was something even the slaves balked at. Thirsty camels drank copiously. Joy flooded through him as he realized that only God could have brought about such a miracle. But stranger still, it was evident that God had also been at work here in Haran before he even arrived.

He held his peace while he watched her watering the camels. *Surely there can be no one more generous.* When she had finished he could no longer restrain himself. "Whose daughter are you," he asked, "and by chance is there room in your father's house for us to lodge?"

"I am the daughter of Bethuel, the son of Milcah and Nahor," she said. Then looking up at him with her light brown eyes flecked with gold and long, curved lashes, she added, "We have both straw and provisions for your animals and plenty of room for you and your men."

At that Eleazar was almost overcome with wonder and amazement. "Blessed be the Lord God of my master Abraham," he said, bowing his head, "who has led me straight to the house of my master's brethren."

He took from his belt the small olive wood box Isaac had given him and drew out the golden earrings and the two bracelets. As he put the bracelets on her arm, he said, "The young son of my master sent these for you."

Rebekah stood for a moment arranging the bracelets and fingering the gold earrings, too overcome with excitement to speak.

Finally with a quick, bright smile, she said, "I have heard my father and grandfather speak often of my uncle Abraham. They will be so happy. I must run quickly and tell them of your arrival." With that she set the heavy jar down in the sand and went running along the worn path back to the city.

When she arrived home and flung open the door to the courtyard, she was immediately confronted by her brother Laban. "Where's the water you were to have brought?" he asked angrily.

"And where's the jar?" her mother questioned. They had all been waiting impatiently for the water she had gone to fetch. It was usually the job of the new bride to bring water for the family, but Laban had objected, saying his bride was not used to such lowly tasks. Rebekah hadn't objected since she loved to be outside and getting the water was one of her favorite errands.

When she hesitated and didn't answer right away, Laban grabbed her by the arm impatiently. "Where have you been? It should take only a short time to get water . . ." He stopped suddenly as he looked down at her wrist and saw the bracelets. Immediately his eyes narrowed into suspicious slits while his mouth twisted unpleasantly. "And where did these come from?" he demanded.

By this time everyone in the family had gathered around, and they were all looking at the bracelets. "Where? How? Who?" they chorused.

Rebekah pulled away from Laban and smiled as she fingered the new earrings. "The most wonderful thing has happened," she said breathlessly.

"You've no doubt been out acting the flirt. Spoiling your chances to marry Nazzim," Laban shouted in frustration.

"Don't you see?" she said impatiently, "My prayer to the God of our uncle Abraham may have been answered."

A stunned silence greeted her announcement and then Laban spoke. His voice was low and controlled but his words shot out like poisoned arrows. "You can't spoil our agreement with Nazzim. There's gold and influence at stake. No simple trader can equal that."

Rebekah was unmoved by his hostile demeanor. "Go see for yourself," she said. "His servant is still by the well with all his camels."

Laban cursed. "By the gods I'll soon put an end to this," he said, whirling around and hurrying out the gate.

The minute he was gone the whole courtyard sprang to life. Deborah reached her first. "Oh my dear child," she said. "How are you so sure this is an answer to our prayer?"

Rebekah pulled back her mantle so her nurse could see the gold earrings more clearly and held out her arm for all of them to see the bracelets sparkling in the morning sunlight. "The servant said these were for me from the son of my uncle. I need no greater proof."

Her old nurse began to wipe the tears of joy from her eyes, but Nahor, sitting under the grape arbor, roused himself to say, "Laban has set great store by this marriage to Nazzim. He'll not be easily turned aside."

Rebekah ran to him and held out her arm so he could see the bracelets. "Grandfather, I am not afraid. I prayed with Deborah and now see what has happened already."

Nahor reached out and touched the bracelets, and with his almost sightless eyes, he struggled to see the earrings. "Have no faith in the gods," he said. "My brother Abraham trusted the unseen God and it brought nothing but heartache to our family. He has no family, no connections. How can he be anything but a poor shepherd?"

Rebekah hugged her grandfather. "I know you don't trust the gods," she said, "but your brother trusted his God, and we will soon hear from his servant what has become of him."

"Don't hope for too much, my dear," he said. "You have your brother Laban to deal with. When he wants something he usually gets it, one way or another."

6

*L*aban had mixed emotions as he hurried toward the city gate. He doubted that the stranger, if sent by their uncle Abraham, intended anything but some sort of reconciliation. Abraham was probably in trouble of some kind and wanted to be reinstated as head of their family. Then the very idea that he had a son by Sarah was preposterous. Sarah had never had a child. What could all this mean?

When he came to the gate he paused. By this time many of the women were returning from the well, and they were all abuzz with amazement at what they had seen.

"A messenger from your uncle Abraham," an old woman gasped breathlessly as she shuffled toward him. She was too old to be shy. She was the go-between in family quarrels and the matchmaker for any young daughter. At times she even condescended to tell fortunes. She carried no water jar, as she went to the well only for the gossip. It was obvious that on this day she felt she had plenty to tell.

Laban was her first target. She clutched him by the sleeve. "Ten camels loaded with treasure," she hissed just loud enough for those around to hear.

Laban pulled away but she lunged after him and clutched his sleeve even more firmly. "You've not heard the strangest news."

Laban turned toward her, scowling but interested. "What do you know?" he urged.

The old woman cupped her hand around her mouth and stretching up whispered, "Be careful. The man lies."

"What do you mean?" Laban could not resist hearing more.

"He says your grandfather's sister, Sarah, has had a son. We know that can't be true. She'd be too old."

Laban was again puzzled. He hesitated while he juggled the information around the known facts. His face took on a crafty look. "You can be sure, old one, I'll not be fooled," he said finally. With that he turned and walked more slowly toward the well.

His mind was spinning with all sorts of possibilities. Who could this stranger be? What did he want of them? He must remember what was at stake. He had seen the gold earrings and the bracelets, gifts fine enough for a bride. He must not let this sway him. Rebekah must marry Nazzim. He must not let her get her hopes up. At the same time he determined to treat the stranger with all the courtesy and hospitality their family was known for.

By this time he could see the camels lying under the almond tree and he could just make out their elegant trappings. If this was indeed a messenger from his uncle, he must be bringing good news, for only a man of great wealth could possess such an extensive caravan. He pushed all his doubts and fears to one side and strode with great dignity the rest of the way.

He noticed a tall, stately older man coming toward him. "You must be that young maid's brother, Laban," he said.

"Indeed I am Laban the son of Bethuel who is the son of Milcah, which she bore to Nahor." He had quickly assessed the importance of the man and his entourage. It was obvious he came with important credentials. Laban was impressed and anxious to extend the required hospitality. "We are waiting and ready," he said. "We are honored to receive messengers from my uncle Abraham."

Laban led the way back to the house through throngs of villagers hastily assembled to see the newcomers, who were reported to bear news of their former neighbor, Abraham. He said no more as he besieged on every side with questions, but when they reached the door to the courtyard, he waved the curious villagers back, opened the door, and motioned to Eleazar. "Come in, come in," he said, "thou blessed of the God of my uncle Abraham. See, I have prepared the house and there is room for all your men and camels."

Laban quickly ordered his servants to help Eleazar's men unload and feed the camels, then bed them down on the far side of the courtyard reserved for animals. He was pleased to see a fine feast being prepared under the sheltered area of the court. It was obvious that friends and neighbors had responded generously and in fact were still slipping extra bread and roast chickens through the servants' door.

Bethuel himself came forward with a pitcher of water and a servant to wash the feet of Eleazar, while Laban ordered the servants to wash the feet of the rest of the men.

By the time the sun was high in the sky and all the niceties had been accomplished, the women had finished preparing the feast. They had placed the last stack of bread on the mat and had withdrawn when Laban came forward and urged the men to be seated. They all gathered around the food and were ready to eat when Eleazar, still standing, raised his hand and to everyone's surprise addressed them. "I will not eat until I have delivered the message I was sent to bring from your relative Abraham."

Laban paused and turned toward him eagerly, while Rebekah and her nurse, with some of her other maidens, came to stand behind a shuttered window where they could hear all that was said in the courtyard.

"I am Abraham's servant," Eleazar began. "I must tell you that the Lord has blessed my master greatly with flocks and herds, silver and gold, camels and asses as well as menservants and maidservants. He has become a very great and important man.

"Furthermore," he continued, "Sarah, my master's wife, bore a son to my master when she was old." At this juncture there was a gasp of surprise and those listening interrupted with cries of joy and exclamations of amazement.

When they were quieted at last, Eleazar continued, "It is to this son my master has given all that he has, and it is for this son a bride is to be found." Again there were such expressions of surprise and excitement that for a time Eleazar could not continue. Even the women listening in the back rooms gazed at each other with bated breath and smiled with knowing nods.

This time Laban, who had become very interested in the story, raised his hand and commanded everyone to be quiet and listen to what Eleazar had to say. When they became attentive Eleazar hurried on. "My master is determined that his son should not marry a Canaanite. For this reason he commissioned me to come here to the country of his own people and seek out a maiden. And so I have come at my master's bidding."

"What made you think any young woman would leave her family and her people to travel so far with a stranger?" The questioner was old Nahor himself, who had stood with great difficulty and was leaning on Bethuel's arm.

"I asked that same question of my master," said Eleazar.

"Yes, yes, what did he say? What was his answer?" Laban leaned forward eagerly.

"He said, 'The Lord, before whom I walk, will send His angel with you, and will prosper your way; and you shall take a wife for my son from my kindred and from my father's house.'"

"But," said Laban, thinking of his sister and their unofficial agreement with Nazzim, "if the maiden is already promised to another and cannot go?"

"Ah then," said Eleazar, "I am freed from my oath. However, since I have come I have been much encouraged."

"Encouraged, how?" Laban demanded.

Eleazar smiled. "When I came to your well, I stopped and prayed, 'O Lord God of my master, when the young virgins come down to draw water, if there is one who, when I ask, will give me a drink of water and then will agree to water my camels also, let this be the one for my master's son.'"

Laban grew uncomfortable and Bethuel shifted nervously from one foot to the other. Rebekah, looking from the window, let out a gasp of surprise and reached out to grasp Deborah's hand. Eleazar seemed not to notice their reactions but continued, "Before I had finished speaking in my heart, Rebekah came with her jar and drew water then willingly gave me to drink and offered to water my camels also.

"I could hardly believe what I was seeing," Eleazar continued. "'Whose daughter are you?' I asked. When she told me she was the daughter of Bethuel of the house of Nahor I bowed my head and gave thanks to the God of my master, who had led me in the right way to take my master's brother's daughter for his son."

Both Bethuel and Laban were silent. They had never heard of a god working in such a direct manner. They also remembered that Rebekah had prayed to Abraham's God. How very strange it was that all of these events had fit together so perfectly. If Eleazar had come just a few weeks later she would have been married to Nazzim.

Could it really be possible that an angel had guided Eleazar and then had also prepared them in Haran for his coming?

Eleazar raised his head and looked around at each one of them as he said, "Now tell me if you intend to deal kindly with my master and, if not, let me know so that I may look elsewhere for a wife for my master's son."

Behind the shutters of the window, Rebekah closed her eyes and held her breath waiting for Laban's answer. It would be the greatest miracle of all if he would agree to let her go. He would not only be missing out on his many plans but would have to somehow inform Nazzim that the agreement had to be canceled.

Now both Bethuel and Laban were in awe of a God who seemed to work so openly and to express His desires so firmly. To hear that even an angel had guided Eleazar was impressive. They looked at each other and knew they could not go against such a demonstration of the strength of Abraham's God. Laban spoke for both of them, "It's obvious this thing proceeds from the Lord, the God of my uncle Abraham. We cannot come against it; Rebekah is free to go with you to become your master's son's wife as the Lord has spoken."

When Eleazar heard this he bowed down to the ground and then rose to his knees with hands in the air and tears running down his cheeks. Words of praise were on his lips for the miraculous way in which the God of Abraham had brought about His will.

When he rose he asked that Rebekah might be brought out and seated in the chair of honor so that he could give her the gifts sent by the household of her prospective bridegroom. Rebekah came, still dressed in the simple garments she had worn to the well. Her mantle of coarse stuff that would not stay in place let her curling hair peep out around her face; her feet were bare and she wore no jewelry except for the earrings and bracelets given her at the well by Eleazar. She hesitantly sat down and then looked around, eagerly wondering what would happen next.

Quickly Eleazar ordered his men to bring out the presents. Right away there was a great stir in the stables where the camels were lodged. Then slowly, one after the other, the servants of Eleazar appeared carrying gifts to be laid at Rebekah's feet. There were trays holding ornate headpieces with carefully worked silver leaves and stylized flowers. There were casks filled with the most exquisite gold and silver jewelry inlaid with large and costly gems. Quickly this was followed by brass and marble incense burners with the incense wrapped in leather bundles decorated with drawings of Egyptian flowers and birds. Beside them were placed alabaster urns with precious and rare fragrances. There was linen from the looms of Egypt, fine textured gauze mantles from Gaza, and embroidered doeskin slippers from the craftsmen of Damascus. There seemed to be no end of the delights.

When Rebekah had at last received all of her gifts, there followed even more gifts for the whole family of Nahor. Even Laban, who was usually thinking of making the best deal and what profit was involved, was impressed. "It's settled," he told his father. "It's only right that Rebekah should marry her cousin."

* * *

Quite unnoticed by any of the revelers, Laban's wife, Barida, was standing in the shadow of the doorway leading into the women's quarters. She had witnessed everything and finally had heard what Laban said. She was angry and upset. She had counted on her father's marriage to Rebekah. She had even hoped that in that event she and Laban could move back into her own home with her father. She was already smarting under the watchful eye of her mother-in-law and she found it most unpleasant. If she could move back into her own home, she would easily manage to be in control, and she had to be in control if she was to be at all happy. To wait until she had sons and Laban's parents were dead would take too long. She must somehow get word to her father so this whole farcical development could be stopped.

All afternoon she paced up and down digging her nails into her arms, pulling her hair, and cursing her evil luck. If she could only get a message to her father in time. She could depend on him to be livid with anger. He would act forcefully and swiftly. Slowly she devised a plan that would have to be carried out under the cover of darkness.

Just as the sun set and darkness descended over the house of Nahor and the village of Haran, Barida put her plan into action. She called her little serving maid to her rooms. "Quick," she ordered her in a whisper, "you must go and warn my father that my husband, Laban, is in the very act of arranging a marriage for his sister with a distant cousin. My father must act immediately or it will be too late."

The girl repeated the message to be sure she could remember it, and then slipped out and headed for the back gate where there would be less chance of being noticed.

Barida's plan would probably have worked but for one mistake. She was so angry she could not resist threatening Laban when he finally returned to their room. "It seems you have forgotten that your sister is promised to my father," she said. "If your plans actually work out, he'll never forgive you for such an insult."

Laban swung around and glared at her suspiciously. "What do you mean, 'if'? There is no 'if' about it. My sister will go with this messenger and marry our cousin. It's better this way."

Barida laughed a cold, cynical laugh. "You forget, it seems, that she was promised to my father. He's counting on it. He's not used to being disappointed."

Laban was instantly defensive. He had known there would be trouble, but he could not resist claiming the wonderful gifts that Abraham had sent. These were gifts to be enjoyed right away, while it could be a long time before he would be able to claim any of Nazzim's wealth. This was a sure thing, while to depend on a scheme involving Nazzim was not so sure. Nazzim could marry Rebekah, and if he was not pleased with her return her the next day, and there would go all of Laban's carefully made plans.

Barida realized she had to act fast. Her father was old and often confused. She couldn't depend on his prompt reaction to the news she had sent to him. She quickly decided to tell Laban what she had done. She was sure he would be afraid to proceed further with his troublesome plans. Given enough time she had no doubt her father would put pressure on Laban and his family so that Rebekah would be forced to marry him.

"My lord," she said with a toss of her head and a strange tightness to her mouth, "my serving girl has already gone to deliver the message to my father that his promised bride is about to be given to another. I have no doubt that he will act quickly to put an end to your crafty plans."

Laban clenched his fists and glared at her in disbelief. He had underestimated Barida, but he had no doubt about Nazzim and his anger and penchant for wreaking vengeance upon anyone who stood in his way. He knew very well what trouble Nazzim could cause. He had been foolishly counting on enough time to work something out. Now there was no time. Nazzim would be descending upon them at any moment. Such was the anger of the man when aroused that he could very well arrange for Rebekah to be disfigured or killed so that if he couldn't have her neither would anyone else. In fact it was possible that under the circumstances he would no longer want her but would not allow her to marry anyone else.

These thoughts raced through his mind as he swung around to face Barida. He grabbed her by the arm and pulled her toward him so that he was glaring directly into her pinched and watery eyes. "By the gods of my family, you will not succeed."

She laughed a harsh, defiant laugh. "Your gods are from Ur and have no effect here. It is my father's god called Sin that rules."

Laban was half-afraid she might be right, and so he let out a vile oath and flung her from him as he left the room.

＊ ＊ ＊

As Laban came out into the courtyard, he found only the women sweeping and kneading the bread for the morning meal. He was about to go on up to the roof when his mother came hurrying toward him. "Laban," she whispered, "I must see you immediately." By the look on her face Laban knew something very serious had happened. Without a word he followed her to the small receiving room off the courtyard.

The minute the door was closed, she leaned toward him and whispered, "I have your wife's maid locked in the provisions room. I don't know what mischief she was about, but I caught her leaving from the back gate. She's crying and threatening terrible things. Of course Barida was sending her."

A look of surprise crossed his face and then he grinned and rubbed his hands together. "You caught her going out the back gate? You did well, very well," he said. "You've saved us a great deal of trouble."

"I'm sure Barida will be upset."

"Barida will be very upset. She needs to be upset. She's already trying to control things."

"Where could she have been going at this hour of the day?"

"I just talked to Barida. She was sending her to Nazzim."

"To Nazzim?" His mother was puzzled.

"It's obvious she intended to stop Rebekah's good fortune. She wanted her father to come and put an end to all our plans."

The mother's hands flew to her face as a look of horror spread across it. "What'll we do? What can we say? Nazzim's very strong."

Laban ran his fingers through his hair and grimaced. "There's no time. Something must be done fast, but what?"

The two stood looking at each other. It all seemed quite hopeless. Sooner or later Nazzim would be sure to win. Stopping Barida's maid gave them time, but so little time. If they were going to do anything, it would take much more time.

Laban shrugged. "I have to go tell Eleazar. He needs to know." With that he turned and went slowly up the stone stairs that led to the roof where the men were still sitting. Laban found them reclining on the stiff woolen mats stuffed with straw, leaning on the cushioned armrests, and drinking his mother's best fig wine. A slight breeze blew and the moon shown through the leaves of the grape arbor with a soft and magical light.

The men were asking questions and mulling over Eleazar's astonishing answers. They were hearing more of their relative and his obvious success when Laban burst into their midst with his dire news.

"We have not been honest with you, my generous friend," he said, looking at Eleazar directly. "My sister has been all but promised to a prominent, very wealthy old man, the father of my wife. It seems that my wife has already made one attempt to alert him to our plans, and we can be sure to hear of his violent reaction soon."

Immediately everyone began to talk and to explain while Eleazar sat in a stunned silence. He could tell by their agitation that this was no simple problem. He had been so happy, so sure of God's guidance and the rightness of all that had transpired. How could this have happened? He well knew the violent reactions of men like Nazzim and their families under such circumstances. It touched their honor at its most vulnerable point, and they would hurry to wreak the most terrible revenge. A wealthy, prominent older man would have resources and be able to devise torments undreamed of by the ordinary citizen.

They were all looking at Eleazer and he had no answers to give. He tried to think what his master, Abraham, would do under these circumstances, and he knew that he would insist there was no escape without prayer for guidance from Elohim. He looked around at their faces and saw that they had no idea of what this involved. They would think it complete foolishness, but he had no other answer to give. He stood and faced them. "I only know," he said, "that I have been guided in a most miraculous way to your house and to your young maiden. Surely the God who guided me here will give us the wisdom we need to meet this difficulty." With that he turned and went down the stairs to join his men sleeping out under the soft night air of the far courtyard.

Laban flung off his headgear in frustration and kicked the clay mugs of wine, making them spill across the tiles in a red streak. "The man is a fool to depend on some mysterious angel or his God. Nazzim has armed retainers and a host of the local gods to come to his aid. I have been foolish to entertain such plans for Rebekah. We will all be attacked one way or another." With that he dashed for the stairs; taking them two at a time, he landed at the bottom not knowing what he should do. When he ventured into the far court, he found

Eleazar and his men already sound asleep.

Laban paused by the door that led to the idol's shrine under the stairs. From around the door came a sweet smell and small wisps of smoke. Laban realized that either his father or his grandfather had taken the matter into his own hands and had implored the old goat-man to intervene in this problem of Rebekah's marriage.

He gently lifted the latch and opened the door a slight crack. In the dim light of the oil lamp, it looked as though the idol was smiling. "So you think you've won," he muttered. "You aren't afraid of Abraham's God? We know what side He's on. He wants our sister for this Isaac."

Laban was about to close the door and go back to the roof when quite suddenly Nahor appeared out of the shadows. He was shuffling along and leaning heavily on his gnarled cane.

"So you're wondering," Nahor said, "who prepared the incense and lit the lamp and for what purpose."

"Of course," Laban said.

"I don't want Rebekah to leave. I never wanted Abraham to leave."

Laban was not surprised. "You want Rebekah to marry Nazzim?"

"No, no, not that old man," Nahor said, thumping his cane on the hard packed earth. "The old idol must do better."

Laban chuckled. "He's smiling in there. What does that mean?"

Nahor came close enough to whisper, "He's about to show us how strong he is."

For a moment there was silence between them as they thought of all that might mean. Then Laban turned and headed for the stairs. "We'll see," he said. He went back up the stairs to the roof, lay down on the straw mats under the grape arbor, and pondered the situation. After rehearsing all the facts in his mind, he came to the conclusion that this time there was no way the God of his uncle Abraham could win. It was obvious the old goat-man favored Nazzim, and it was only a matter of time before Nazzim would come to claim Rebekah. No matter how clever this Eleazar might be, there was not enough time for any plan he might devise. Laban shifted to a more comfortable position, but he could not sleep.

**7**

*E*arly the next morning Eleazar woke his men and ordered them to prepare the camels for departure. This did not take long and they were soon gathered for the repast Bethuel and Laban had promised them. The sun was just coming up over the roofs of the nearby houses and somewhere over the far wall a rooster began to crow. One of Laban's shepherds knocked on the courtyard door and handed in a kidskin container of fresh goat's milk, while fresh bread was passed around with chunks of tart smoked cheese. The men ate with relish and then sat silently waiting for Eleazar to tell them what they were going to do.

Eleazar ate calmly and with unusual deliberation. When he had finished, he turned to the three men of Rebekah's family. "It's obvious to me that we must leave immediately. I have accomplished all that my master commanded."

Rebekah's mother stood in the shadows, and when she heard what he intended to do, she let out an anguished cry and rushed forward. "Please, I beg of you, let my daughter stay with us awhile. It's so far to Canaan. We may never see her again."

Eleazar answered slowly, "Do not keep me. I understand your concern. I wish it could be an easy matter. However, you have seen how my way was prepared, and now it is clear to me that the time has come to return to my master."

Then Bethuel, who saw the wisdom of the man's decision, stood up. "We must send for Rebekah," he said, "and let her decide." With that he led the men of the family to the visiting room and sent the mother to bring Rebekah.

When they were by themselves, Laban said, "This seems to be very wise. If they linger even a short time, Nazzim will be down on us with his men like a pack of wolves."

"But if she goes with him, old Nazzim will never forgive us," Bethuel said.

"When Nazzim hears what we have tried to do, he may decide not to marry Rebekah just to punish us," Laban admonished.

"You were so eager to marry her to Nazzim. Why have you changed?" Nahor's voice was thin and petulant.

This silenced them for a few moments while Laban thought about the strange events that had conspired to change his mind. He had been influenced by the gifts, but it was more than that. He found it hard to put this feeling into words. Finally glancing around as though to be sure only his father and grand-father were listening, he whispered, "It's Abraham's God, Elohim. He seems to be able to arrange things. It somehow frightens me to go against His will."

"So it is agreed that we will leave it to Rebekah to decide," said Bethuel.

"She's not shy like some," Nahor said. "She knows what she wants, and if she doesn't want to go, she won't. She probably won't want to go, especially not in such a hurry."

Laban resumed his most crafty look, usually reserved for dealings in the market. "You must see how brilliant this is," he said. "If she decides to go, we'll blame it all on her, and by the time Nazzim hears about it, she'll at least be a day's journey away."

There was a soft knock on the door, and when Laban opened it he saw his mother standing with his sister in the shadows. Laban drew himself up, and with a voice that suddenly sounded unusually kind and conciliatory, he welcomed them into the small reception room.

Rebekah stood looking around the room with amazing composure. In just these few hours she had gone from the carefree, fun-loving daughter to a confident young woman who could make difficult decisions.

Laban closed the door. Turning to his mother, he said, "Have you ex-plained to her what Eleazar has proposed? Does she understand what may happen if we do not go along with his plan?"

To his surprise it was Rebekah who answered with a slight lifting of her chin and a note of disgust in her voice. "Of course I understand. I'll never marry that terrible old man your ugly god picked out for me."

"We must not speak against the old goat-man," Laban admonished. "He can wreak terrible revenge."

To everyone's surprise, Rebekah grinned. "He's not very strong if Nazzim is the best he can produce."

"You have to admit he's rich and probably would not have lived very long. Two very good recommendations for any husband." Laban was stern and defensive.

"There's no need to argue," Rebekah assured them. "I'll go with this messenger from my uncle and marry the young man who has been so obviously chosen for me by his God."

Laban stood studying her for a moment. He knew his sister very well. Often she was sweet and obliging, but there were times when she asserted herself in what he considered a stubborn and even manipulative way. He nervously pulled at his short beard as he admitted to himself how often his whole family had been known for their ability to bend and twist even difficult situations to attain their own ends.

He shrugged and walked to the door. "Wait in here," he said, "and I'll bring Eleazar so we can discuss this more thoroughly."

✳ ✳ ✳

Eleazar had asked to meet with Rebekah, her nurse, Deborah, her hand-maidens, and her immediate family. When they were all assembled, old Nahor rose with difficulty and with a quavering voice confronted Rebekah. He voiced the question for the last time. "You are the light of this house, the joy of my old age. Will you choose to leave all of us and your life here to go with this messenger of my brother?"

"It's best that I go, Grandfather," she said, looking at him sadly but not moving to embrace him as she normally would have done.

"But my dear child, you know the story of how my brother, Abram, who's now Abraham, left us, broke up the family to follow this God of his. Now he wants to take the very apple of my eye for his son. It's too much. He asks too much."

Laban began to be concerned that the old man would persuade her to stay, so he broke in, "It's quite simple, Rebekah. We'll abide by your decision. Will you go with this man and marry the young son of our uncle, yes or no?"

Rebekah looked around at all of them and then focused her gaze on Eleazar, who had been sitting silently in the seat of honor. "I intend to go with this man and marry my cousin."

As she said that, her mother gave a cry and ran to embrace her. Nahor turned his face away and wiped at his eyes, while only Laban looked relaxed and pleased.

"My father," Bethuel said at last to Nahor, "will you give her the family's blessing before we send her away?" Nahor frowned and coughed and motioned for Bethuel to pronounce the blessing. He had not forgiven his brother, Abram, for leaving, and he could not bless this taking of his favorite granddaughter. It gave too much the look of compliance.

Bethuel, without hesitation, called for Rebekah to come kneel before him. As was the custom he placed his outer, fringed garment over her head and lifting up his eyes, he said, "Thou art my much loved daughter. Be thou the mother of thousands of millions and let thy seed possess the gate of those that hate them." He had remembered that she would be traveling to a strange country and her children would no doubt need strength and courage to face those who would hate them just because they were different.

The camels were ready, and her handmaidens were gathering up their things and the belongings Rebekah had said she would take. It was important to leave before the sun mounted too high in the sky and it became hot and uncomfortable to travel. Even more important was the necessity of being well on their way before Nazzim discovered he had been robbed of his bride.

While her handmaidens were busy, Rebekah's mother took her to one side. Usually a prospective bride had hours of instruction. Rebekah's mother was frustrated with the turn of events that gave her no time to give much advice. "Aye, aye," she moaned, clutching her mantle across her trembling mouth. "If I had known how it would be, I would have been wiser. How you will manage I don't know."

"Mother, I'll manage very well. I'll be quiet and demure, the perfect young bride."

The mother held her at arm's length. "You are too young, too impulsive. How will you manage?"

Rebekah saw the tears beginning to gather in her mother's eyes. "So you wish I were marrying that old man Laban chose for me?"

"Ayeeeee," her mother objected, throwing her hands in the air. "I would rather see you dead than married to such a one."

"Eleazar says my young cousin is handsome, very rich, and generous." Rebekah held her arm out and twisted the bracelets back and forth with obvious delight.

"His mother, our Sarah, died. Who will show you what to do? How will you manage?"

Rebekah shrugged and looked at her mother with amusement. "Look, I'll show you." With that she pulled her mantle around to cover her face so only her eyes were showing. She lowered her head and took small mincing steps as she had seen the local brides do so often. "I'll be the perfect bride. You needn't worry. I'll be shy and quiet." She spoke the words in a low, diffident manner that surprised her mother.

"There, that is right," her mother said, smiling. "That is the way. A bride must remember these things are important."

Rebekah stopped and looked with delight at her mother. Her eyes sparkled with mischief as she reached out and hugged her. "I will do everything right until they are used to me and then . . . I may surprise them with my true self." Here she flung back the mantle and with quick springing steps danced across the room.

"Too much freedom. I gave you too much freedom," her mother cried as she sank down among the colorful bedrolls all neatly stacked in the corner of the room.

Rebekah saw that her mother was really disturbed and she felt remorseful that she had caused her so much concern. "Come, Mother," she said. "I promise I'll be shy, quiet, and modest just as you would wish."

"You'll keep your face covered . . ."

"I promise. I'll do everything just the way everyone expects."

With that her mother struggled to her feet and brushed her gown to straighten it, adjusted her mantle, and then with one long, fond look at her daughter, said, "There's one consolation, you're going to close relatives. You'll be safe—no talk of divorce, beatings, or turning you out." She sighed and wiped two large tears from her cheeks, then in a burst of emotion she embraced Rebekah and clung to her sobbing.

There was the sound of running, then voices low and insistent. Slowly her mother released her as she whispered, "It's time to go. It's bad luck to keep men waiting."

With that, the two went out to join the others in the courtyard.

\* \* \*

At the very last moment Rebekah's mother called Deborah, Rebekah's old nurse, aside. "Here," she said, handing her a small, tightly wrapped bundle. "These are the swaddling clothes I wove with my own hands for my daughter's first child."

Deborah took the soft, flaxen bundle and was about to put it in with her things when she felt something hard slightly protruding from the cloth. She gave the mother a questioning glance.

"It is nothing, nothing to concern you," the mother said as she looked around furtively. She nervously pulled Deborah aside to where none of the others could hear what she said. "You understand. I will not be there to help her. She may need this." She reached out and pulled at the soft cloth until it covered the hard, dark object completely.

"A small goddess?" Deborah asked.

The mother nodded and whispered, "One made by old Terah in Ur."

"But . . ." Deborah knew she would be severely punished if it were discovered that she was leaving with one of the household fertility gods. The ones from Ur that had been made by Terah's workmen were especially prized.

"They are expecting many children," the mother said, giving Deborah a knowing look. When she saw that Deborah didn't quite understand, she leaned forward and whispered, "God forbid but she may be like our kinswoman, Sarah." With that she drew the mantle across her mouth to stifle a sob.

Deborah was immediately filled with compassion. She tucked the package into the small bundle of her belongings. "Don't be afraid," she said. "I'll be there to take care of her."

With that the mother impulsively grabbed both of Deborah's hands and kissed them. "You must care for her in my place."

"I swear by the gods of Ur, she will lack nothing." The two women exchanged a long, meaningful look and then went together out into the busy courtyard.

It was immediately obvious that Laban was nervous and impatient. He, more than the others, was well aware of the conflict that could result if Rebekah did not get away as quickly as possible. He was frantically urging, cajoling, and insisting that they hurry. As a result it was within the hour that Rebekah mounted her camel and was ready to follow Eleazar and his men out the city gate and down past the well where she had met him such a short time ago.

Her mother and the servants ran along beside the camels until they came to the well, and then they stood weeping and waving as long as they could see them.

Rebekah had a moment of sadness as she realized that she was actually leaving her family and everything that was familiar. She turned to look back again and again; the familiar faces were all the more dear as they gradually faded from sight. Even more touching had been her old grandfather standing at the door of the courtyard with Bethuel. He was too old and feeble to follow them to the well. She would always remember that just before she mounted her camel he had reached out to her and whispered, "Abraham's God has won again, and perhaps it's for the best."

*  *  *

Rebekah was flushed with the thrill of adventure and young enough to spend very little time grieving over leaving her family. It never occurred to her that it would be very difficult, even impossible, for her to repeat this trip and come to see them.

As she and her handmaidens rode along, they sang and from time to time called to each other remarking on the emerging wonders around them. Eleazar was thoughtful enough to ride back and explain many things about the landscape they were passing or the customs of the people they were about to meet. The camping in the early evening was the favorite time for everyone. They loved to sit around the campfire enjoying the snap and crackle of the burning twigs while watching for the rising moon. Then, long before daybreak they were up and mounted ready to ride again. They must make the most of the cool hours before the sun rose.

Rebekah asked many questions and Eleazar was able and willing to answer as many as possible. She was curious about the reason her uncle had chosen to leave the rest of the family. She wanted to know why they were living in tents away from the cities. She knew very little of her cousin Isaac, and of course she was most curious about him.

"Isaac is very handsome," Eleazar told her. "Perhaps his most outstanding quality is a special charm that makes it easy for him to make friends. If someone doesn't like him, it bothers him. He's not content until he has managed to make that man his friend. He admires his half-brother Ishmael because he is a rather rough fellow who hunts and fights and is good at besting any opponent, but I find Isaac easier to live with."

When they retired to their own tents, the talking didn't stop. Each one came with new questions and some came with answers. One of the handmaidens, Tesha, had the news from her camel boy that Isaac had never gotten over his mother's death. Rebekah fingered the bracelets she was wearing and thought about what it must have meant for Isaac to have sent her such dear treasures. Just wearing the bracelets made her feel a special kinship with her aunt Sarah.

She was learning many things about her aunt and each revelation made her more real. She knew that Sarah had been barren for many years. She could just imagine how difficult that would have been for her. Everyone believed only evil women or women under some terrible curse from the earth goddess were barren.

Rebekah spent some time thinking about blessings and cursings. Words had real power. Even a powerful curse written on a small bit of parchment and buried in a secret place could make someone ill.

Blessings could be just as powerful and would help a person overcome any difficulty. A blessing given by a parent or a priest was very strong. Usually only the sons in the family, and especially the firstborn son, received any blessing from their father. How amazing it was that her father had given her his blessing. It was more precious to her than great riches.

She was to be the mother of many. There would be no barrenness for her. She would give her husband strong children. She had been given that promise in the blessing of her father.

Then the strange blessing. What did it mean? "Let thy seed possess the gate of them that hate them." She pondered on this a good deal. She knew very well that whoever controlled the gate of a city was in charge. So she finally decided it meant that even though the people within a city hated her descendants, her descendants would be in control of things. What an amazing, wonderful blessing.

She was elated with the blessing until she began to ponder on why the people of any city would hate her descendants. This was a great puzzle. It was only much later that she began to glimpse the larger meaning of the strange blessing.

She had a small brass mirror, which she looked in from time to time. The handmaids were always borrowing it. It was blurred and shaky but you could get some idea of how you looked. She had heard all her life that her aunt Sarah was the most beautiful woman in Ur and she worried that Isaac would think her too plain and ordinary to take her place. Maybe he would be sorry he sent his mother's gold jewelry to her. She wondered if she would ever be to him what his mother had been, and how would she know.

Then she would think of Nazzim and how strange it was that only a short time before she had no hope but to marry him. The God of Abraham was indeed strong, and He obviously paid attention when even a maid prayed earnestly to Him. She felt a warm glow, a happy feeling of discovery. This God, who seemed to be known only to the men of her family, cared about her and had rescued her. She determined to give Him first place among the gods and to discover as much as possible about Him from the family of her uncle Abraham.

\* \* \*

Though Eleazar pushed his caravan as fast as he thought wise, he indulged in considerable restraint for the sake of the young bride and her maidservants. As it developed, it was almost a month before they neared the area where Abraham was camped for the summer. Now when they pitched their tents for the night and sat around the fire waiting for the moon to rise or looking for the star clusters they called the seven sisters, Rebekah began to ask specific questions about Isaac. Eleazar had waited for just such a time to tell her the things he thought she should know about her bridegroom.

One night he told her how Abraham had taken Isaac up on Moriah to sacrifice him. Rebekah's eyes grew round and questioning. "He would have sacrificed his only son, the son he and my aunt had waited so long for?"

"Abraham will withhold nothing from his God," Eleazar explained.

"But my aunt, what did she say?" Rebekah was obviously puzzled. Usually it was the pagan Canaanites who sacrificed their children. It had never occurred to Nahor or Bethuel to sacrifice a child to the old goat-man. They didn't really believe in his powers that much.

Eleazar was silent for what seemed a long time. He poked at the fire and studied the stars as though he didn't intend to answer. Finally turning to her, he said, "She didn't like it. She didn't like it at all. There was a terrible scene as you can imagine. I must say I couldn't blame her. All of us in the camp thought it was too much."

Rebekah was leaning forward eagerly waiting to hear the outcome. Her maids—who had been preparing her bed and setting out her toiletries on the smooth, cool sand—stood motionless, quite shamelessly waiting to hear what happened next.

"And my cousin Isaac, what did he say?"

"I was not there to see it. I have only heard what happened, but the lad trusted his father."

"And my uncle found he could not do such a thing. He could not sacrifice the son given so miraculously." Rebekah could not wait for Eleazar to tell the story. She wanted Abraham to rescue his son even at the last moment.

"No, that is not what happened," Eleazar said rather sharply. "It was an angel sent by Elohim that rescued him." There was a gasp and rustling sound as the handmaids left their work and came closer so they could hear this strange tale.

"Abraham had tied the boy to the altar and was raising the knife . . ."

With a cry of horror Rebekah hid her face in her hands and turned away, not being able to bear what she was sure would come next.

At this Eleazar rushed ahead to relieve the tension. "It was an angel of Abraham's God that saved the boy. He cried out and told Abraham not to harm his son. 'For now I know that you fear God,' he said. Then a strange thing happened, Abraham looked and to his surprise saw a ram caught in a thicket. He freed Isaac and sacrificed the ram in his place."

Everyone was quiet as they marveled over the strangeness of the story. "And that is all?" Rebekah asked. "There was no explanation of why this had to happen?"

Eleazar looked surprised. "That much of the story is all I usually tell. It is enough for most folks."

"I want to hear it all," Rebekah said. "I must hear it all if I am to understand my husband and his family."

"Well, it seems the angel called to Abraham a second time."

He hesitated and Rebekah urged him to go on. Her handmaidens clustered even closer so they would not miss a single word. "And . . . what did the angel tell him?"

"The angel gave him a special message. Abraham has treasured this message and repeated it often as though he is constantly pondering its meaning."

"And . . ." Rebekah said again.

"What the angel said was wonderful. He said, 'Because you have done this thing and have not withheld thy son, thine only son, I will bless you and multiply thy seed as the stars of the heaven, and the sand which is on the sea shore; and thy seed shall possess the gate of his enemies.'"

"That was part of the blessing given me by my father," Rebekah said. "How strange."

"That has been an age-old saying of those who wish to give a meaningful blessing, but no one has ever heard such a promise from an angel of Elohim. This was different."

"Is that all?" Rebekah asked.

"No," Eleazar answered. "It seems you will pull every bit of the blessing out and examine it before you even meet your intended groom."

"I must know it all. The good and the bad. Was there nothing bad predicted for them and their descendants?"

"Nothing bad but something even stranger. Something we have all pondered from time to time."

"Tell me," she said. "I must hear everything before we arrive."

Eleazar looked around at them all, and when he spoke there was a break in his voice as though it were such a precious thing that merely speaking of it moved him deeply. "The angel said, 'in thy seed shall all the nations of the earth be blessed because you have obeyed my voice.' His name had earlier even been changed from Abram to Abraham, father of a multitude."

A great silence followed as everyone pondered the meaning of the angel's words. Finally the handmaids rose and silently went about their work. Then Deborah followed them to make a last check of the tent and sleeping arrangements before retiring for the night. Only Rebekah remained by the fire. Eleazar, glancing at her, noticed tears in her eyes and knew she could not speak. "I understand," he said at last. "You are the one who will bear the child who will fulfill all these promises made to Abraham. It's not a simple thing to have been chosen for such a purpose."

It was a long moment before Rebekah could speak. "I'm but a simple, ordinary maid, not one to be responsible for such glowing promises."

For the first time Eleazar understood how overwhelming all of this must seem to her, and a great compassion filled his heart. Rebekah was so beautiful and had such a confident air, he had not thought of her as being overwhelmed by any situation. Now he realized that she could be very vulnerable. "I rather think Elohim knew just exactly what He was doing when He chose you to be Isaac's bride."

"I . . . chosen?" she asked.

"Of course. Were you not the one who gave me drink and then also watered my camels?"

"That was but a simple thing."

"Were you not the one who agreed to come with me on such short notice?"

"Yes ... but ..."

"That was the sign I asked for, so that I would know whom Elohim had chosen."

Nothing more was said between the two, and after a while when the night breeze grew strong enough to make the fire flare up, the tents billow, and the tethers creak and groan, they each rose and went quietly to their own place for the night. Eleazar went quickly to sleep, but Rebekah lay awake long past the moonrise pondering all that she had heard.

* * *

When they reached Jericho, Eleazar told them it would be only a short time before they would arrive at their destination. He also told them he had made arrangements for them to visit the famous bath where Rebekah would be prepared and anointed for her wedding night. There were women who were clever at arranging the hair, decorating the fingernails with small flowers done in kohl, and rubbing fragrant spices into the skin. The perfumes were rare and costly, but Eleazar had a whole purse, which he gave to the attendant, admonishing her to spare no expense. "This is to be the bride of my master's son and my master has ordered me to do this."

While the women were involved in preparations for the meeting of Rebekah and Isaac, Eleazar took care of some of his own business. The most important bit of business was to find a lad who would carry a message to Abraham's camp telling of their arrival. He could not tell the day, but he could report on where they were and when they would leave. This would give Abraham's men some idea of what day they would arrive.

When it came time to leave Jericho, Eleazar came with the camels and his retainers to pick up the women. He could see that Rebekah was not only impressed with all that had been spent on her but was a bit frightened. He realized that she was just now beginning to face the reality of her situation. Undoubtedly she was fearful of meeting this stranger who was considerably older but was to be her husband. He tried to think of something that would reassure her, help her to understand that only happiness lay ahead for her in the camp of her uncle Abraham.

"You are indeed lovely," he said.

"Will my husband be happy with me?" she asked.

Eleazar hesitated only a moment and then he said, "Isaac, as you know, means laughter, and he is one who makes it his business to be happy. He will indeed be pleased with you."

But Rebekah couldn't help but wonder.

**8**

*I*saac had counted the days it would take for Eleazar to make the journey to Haran. He knew it was hazardous and long, taking about twenty-five to thirty days. He had estimated by the moon's fullness and then its fading that enough days had passed for Eleazar to have arrived at his destination. Then when it occurred to him that he had no way of knowing how long it would be before he would start back, or if his trip had been successful, he stopped counting.

As the days and weeks went by, he became more and more curious about this cousin who was to be his bride. He tried to picture her, but only questions and problems filled his mind. He decided it was almost too much to hope that she would be as beautiful and as adventuresome as his mother had been. On the other hand, he had to admit to himself that even his own mother would not have come so far to marry someone she had never seen.

Gradually it occurred to him that Eleazar might be successful simply because the young woman was so undesirable or ugly no one had wanted to marry her. If she were really attractive, she would have so many suitors she would never agree to taking a chance on a distant relative she had never seen.

Then what would they do if after she had come so far they found her to be totally unsuitable? Under most circumstances, if a bride proved to be lacking in some way, she could be sent back to her parents. He had heard of one such case where a new bride could not bake bread without burning it, and she was sent back to her parents immediately in disgrace.

With a sinking heart he realized this could not be done with a cousin who had come so far to marry him. Also, since his father had made such a point of trusting Elohim to lead Eleazar to the right woman, there could be no question of not accepting her.

He understood his father's concern that he not marry any of the local women. It would have been an impossible situation. Their lives and ways of living were so different. His half-brother Ishmael had many sons but the women he had married were a great trial to his father. Abraham was obviously determined to avoid that mistake a second time.

He was always amazed at how completely his father trusted Elohim. Abraham seemed to have no doubts that in spite of the difficulties, their prayers would be answered and the right woman would be found. It was his father's way to first find Elohim's will in a matter and then to trust completely in the outcome. He himself had not this certainty. He would have to wait and see what happened.

On this night he had been restlessly tossing and turning as he mulled over the possibilities. Finally he rose and quietly strapped on his bone-handled dagger, flung his cloak over his shoulder, and, as was his custom, walked out into the crisp, early morning darkness.

He walked toward the rocky heights that led to the Valley of Salt and his father's well at Beersheba. "When Eleazar comes," he reasoned, "he will probably be coming down from the highlands on one of these paths."

He walked slowly, pondering the strangeness of his life and the importance of the events that were about to take place. He kept to the low trails where the paths were clear and distinct from constant use by his father's sheep. Floating up and around him on the crisp morning breeze were the odors of fragrant herbs that gave off their most pungent aroma when crushed underfoot. He marveled at the constantly changing fragrance. At one time it would be the sharp scent of thyme; another, the stringent odor of sage or yarrow. All the time he was plunging farther and farther along the path leading to Beersheba.

Gradually he became aware of someone breathing heavily and at the same time the soft pounding sound of running feet. He stopped and looked around. Though the sky was lightening, he could see very little because of a fog that hung low in the valley below him and on the path ahead of him. He stopped and listened. It was evident that someone was on the path ahead of him and running toward him.

Suddenly a part of the mist darkened and as Isaac stood still and waited, the figure of a young boy emerged. The boy looked surprised and then frightened. He was breathing hard and couldn't speak. He leaned against the rock wall that rose up on one side of the path and looked questioningly at Isaac.

"Where could you be going in such a hurry and so early in the morning?" Isaac asked.

"I have an important message to deliver and I was told I should go quickly."

"And whom may I ask is the message for?" Isaac questioned.

The boy looked puzzled and then smiled. "I don't suppose it would hurt to tell. It's not that sort of secret message."

"Then tell me where you're going. These are my father's grazing lands and . . ."

"Then your father must be Abraham."

"My father is Abraham," Isaac said. He was instantly alert and excited. He realized the message could have something to do with Eleazar. "Was it a man named Eleazar who gave you the message?" he asked.

"Yes, it was," said the boy with a puzzled look.

"Did he have any women with him?"

"Oh yes, a very fine lady by the looks of her camel's trappings."

Isaac could hardly contain his excitement. "Did you happen to catch a glimpse of this young lady?" he asked hesitantly, knowing it was not customary to ask so openly about a young woman.

The boy hesitated and quickly Isaac reached in his knapsack and held out a big chunk of smoked cheese.

The boy grinned and reached for the cheese. "I did catch just a glimpse of her. This Eleazar was giving me instructions and she leaned forward to hear." He stopped and took a big bite of the cheese.

Isaac reached out and held his arm so he couldn't take another bite, "So you saw her . . ."

"Yes," the boy said, realizing he would not get loose until he had told more. "A wind blew up and caught at her mantle," he said, "and before she could pull it around, I did see her."

"You saw her?" Isaac asked with growing curiosity.

"I did. I saw her. Well, to tell the truth, it was just a glimpse."

"And . . ." Isaac tightened his grip on the boy's arm.

"She knew I had seen her and at first she looked frightened. Then she smiled. For a moment I swear it was like the sun was shining."

"She smiled? Why?" Isaac asked.

"I don't know. Anyway before I left, when no one was looking, she motioned me over to where she was sitting so tall and splendid on her camel. 'Here,' she said, 'take this and forget what you have seen.'"

The boy reached in his leather pouch and pulled out a perfectly round flattened piece of gold. It had a delicately etched palm tree and some letters. Isaac saw at once that it was the kind of charm women wore as decorations framing their face. She obviously had been concerned enough to part with one of the coins in her headpiece. He felt a twinge of guilt to think of how he had pried her little secret out of this simple boy.

His feelings of remorse quickly passed as there was one more question he must ask the boy before he let him go. "Where was Eleazar when he gave you this message?" he asked.

"In Jericho," the boy answered with an obvious impatience to be off.

"Then go quickly. If you follow this path, you will come to the brook Besor and you will see the tents of Abraham spread along its length. I'll see you in my father's tent, and it will be as though we had never met."

The boy quickly stuffed the rest of the cheese in his mouth, brushed past Isaac, and hurried off down the path and disappeared into the mist.

\* \* \*

As Isaac hurried back along the path, his mind whirled with the preparations that must be made. "A fine lady, on a camel with elegant trappings," the boy had said. For the first time he worried that living in a tent might seem too difficult for her. He would, of course, take her to his mother's tent.

He knew that his uncles lived in the city and only went out to the fields to plant and herd their flocks. She probably preferred the city. He paused and tried to imagine how their camp would look to someone who had always lived in the city. To him the time they spent out in the fields was wonderful, but to a wife it could look very different.

*I must hurry and set my mother's tent in order. She must not have reason to despise anything that belonged to my mother.* He started to run and was back at the camp in an amazingly short time.

He went directly to his mother's tent, and on lifting the flap paused to look around. He was mesmerized by the familiar odor of jasmine mixed with musk and patchouli that still filled the air. A soft linen robe lay just where she had left it thirteen years before when she went up to Hebron where she had died. It was flung across the carved chest she had brought with her from Ur. Her fine brass mirror hung by a leather strap from the tent pole, and her incense burner had tipped over beside the fire pot. He removed the stopper

75

from an alabaster jar to smell the contents. It was her favorite fragrance, the rare and expensive patchouli.

In one corner, neatly stacked, were her cooking utensils. A tripod and goatskin container for making leban from the sweet, fresh milk of the goat, a wooden bowl for kneading bread, a clay bowl that had always held the bubbling ferment that made her bread light and fluffy. There were a few tongs and ladles and clay jars holding flour and smaller ones holding her spices. Hanging above from one of the tent girders were strings of dried beans, peppers, and clumps of garlic and onions. She had always cooked for her family, and Isaac wondered if the young girl Eleazar was bringing would do the same.

He paused beside her loom, which held a partially finished piece. He rubbed his hand along the well-worn beams while he looked around the room. He tried to imagine someone young and beautiful moving among his mother's things. He thought he would despise her if she should not like his mother's belongings. How could he endure it if she insisted that she wouldn't cook and had his mother's treasured, carefully collected cooking things removed. He suddenly wished he could be free of the whole complicated business. He would much prefer remaining as he was. He had to admit he had been lonely, but that was not as bad as having some disagreeable young woman making demands on him.

He immediately felt remorse. He realized that he had no reason to think of her in such an unkind way. In fact, he could almost picture her now. She must be quite young and terribly brave. There was so much she didn't know, and yet she was coming and trusting all would go well with her. How charming the little scene. Her mantle blowing off and her laughter until she noticed the boy had seen her. He liked it that she had laughed. She was naive but resourceful. Imagine pulling off one of the gold ornaments from her headpiece to be sure the boy gave only a good report of her.

Suddenly and quite unexpectedly, he felt a lump in his throat and tears sprang to his eyes. He had been deeply touched by this show of bravery in his little bride. He felt a strange new urge to protect her. There would be so many things for her to adjust to. She had probably known that would be true and yet had decided to come. She had trusted him and he must not fail her. Even if she moved his mother's things around, or wanted to get rid of some of them, he would not be resentful or angry. She had given him an unconditional trust and he must give her all the love she deserved.

Isaac was more accustomed to walking out in the evening than in the morning. At this time of day there were the soft sounds of birds nesting, the rustling of little animals hurrying to hide, or the whispering sound of grasses ruffled by the evening breeze. He would watch as the sun, large and luminous, lighted the huddled walls of Gerar in the west and in the east the moon rose pale and fragile in the still blue sky.

The fields that he walked across were the same, but now he found himself watching the horizon and listening for the jangle of the trappings that announced a camel caravan. It had been two days since he had encountered the young boy who brought the good news of Eleazar's return. Two days of wild excitement in his father's camp. Vast preparations were being made to welcome Bethuel's daughter, his bride.

He didn't want to meet her for the first time with everyone watching. He wanted it to be something unique and private. He knew they were all anxious to see if she was beautiful and if he was going to love her as his father had loved Sarah. He knew he couldn't avoid their curiosity, but first he wanted to greet her himself. He wanted to spare both of them any embarrassment.

There was so much to be decided and so many adjustments to be made. He at least knew the plans being made. She was to stay in the bridal tent with her maidens until they had time to get acquainted, and then Isaac would take her to his mother's tent. In no part of the plan was there room made for this meeting that he was hoping for.

He was so engrossed in his thoughts that it was some time before he heard faint and far away the jangle of a camel caravan's approach and the call of the Bashi driver. Looking up he saw a splendid caravan coming around the bend from where it had been hidden from view by a huge rock formation. The caravan of his father's servant, Eleazar. He hurried toward it. The camel with the elegant trappings, a colorful array of tapestry, tassels, and bangles, had to be the camel of his bride.

As he approached, the caravan came to a stop. To his surprise the decorated camel came a few steps farther and then, in response to a sharp command given in a lilting, feminine voice, it knelt.

Quickly and with amazing agility, a small person alighted and came forward with a confident air that astonished Isaac. At first he thought it must be a young man coming with some message, but then rather suddenly a thin veil was drawn over the face. He stopped, baffled by the emotion he felt. This was undoubtedly his bride. How mysterious and exciting, even frightening, she seemed. She didn't wait for the man to make all the moves. She seemed totally at home and unafraid.

As he hesitated she came toward him, and he heard her softly intone his name as though she were saying it to herself. "Isaac, laughter," she said. She was veiled, but the veil only added beauty and mystery to the young face he saw before him, lit by the sunlight. They looked at each other seriously and long. Isaac had expected a painted prettiness, but instead he saw a young girl who held some secret charm, whose eyes were large and challenging, whose mouth was generous and the face angular. Suddenly the eyes crinkled and the lips parted as she laughed. "How handsome you are, my cousin," she said.

With that she leaned forward and, as was the custom of cousins, kissed him on both cheek—first one and then the other. "Come ride with me and lead us to your camp," she said. With that she led him back to her camel. "It's easy to get off," she said, "but quite impossible to get back on without help." She held out her hand and in a daze he took it, marveling at its softness and strength. With the swiftness of a young mountain goat, she scrambled up the footholds and back in place behind the driver's seat. Leaning down and taking his hand, she guided him into the seat of the driver.

Isaac was charmed and delighted with the turn of events. As he answered her many questions, he was aware of a steady parade of impressions going through his mind. He had hoped for a pretty wife and instead he had been given this fascinating young woman. She was interested in everything and had an exuberant joy even his mother had not had. He couldn't have explained her to anyone. You wouldn't say she was pretty. That was too tame and too prosaic. She was so much more than pretty. Just to see her smile was more beautiful than any sunrise he had ever seen. Most of all she obviously liked him. He had read it in her eyes just before she kissed him. His cheeks still tingled with her kiss and her subtle perfume floated on the air around them.

All too soon they were met with tambourines, drums, and flutes being played by a jolly procession of young men and women from Abraham's camp. They guided them into the center of the dark tents, and there Isaac was helped down and led away to the men's guest tent while Rebekah was welcomed by the women. Before they were parted, Isaac had paused just long enough to smile at her. As he did so he noticed that one of the coins that cascaded down from the caplet that she wore was missing. Again he was deeply moved. At that moment he knew that he loved her as much if not more than he had loved his mother.

* * *

Over in the city of Gerar, Anatah paced back and forth in terrible frustration. She had been hearing for weeks that the servant of the desert prince, Abraham, had gone back to the family in Haran to find a bride for Isaac. She had comforted herself with the thought that no young woman would choose to travel such a long distance to marry a man she didn't know. If such a person did come, she was sure to be ugly and old. Too old to get a husband any other way.

When her informant came running to tell her that a caravan had arrived with elegant trappings and a young bride for Isaac, she was furious. She had entertained thoughts of bribing someone to make friends with the young bride and then make sure that nothing she did succeeded. If she went riding, they were to see that she came home covered with mud from a mysterious accident, or if she baked something, they were to secretly put the powder of bitter herbs in the mix. She even thought briefly of poisoning her.

She had hoped to carry out these plots before the marriage was consummated. When she heard that Isaac had taken his young bride to his mother's tent, she knew there was nothing she could do except wait and see if the marriage succeeded.

From the report of his happiness and her joy, there was no chance of the marriage proving to be a failure unless they were childless. Children would be very important in this marriage. She knew that the father, Abraham, had a promise from his God that he would be the father of multitudes. If this marriage did not produce an heir right away, then surely Isaac's love for her would fade and he would send her home to her family.

She determined to give the earth goddess one last chance. In desperation she hurried to the niche beside the lily pond and confronted the ugly little image. "You must know already of your failure," she said. "Isaac has married the woman. If he has a child by her, I will have lost him forever. You must see that she is never with child. She must never conceive."

With that she felt much better. She gave the little image a hard look before turning and heading back to the receiving room. Her brother Abimelech, who had taken over the title and the crown after his father's death, was hearing some complaints from his shepherds.

She listened only long enough to hear that their complaint was against the shepherds of the great and wealthy Abraham. He had too many animals and was right at that moment digging more wells to obtain the water they needed. "There is a law that if anyone digs a well, they can claim the land around the well," said the king. "This Abraham and his son Isaac are going too far."

Anatah waited to hear no more. She had all the information she needed. She would get at Rebekah through her faithful informants and at Isaac through her brother Abimelech.

"Let his God bless him," she muttered. "The more he is blessed, the more crowded the land will become, and the sooner he will be driven out." *If our gods and our people are not good enough for him, then he should be forced out one way or another.*

*J*ust as the moon rose over the distant mountains, Isaac brought Rebekah to his mother's tent. "It is our custom here for the bride and groom to remain secluded for eight days," he said. "Is this also your custom in Haran?"

She was sitting on a soft, fringed cushion looking over a round tray woven of the stiff, broad grasses from the brook and piled with dried dates and figs. He was surprised that she didn't seem frightened or shy. She glanced at him and then went back to looking at the dates. Her gold bracelets jangled as she reached out and plucked the date of her choice and then took a small bite before again looking at him. "Of course. The old women say it's to give time for the trouble-causing demons to leave."

"Do you believe there are trouble-causing demons?" Isaac asked.

She took another small bite as she glanced around the tent and contemplated the answer. "It could explain why some people have so much trouble."

"Do you think that is why someone like my mother was barren for so many years?"

"That's the kind of thing the demons are supposed to do."

"You don't seem to be very concerned about them."

"I'm not," she said, looking directly at him and at the same time licking the sticky sweetness of the dates from her fingers.

"You aren't afraid of anything, are you?" He reached for the damp, perfume-scented cloth that was draped over the side of the tray, intending to wipe away the offending syrup. She took the cloth from him and wiped each hand slowly and with an obvious enjoyment of the subtle fragrance. "Oh, I am afraid of some things, but not of being barren."

"You're not afraid of being barren? I thought every bride was afraid of that."

"Well, I'm not," she said as she carefully folded the cloth and put it back on the side of the tray. "I had a special blessing given me before I left Haran. I will have many children."

"And I too have promises. No trouble-causing demons can come against the promises of Elohim to my father."

"I'll tell you what I think." She looked around again as though to make sure no demon lurked in the dark corners of the tent. "I think it is the old women who like to frighten new brides. They love to tell horrible stories. It's always the poor young bride who turns out to have the ears of a donkey or talons like an eagle instead of fingers." She held out her two arms and looked at her hands. "It would be awful," she said, looking at him and grinning.

He captured one of her hands in both of his. "You have beautiful hands," he said. "I noticed them when we first met and you brushed your hands against your veil."

"And you have eyes that say many lovely things even before you speak."

"We will have no problems," he said. "Our children will be wise and prudent."

"They will all be handsome and generous," she said as they both laughed with the delight of discovery.

Isaac could hardly contain his joy. Joy in the realization that he was no longer alone or lonely and joy in realizing that he had trusted his father and Elohim and they had not failed him.

＊ ＊ ＊

As the days passed, Isaac found it even harder to believe his good fortune. His little bride was full of happy surprises. She responded to his attention with dancing eyes and coy glances that made their nights magical. She never seemed to tire of him. At the same time he marveled that she never bored him. *Perhaps it's because she's busy. There's always something that interests her.*

Early in the morning he would wake to hear singing coming from the tent that had belonged to his mother and was now Rebekah's. It was a hypnotic, rhythmical tune that went along with the swinging goatskin that produced the morning's butter. Then there was the sharp slapping sound that meant flat cakes were being turned on the outdoor clay oven. It made him smile as he lay back against the straw-filled headrest. There would be only a few minutes before she would appear with buttermilk and bread cakes dripping with honey butter.

As she knelt, placing the straw mat with its delectable offering beside him, he was aware of the subtle fragrance that always filled the air around her.

It was not the patchouli of his mother but some mysterious blend that hinted of Damascus or the markets of Mari.

He was charmed by her way of reaching out and taking hold of his hands before he could reach for the food, then bending forward to kiss him. He could see that she was amused by her own boldness as she sat back on her heels, hands folded in her lap, and grinned at him.

It was not the custom for a wife to be so forward, but when she saw that it pleased him, she seemed to delight in continuing the practice. He was amazed at how quickly she determined his likes and dislikes. She was a careful observer and so fitted in without being told. He knew his mother would have liked her and would have been happy that he was no longer lonely and grieving.

When it came time for him to again spend long days with his men, he became concerned. What would she do? How would she spend her time in this strange camp that was so different from anything she was used to?

He finally decided it was a foolish concern. She seemed to find even the rocky, sand-strewn desert fascinating. "There are lovely flowers here," she said on one occasion, holding out a long spike with clusters of pink-winged fruit.

Isaac took the flowers from her and pointed out the six membranous wings surrounding each small nubbed bit of green. "In the summer," he said, "these small wings dry out and then the wind blows the winged seeds to new places."

He broke off one of the leaves and handed it to her. "Here," he said, "taste it. The shepherds like its refreshing taste."

She nibbled at it and was surprised to find it quite sour but strangely invigorating. "Are there other plants like this?" she asked.

"In every season there are new surprises," he said. "Now that the rains have stopped, we will see some of the most beautiful ones."

"Are there flowers in the dry season?"

"You'll find a few. Some are even my favorites. We'll make time to go look for them if you like."

"Oh," she said, "I'd love that."

\* \* \*

Actually Rebekah had not found the adjustment as easy as Isaac had assumed. She had taken for granted that the most difficult part of her marriage would be the long journey by camel from Haran to the place where they were camped. She had been totally unprepared for this barren, windswept expanse of sand and low shrub.

She had seen it for the first time when their caravan left Hebron. Coming down from the heights, on a well-worn mountain path, she noticed with pleasure the terraced plots of gourds and grapes, and then the dusty green leaves of the olive trees that bordered the path. However, at a projection of barren rock that rose above the surrounding trees, she was suddenly able to view the desert that stretched before them in every direction as far as they could see.

Every so often jagged, ugly mountains broke the dry, gray loess into sections. There were few trees. She could see a number of acacia trees and a few tamarisk trees, but the dusty palms grew only in clumps near the occasional springs. It was a world of gray rock and dull sand with shrubs and small trees all the same color.

She had been forced to admit to herself that this was not going to be easy. However, all her life she had chosen to look at the bright side of any situation and now was no different.

Then she had seen Isaac coming across the field to meet them, and everything changed. When she saw the admiration in his eyes, the handsome lift of his head, and the strong brown muscles of his arm, she was immediately charmed. She had forgotten all of her fears and was prepared to enjoy her new life in this strange place.

As the months passed Rebekah was surprised at her own happiness. She found Isaac's delight in her a never-ending miracle and the slow pattern of life in her uncle's camp much to her liking. There seemed to be few restrictions. She could organize her maids to gather herbs for the evening stew, hunt wildflowers, or single out a sheep as a special pet. She was usually up to enjoy the sunrise over the eastern peaks and in the evening she sat with Isaac on soft goat-hair cushions at his tent door. Together they watched the sun slowly descend and then with a final burst of color disappear behind the distant palms leading to the city of Gerar.

There was only one flaw. Isaac was already forty years old and everyone was anxious for them to have a child as soon as possible. When asked, Isaac always said, "There's no need to worry. I have my father's blessing and he was promised descendants as the stars and as the sands of the sea."

However, when a year had passed and there was no sign of Rebekah's being pregnant, eyebrows were raised and questions whispered. Abraham had been married to Keturah eleven years and they already had three robust little sons and were expecting another child.

"There's no reason to be afraid," Rebekah was heard to say. "I have the blessing of my family. I am to be the mother of whole nations."

In spite of these reassuring sentiments, some watched carefully to see whether, if this situation continued, Isaac would take another wife or a concubine as his father had done.

When Keturah's son was born, Keturah cried for joy and Abraham hosted a great party to celebrate. "We will name this child Median because there will be many more," he said. He was well aware and sensitive to Rebekah's feelings, but he felt sure that time would give them the child that had been promised. He could barely remember the anguish he and Sarah had suffered over her childless state. It now seemed so easy to produce a child.

Rebekah came to the party but was seen to weep openly when she was given the child to hold. "Let me be fruitful like Keturah and not barren like Sarah my kinswoman," she whispered.

Several of the women heard what she said and reported to Isaac. He was immediately disturbed. He ordered them to refrain from any mention of children and to see that she found some distraction that would temporarily take her mind off the problem.

Deborah was the first to respond. She had been brought to Nahor's house in Haran as a young girl to care for Rebekah when she was a baby. "It is better that she be a nursemaid to your little girl than starve in our home," her mother had said. From that time on she had been an important person in Rebekah's young life. She was cheerful, rather ordinary, and wise beyond her years. Rebekah could be sure of her total love and devotion.

She was the first to grasp the seriousness of Rebekah's dilemma. She could see that with the father, Abraham, expecting descendants as numerous as the stars, it was important for Rebekah to become pregnant as soon as possible. Since she was naturally wise in the ways of herbs and potions, she immediately began to think of a solution.

Within the hour she secretly called one of the young shepherds and insisted he go find some small, spiky leaves from any of the vervain bushes. With them she intended to brew a potion that was sure to induce pregnancy. To her great disappointment, he returned with the news that such bushes were only to be found on the high slopes around Hebron.

Deborah was not one to be easily defeated. "Go hunt until you find a mandrake," she said. "This will always bring results." As it happened it was not the shepherd who found the mandrake but one of the shepherd's wives. She had been going to keep it for her own use, but since she already had five young children, she decided to give it to Deborah with instructions that if placed under Rebekah's sleeping mat, she would be pregnant before the new moon.

That night while Isaac was sitting with his father and the men around the fire, Deborah called Rebekah into the tent. "Look," she said. "See what one of the old women brought me this afternoon." To Rebekah's astonishment, Deborah reached into one of the baskets and pulled out something carefully wrapped in sheepskin. With her eyes dancing and her fingers flying excitedly, she unwrapped the bundle and exhibited a perfectly shaped mandrake. "See," she said, "now you will be with child. The old woman said these are not hard to find here in the desert."

Rebekah had heard of the strange magic of the mandrake but had never seen one. Its dull leaves and whitish-purple blossoms were wilted, but the forked root was strong and healthy. "See," Deborah said, "it does look like a little person."

Rebekah picked it up and held it at arm's length. "It's an ugly old thing. What am I to do with it?"

"Be sure to keep it in a safe place and sleep with it under your sleeping mat every night," Deborah said. "You won't have to worry anymore about getting pregnant. This is the very strongest magic there is."

"I have often heard the surest magic was to keep one of old Terah's small fertility images under the sleeping mat. It's too bad I didn't bring one with me."

Deborah didn't answer right away. She had thought of bringing out the small image Rebekah's mother had given her, but she was afraid it would not be welcomed by either Isaac or Abraham. It was better, she thought, to use the more natural herbs and potions. Surely with the mandrake, Rebekah would be pregnant within the fortnight.

When the fortnight had passed, Rebekah was still not pregnant, and when three more months had passed, it was whispered that Keturah was again pregnant, but Rebekah was still barren.

Abraham had now turned all the business of raising their vast herds to Isaac who was fast mastering the art of making a profit, as well as making decisions for his family.

When the rainy season came, Isaac announced that they would be moving to Gerar. "You will like it in the city," he said to Rebekah. "Short visits can be pleasant; to stay longer means getting involved with their feast days and temple celebrations."

Moving to Gerar was not very complicated. They left the tents as they were and moved into the large stone house that was kept ready for their return by servants. Once they were settled, Rebekah and her maidens spent most of their days in a leisurely fashion while Isaac and some of his men still rode out to inspect his vast herds.

The women spent much time in the mornings at the public bath. Here they met many of the women of Gerar and took pleasure in hearing gossip from places as far away as Egypt. Even more exciting were the visits to be made in the afternoon to the homes of women of wealth and leisure.

It was on a cold, cloudy morning that something happened to spoil not only the trips to the bath but the whole visit to Gerar. On this morning Rebekah and her maidens had especially looked forward to relaxing in the warm fragrance of the steam rooms and pools. The maids had just finished spreading out her sponges and pots of cream and were heating olive oil over a little fire pot when there was a great commotion at the door. Women began to whisper and gather their food and toilet articles into their baskets and then slipped quietly out a side door.

Rebekah sent Deborah to find out what was causing the commotion. Within moments she was back and urging everyone to gather up their things and follow the others out the door.

"Leave?" said Rebekah. "Why should we leave?"

"It appears that one of the king's sisters is coming with her women and children. The women say they always leave so she can use the whole bath."

Rebekah laughed. "How silly. There should be room for both of us."

"That's not the matter. There's room but the princess must not bathe in a room with . . ."

Rebekah laughed. "She must be very old and ugly to want to be alone."

"Old and ugly, who are you saying is old and ugly?" The princess stood in the doorway holding what appeared to be a small boy while two little girls clung to her skirt.

Rebekah stood looking at the woman but could not speak. She was taken aback by her regal demeanor and her haughty manner. She wanted to apologize, but the words wouldn't come.

"Who are you and what is your name?" the princess demanded, setting the little boy down by her side.

"I am Rebekah the wife of Isaac, the son of a great desert prince named Abraham," Rebekah said.

At her words the whole demeanor of the princess changed. A look of cunning came across her face, her eyes narrowed, and she stood shamelessly studying Rebekah. "So you are the bride of Isaac," she said. "You have come from Haran. I've heard of you."

"You honor me," Rebekah said, avoiding the woman's piercing stare.

"Where are your children?" she asked. "I've heard much of the promises made to this 'prince,' as you call him, by his God."

Rebekah felt the drops of sweat run down her face while her hands and feet felt suddenly clammy and cold. Her stomach twisted and churned and a terrible nausea came over her. She shook her head but no words came.

The princess tossed her head in the air and smirked. "I would guess that you have none. It's too bad. Your husband will have to do like his father and get another wife."

"You're right," Rebekah said at last as she regained her composure and looked at the princess without flinching. "I have no children but I have promises."

"Promises?" the princess asked. "Who has given you promises?"

"The God of my father-in-law Abraham, Elohim, He has promised."

The princess laughed a hard, harsh laugh. "You'll eventually learn, it's only the earth goddess that makes a woman fertile and can give her children. What proof do you have that this God of your people has ever given anyone a child?"

"Sarah, the mother of my husband, trusted Elohim and she was given a child even in her old age."

The princess grimaced and tossed her head arrogantly. "In her old age and only one child. Look, I have three children and am expecting another before the barley harvest. This is what my goddess can do."

Rebekah burst into tears and turned away. Deborah put her arms around her and tried to comfort her. At that the princess motioned to her serving girls. "We are not staying," she said. "This woman no doubt has her bellyful of demons. She will destroy everything she touches."

With that she picked up the little boy and started toward the door. Suddenly she hesitated and came back to where Rebekah stood. "Tell your husband that you met a princess named Anatah today who has three children and is expecting her fourth. He will understand."

As the sound of her footsteps died away, Rebekah ordered her handmaidens to gather up everything; then, leading the way, she hurried out the door and down the familiar, narrow lane to their house.

Isaac had just returned and was disturbed to see his dear Rebekah so distraught. "I won't stay here another night." Rebekah sobbed. "I want to go home, back to the tents."

It was only after they were back in their own familiar tent beside the Besor that Rebekah was able to tell him what had happened. When she told him the name of the princess, his face grew grave and troubled. "She says one must pray to the earth goddess for children," Rebekah told him.

Isaac said nothing, but he wondered at the ways of Elohim that He let this goddess get the best of Him in this way.

Deborah had been so sure the herbs, potions, and mandrake would bring about Rebekah's pregnancy that she had kept Terah's little goddess hidden away. Now she felt the little image was Rebekah's last hope. She knew that Abraham and Isaac would frown upon resorting to such desperate means. She herself viewed the little image as something that ought to concern only the women. The men would not understand that without the help of the goddess, Rebekah would never become pregnant.

In the darkness she felt under her sleeping mat and pulled out the soft, woven cloth given her by Rebekah's mother. With slow, careful movements, she unwound it and at last held the small image in her palm. She could feel its cool smoothness, the rounded stomach, and the straight, almost rigid legs. The nose was sharp and the head small. She wanted to look at it. The moon was full, and so without waking the other serving girls, she crept out of the tent into the bright moonlight.

Sitting with her back to the tent, she held the little figure in the light so she could get a better look. *She's ugly,* she thought with surprise. *I would have thought she would be beautiful. Everything about her is so carefully chiseled but the head and face are almost carelessly done.* The eyes were two slits and the mouth another slit, while the nose seemed to have been pinched into shape.

It seemed rather strange to Deborah that the carefully rounded stomach and the prominent V where the legs came together were the only parts well done. *It's as if the head is unimportant and only the childbearing parts are to be valued,* she thought. She had to admit to herself that to most men, a woman was worse than useless if she could not bear a child.

The next morning when the other women had gone about their chores and she was alone with Rebekah, she brought out the carefully wrapped packet. "You have wanted an image of the goddess from Ur and here it is," she said as she carefully unwrapped the packet and handed her the small figure. "It was given to me by your mother before we left Haran."

"My mother gave you this?" Rebekah asked as she turned the little figure around and looked at her from every angle.

"She wanted to be sure you had all the help you might need."

Rebekah was so moved she couldn't speak. Two tears dropped on the small goddess and she impulsively kissed the ugly face. "It must be one of the images my great-grandfather, Terah, made before he left Ur," she said.

"It was one of your family's most treasured possessions. Only your mother's great love for you could have persuaded her to part with such a prize."

Rebekah smiled through her tears. "Now I know I will have a child. This is a sign, a good omen."

"I should have given it to you years ago, but I knew that Isaac and his father would not approve."

"Of course, they are men," Rebekah said. "They don't understand such things. Their God is for men and now I know, it is only a goddess that can give a child."

Rebekah studied every feature of the small image, then kissed it again and tied it into the soft folds of her mantle. "And what is this cloth it came wrapped in?" she asked.

"Those are swaddling clothes for the baby. She wove them herself of the finest threads."

With eyes shining and hands trembling, she carefully folded the soft, white cloth. "It's my mother's own weaving," she said.

From that time on, Rebekah depended on the little image from Ur and gave up all hope of any help from the God of Isaac and Abraham. She asked two things of the little idol, first to give her a child and second to keep her husband from taking another wife as his father had done.

Surely now she would have a child.

*T*en years had passed since the fateful visit to Gerar, and since that time Rebekah refused to go near the town. Even though Keturah and her children went often with Abraham, still Rebekah would not go. "I can deal with my problems better in familiar surroundings," she said.

She meant that the people in Abraham's camp were all very supportive and many of them secretly brought her special herbs, potions, and charms that were to be a sure cure. She accepted all advice and welcomed all concoctions no matter how disagreeable they might be. She secretly felt that in time, after she had suffered enough, the goddess would take pity on her and give her the child she so desperately yearned for.

As time passed with no results, she began to beg Isaac to take one of her handmaidens as his mother, Sarah, had given Hagar to Abraham. "This will give us a child," she said wistfully.

Isaac rejected all of her suggestions. He stood firm in his belief: at the right time Elohim would grant them the child that had been promised. He was so sure of the promises given to his father that he never doubted that Rebekah would soon be with child.

Then something happened that caused even Isaac to doubt and begin to question everything he had taken for granted. His half brother Ishmael came riding into their camp with regal pomp, splendor, and show of wealth. His twelve sons rode on each side of him while his wives and their servants stretched out into the distance behind him.

With a great flourish of filial deference, Ishmael bowed low before Abraham, then raised the hem of his father's garment and kissed it. As he rose and stood aside, each of his sons came forward and did the same. Abraham was deeply moved. Ishmael was tall and handsome and his sons were strong and agile. More than that, Ishmael had brought gifts from the rich coffers of Egypt: rare perfumes, ornate jewelry, robes woven with intricate designs, incense, casks of unguents and fragrant oils.

"I have come to see my father," Ishmael said.

Though Abraham and Isaac ordered guest tents to be set up, Ishmael insisted on raising his own tent for himself. It was not woven of dark goat hair but was of skins sewn together and lined with fragrant drapery of Egyptian make.

Everything he owned seemed to be made with the very finest craftsmanship. His clothes were of Egypt's most costly linen and he wore a pectoral of precious stones set in polished brass. His sandals were gilded leather and his cloak was fringed.

Abraham ordered a great feast and the men sat long into the night around the fire discussing all that had happened to them and remembering the past. When it grew very late on the last night and everyone had drifted off, leaving only Isaac and Ishmael alone, the discussion took a more personal turn. "I was jealous of you," Ishmael said at last. "You were to have the blessing and were to be given the birthright."

Isaac grew very still and pensive. When he spoke it was with an air of real sympathy and understanding. "I didn't understand at first but now I do. For thirteen years you had been my father's firstborn and the delight of my mother. When I was born, everything changed for you, didn't it?"

"Yes. I never had known that Hagar was my mother until then. It was a terrible blow."

"And then my mother sent you away. That must have hurt the most."

There was a long silence and then Ishmael spoke in a low, tense but controlled voice. "No, the greatest hurt came in knowing I was not to have the blessing of the firstborn or the birthright."

"And I suppose you are still pained."

Ishmael laughed a hard, forced laugh. He broke in half the small stick he had been absentmindedly holding and threw the pieces into the fire. "No, no, I am not pained anymore," he said.

Isaac was surprised. "You no longer want the blessing or the birthright?"

Ishmael laughed again. "Look at me. I have more flocks and herds than my father, my sons own towns and live in stone castles, my coffers are full of gold and silver. I want for nothing. What greater blessing can my father give me?"

Isaac reached out and filled Ishmael's cup with more wine. "And," he said, "you have not mentioned your twelve strong, handsome sons or that I have none. If anyone is going to be the father of nations, it seems obvious; it will be you."

Ishmael toyed with the fringe on his cloak and smiled. "I wasn't going to say it, but it does seem rather obvious who has the blessing and the birthright."

"It has been almost twenty years since I married Rebekah, and in all this time we have not been blessed with even one child."

"Can you still be expecting Elohim to give you a child?"

"Yes," Isaac said slowly. "He is our only hope and He has promised."

Ishmael's eyes opened wide in astonishment. "You believe then. All that our father has spoken, you really believe."

"Yes," he said as a look of intense pain crossed his face.

They remained silent for a few minutes listening to the snapping of the thorns in the fire and the whirring of bats above their heads. Finally Ishmael roused himself to go and then, being reminded of something, sat back down. Impulsively he leaned over to look more closely at his brother and said in an almost kindly manner, "You could get another wife, you know."

"No," Isaac said with surprising force. "Elohim has promised and I will hold Him to His promise."

Ishmael was startled. He didn't answer for a few minutes but he was puzzled. "What makes you so sure you can trust this Elohim of our father?" he asked at last.

"I have learned through painful experiences that He can be trusted. However, one may have to wait until all hope is gone."

"I don't understand," Ishmael said.

Several minutes passed. Isaac seemed to be struggling within himself, not wanting to share something so personal. "You must have forgotten," he began finally. "I am the son of a mother who was ninety years old when I was born. She and my father had given up all hope. She laughed at the angels who told my father she would conceive."

"But you weren't there. You've just heard about it. You've had no personal experience with this Elohim."

Isaac stood and helped Ishmael to his feet. He placed his hand on his brother's arm and seemed about to say "good night," then he hesitated. "It's true, I was not there, but when the bigger challenge was given, I was very much there."

"You mean the sacrifice. I didn't understand that either. If you were

Elohim's chosen, how could He take such a chance? You could have been killed."

There was now a long pause as Isaac seemed to be reliving the whole episode. When he spoke his voice was low and his words measured. "I was actually tied as an animal is tied for sacrifice. He placed me on the altar." He did not look at Ishmael but off into the distance as though he was seeing all that happened. "Our father actually raised the knife."

"Do you really think he would have been able to kill you?" Ishmael whispered in a hoarse voice.

"Of course," Isaac responded without hesitation. "Our father was serious. If Elohim told him to do something, he would do it."

Ishmael shuddered. "I'm glad I was not the chosen or blessed of my father. Do you sometimes wish he had picked me and let you be free to do as you pleased?"

Isaac kicked at a stone until it spun loose from the sand and went rolling down a small incline. "No, if I escaped the fright of the sacrifice, I would have also missed the joy of the ram in the thicket."

"So you think Elohim put the ram there?"

"Of course, it was the angel that told my father not to harm me. He had already raised the knife when he saw the ram in the thicket."

"I have been told our father gave the place its name," Ishmael said. "Jehovah-Jireh . . . the Lord will provide."

The two stood by the fire mulling over their conversation and the strangeness of their lives. At last Ishmael heaved a sigh of relief as he said, "I now understand many things, and it is good I was not chosen by my father for the birthright or the blessing." The two embraced and then without another word walked silently away from the fire into the shadows and each to his own tent.

\* \* \*

Isaac did not go right to sleep. Instead he lay wide-awake watching the tent cloth billow and fold and hearing the tent poles creak and groan. He found himself puzzling over the birthright and the blessing. What were they worth when it seemed that a man like Ishmael could find the same results without the restrictions and discipline? Ishmael prayed but he didn't presume to hear the voice of Elohim. He had entered into the covenant through circumcision, but he was not to have the birthright or the special blessing, and so it seemed that he wasn't expected to regulate his life in such a strict way.

The more he thought about it, the more he grew confused. Ishmael did not have to live apart from the men of the cities. He could even keep an idol in his house and not feel guilty.

He remembered asking his father about the blessing and receiving a very strange answer: "It is not just that we are to be blessed but that through us the whole earth will be blessed," his father told him.

It was only after Ishmael had gone that Isaac learned the real purpose of his visit. He had come to ask Abraham for a blessing on his twelve sons and also to tell him that Hagar had died. He had buried her in an ancient, pagan temple on the coast of the Red Sea. This temple was built around a strange stone that had fallen from the sky and was considered sacred.

* * *

Several days passed before Isaac rode out to check on the men who stayed with the herds. He and his men rode up the dry riverbeds and circled the jagged mountain ranges to come at evening to an oasis where his herdsmen were camped. He found them all doing well with no reports of sickness or attacks from wild animals. He ate with the men, and when the moon came up he unrolled his pack and slept out under the stars close to the fire.

He often studied the stars, remembering always that his father had said Elohim had promised him descendants as the stars. Sometimes he would hold a fistful of sand and watch it pour in a thin stream onto the hard-packed earth. "Your descendants shall be as the sands," had been quoted to him over and over again. What did that mean, he wondered, if your wife was barren and had been barren for twenty years?

At times he had thought his father had made a mistake. Now he was almost sure of it. For Ishmael to have twelve sons was almost sure proof of Elohim's preference. Then there was also Keturah, who already had four sons. Surely if the promises were to come down through his line, he should have at least one son by this time. Was he, Isaac, still the one to have the birthright and the blessing?

When he reached home he went straight to the tent of his father and was relieved to find him alone. The servants had built a fire in the fire pot and Keturah had a delicious stew cooking in a stone dish on the top. Abraham sat holding the big folds of bread, waiting for the moment when he could dip pieces in the soup. This was his favorite dish.

He quickly pulled out a cushion for Isaac, and tearing the bread in half gave him the larger part. "You have been out riding and will find this stew very tasty," he said.

Isaac accepted the bread and sat down but said nothing. Abraham watched him for a few moments and then asked, "Is something troubling you, my son?"

"I am almost sixty years old, my father, and I find that there are many things I have taken for granted and have not understood."

Abraham almost laughed until he saw the serious look on his son's face. "What have you not understood?" he asked.

After a long moment of silence, Isaac looked up at his father with such a look of pain that Abraham was shocked. "The most basic thing in our lives. It is the blessing Elohim has promised. What is it? How do you know I am the one to receive it?"

Abraham's hand holding the bread stopped in midair. He turned to give Isaac a stunned look. He had always assumed that Isaac understood everything. He was such a devoted son and so careful to abide by the simple rules Elohim had given them. "You have done everything I have ever asked of you," Abraham said. "You went up Moriah with me and let me tie you to the altar without crying or saying a word. You agreed to let Eleazar go back to Haran to find you a bride. What have you not understood?"

Now tears were in Isaac's eyes. "Don't you realize? I did those things because I loved you and you asked it of me."

Abraham was visibly shaken. He placed the bread on the rim of the fire pot, pushed his headpiece back, grasped his beard, and frowned. For a moment he was speechless. He studied Isaac as though seeing him for the first time. When he spoke it was hesitantly. "My son, you are the child of promise. It is you who will receive Elohim's special blessing. Don't you understand that?"

"I have heard the words, but I don't know what this blessing is and why you think I am to inherit it."

Both men looked into the fire but seemed uninterested in the stew pot that was giving off a delicious fragrance. The large pieces of bread had been forgotten.

"To explain," Abraham said, "I must start way back. You already understand that Elohim, the one God, has always existed. Men discover Him; they don't invent Him. This is His world. He created it and everything in it."

"He existed back before Noah and the great flood?" Isaac asked.

"Of course. He let the flood happen because men had become so evil."

"And Noah? Why did He save Noah?"

"This is the first thing we have learned about Elohim. When He wants to do something in His world, He always chooses a man. Noah was chosen and I have been chosen as you are also chosen."

Isaac was gazing at his father intently. "What does it mean to be chosen?" he asked. "Chosen for what?"

"We don't always know. We must listen to Elohim and do what He tells us. We must know that He exists and that He has something of importance for us to do."

"And Noah? What happened to him?"

"Noah obeyed Elohim and his family was the only one saved from the flood."

"And his blessing?"

"He and his family were saved and he was given the rainbow as a very special gift from Elohim."

"I know about the rainbow. Elohim will never again destroy the world with a flood. You used to tell me that after the rains."

"Our family history tells us more about Noah. He was saved because God saw he was righteous and because he listened to God and believed in Him. But we also know that Noah left rules for us to follow if we would be righteous."

"We have the rules of Noah?"

"Of course. Our people come from the line of his son Shem, and they settled just below the mountain where the ark landed. The village of Haran is not far from that mountain. Shem lived to be very old. I can remember seeing him when I went north on trading trips with my father."

For a long time the two sat without saying anything. The moon rose and the fire died down. The sounds of mothers quieting their children could be heard, and then the soft, hurrying footfalls as someone walked by the tent. At last Abraham spoke. "It's not difficult. One who would know Elohim must believe that He is and that He is a rewarder of them that seek Him."

"And," said Isaac, "what are His rewards?"

"For each man they will be different, but for me and my family it is plain.

I am to be given this land and descendants as numerous the stars. I will be blessed and in turn will be a blessing."

"It's that simple?"

Abraham smiled. "It's as simple as a friendship. He has chosen to love me."

"But I have no children. Rebekah is crushed with the burden of it all. She feels she has been rejected. She's miserable."

"My son," Abraham said, after a pause, "have you asked Elohim for the child?"

"No," Isaac said finally. "I thought it was something that happened normally without asking."

Abraham picked up his piece of bread and dipped it in the stew, then bit off the succulent morsel and motioned for Isaac to do the same. When he had eaten almost all of the bread, he reached out and grasped Isaac's arm. "My son," he said, "it's important to ask Elohim for the things we need and want. Then when they come, we know they come from His hand and not from our fleshly efforts or an idol's fancy. We thank Him for the gift and are satisfied."

The fire had died down to a pile of glowing coals. The stew pot was almost empty and the bread was gone. Isaac rose to go and then hesitated. "Even though I have no children, you still believe all this will come to pass."

Abraham rose and came to where he could look at his son, who now stood in the soft, full light of the new moon. "I have no doubt, no doubt at all."

With that Isaac turned and went through the darkness toward his tent. Abraham stood watching him go until he was lost in the shadow of one of the tents.

*I*saac was once again camped at the oasis called La-Hai-roi, a place considered holy as it was here that Hagar, the mother of Ishmael, had seen the angel and been comforted. Hagar had named it Beer-La-hai-roi, or the well of Him that liveth and seeth me. Since that time, it had changed a great deal. Now there were tall palm trees and the well had a worn stone curb. It was a favorite stopping place for caravans going up to Hebron or over to Gaza.

Isaac had moved to this site not only because it was such a pleasant spot, but because he hoped the same angel that had brought such comfort to Hagar would again appear to bless and comfort Rebekah.

Actually it was in this place they reached the final crisis. First, it was here that Rebekah became obsessed with the problem of Sarah and her handmaid Hagar. Every way she turned she was reminded of Hagar's trauma, which had been acted out in this very place. She felt first the agony of Sarah who had been barren all of her life and at almost ninety was still childless. Then she was haunted by the frustration of Hagar who, while carrying a child for Sarah, had been beaten by her so that she had run away and had come here to this well.

"Why," Rebekah asked Isaac, "did Elohim let Hagar get pregnant so quickly? If He had just let Sarah have a child instead, things would have worked out much better."

During the visit of Ishmael, Hagar's now grown son, she had become increasingly aware of her problem. All of his wives had seemingly produced sons with no difficulty. They were plump, jolly women who thought it the very simplest thing to get pregnant and have a child. When she had asked them what herbs or magic potions they had used, they laughed and winked at each other as though it were a silly question.

Finally there was Keturah, who had never had to eat the strange, bitter potions or go through difficult ordeals to become pregnant. She had been able to fit right in with Ishmael's wives, discussing the trials of the birthing stool and the joys of nursing her little sons.

Rebekah's handmaids had tried to encourage her by pointing out that she still had the firm, pointed breasts of a young girl and her stomach was only gently rounded. These wives she so admired, they said, had thighs that spilled over their saddles and were so heavy they swayed the backs of their donkeys, their breasts were like filled wine jugs, and when they smiled there were teeth missing.

"But they are honored and respected," Rebekah reminded them. "They gave their husbands sons."

Now, on this night, Rebekah was even more distressed. She had taken so many vile smelling potions and had ordered so many charms that she was exhausted with the effort. "I used to be so happy, so excited about everything," she said to Deborah. "Now I think only of getting pregnant. I must have a child. I couldn't bear for Isaac to take a woman like his father took Hagar."

In the midst of this discussion, they heard someone approaching and Deborah lifted the tent flap to peer out into the darkness. Seeing that it was Isaac, she let it fall and hurried back to Rebekah. "Now, now," she said, as she coaxed a few curls into place around Rebekah's face, "it's your husband, Isaac. You mustn't let him see you this way." Then she quickly snatched up the fire pot and sprinkled some citrus peels on the coals to make a pleasant smell.

Just as Isaac appeared out of the shadows, Deborah disappeared out the back of the tent. Rebekah usually ran to meet him and had some happy event to recount. Now she rose from the cushions where she had been sitting, but did not smile. Though she held out both hands as usual, he could see there was something wrong. "My love," he said, putting an arm tenderly around her and leading her back to the cushions, "what's wrong? What has happened?"

She tried to smile but instead quickly turned her head away so he could not see her eyes filling with tears. It was then he saw the clumps of herbs and weeds, the gourds that were strewn around with vile black potions dried in them. The smell was no longer the sweet fragrance of jasmine or sandalwood but some rancid, putrid odor that almost choked him. "What has happened?" he said, peering into the darkness as he tried to assess the situation. "This is like the cave of some fearful witch."

At that she pushed him away and scowled. "I've tried everything. All these awful potions to drink or eat or be bathed in." She flung out her arms in a gesture of helpless frustration. "It's no use. I can't do even the simplest things that other women do so easily." At that she crumpled down among the cushions and sobbed great wracking sobs that tore at Isaac's heart. He had never seen her cry like this before, and he couldn't imagine what had brought about such disaster. His lovely, smiling little wife had somehow been deeply hurt, and he meant to get to the bottom of it.

"Is it me? Have I done anything to hurt you?" She couldn't speak but shook her head. He became more frantic as he asked, "Has someone hurt you?" Again she shook her head but sobbed even more wildly.

He sank beside her and held her tight while he spoke soothing words, brushed back her hair, and tried to see her face. "Tell me, you must tell me what has happened," he insisted. She shook her head but could not answer.

In a veritable frenzy Isaac shouted for Deborah. The old woman must have been standing just outside the tent, for no sooner did he call than she appeared. "What has happened to my wife? Who has hurt her so?" he stormed.

Deborah had never seen Isaac so agitated. She stood speechless, not knowing what to say.

"Come, come," he said. "Why has she been eating all these strange things, and what is this terrible odor?"

At that Rebekah pulled away from him, and without bothering to straighten her mantle or wipe the tears from her cheeks, she blurted out, "I've been drinking ugly potions, gathering rare herbs, boiling foul smelling ointments, and still I'm not with child."

"My lord," Deborah said, coming to her defense, "she has indeed tried everything. Even the Egyptian cures."

"Egyptian cures?"

"Ishmael's wives brought me special gifts when they heard of my trouble," Rebekah said.

"What sort of gifts?" Isaac asked.

"Some giant beetles called scarabs. They were dried and you mix them with lentils."

"Beetles! Why beetles?" he said.

"They are believed to have strange and wonderful powers," Deborah said. "At the beginning of the wet season, they suddenly appear and then they disappear when it's dry. They say that when they're eaten, they can make a person live long or become pregnant."

"They also brought huge frogs to eat." Rebekah made a grimace of distaste.

"You ate frogs?"

"An old Egyptian woman from Gerar told us these large frogs will always bring children," Deborah explained.

"I only ate the legs," Rebekah said. "Then someone told me not to eat them anymore or my children's eyes would bulge out."

"I don't understand." Isaac looked puzzled and confused.

"My lord," Deborah said, "these special frogs are called matlametlo. They hide in the root of a bush in drought and come bursting out when it rains. The Egyptians believe these frogs can bring new life."

"I thought we agreed we'd wait for Elohim to give us a child," Isaac said finally.

For a moment there was silence as both Rebekah and Deborah realized that Isaac could not understand their frustration. He seemed so sure. He apparently had no doubts that at the right time Rebekah would fulfill the promise and become pregnant.

"It's quite obvious to me Elohim's a God for men, not a woman," Rebekah interjected gently. "I've prayed and waited twenty years and nothing's happened."

"My mother . . ." Isaac began.

Rebekah jumped up. "I'll not suffer as your mother did. I can't endure a Hagar. I'd rather die."

"Who has even suggested a Hagar? I've never considered taking another wife."

"I know what will happen if I can't have a child."

"We must be patient and wait."

Rebekah ran to the sleeping mat rolled out in the corner and, kneeling down, drew out the small, carefully wrapped packet. Then coming back to kneel beside Isaac, she said, "Here's what women depend on who want children." She unwrapped the packet to reveal the small image of the fertility goddess of Ur.

Isaac drew back as though he had been slapped. He frowned and shook his head when she tried to hand him the little image. "Where did this ugly thing come from?" he demanded.

"Rebekah's mother gave it to me as we were leaving," Deborah said.

"And you brought this from Haran?"

"Yes, my lord. It's one of the small images from Ur made by your grandfather Terah. It is very powerful in matters that concern women."

"From Ur?" Isaac said.

"My family in Haran kept favor with all the gods," Rebekah said.

Isaac jumped to his feet in great agitation. "We must destroy it quickly before my father hears of it. He'll not be pleased to know there's such a thing in our camp."

"No," Rebekah cried, hiding it behind her back. "I'll die childless without her. Even the shepherds and their wives know one must depend on a goddess to have children."

Isaac frowned and pulled at his beard. His eyes were piercing and stern. "And who would you thank for a child gotten by such means?" Both Deborah and Rebekah shrank back, but Rebekah still kept the image behind her back, clutched firmly in her hand.

"It must be destroyed. Come, give it to me. I'll have it done away with." He held out his hand, but Rebekah clung to it with all the more determination.

"You are afraid of your father," Rebekah cried, turning her face away so she would not have to see the look in his eyes. "This small image will do no harm and it is my only hope for a child."

"So," he said, "you are depending on a lifeless bit of molded clay instead of the living, creator God." He struggled to understand this strange turn of events.

At that Rebekah brought her hand out where she could look at the small image more closely. It was, as he said, rather ugly but carefully molded of brown clay. "You must not think of destroying it," she said. "It's very old. The only thing I have that was made by my great-grandfather. It's quite precious."

"If you're depending on this ugly clay image to give you a child, who knows what you'll get. We can be sure it will not be the child Elohim has promised."

Rebekah gave a startled cry. "How can you say such a thing? This is my last chance. I can't give it up." With that she sank down among the cushions and buried her face in her folded arms with the little image still clutched tightly in her hand.

Isaac squatted beside her and spoke gently. "Surely you can see that this lifeless bit of clay can't give you a living child."

Rebekah straightened up and held the image out where she could see it again. For a long moment she was silent, taking in its pinched face, slitted eyes, slightly rounded stomach, and the legs tightly pressed together. "If I give her to you, are you going to destroy her?"

"She must be destroyed. Even if my grandfather made her and she is very old."

"Why can't I keep her and you pray to Elohim for a child?"

"And if the child comes, who will you thank?"

Rebekah stared at the little image in her hand as though she were seeing it in a new light. "I would thank Elohim."

"And the little image?"

There was a long silence. When she spoke it was so softly Isaac could hardly hear what she said. "I'd think the little goddess had somehow brought it about."

"And what would you tell the other women?"

Tears came in Rebekah's eyes. "I would probably loan them the little goddess if they could not get pregnant."

"And the child? What would you tell the child?"

Rebekah began to sob softly as she studied the ugly little figurine. Her tears splashed on its pinched face, and she wiped them off with a corner of her mantle. She could not speak. She covered her face with one hand, and with the other held the image out to Isaac. "You can do with her as you please. I cannot bear to destroy her myself."

Isaac took the little figure and stuffed it quickly into his belt. "Don't be afraid. I'll see that she is destroyed. Then I'll make special entreaty of Elohim for our child."

Rebekah turned and buried her face in the cushions and wept while Isaac motioned to Deborah to comfort her. "I'll be back later, but now I must tend to this thing lest she change her mind."

* * *

News leaked out about the small idol and Isaac's entreaty for his wife. The whole camp waited and watched to see what would happen. They feared for Rebekah's sanity and were divided as to what harm could have been done in letting her keep the small image. "It was made in Ur by old Terah. It undoubtedly held special powers," some said.

Others were shocked to hear that right in the tent of Isaac's wife such a thing had been hidden. As it turned out, when within a few weeks it was discovered Rebekah was pregnant, both groups rejoiced and marveled at such a miracle.

Wonderful predictions were made as they contemplated the birth of this child. "Of course it will be a boy," they all agreed.

* * *

From the very first, the pregnancy was not the joyful event they all had envisioned. When Isaac threw a great feast to celebrate and invited all their friends and relatives, Rebekah was confined to her tent. The very smell of roast lamb or a bowl of lentils made her dizzy and nauseated. She could drink only warm water and could eat only the rounded loaves of plain bread. "The child will never develop," the old midwives predicted. She must eat.

They plied her with every kind of choice morsel, to no avail. The roasted pigeons were turned away at the tent door, and the very smell of the savory stew she had once loved made her even more ill. Finally dried figs were brought, and succulent melons, but nothing solved the problem.

In the fifth month, when she was finally able to eat, she began to suffer from a new problem. "I feel that something is very wrong," she would say. "There's a constant twisting and tugging day and night in my stomach. I can't sleep. I can't even sit comfortably."

Again the midwives gathered, and they too had to admit it was unusual. When they put their hands on her stomach, they could feel the violent movement. "She has no rest day or night," they reported.

For Rebekah it was not only a time of frustration and pain but also a time of puzzlement. "This is not the child of the goddess but the child my husband prayed for to Elohim. Why should it be this way? I've done everything my husband asked of me. I let him destroy the little idol and now I am in this torment. Why has this happened?"

Some women suggested it was the revenge of the earth goddess and others refused to admit that anything was unusual. Isaac was as deeply perplexed as Rebekah, and so at last he went to his father, Abraham, and asked what should be done. "I have no doubt, since it is in Elohim's hands, it will turn out all right," Abraham said. "However, if she is concerned then tell her to inquire of Elohim."

"But she is a woman and . . ."

"My son, I learned a great lesson from Hagar. The angel appeared to her and comforted her. She was an Egyptian, she wasn't familiar with our ways, and yet her prayer was heard."

Isaac sat awhile longer with his father and then excused himself and went back to tell Rebekah his father's astonishing response. Rebekah was still sitting by a small fire of thorns, rocking back and forth, her arms folded over her stomach in an effort to get some relief. Deborah and two of her handmaidens were with her, but when Isaac appeared they quickly left. Isaac sat beside her and waited for a few moments before speaking.

"And what does your father say?" Rebekah asked at last.

"He says for you yourself to go inquire of Elohim. This is the only way you will be comforted."

"I inquire? I remember asking for a husband when my brother Laban was going to have me marry an old man named Nazzim."

"And what happened?"

"Eleazar came and rescued me."

"Then you did inquire of Elohim?"

"I didn't know anything about Him. I just knew He was the God of my uncle Abraham and I was desperate."

"For my father it is all very simple. When I was a child he used to tell me to go talk to Elohim just as I would come to him."

"Go to Elohim? How do I go to Him? We can't see Him. I'm just a woman. I can't build altars or make sacrifices."

"That's what's so strange. My father builds altars and makes sacrifices, but he also talks to Elohim as though He's his friend."

They said no more about the problem but sat by the fire until it had burned down to a few glowing coals. And then Isaac picked Rebekah up and carried her in and placed her on the mat Deborah had rolled out. He rubbed her back and cradled her in his arms until he could hear the soft, steady breathing and knew she was at last asleep. He stayed with her until morning and then quietly slipped out to meet his men who were going to check one of the new wells that had been dug.

\* \* \*

Rebekah pondered the strange turn of events. Though she had heard the story of Hagar many times, it had never occurred to her that a woman could talk to Elohim in the same way she would talk to her grandfather or her husband. When she had cried out to Him in Haran and asked Him to rescue her from marrying Nazzim, she had prayed no formal prayer. It had been simply a plea for help. When Eleazar came, she had assumed it was all in answer to Abraham's prayer for his son.

She went over in her mind the names she had heard for this God of her husband. Isaac referred to Him as El Shaddai when he talked about His power and strength and El-Elyon, or the most high God, when explaining that He was above all angels and powers of the air. She had heard Him also called Jehovah-Jirah, the God who provides, and Elohim, the creator God. She must think first of all what name she would call Him if she was to do this unusual thing.

As the days passed she decided she would feel more comfortable talking to Him as Elohim, creator God. She had been reminded that He had made the flowers she loved and had caused the sheep to birth the little lambs. He had made the water that flowed by in the brook Besor and even the sun and the moon with all their beauty. All of nature began to take on a new aspect to her. She was coming to know the creator God by the beauty He had created, and she felt a growing wonder and love for Him she had not thought possible.

Finally on a day in early spring, while out looking for fresh herbs, she came upon a lovely sight. She had grown tired and wandered off from the others. She was about to sit on a projection of rock when she saw flashes of bright red on the northeastern slope of a rocky hillside. Upon investigation she found a cluster of tulips. They were a brilliant red and were known by the shepherds as bloody tulips.

Isaac had pointed out the plant when it was but a single thin waving leaf. "In three or four years," he had said, "if conditions are favorable, the plant will put out three leaves. Soon after that a single spike will begin growing from the center, and in a very short while there will be the most beautiful red tulip."

She had often seen the thin waving leaf but never the tulips Isaac had described to her. Now she knelt to see the lovely, delicate flowers more closely. She sat back on her heels and marveled. It was such a lovely sight. Several were open, but others were still closed. They were not to be picked, as they would soon die and the bright petals fall. She could hardly contain the wonder of the moment. It had taken these little plants three or four years to produce these bright beauties. How much like herself, she thought. This little plant had taken so long to come to this moment of fulfillment and it had been fashioned that way by Elohim. How very strange and wonderful.

Isaac had said his father often told him there was a pattern in nature. It was left up to man to learn the patterns and not waste time begging Elohim to change the pattern. This little flower would come in its season and not before. Isaac accepted this and was not bothered by periods of waiting that so disturbed her.

As she sat looking at the delicate red flowers, she understood that she too was being fruitful at the appointed time, when the conditions were right. A great joy filled her heart. She felt that Elohim had let her find the lovely bright flowers just to give her this message. "Then why," she asked, "am I in this torment? Why, if this is Your plan, should I have no peace?"

She had not expected an answer, but to her surprise she heard a voice speaking to her. It was distinct and the message was concise. "Two nations are in your womb," the voice said. "The one people will be stronger than the other, and the elder will serve the younger."

The voice ceased but the words "the elder shall serve the younger" echoed in her mind over and over as she pondered what it might mean.

Slowly she got to her feet and hurried to find Deborah and her other maidens. She didn't join in the happy banter and didn't even ask what herbs they had found. She was totally preoccupied with what had happened to her and the message she had been given.

When she finally arrived at her tent, she entered the cool darkness and sank onto the cushions completely exhausted. Almost immediately, her small serving maid, Tesha, came, and she sent her to find Isaac. She could hardly wait to tell him all that had happened to her. Elohim had spoken just as Abraham had suggested, and the message was strange and wonderful.

She had expected Isaac to be as excited as she was, but to her chagrin, she found him paying very little attention to the message. Instead, he was mainly pleased that she was no longer anxious. "But what does it mean?" she asked. "The elder shall serve the younger?"

Isaac puzzled over it a moment. "Are you sure that is what you heard?" he asked hesitantly. "It doesn't sound right. To have twins would be unusual, but it would be against all tradition and custom for the elder to serve the younger."

Rebekah looked down at the cushion and fingered the fringe. "I was so sure . . . but . . ."

Isaac hugged her. "It's going to be all right. Everything's going to be all right," he said. "Whether you have one child or two doesn't matter; you are going to have a child and that is what is important."

She pulled away and looked at him. "But I was so sure..."

"Of course, I understand." He pulled her to him and gently kissed her forehead where her mantle had fallen away. "This is all so hard for you but it will all be over soon."

Rebekah pulled away and took some time adjusting her mantle. She didn't want him to see how disappointed she was. She had expected such a different reception. He patted her hand and then rose and strode out through the opening in the tent.

She sat very still pondering all that had happened. How had she thought Elohim would really bother to speak to a troubled woman? No matter what Isaac had said, it was evident he didn't really believe Elohim had actually bothered to speak to her.

She gave a groan as the churning and twisting suddenly seized her. She bent over, clutching her stomach. Sweat broke out on her forehead as she stuffed the end of her mantle in her mouth and bit down hard. He was right about one thing: it was getting close to her confinement. It wouldn't be long now. However painful the birth might be, it would be a relief to be rid of this constant upheaval.

As quickly as the struggle had seized her, it stopped, and she sank back into the cushions exhausted. She stretched her fingers out over her bulging stomach and breathed deeply. "I was so sure," she murmured.

* * *

It was within that week that the birth pains began and the birthing stool was moved into her tent. Deborah hurried to get the folded swath of fine linen for the swaddling clothes while others busied themselves getting extra water from the well and the salt for rubbing the newborn. They stopped only to spread the news that Rebekah was about to have the long-awaited child.

Rebekah had been on the birthing stool for a considerable time and the midwives were beginning to get anxious when Deborah, who was holding her hand, felt her grip tighten. "The child is coming," she said just as Rebekah let out a great cry and, weeping, clung to Deborah.

Within minutes the old midwife held up a screaming, struggling infant. "It's a boy! He's healthy and strong," she shouted.

"He's covered with soft red hair like a lion's cub," another exclaimed as she rubbed the child with oil and salt and wrapped him quickly in the swaddling clothes, ready to take him outside the tent where Isaac waited impatiently.

"There is yet another child coming. I saw a hand clutching the heel of this one," the old midwife had exclaimed, but no one but Rebekah heard her. The women had all followed the first midwife outside the tent. Isaac was given the child. Immediately the somber mood changed and there was dancing and singing and exclaiming over the rugged health of the child. "He is beautiful to see with soft, red hair and a strong cry," they chanted and sang.

Even when one of the serving girls rushed out to tell them another child was being born, they paid no attention. Isaac was laughing and exclaiming over the child he held. He wept tears of joy and cried with a loud voice, "This is the child of promise, my firstborn, the child who will inherit the birthright and the blessing. We will call him Esau because of his redness."

In the tent Rebekah held out her arms and asked to hold the second child, who had arrived quietly without the attention or fanfare of the first. There had been no swaddling cloth to wrap him in, so he was hastily rubbed with oil and salt and wrapped in Rebekah's head cloth. The old midwife studied him a moment. "He's a scrawny, poor one, not healthy and strong like the other."

Rebekah hungrily clasped the small bundle and cradled him in her arms. She studied his little face. His eyes were shut tight, giving his features a worried look that tugged at her heart. She marveled at his small, perfect ears and ran her finger around his face and gently touched his mouth so that he gave a small sucking motion. She smiled as she examined his tiny hand and thought how the midwife had cried out that his hand had been clutching the heel of his brother.

Tears came to her eyes as she realized that this small one was being totally ignored. Everyone had now left her alone in the tent while they celebrated and rejoiced over his brother. She could hear the clamor and now drums beating and the ram's horn blown to announce the importance of the occasion. From time to time, loud and clear, she heard the strong, lusty cry of her firstborn.

She laid her cheek against the soft dark hair of her neglected child and let her tears fall freely. *No one cares about this lovely child, and no one has even come to give him a name.* She rocked back and forth studying his little form with wonder and delight. *There really have been two babies struggling in my womb. Two nations, the voice called them. And it was said the elder shall serve the younger.*

If it really was the voice of Elohim, surely He would reveal His will to Isaac and his father, Abraham!

She felt the soft little hand of her child curl around her finger. Looking down she remembered again that it was this hand that had grabbed the heel of his brother. She laughed a tight, bitter laugh. "We will call you Jacob, the supplanter, the cheater of his brother, the heel grabber," she murmured in utter frustration. "We will see if even Elohim can manage to give you the blessing and the birthright when your father has already announced it will go to Esau."

It was some time later that Isaac discovered another child had been born. "What will we call him?" he asked Rebekah.

"I have already named him Jacob," she said, hoping he would get the subtle message and remember the prediction.

He looked puzzled for a moment and then smiled. "You can name this one; I have already named our firstborn Esau."

*I*t was spring and the time was fast approaching for celebrating the fifteenth birthday of Isaac's twins. It was also a happy, joyful time, for during these years Abraham and his family had prospered in a most astonishing way. The winter rains had been abundant and one saw bright clumps of flowers thriving in unexpected places and even more surprising, large patches of winter wheat.

Abraham had used the learning of Ur to produce this miracle. In Ur the land was barren except for the areas that were irrigated. "Any land will become fruitful with water," he said. "Dig wells, take advantage of the winter rains, and this will no longer be barren land."

Not only had the land become productive, but his flocks of sheep and goats had multiplied in an amazing way. The fine quality of his wool was acclaimed and sought after, not only in the cities along the central ridge but also in the coastal cities as far north as Byblos, Ugarit, and Carchemish. The scraped and treated sheepskins were often carried down into Egypt where they became sandals, cushions, and even vellum for writing.

Abraham had become a man of vast and enviable wealth. This was to be both the source of his great satisfaction and his growing problem. The men of the cities and the traders along the caravan routes looked at him with greedy eyes. It all looked so easy and they coveted the same success.

It had also been more than thirty-five years since Keturah had become Abraham's concubine, and in this time she had blessed him with six strong, healthy sons. They were quick to learn, and he had observed with pride how easily they could master any physical feat. In competitions of brawn or muscle, they all excelled.

Two of them, Ishbak and Shuah, were about the same age as Isaac's twins. Abraham had noticed with growing concern that they tended to seek out Esau for their adventures but ignored Jacob. As a result, Jacob was more inclined to be in his mother's tent learning her tricks of making a succulent lentil stew or helping to turn a young lamb on the spit. *The boy must be lonely at times,* Abraham thought.

When the men sat around the campfire in the evening, Jacob kept to himself and only listened to the men talk. Esau and the sons of Keturah were always in the midst of any discussion. They never seemed to lack tales of adventure that involved both skill and raw courage. Abraham was too old now to enter into the heady excitement of either the hunt or the games of physical skill, and so he too sat and listened and watched.

He noticed how Isaac's eyes shone with pride as Esau fearlessly wrestled and sometimes even bested the sons of Keturah. He would challenge them to target practice with their bows and arrows just so he could see Esau excel. He could not restrain himself from bragging about the attainments of his handsome son. He never seemed to notice Jacob. It was as though the boy didn't even exist, and yet Jacob was much more like Isaac had been at the same age.

As the competition between Keturah's sons and Esau grew more fierce, Abraham saw with alarm that what had at first seemed good and healthy had grown almost ugly and destructive. It was slowly disrupting the peace of the camp. Rebekah and Keturah were no longer friends. They watched their sons from a distance and became bitter if their sons were not the favored ones. Isaac was unwittingly a part of the whole dilemma. He was so proud of his more aggressive son, Esau, that he was often unfair to Keturah's sons and totally oblivious to the needs of his second son, Jacob.

Abraham had long ago explained to Keturah that her sons were not to receive the birthright or the blessing. At first she had accepted this without anger or resentment. However, as the competition grew between her sons and Esau, she began to pout and cast dark looks at Rebekah and Isaac. She had even tried by cunning and craftiness to turn Abraham from his intentions.

When Abraham commented with delight on some special dish she served him, she would motion for her son Jokshan to come and tell his father how he had managed to trap the bird. "Your son Isaac has never done such a thing and at such a young age," she would say with pride as she pushed her son into the firelight.

The boy would quickly come to stand before Abraham, still holding his throwing stick. His eyes seemed to glint in the firelight with anticipation of his father's approval. His head was held high with a certain haughty assurance. "See, we named him right, Jokshan, fowler," she would say. "He will never go hungry."

113

Abraham was well aware of her strategies as she pushed forward her other sons in the same way, but he never minded. He admired the boys and loved their brash assurance. Isaac had never managed such an air of confidence.

However, there was one area in which he was always disappointed. He had a habit of asking these sons to come and sit with him, anticipating a lively conversation. "Have you ever wondered how a bird can fly?" he might ask, expecting some interesting conjecture. Instead the boy would look at him with wide, puzzled eyes and frown slightly.

"It's not such useless puzzles he's concerned with," Keturah would explain after he had gone. "He doesn't waste time dreaming about things that don't matter."

Abraham had to conclude that all of Keturah's sons were of the same practical bent. They excelled at doing and producing visible results and had no time for what seemed to Keturah "idle talk." He realized that Isaac of all his sons was of the most thoughtful disposition. He always enjoyed a good discussion, and Jacob was the same, while Esau was more like the sons of Keturah. It surprised Abraham to see such differences in his own family.

✳ ✳ ✳

On a night in early spring, Abraham was gradually wakened by the creaking of the tent poles as they tugged against the tethers. A cool breeze had sprung up. The moon was full, and outside the tent were whole splashes of light. The stillness was broken only by the bleating of some of the young lambs separated from their mothers. He rose with difficulty, realizing how feeble he had become. He unfolded his shawl that had served as a pillow, wrapped it around his shoulders, and went to the tent door. It was a rare time that he was ever alone, and he knew that one needed to be alone at times to unravel some of life's mysteries.

He had much to ponder. The time was fast approaching that he must make a decision; he must do something about Keturah and her sons. He could remember how excited he had been when Keturah seemed to be able to produce sons one after the other with no trouble. After Sarah's long time of barrenness, he had viewed this as something wonderful and even mysterious.

Now he saw things differently. He knew he would not live much longer, and after he was gone, where would this struggle and competition lead them? There were six sons of Keturah and Isaac only had two. Keturah was encouraging her sons to edge out those of Isaac, if not for the blessing then for the birthright. He had even known instances where the sons of a concubine had murdered the sons of the legitimate wife just for the advantage.

It was evident he must move quickly, make some hard decisions. Isaac was the immediate concern. He must not be displaced, but after him what would happen? Esau, Isaac's firstborn, seemed only concerned with practical matters, while Jacob was just the opposite. Why hadn't there been just one son for Isaac with these two qualities perfectly blended, he wondered.

He held tightly to the tent pole as he lowered himself to the sandy floor. He must settle this in his mind before daylight, and then he must act. He could already feel his strength ebbing, his voice getting softer, and his eyes dimming. Who could guess how long he had before he would be gathered to his people in the great and strange land of the dead.

He tried to go back over the years that had gone so quickly. He wanted to remember each of the sons of Keturah so he could deal justly with them. He realized that as he had grown older they all tended to blur together without separate identities.

There was Zimran, meaning celebrated. Abraham was always embarrassed to think how he had almost forgotten Isaac in his joy at this son's birth. During the twenty years that Rebekah had been barren, Keturah had been having children. Jokshan, the fowler, came next then Medan, judgment. Keturah had insisted on the name because she had pressed him to make a judgment in favor of her son as opposed to Isaac's claim on the birthright.

Some time had passed after that before she had presented him with Midian and then Ishbak. The last son she had named Shuah, depression, because he had been born at the same time as Isaac's twins. With Isaac's twins everything changed. He had heirs and her sons could no longer be considered. Keturah had grown depressed and even bitter.

As much as he loved the boys, it was evident that he must send them away. He would give them each a generous settlement and send them with their mother back to her father, their grandfather. They would be more than welcome there as the old man had produced only daughters. He determined to do it quickly while he was still of sound judgment and in control of things. There was not much time left and things must be in order so there would be no conflict after he was gone.

He knew it would not be easy. Keturah would cry and the boys would complain among themselves. They would not dare to openly come against him. However, if things were not settled now, once he was gone and Isaac was in charge, there would be constant trouble.

He thought of Isaac, and as happened so often these days, he was reminded of their trip to Mount Moriah. Layers and layers of meaning kept coming to him in these years since it had all happened. There was nothing unusual in his taking his son to sacrifice him. This was done quite often by his Canaanite neighbors for seemingly trivial reasons. A child or young person might be sacrificed for the success of a trading venture, the erection of a house, or even to clear a man's conscience before his household gods.

One of the things that made their sacrifice so different from his was that they usually had many sons and he had only the one special son of the promise. Ishmael, his firstborn, was not even considered. It was obviously a test of some sort. He had realized at first that in presuming to be a friend of his God, it was to be expected that at some time that obedience would need to be weighed and evaluated. Mount Moriah may have been that evaluation.

It was also different because he had been told to go to a specific place, Mount Moriah, to make the sacrifice. The usual procedure was for the sacrifice to be made close to the man's home. Friends and relatives would be notified and a feast would be prepared and served once the ritual was over. None of these things were part of his instructions.

Of course the final difference was that the boy was not sacrificed after all. If he shut his eyes, he could still see his son's trusting gaze, feel the raised knife in his right hand, the place marked with his thumb where the knife would fall. There had been the sudden rigidity in his raised hand and the voice telling him not to harm his son. Then the miracle of seeing the ram in the thicket.

He remembered telling Isaac when he had asked about the lamb for the sacrifice, "The Lord will provide." Of course there had been no lamb and he had tied his son, placed him on the altar, and raised the knife before the ram had appeared. The usual procedure would have been for the sacrifice to be carried out regardless of what he heard or felt. He'd never heard of anyone untying and releasing the sacrifice. If he hadn't been used to listening for Elohim's voice, he would have gone ahead and sacrificed his son. He buried his head in his hands and wept. Even as an old man the memory moved him deeply. His son's trust, Elohim's faithfulness, and then the realization that his God did not want His people to sacrifice their children.

116

Very slowly the memory faded and he was again aware of the night sounds, the dark sky punctured with bright stars, the smells of damp earth and growing things, and finally the fresh breeze that toyed with the tent flaps and lifted the sand at his feet. *Yes, I must send Keturah and her sons away. Isaac would not have the strength to do it. He would give in to their pleading, might even give them his birthright.*

With great effort he raised himself, dusted the sand from his robes, and turned back into his tent. He rolled his shawl into a pillow and eased himself down onto his mat and was soon fast asleep.

The next day he woke with a new feeling of urgency. He had to accomplish all that needed to be done. He must make his announcements soon and carry out his decision quickly. Keturah and her sons must be sent away as soon as possible. First, he would have to tell Keturah. Then he would have to make an announcement to his immediate family and close tribesmen.

Before he took any action, he called Eleazar and conferred with him. He must not offend his friend who was Keturah's father, and he did not want his sons to feel that he had been unfair.

When Eleazar came, Abraham did not ask his advice as he often had done in the past; instead he simply told him his plan. "You must take several trusted men and ride as quickly as possible to my old friend, Keturah's father. You will tell him that I am soon to be gathered to my people and I must leave my camp in order."

Eleazar started to object but was silenced by Abraham's stern look and upraised hand. "You will tell him," Abraham continued, "that while I have a son to manage my affairs when I am gone, I know that he has none. He gave Keturah to me at a time when I needed her; now I am ready to return her with her six sons and such of my wealth as they will need. They are good sons and grandsons and will bless him in his old age."

Eleazar was gone for a fortnight, and when he returned he had nothing but good news to impart. "The old prince welcomed me as though I were a brother," he said, "and when I told him your decision, he wept." His daughters were all married and gone and both his trading business and his herds were being managed by hired strangers. He was being raided and terrorized by robbers and he expected at any time to be taken prisoner and have all his wealth snatched from him.

Now when Abraham called Keturah and told her of his decision and the problems her father was having, she didn't object. She had quickly seen that it would be to her sons' advantage to be in a secure position. However, Abraham was amused to see how shrewd she was in bargaining with him. "She makes decisions like a man," he confided to Isaac.

There was much discussion and argument among Keturah's sons until they finally concluded that in all that was planned, they would be the winners. In the end they were impatient to leave and actually resisted the effort of their father to send them off with dancing and singing and huge feasts. They bragged and strutted about with a new sense of their importance.

Esau welcomed their leaving, but Jacob had a different reaction. For the first time he fully understood the importance of being the firstborn, of inheriting the birthright and the blessing. These were things he valued all the more since he felt they could be denied him.

Many times he had heard his mother telling of his birth and the word she had received from the Lord. To her it was all settled—he, Jacob, was to have the blessing and the birthright. However, he knew that his father had paid no attention to anything his mother had said. He was assuming that Esau would have both the birthright and the blessing.

To make his situation even more bitter, now both Zimran and Jokshan taunted him, saying, "It's your brother, Esau, who will inherit everything. You will only prosper in his shadow." At this they would nudge each other and smirk. He noticed with growing frustration that they treated Esau very differently. Since he was to receive the blessing and the birthright, they wanted him as their friend.

He understood quite well why the sons of Keturah were being sent off to their grandfather. This was how things were done. The firstborn son must have no competition. He wondered how long it would be before a choice would have to be made between himself and his twin brother. What would happen when his mother and father at last confronted their very different ideas of what should take place? Of course nothing would happen until Abraham died. When he died, everything would eventually be brought out into the open, and there could be some terrible conflicts.

## 13

*J*acob watched Keturah and her sons leave with a feeling of relief.

The last few days had been filled with feasting and packing, some crying, and more advice given back and forth. At the last, Keturah was concerned for Abraham's care. He was not strong now and would need constant attention. "He must have warm broth on waking in the morning and fruit in season," she told Rebekah. "Perhaps you could have Jacob tend to these things. He is the only one who doesn't have something important to do."

Rebekah was ready to give a quick retort and then thought better of it. The suggestion was good even though the snide remark was not. In this simple way it came about that Jacob was chosen to spend time with his grandfather and to minister to his needs.

Several days before Keturah was to leave, Jacob was brought to his grandfather's tent. Abraham had only been told that one of the twins would stay with him and would take care of any needs he might have. He had obviously assumed it would be Esau. He had muttered something about having envisioned "feasting on some of the boy's venison." More than that, it was obvious that he had looked forward to spending time making sure Esau was grounded in the basic beliefs and history of their family.

When Jacob appeared, Abraham could not help but show his disappointment. He even spoke to Isaac about it, but nothing could be done. Esau was not only absent on hunting trips but had begun to spend time courting a young Hittite maiden who lived in the city of Kiriath-arba (also called Hebron). "We are not pleased that he is so interested in a Hittite, but there is no one else for our sons here," Isaac explained.

Before Keturah left, she took Jacob and showed him all that he would be responsible for in caring for his grandfather. She was concerned that Abraham not only have the proper food but that it be cut in pieces easy to chew; the sauces for dipping his bread should be seasoned with mint and basil; while for his stomach's sake he must have cardamom in warm camel's milk. At night

Jacob must warm a stone to put at his feet.

The instructions went on endlessly until Jacob was afraid he could not remember everything and begged to be released from the responsibility. He went first to Rebekah, who was preparing some birds for their dinner. He begged her to make some other arrangement. "No, no," she said. "This is a good time for you to learn everything you must know if you are to have the birthright and the blessing."

"But Esau said . . ." he began.

"We are not listening to Esau or anyone else," his mother retorted. "It was Elohim Himself who spoke and told me the younger was to rule the older. That should be enough for you. Don't listen to all these people who didn't hear the voice."

"But my father . . ." Jacob said.

Now Rebekah stood up. The bird she had been plucking dangled from one hand, and with the back of the other, she pushed away a stray curl that had crept from the tightly wound head cloth. For a moment she just stood looking at Jacob, and then she frowned. "I'm going to tell you something you must never forget," she said. "You are the chosen one. You are the one who will receive the blessing and the birthright. I don't know how it will come about or when, but that's what's going to happen."

She pulled off a few more feathers, then handed the bird to one of the serving girls. "Come," she said. "I, myself, am taking you to your grandfather. You must listen to all he has to say. You must remember everything. He'll not live long and these things he knows must not be forgotten."

"But," Jacob objected, "we have been told these things many times."

She held out her hands for one of the serving girls to pour water from the pitcher over them, then wiped them on the end of her mantle. "Come now," she said. "When your father dies you must be the one to carry on the wisdom and the meaning of your grandfather's belief. This is just the training you'll need."

When they came to Abraham's large tent, she confidently raised the flap and pushed Jacob before her into the tent. "Here, my father," she said, "is Jacob, the lad who will take care of you. He's very clever and so will want to hear all that you can tell him of our family and our God."

She stood smiling and confident while Abraham raised his head and looked at them with a steady, piercing gaze that frightened Jacob. Jacob hung back until his mother again pushed him toward his grandfather. "Here's your grandson who will serve you, and you in turn must teach him."

With that she gave Jacob another push, raised the tent flap, and left the two alone together.

Abraham cleared his throat and looked at the boy. He had always noticed Esau, and this was the first time he had ever seriously considered Jacob. "Boy," he said, rather kindly, "come sit here beside me and we'll get acquainted."

Jacob hurried forward, and bending over his grandfather's hand, he raised it to his forehead in respect, then quickly he edged onto a leather cushion that was far to one side of his grandfather.

"No, no, boy, come sit here where I can see you," Abraham said, thumping a cushion at his side. "First, you will tell me something important about yourself and then you may ask me anything that puzzles you."

Jacob told him that he was not a hunter like his brother nor was he as strong and handsome as his brother. "I have no talent for anything, it seems, but cooking like a woman," he said.

To his surprise Abraham laughed. "To learn to cook is a good thing. If I could cook I would not be dependent on anyone."

Jacob relaxed. He had always seen his grandfather as large and impressive. Men listened when he talked, bowed over his hand in respect, and at times even kissed the hem of his robe. They always seemed to be eager for his advice.

In the past, when he had been invited to the large tent, he had been lost among the sons of Keturah and the many visitors. He had stood back and watched his grandfather with awed amazement but had let Esau and his father do all the talking. He always hoped he would not be noticed.

Now there was a strained silence as the two studied each other. Jacob knew from experience that his grandfather was looking for some family resemblance. That's what everyone in the family did. He was always compared to some relative who still lived in Haran.

Abraham stroked his beard and frowned. "And now it's your turn," he said. "Is there some question you would like to ask of me?" His voice was deep and formal, but his eyes under the gray, feathered brows were kind.

Jacob squirmed. He did have a question he had wanted to ask but was afraid it would seem silly. He looked around the tent and back at his grandfather. He wished he could think of something that would impress him. He had many questions, but he could only remember one at this moment. "Why did our family leave Ur of the Chaldees?" he asked finally.

To his surprise his grandfather's face lit up with delight. He smiled and looked over at Jacob with growing pleasure. Jacob remembered his saying that curiosity about the right things was a sign of teachableness and intelligence.

"To answer properly will take some time, but leaving Ur was the start of everything," Abraham said. And then he was off, weaving an amazing story of the family history.

In the days that followed, Jacob learned many things, but most of all he developed a growing understanding of the importance of the birthright and the blessing. He didn't tell his grandfather that his mother insisted that Elohim had told her that he, not Esau, was the one to receive the blessing.

Gradually the questions he asked his grandfather were about the meaning of the birthright and the blessing. The birthright was easy; it had to do with inheritance. But the blessing was something both wonderful and mysterious. A man with such a blessing would never feel inferior. He could not help but succeed at anything he attempted. Without his even trying, things would bend in his favor.

The more he thought about it, the more he wanted it. It became the thing he thought about in the daytime and dreamed of at night. It seemed to hang in the very air before him, elusive and yet somehow promised to him if he could believe his mother.

He was bright enough to realize that he could not just go to his father and reason with him. If his mother hadn't succeeded in convincing him, nothing would. His father never deviated from the rules. It was traditional for the firstborn to receive both the birthright and the blessing, and so Isaac never questioned the rightness of it.

Esau would have to die or renounce the whole thing before it could logically come to him. That Esau would die was impossible. He could even wrestle wild animals and never get a scratch. To imagine that he would willingly give up such a prize was unthinkable.

* * *

It was near the end of the summer that Abraham grew so weak he had to be carried to the door of his tent to greet the many dignitaries who came to visit. News had spread that he was not going to be with them much longer, and they wanted to see him, talk to him, get some last words of advice and wisdom. He welcomed everyone and patiently listened to their stories, but at the last it was Isaac he wanted to see. "I will not be here much longer," he said. "I've taught Jacob much that is important of our God and our people but Esau . . ."

Isaac nodded. "Esau is not like us. He doesn't spend time pondering the nature of our world or why we are here. He takes everything for granted. He's the practical one; he isn't disturbed by the things that disturb us. I've always admired this in him."

Abraham was silent and Isaac felt disapproval in his silence. When he spoke it was with a tinge of sadness in his voice. "I leave you, my son, to teach him all that he must know of our people and our God. If he is not taught, he will have to start all over again learning the truth about our God and what He wants from His people. He will find it easy to blend in with the people around him. It will be easier to join in the lewd rites of fertility with their sacrifices of sons and daughters to appease the gods of the rain. He will bow down out of fear to the snake and the bull."

Isaac shifted uneasily. He realized that Esau had little time for learning their family heritage and the ways of his father's God. He felt remiss in not teaching him all that his father had taught him. Time had gone so fast. He had not realized the boys were so old or that his father could actually be leaving them. "I will start this very day to teach him all that you have taught me," he said with a catch in his voice.

It was not as easy as he had imagined. Esau was much more interested in the ways of the quail in the spring and the gazelle at the salt licks. He eagerly listened to the rough shepherds as they sat around their fires in the evening discussing old superstitions and charms to fend off the evil eye. He seemed more a part of the earth than of the airy realm of debate and introspection. *I will have to find a way to interest him in more serious things,* Isaac thought with a twinge of alarm.

\* \* \*

Abraham lived through the cold winter months with the chilling rain and dark skies, but when spring came he took a turn for the worse and on a bright sunny day in the month of Nisan he died. His death was peaceful. One moment he was holding the morning's gourd of honeyed camel's milk and the next his hand had relaxed. The gourd fell to the mat and the white mixture spread out over the bright folds of his robe. He slumped back. For a moment his face had a look of pleasure. His hand upraised briefly as though in greeting and then he was gone.

Isaac had just come into the tent. He knelt beside his father, and frantically called his name, rubbed his limp hand, and tried to get some response. Jacob stood beside him, stunned and afraid. "Go," his father ordered, "get Eleazar, find your mother. Esau must be found and told."

Jacob found Eleazar first. He was sitting with some of the merchants from Gerar who had come to bargain for lambs for their spring festivals. When he heard the news, he quickly excused himself and rushed to Abraham's tent. On the way he told others, and within a short time the whole camp had gathered around the tent or crowded inside. Esau came pushing through the crowd and stood still holding his throwing stick as he looked at the frantic scene. He knelt beside his father and took one of his grandfather's hands in his and wept. "I didn't know," he sobbed. "He was so strong. How can he be gone so soon?"

Jacob found Rebekah sitting at her loom. She was not surprised. She had anticipated this for some months. She stood up and clung to him for a few moments and then stiffened. She seemed to be contemplating something. "My son," she said, "this will not be easy. I will give you the winding cloth Sarah wove long ago for his burial. You will take it to your father, then prepare yourself for the walk to the cave of Machpelah."

\* \* \*

The long procession wound up through the waddis and then climbed to the higher ground crested by the small village of Kiriath-arba. As it went along, people from great distances heard the news of the strident, urgent blowing of the shofar and came to join the procession. Abimelech, the king of Gerar, sent mourners dressed in sackcloth, with their faces streaked with ashes, their bare feet moving in patterns timed to the dull beat of the drums of death and their wails of practiced grief. Children ran along beside the procession, while old women and young mothers holding babies or clutching a young child by the hand lined the path to watch them go by.

Isaac and his sons led the procession while his men took turns doing the honor of shouldering the slab on which lay the wrapped body of their patriarch. Isaac for the first time carried the staff that had belonged to his father and wore the ring that bore the family emblem.

When they reached the caves that Abraham had bought so long ago to bury Sarah, they found Ishmael and his sons waiting, and coming within the hour were the sons of Keturah.

At the mouth of the cave, after the great stone had been rolled away, Isaac called Esau to him and said, "Today the mantle of my father falls on my shoulders. His staff is in my hand and his ring on my finger, and with it his blessing and the birthright. Let it be known that when I go to my fathers, my son Esau will, by right of the firstborn, inherit the birthright and the blessing of my father, Abraham, and all his people."

Jacob did not wait to hear more but pushed his way through the crowd, hot tears almost blinding his eyes and a heavy pall of utter rejection crushing down upon him. He went a short distance and climbed up on a rocky projection where he could see the whole thing. He expected someone to miss him, to call out for him when the sons all went with his father behind the bier into the darkness of the cave, but no one did. He jumped down from the rock and stood to one side, almost swallowed up by the crowd and ignored.

He did not linger but slipped away unnoticed down a back path that led back down to the Negev. Once out of sight he began to run, not caring where he went. When at last he was totally exhausted, he found a cleft in one of the rocks, wedged himself into it, and hunched down out of sight and out of the glare of the afternoon sun.

At first he felt only the riot of emotion that rose up in his throat like gall and pounded in his temples. He was beyond tears. He ached with a terrible grief, a feeling of bereavement that went beyond the pain he felt at the loss of his grandfather. His grandfather had loved him, and his feeling of loss was intensified by the realization that his father hardly noticed him in his love for Esau. Hot tears stung his eyes as he remembered all the times his father had reached out to Esau with pride and acceptance and didn't even notice him.

He couldn't bear to think of telling his mother that he had left the crowd. She would be so disappointed. "You have to be strong," she would say. "Don't hang back. You have to make things happen the way you want them." Esau took things for granted. He just assumed he was to be the chosen one.

In the end he didn't tell his mother. He waited to return home until he could join the mourners and arrive unnoticed. She assumed he had been a part of the whole event until she questioned Esau. "I didn't see him," Esau confessed. "He must have left early."

Then there was no escape. "Why were you not with your father?" she asked with a suspicious look he had grown to dread.

He tried not to answer but she reached out and held him by his cloak. "You know I've told you that you're the one to have the birthright and the blessing. You have to believe it, act like it."

He pulled away and stood struggling to control a whirl of emotions. He could not endure her knowing how much he cared. It was better she think he was a brash and careless fellow who didn't value the birthright or the blessing, who didn't notice his father's rejection. He winced, expecting the usual lecture but instead he only heard her sobs—angry, frustrated sobs. He lunged for the tent door and fled out into the moonlight.

*  *  *

It was several days later that Jacob collected some garlic, onions, and lentils, borrowed his mother's fire pot, and proceeded to make a succulent stew. He was never impatient but took the time to let the flavors blend and mingle, the steam rise with the familiar, inviting odor. He enjoyed the whole activity. He could do some of his best thinking waiting for a pot to boil.

Now he squatted beside the pot and idly stirred the stew with a wooden stick he had specially carved for this purpose. As usual he let his mind wander. Esau was out hunting. If he brought down an antelope, there would be a big celebration with plenty to eat when the animal had been cleaned and set to roast over the fire. Jacob frowned, remembering many such feasts. He much preferred the delicately flavored stew to the torn flesh, soured milk, and bread of such meals.

These days his thoughts were often on his bitter feelings toward his brother. He knew that among some people twins were viewed as bad luck. They never let both of them live. He would have been the one left to die. Esau was strong from the start and the firstborn. However, in some places it was the firstborn who was sacrificed. He thought about that for a while. He mulled over the possibility that his father might sacrifice Esau as Abraham had set out to sacrifice him. But Abraham had decreed that their God did not want humans sacrificed. Abraham had made this plain in all of his teaching.

This was one of the astonishing things about his grandfather. Abraham really wanted to please Elohim. He didn't depend on custom or what people expected; he spent his whole life doing only what Elohim wanted. It was like this strange, unseen God was really his friend; he depended on Him like a brother.

Just as his grandfather wasn't like other grandfathers, so, also, his mother wasn't like most women. She insisted it was his father's prayer that had moved God to give them the twins, but it was her prayer that had brought the strange answer, "The younger will rule the elder." She believed this. She couldn't understand why no one would listen to her. Isaac had told her to go question Elohim, and when she did and came back with the answer, he obviously didn't take it seriously.

Being twins maybe they should split the blessing and the birthright between them. Jacob had long ago resolved that if given the chance, he would snatch at least one of them away from Esau. He thought about it. Esau could have the birthright; it was the blessing he wanted. Or if Esau got the blessing, then he could have the birthright.

As he lay back against the base of the large projection of rock, he was about to doze off when he heard a low whistle. Looking up he saw Esau, hot and dusty, about to dip into his stew.

"No, no, no," he shouted, jumping up and snatching the piece of bread from Esau. It was dripping with stew and Esau had just missed popping it into his mouth. "You have your birthright and your big feasts; you'll not take my stew without paying some price."

Esau laughed. "A price for stew?"

Jacob stood his ground. "Why not?"

"It's so easy to make a stew and besides I'm hungry. There'll be no big feast. I didn't find any game."

"You can't have everything just because you're the firstborn." He said this with a sneer as he positioned himself between Esau and the coveted stew.

"I hope you're not going to go on about the birthright again," he shouted. "I'm starving. I won't live to inherit anything if I don't get something to eat."

"You've just been gone two days . . ."

"Two days with nothing to eat. There's a famine brewing out there. What good is it to be firstborn if one dies of starvation?" He pushed Jacob aside, squatted beside the pot, picked up the bread, and was about to dip it in the stew.

With all his strength Jacob pushed his brother into a small clump of thyme. "Exactly; what good will the birthright do you if you starve?"

Now Esau was frantic with hunger. He could smell the stew and this drove him to even more desperate measures. "What do you want? I'll give you anything, my throwing stick, my knife, even my sling, just let me have the stew."

Jacob laughed a hard mocking laugh as he looked down at his brother groveling before him. "There's only one thing I want and you'll never part with it, so you won't get the stew if I have to dump it out on the ground."

"You wouldn't!"

"I would."

"You can't be talking about the birthright?"

"That's the only thing you have that I want."

Esau sat up and stared at Jacob in astonishment. "I think you're serious."

"Of course I'm serious. You can have the whole pot in exchange for your birthright."

Esau laughed. "That's easy. As you said, what good is the birthright to a dead man."

Jacob's eyes flashed and he cracked his knuckles as he did at times of great excitement. "You'd really give your birthright for my stew?"

"Why not? I don't even know what a blessing is and the birthright . . ." He shrugged. "That's a long time off and I'm starving."

Jacob squatted down beside him. "You're serious? You won't go back on your word?"

"No, no. You can have it. Now give me the stew."

When Jacob went to his mother's tent and told her of the bargain, she didn't immediately congratulate him. Instead she stood, head tipped to one side, eyes narrowing, and her lips pursed as she evaluated the whole thing. "That sounds like him. He doesn't really value such things. He just lives for the moment. He'll more than likely forget he ever made such a deal," she said. "You'll have to keep reminding him."

*That's easy,* Jacob thought as he put the fire pot and the empty bowl back in its place. *He promised and I won't let him go back on his promise.*

\* \* \*

In the days that followed, everyone but Jacob forgot about Esau's promise. They were all too preoccupied with the news he'd brought. "Everything's drying up," he said. "There are no animals like there used to be."

Isaac's shepherds began reporting the same thing and traders coming through with their caravans added ominous details. "If it weren't for the wells dug by Abraham," they said, "both men and their beasts would be dying."

"There have always been famines," Isaac reminded his family. "Some have been worse than others. One of the worst was in the time of Sargon the great. All of the northern reaches of the Tigris and Euphrates were laid waste. That's when our ancestors fled to Ur in the south."

"Does that mean we should go down to Egypt till the famine's ended?" Esau asked.

"It's difficult to be strangers among a strange people," Isaac said. "Our ancestors never went back north until Elohim spoke to Terah, my grandfather. One must be careful in making such moves."

Finally, Isaac decided to ride into Gerar and talk to the king. He needed to find out what plans he was making to last out the famine.

He found the king in his treasury overseeing the delivery of payment for bags of wheat he had just received from some Egyptian traders. After their greetings, the king led Isaac to his audience chamber and invited him to sit with him. "We have much to discuss," he said. "I hear your herds of cattle and sheep have not been touched." The king spoke with raised brows and a narrowing of his eyes that gave him a crafty, puzzled look. "What is your secret?"

"Wells," Isaac said. "My father dug many wells."

"I don't understand," the king said.

"With wells you can irrigate and grow crops without the rain."

The king frowned. "That sounds dangerous to me."

"What do you mean?" Isaac asked.

"Surely such a thing will bring down the wrath of the goddess Anat and all the other gods."

"Then what is your plan?" Isaac asked, puzzled.

"We'll continue to entreat Anat; she's in charge of such things. Of course we'll continue to get grain from Egypt as long as they'll sell it to us."

"When we finish digging the new irrigation ditches," Isaac said, "we'll be harvesting a lot of grain and can spare some to sell in your market."

"It's your wells, you say, that make this possible?"

"In Ur of the Chaldees there was very little rain. They had to irrigate. There are great rivers of fresh water underground that your people can learn to use."

"No, no!" the king said almost in alarm. "We must not offend the goddess. However, we would not mind buying the grain from you."

Isaac looked at him and saw that he could not understand. He would never be in favor of getting water from the ground when their goddess had not sent the rain. To him it would be blasphemy.

As the king rose, he turned to Isaac. "Come, move into our city," he said. "Perhaps we can work together to fight this famine."

And so Isaac and his family moved to Gerar. The king proved to be generous. He moved some of his own family out into smaller quarters so Isaac and Rebekah and their family and servants could move into houses adjoining the palace.

"You will come and sit every day with me," Abimelech said. "Your family will be like my family. This famine is sure to pass, but in the meantime we may need each other."

Rebekah had not forgotten her former experience with the king's sister Anatah. Now she was surprised when this same sister invited her to come sit with her women whenever she chose. Rebekah would have much preferred going down to Egypt.

When the spring finally came and there had been no winter rain, Isaac began to seriously consider moving down to Egypt. He called his men together and said, "If we stay here, we will have to depend on the wells and building irrigation channels. It will be hard work and in the end we may all starve."

"We are ready to move. When can we leave?" they immediately asked.

Isaac held up his hand and signaled for silence. "We must not make such a move without first getting guidance from Elohim."

They were all aware that he had been fasting and praying, spending most of the day and far into the night on his face before his father's God. Now for the first time, they understood his concern and they began to wait anxiously for his answer. Most of them believed it was already obvious what should be done. They would have no real choice but to go down to Egypt where the Nile could be trusted to fend off any famine.

When the day finally came that Isaac announced the answer that had been given him, they were all speechless with amazement. "We are not to go down to Egypt," he said. "We are to stay right here and trust Elohim to take care of us. We still have the wells that have not run dry, and we can continue to build irrigation ditches as they have always done in Ur."

He said no more but turned and went back into his tent. He had seen them frowning with puzzled, questioning looks and real fear clouding their eyes. He heard their murmuring and then quite clearly he heard one of them say, "Can we trust him to really hear from Elohim like his father? This goes against all our better judgment. To go to Egypt is the only safe thing to do."

# 14

*I*saac himself could hardly believe what he had heard from Elohim. It was so different from what he had expected. He was well aware of everyone's reaction. He could see it in their eyes as they looked away—they were frightened. What he told them was not based on common sense. To stay on in the midst of the worst famine any of them had ever experienced sounded like the most foolish thing they could do.

Rebekah had been so sure they would be going down to Egypt that she had been quietly packing and was ready to go. Now she couldn't help wondering if Isaac was making a big mistake. If Abraham had been there and told them they were to stay, that he had heard this from Elohim, it would have been different. Isaac's speaking with such sureness didn't impress her. "You know we will all starve if we stay here," she said finally.

Esau was the only one who agreed with his father. He didn't want to leave because he was totally entranced with one of the Hittite maids of Kirjath-arba.

Her name was Judith. He had seen her dancing with the maidens at one of the festivals honoring the goddess Anat. She danced handling a large snake that wound around her arms and encircled her waist. She not only danced with a fascinating, snakelike undulation, but she was also able to make the large snake obey her every command.

Esau was fearless in confronting the lions or the panthers that prowled the jungle of the Jordan. He had been known to wrestle one of the lambs from a large bear, but he avoided and feared the snakes. He had killed many of them as they reared up in his path and glared with their cold, beadlike eyes, challenging him. He knew that they were stealthy and deadly, and to see a young beauty like Judith tormenting and flirting with the big snake fascinated him.

He had waited until the performance was over and then, jumping down from the wall where he and other young men had been sitting, he confronted her. "Are you not afraid?" he asked.

"No," she said as her eyes narrowed and she tossed her head, studying him all the time. "The snakes I can control," she said, "but a young man like yourself is the real danger."

He only later learned what she meant. She had been dedicated to the goddess as a very young child, and it was the only life she knew. Esau understood but was determined to have her for himself; to leave for Egypt at this time would spoil everything.

Jacob's reaction was different. He was among those who crowded into his father's tent to hear what had changed his mind. It interested him because it was so unlike his father. His father was never one to speak with authority. He was always looking for some peaceful way around any disagreement. Now here he was insisting on a plan of action that was definitely unpopular.

"It was the Lord Himself who appeared to me," Isaac had said. "'Do not go down to Egypt,' was His message; 'I will be with you and will bless you.'" They were all so shocked and confused that none of them remembered hearing the rest of the message, though Isaac had repeated all of it. For Abraham's sake his seed was to multiply as the stars of heaven and all the land that had been promised Abraham would be given them. And, as had always been promised before, in his seed would all the nations of the earth be blessed.

While they sat too stunned to question the vision, Isaac told them that Abimelech, king of Gerar, had also urged them to stay. "He is very friendly," he said. "Even he says we can trade with them as long as the food lasts."

In this way Isaac's family gave up all thought of moving down to Egypt. Reluctantly Rebekah unpacked her things and started to make the large fortress next to the palace into a home.

The balcony that jutted out on the side of the king's palace was a delightful place. There had once been a grapevine that twined up and over, forming a shaded area. Now the vine was leafless and dry but offered strong limbs on which to hang her cages of pigeons. The herbs she used for cooking were soon growing in the clay pots, which could be easily watered. She had basil, cumin, coriander, and mint. With these herbs she could make many different dishes of the meat that was still plentiful.

It soon became quite evident that even the king and his family had begun to suffer from the famine. Instead of the lavish feasts that had been held in the past, now there were only a few dates served on dry reed mats, and the last of their store of wine was carefully portioned out.

The king's sister Anatah still held afternoon parties for her friends, and the women of Isaac's family were always invited. The entertainment was usually gossip, village dancers, or sorting through the merchandise of traders from Egypt who brought jewelry, cloth, perfumes, and scarce herbs.

On one of these occasions, Abimelech had arranged with his sister to sit behind a curtain where he could see the women of Isaac's family. "I have heard that even his serving women are doe-eyed and shapely," he confided to his vizier. "His sister is reported to be a great beauty." His eyes narrowed and he pulled at his short beard as a lustful grin played across his face. "I need a distraction right now. This woman may be just what I need."

When the time came for the visit, Abimelech could not take his eyes from Rebekah. "She is the sister I have heard about," he whispered, "and indeed she is all that I've been told. I'll have my chief steward speak to Isaac at once."

When Anatah heard what he wanted, and was given the description of the woman, she was appalled. "The woman you are so interested in is not his sister but his wife," she insisted.

"Impossible," her brother stormed. "I have carefully investigated and my friend Isaac says she is his sister."

Anatah was not to be outdone. She had spent several hours every day on the palace roof hidden behind a screen where she could watch what went on in the apartments of Isaac and his immediate family. What she saw both intrigued and angered her. Their balcony was wide with a couch, large storage jars, a loom, and several reedy cages for pigeons. Off to one side was a fire pot, which was always lit in the early afternoon by a serving girl. Soon after this, a woman she knew as Rebekah, Isaac's wife, would come with a tray, squat beside the pot, and make what looked like a delicious stew.

Even from her vantage point, Anatah could smell the tantalizing aroma. It was obvious Rebekah was making the most of what she could still find as the famine had undoubtedly hampered her usual procedure. There was no bread and no small grains in this mixture. All this interested the princess, but what followed made her resentful and angry.

Isaac, still handsome and virile, would appear and come striding through the curtained doorway, calling out some cheery greeting. Rebekah would jump up, push her hair back from her face, and, laughing, run to him. Sometimes she flung herself into his arms and, pulling his face down to her, would kiss him enthusiastically.

Other times they seemed to play a game where she flirted brazenly and he pretended not to notice; he even went to investigate the steaming pot. All the time it was evident to Anatah that he was very aware of Rebekah and was enjoying her attention. It always ended with both of them tumbling together with laughter and frenzied excitement on the couch. Only after a time, when they lay exhausted and spent, did she rise and ladle some of the fragrant mixture from the pot into a bowl and bring it to him.

He never took his eyes from her as he ate. He listened and nodded, sometimes laughed, and even examined some new piece of jewelry or apparel. It was at this point Anatah turned away; she had seen enough and she was desperately jealous. She had never had a man really notice her as a person. Though she had practiced every ploy in the art of seduction that she had learned in the temple of the goddess, she had received only jewelry for her efforts. With her husband there had been children, including three tall, handsome sons, but never anything really caring and personal.

When her brother refused to believe this was indeed Isaac's wife, she determined to prove it to him. She would bring him to this rooftop, or, better still, to a window in his own apartments and let him see for himself.

The plan succeeded far beyond her imagining, and she could not have been more pleased. Her brother was at first incredulous, then amazed, and finally angry. "This Isaac has dealt deceitfully," he muttered. "He could have made me look foolish. He has obviously been willing to risk someone lying with his wife and having to be stoned for the offense."

"My brother," Anatah said after she had enjoyed his ranting sufficiently, "it's no more than his father, Abraham, managed with your father. You should have been more cautious."

"It's true! His father did deceive us in the same way." Abimelech frowned and sat down among the cushions of his couch. Taking off his crown he absentmindedly sat, turning it in his hands as he thought. The crown had been worn by his father, and as he looked down at it, he thought bitterly of how both his father and he himself had been deceived by this family. With a sudden swift movement, he put the crown back on his head and adjusted it so that it felt comfortable. He stood up and glared at Anatah. "I will see this so-called friend of mine and have it out once and for all. I'll not punish him openly, but I'll see that many difficulties are placed in his path." As he left the room he muttered to himself, "Why should the gods give two such beautiful women to one family?"

Anatah, hearing him, turned away. "They don't even worship the goddess," she said, frowning. She was still in love with Isaac, and it made her furious that he had been able to find such a beauty and have two handsome sons without once acknowledging the goddess. She had been taught that such people would be cursed with barrenness, their land lie fallow, and their animals give no milk. She believed that only the goddess could control the vital, life-giving force. Only she could bless a woman with children, flocks with young, and make dead, brown seeds spring to life.

\* \* \*

In the days that followed Isaac worked with his men to combat the formidable creeping blight of the famine. "We must dig ditches and raise water from the wells to fill them. In this way we can sow the seed that we have and be assured of a harvest even without the rain," he said. "When the land has water, things will grow."

Every day his men rode out and kept the water flowing in the irrigation ditches. Gradually they saw the seeds they had planted sprout and miraculously begin to grow. They hardly noticed that the king's men rode out to see what was happening. They had mixed opinions. To some it was miraculous, but to most of them it was unnatural and against their religion. Only the gods could send rain, and to trick them by getting water from the ground was dangerous.

Abimelech paid little attention to their reports. He could not believe the work of mere men could defeat a famine that had obviously been sent by the gods. "Come see for yourself," his men challenged, but he had other things to do. So it came as a great surprise when it was reported that Isaac and his men had reaped a hundredfold harvest and were willing to sell grain in the markets of Gerar.

He still held a grudge against Isaac for deceiving him, and he had expected him to have nothing but evil fortune. Now to find that he had succeeded in producing an abundant harvest in the midst of a famine was an outrage. Furthermore, when it was reported to the king that Isaac had given credit to his God, saying, "It is Elohim, known also as El Shaddai, who has caused me to be blessed," he was furious.

"It is an open affront to our gods. Anat and Baal will not forgive such a challenge to their power," the people began to whisper among themselves. Then the king called a conference with his advisers and finally with the priestesses in the temple of Anat, and they all agreed that something must be done.

They first secretly told the people to refuse to buy the grain Isaac's men had grown, but the people were too hungry to listen. Even in the king's household, when Egyptian grain ran out, his servants bought the despised grain from Isaac's men. "He has gotten too strong for us," the king lamented. "With his wells and grain, fat cattle, and ready water, he may as well be king."

With that thought, a conspiracy grew labeling Isaac an enemy of the gods and goddess of their people. "He has grown wealthy with his wells and water," the people said. "He has benefited from the drought. Worst of all, he has given the credit to his God."

Abimelech was ready to listen to the advice of his sister Anatah. "It is useless to punish Isaac," she said. "The problem is bigger than his wells and the harvest. We must show that our gods are stronger than his."

"How do we do that?" the king asked.

"We must entreat the goddess and Baal to bring rain. Surely they will want to triumph over this alien God."

"He is not totally unknown to us," Abimelech said. "We have in the past worshiped El."

"But He did nothing for us," Anatah said, frowning. "He may have created things, but He doesn't control them. It is Anat and Baal that have always responded to our prayers and gifts."

In the end it was decided to defeat Isaac's plans by stopping up the wells that had been dug by his father, Abraham, and were the source of his success. The counselor who thought of this solution was honored by the king and given the high position of the "king's friend."

It did not take long for Abimelech's men to ride out and with shouting and singing fill the wells with sand and stones so it would be almost impossible to reclaim them. They trampled down the irrigation ditches and crushed out the newly sprouting growth and then rode off in triumph to tell the king.

Isaac's men had watched with horror and anguish. It was not easy to dig a well in this land where the soil was dry and unyielding. They could not understand what was happening. Why would people suffering from famine destroy the only source of relief? They had wanted to fight, but Isaac held them back. "Let them go; we wouldn't win that way. They would still stop up the wells and some of our men would be killed."

To everyone's amazement Isaac refused to be discouraged. He had wisely hoarded some grain for seed so that when given another chance, he would have something to plant. No matter how Rebekah begged for even a handful of grain to make bread, he would not relent. "This grain is still going to keep us alive and bring us great prosperity," he said.

When his sons asked what he meant, he explained, "When we again have water and can open the channels to irrigate, we will plant this grain and for each kernel planted we will reap a hundredfold."

"And," said Jacob, "they will give us of their riches in exchange. Everyone has to eat to live."

Isaac smiled. "While they are pleading with their goddess for relief from the famine, we will be busy using the gifts Elohim has given us to actually accomplish it."

*  *  *

While Isaac rode out into the desert each day with his men and worked long hours in the sweltering sun to unstop the wells, the people of Gerar were totally caught up in a frenzy of a different sort. They hoped to bring back prosperity and stop the famine by placating the goddess Anat. "She has the power," they said, "to send the rain and make the land blossom again."

Her priestesses dressed faithfully in their ornate robes and sang and danced before her image in the temple courtyard. They poured precious oil on the altar before her shrine and encouraged the people to sacrifice some treasured ornament or a perfect animal to show their love and devotion to her. "When she sees that we trust her and love her enough to offer our best to her, then she will bless us. Our vats will be filled with oil and our granaries will burst with wheat and barley, our cattle will give birth to perfect young, and our grapes will hang in thick clusters," they repeated over and over to reassure themselves.

When the famine grew worse, the high priestess went into seclusion before the goddess. The temple was not large, but it had a courtyard paved in worn, irregular stones. Off to one side was a well with a carob tree shading its dark depths. The temple was of chiseled stone with a long, red curtain that covered the doorway and hid the altar that lay before the niche where the statue of the goddess stood.

Now while the drums rolled their dirge and the shofars blared their alarm, the priestess stayed hovering over the latest sacrifice. She chanted and circled the altar, flinging incense and special dust that made the fire burn with an unnatural green glow. All this time the people of the city stood crowded together in the courtyard, peered eagerly over the wall, or pushed and squeezed in at the gate. They were anxiously waiting for any word of encouragement.

When she finally came out and stood before them, she spoke in a strong, vibrant voice and her words hung on the air with the terrible atmosphere of doom. "The goddess has spoken," she said. "We have not given our best, she says. Only the best sacrificed on her altar will move her to have compassion on us. Are you ready? Will you sacrifice your greatest treasure?"

"We will. We will." The shout rang out as the people fell to their knees and wept with the awesome challenge. They buried their heads in their hands and rocked back and forth as each imagined sacrificing some prized possession. They loved the joy of surrender to this great cause. They shuddered as they hoped it would be their secret treasure the goddess would choose. What renown and honor would be theirs if some sacrifice on their part would bring about relief from the famine?

Again the priestess entered behind the curtain and stood before the altar. Her voice rose and fell as she repeated the incantation that was to summon the goddess. Then came silence. Even the people grew silent and still as they waited.

Finally, with a dull thudding sound, the drums of fate began to announce the reappearance of the priestess. The shofar was blown and the curtain parted to show her with hands raised, standing before the shrine of the goddess. Slowly she turned and with slow, deliberate motions advanced toward them. Her eyes were glazed, and when she spoke it was as though someone else were speaking through her.

This time her pronouncement was greeted with shock and disbelief. The priestess announced that Anat was a goddess so strong and powerful that she could not be moved by the usual sacrifices. Something of inestimable value to all of them must be sacrificed.

"What do we have? What more can we give?" the people whispered among themselves with dread.

"Your greatest treasure you have withheld. Until you sacrifice the brightest and best of your children, Anat will not be moved. She is in control of the mystery that gives life to all things. The life force is within her hands to give or withhold. We are but as ants in her sight, and our pain is not her pain. She is not to be summoned but only entreated. We must give her what she asks, and she asks for the sacrifice of your children. Will you sacrifice your children?"

For a moment there was stunned silence. At times in the past the goddess had expected such devotion, but not in their generation. Just as the silence was growing awkward, a voice from the crowd shouted, "We are ready. We will sacrifice." At that the chant began, "We will sacrifice, we will sacrifice."

In just this way began the daily sacrifice of not just jewelry and gold but perfectly formed young children, for the goddess would have nothing but the best.

A week passed and then a month, with no break in the famine; no rain and no relief from the terrible hunger. Once again the priestess called the people together. She had an announcement of great importance. The goddess had spoken and there was both good news and bad. The good news was that the goddess was ready to act on their behalf and summon the great life force to the earth so that seeds would sprout and vines put out their shoots and the animals birth strong, healthy young.

The bad news was that this last time the goddess must have not just the gold and silver, the blood of animals, or the more precious blood of their children, but she must have royal blood. Only this was a fitting sacrifice for the great Anat.

While the people waited in an anxious silence, the priestess continued. "The royal family will draw lots, and the family that draws the dark stone will prepare their oldest son to be sacrificed."

That evening just at sunset, the lots were drawn and the lot fell to Anatah, the king's sister. It was to be her oldest and most favored son that the goddess was demanding. Anatah was stunned and then frantic. "Not my son!" she was heard to shout. "Take the sons of slaves or strangers, but not my son."

"Hush," the priestess hissed. "It is an honor you have been given."

"The honor can be given to someone else," she stormed. "I'll not let her have my son."

*I*saac and his family watched from the roof of their house as the sad procession of the king's family returned from the temple and the terrible pronouncement of the priestess. They could make out the form of Anatah and her three sons, now young men, walking beside her. She would not deign to weep or cry out in protest before the people but walked with slow, dragging steps as though in great pain. Her eyes stared straight ahead, her chin was up, and her back held straight and rigid with controlled tension.

The king, Abimelech, led the way through the crowd that parted before him. As he approached, the people grew silent. They wondered what the princess would do. They looked at the handsome young men and some of them turned away weeping.

Because of the severity of the famine, the princess had only a short time to prepare her son for his ordeal. There were no parties now at the palace; the gates remained closed and the shutters drawn. The whole city appeared to be in mourning. As the fateful day approached, women gathered at the palace gates, weeping and pouring ashes on their heads. Merchants offered great treasures to be given the goddess in the young boy's place. From the palace itself there could be heard hysterical weeping both day and night.

"It is too much," Isaac said at last. "What makes them think there really is a goddess or that she controls such things as famine?"

"Maybe an angel will appear and a ram be taken in his place," Jacob said.

"There'll be no ram and no angel," Isaac said.

"How do you know? You were saved."

"Our family has had long experience with these things. I can assure you there is no goddess."

"But everyone believes in her," Esau said. "There are all these temples built in her honor and people sacrificing to her."

"I have told you many times, there is only one God; all other gods are either demons or imagined creatures. My own grandfather, as you know, made images out of clay in Ur and people worshiped them."

For a moment there was silence as his sons thought about what he had said. It seemed impossible that so many people could be mistaken. "Why would they choose to worship something that was false?" Jacob asked at last.

"People want something they can see and touch and manage. Something that makes sense of their world as they imagine it to be. To believe in a God who is unseen, who is Spirit, does not suit them."

"Then we must tell them," Esau said. "The young prince can be saved." He jumped up ready to go to the rescue.

"Esau, my son," Isaac said sadly, "it's not so easy. It's fashionable to believe in the goddess. People like the festivals and it seems logical to them. The temples and their believers are very powerful. You well know it's dangerous to openly voice a disbelief in the goddess. It is entirely possible that instead of the young prince being sacrificed, one of you could be taken."

The boys knew this could happen. Often during times of crisis, men captured in battle or strangers were sacrificed. "I've thought sometimes," Esau said, "that Elohim might ask you to sacrifice one of your sons, and since I am the firstborn, it would be me."

Isaac's eyes filled with tears as he reached out to Esau. "Come my son, let me explain." Esau came hesitantly and sat before his father. Isaac took both of his hands in his and for a moment studied his son's eager, young face. "I have never fully understood just why Elohim told my father to go to Moriah and sacrifice me. I do know this, that my father always taught, after that experience, that our God did not want the sacrifice of any human being."

Though his sons had heard him say this other times, they had never really understood. Now, here in Gerar, with the eminent sacrifice of one of the young princes, it had new meaning. They knew the young princes and had spent many afternoons playing Egyptian board games with them. Being young and optimistic, they felt sure that somehow the young prince would be rescued. It did not seem reasonable that the king would actually let one of his nephews be sacrificed.

As the time drew near, it became evident that public sentiment had changed. Now there was rejoicing and singing honoring the prince who was to save them from the famine. Even the family in the palace was swept up in the euphoria of the occasion. When the prince rode out, he was now greeted with poets chanting his praises and young girls reaching out to touch the bridle of his horse or bending down to kiss his feet. "He has been chosen," they whispered. "The goddess has chosen him to save his people from the famine."

His mother, Anatah, was greeted with such love and admiration it was hard for her to continue in her grief at losing her son.

On the day of the sacrifice, Isaac and his family again watched from the roof of their house. They saw the drummers and trumpeters form at the gate before the palace. Then the singers followed and finally the young man himself. He was seated on a white mule that was decked in throws covered with priceless jewels. His garments were of the finest Egyptian linen and on his head was a gold circlet signifying his position as prince in the king's household.

He looked neither to the right nor the left and seemed not to even notice the crowd that chanted and sang and shouted his name over and over. "He has been given strong herbs so he will not weaken or cry out," Isaac said, turning away. "He must not be seen to fear what is about to happen to him."

Jacob and Esau, looking at their father, suddenly realized that he was reliving his own feelings as he had gone with his father up to the altar on Moriah. It was obvious he felt deep sorrow in the young prince's fate. It was all so tragic. Their father knew there would be no angel and no ram in the thicket for this young man and he could hardly bear the pain of it. When he looked at them, his face was drawn and gray and his eyes were dark and piercing. They had never seen him so disturbed.

He stood rigid and silent, listening to the shouting and singing from the street below them. Then when the big drums of fate rumbled in the distance and drowned out the noise of the street, he buried his face in his hands. An ominous silence followed and then a burst of singing, horn blowing, and drums rolling in a quick staccato beat and they knew it was over, the sacrifice was complete. The people were ecstatic with joy. They danced and sang while free wine from the temple wine cellars was passed around. The fearful deed had been done and now they knew the goddess would relent and end the famine.

"My sons," Isaac said, finally putting his arms around each of them and drawing them away from the sight below, "never forget, our God does not want the sacrifice of children or of princes or of just ordinary young men. He does not want human beings, made in His image, sacrificed."

The next day Isaac rode out with his two sons to the place where his men were preparing to re-dig one of his father's wells that Abimelech's men had stopped up. It was going to be difficult if not impossible. The sun was blistering hot and the well filled with large stones. "We have no choice but to unstop the wells," Isaac said, as they rode on to inspect the other wells that had also been filled in with sand and debris. "We will all starve without water and food," he said.

After Isaac and his sons had ridden on, the men went back to their digging. It was hard, backbreaking work and they were making very little progress. Then one of them, who had jumped up onto a pile of the rocks, called out, "See that cloud of dust? It's the men from the king coming to fight over the well."

He was right. Within minutes the well diggers were surrounded. Men with helmets and breastplates of leather waved spears in the air and threatened them. "In the name of the king," the leader said, "this unlawful activity must stop. Throw down your picks and spades or we will add your dead bodies to the debris in the well."

Isaac had told them not to fight. "They are too strong for us," he had cautioned. However, his men were so frustrated and angry at the senseless waste that they picked up rocks and began to throw them with deadly accuracy. The fight lasted long enough for several of the king's men to suffer crippling injuries and Isaac's men to retreat with two of their men suffering from arrows imbedded in the flesh of their arms and legs.

In this way a daily struggle began between the king's men and Isaac's servants. Even when Isaac tried to stop the carnage, tempers flared and the battles around the wells grew so intense no work was done. Instead of being grateful for the grain and the water, the people of the village became angry and resentful. They began to grumble and complain to the king, "This Isaac and his men must be driven out."

It made them even angrier to have to admit to themselves that in spite of their sacrifices and offerings to the goddess Anat, they still had no rain. Instead it was Isaac who had prospered. This was more than they could endure. "Their wells are an affront to the goddess and their prosperity unnatural," they said.

Without further ceremony, Abimelech called Isaac to him and told him that he and his family, relatives, and servants must all leave Gerar. "You have grown too strong for us," he said. His eyes were dark and his mouth twisted into a grimace.

It was obvious that he had come to almost hate this man who had once

144

been his friend. He now saw Isaac and his people as a threat. They were a constant irritation of one kind or another. They did not worship in the temple of the goddess; they did not believe in making sacrifices to the goddess. Worst of all, Isaac had lied to him about his wife.

The story had gotten out and it made Abimelech look foolish. Now by digging in the earth for water, they were ignoring the prayers and sacrifices that had been made to placate the goddess. Baal, the god of lightning and thunder, could also be preparing to wreak havoc among them for letting these strangers ignore his authority.

Abimelech did not care where they went or what they did as long as they were no longer right at his door causing a constant disturbance. "It's better," he said, "for people to separate if they do not agree on important things."

Isaac was saddened but he understood. He reminded himself that though Abimelech and his people had once known of the true God, El, He had long been forgotten for the more popular gods and goddesses. Now it had come down to a more practical matter; they wanted gods they could understand and manipulate, even if at times it cost them their dearest treasures.

In anger and frustration, Abimelech not only drove them from the city but sent his men to guard the site of Abraham's wells they had stopped up. Isaac's men must not be allowed to dig there again.

The king was just beginning to feel a sense of power and elation when his shepherds came to tell him that instead of being discouraged and giving up, Isaac's men were out in the valley digging a new well. "They are stronger than all of us," his men reported. "They say they have a right to dig, but we know that whoever digs a well can also claim the land."

\* \* \*

Isaac had indeed conferred with his men and they had decided to dig a new well. "It may be easier to dig a new well than to clear the rubbish out of the wells that have been filled in," he said.

"Won't they come and destroy any new well?" Esau asked as they rode out together to see the progress being made on the digging.

"They may, but we will always leave some of our men to guard it. Only when we have the wells to supply us with the water we need will we be freed from the fear of famine."

Isaac's family and servants had moved back into their tents beside the brook Besor. The brook had now gone from a sizable stream to a slow, sluggish trickle of water. The springs that fed it had dried up and the irrigation ditches that Isaac's men had dug in the past were dry and parched.

"My father often told us that in Ur they could not depend on the rain," Isaac said. "They had to dig ditches and channel water if they wanted to grow anything. There is water in the earth and it is water that enables the seeds to sprout."

On this day in the early fall, they were again riding out to inspect the progress on the new well. As they came near the place where the men were digging, they could hear the rhythmic chanting that encouraged the diggers. They could see the tripod with the rope of strong twined camel's hair and hemp that reached down into the hole where two of the men were digging. The chanting and singing urged the diggers along as they sent up baskets of earth. The digging was so arduous that periodically the men in the pit would be hauled up and two others sent down in their place.

The ground was blistered and dry and their progress was slow. "Each day the shepherds of Abimelech come riding to see what progress we have made," the men reported. "'Just as we filled the wells of your father with sand,' they always chant, 'so we will fill this when you are finished.'"

"And do they try to stop the digging?" Isaac asked.

"No, they just laugh and joke and ride around letting their mules kick up the sand. Some of them even throw stones down in the well at the diggers before they ride off."

Isaac was disturbed, but he hoped that when they saw they could not stop his men from digging, they would give up and leave them alone.

This was not to happen. They would not be so easily discouraged. However, it was a full two weeks later that they felt the full force of Abimelech's anger.

The diggers had finally handed up the last basket of sand and were actually standing in water up to their ankles, before they were hauled up amidst great rejoicing. "It will take time, but now we can again dig the channels for water and plant the seed," they shouted.

Their joy was short-lived, for when Abimelech heard Isaac's men had actually dared to dig a new well and had found a plentiful supply of water, he became terribly angry. He immediately ordered his men to close the well. "It's unnatural," he said. "It is Baal that waters the land. We are not to rob him of his work. We must entreat Anat to persuade Baal to send rain, not dig in the earth."

When word reached Isaac that at the new well there had been fighting between his men and Abimelech's, he was greatly troubled.

"They claim the water," one of his servants reported. "They say the land is theirs and the water is theirs. Every day they come and we fight them off."

"I understand their concern," Isaac said. "They know that any man who digs a well can also claim the land. We must not fight them. Instead we will move to a new site farther away from them and dig another well."

"But it is so difficult. We already have the ditches dug and some of the seeds planted," they complained.

"We'll call the well Esek, or contention, because there has been strife over it, but we will move on and dig another well."

Once again, at Isaac's insistence, they began to dig another well. For a time Abimelech's herdsmen only came by to harass and torment the well diggers. They did not claim the well until it was dug and the men were celebrating. Then with a force of armed spearmen, they descended upon them, drove them off, and claimed the well as their own. They had no need for the irrigation ditches and so trampled them down.

"We will call this well Sitnah, or hatred," Isaac said, "for it is evident they hate us."

Isaac now began to look for a place that would not be disturbed or claimed by Abimelech. He wanted no more trouble. The next day they broke camp and traveled to a small oasis outside the area Abimelech's men usually patrolled. It was a small oasis with palm trees that was no longer visited by caravans and so was empty of any inhabitants. "Here we will dig again," Isaac said, "and this time we will have peace."

It happened as Isaac had predicted. They found plenty of water and Abimelech's men no longer bothered them. "We will call this place Rehoboth," Isaac said, "for the Lord Himself has made room for us."

In spite of the fact that the oasis was beautiful and peaceful, Isaac was restless. He remembered hearing that in his father's time there had been strife with the older Abimelech over a well his father had dug. His father had settled it by not only giving a gift of sheep and oxen to Abimelech but by setting aside seven ewe lambs for the king. "These will remind you of the covenant between us," Abraham had said. "This well and this land will be mine." Abimelech had agreed and the well had been named the well of the oath, or Beersheba.

Isaac wondered what had happened to the well. Surely Abimelech would feel obligated to honor an agreement made in such a formal way. It was only a short time later when a caravan from the north chanced to stop by their oasis, that he heard news of the well. The caravan had just come from Beersheba and the men were complaining that the well there had been filled with stones and rubble.

"Who owns the well?" Isaac asked, just to see what they might answer.

"They say there was an agreement with the people in the area, including the king of Gerar, that the well would belong to Abraham and to his descendants."

Isaac listened with growing excitement. He could remember seeing his father build an altar and plant a grove of trees near a well he had dug in that very place. He even vaguely remembered the formal ceremony naming the well and establishing his ownership.

By the next morning, just as the caravan started on its way, he had decided to go and see the well that must now, by all rights, still belong to him and his family.

It took a week of preparation before he and his two sons and a group of his men were able to start out along the well-traveled caravan trail going north.

Isaac had looked on this not as just a casual venture but more as a spiritual journey. He hoped that by returning to this place where his father had not only dug a well but had built an altar and worshiped, he would find peace from the anger and frustration of these last years. He had not understood why it was necessary to waste so much time fighting over the wells. It had been Elohim who had told him not to go down to Egypt. Then why hadn't He made things a little easier?

He had not been angry at Abimelech. The king was just exercising what he believed were his rights. However, he had been disappointed that his God had not made a better showing for Himself. It should have been so easy for Him to help his men defend the wells they had dug with such effort.

As he rode along the worn trail, he was reminded of all that had happened to him. Much of what had happened had also happened to his father when he had spent time in the city of Gerar. He should have known better than to deceive the king by saying that Rebekah was his sister, but the digging of the wells had been different. It had seemed a natural, intelligent solution to the famine. It was something he felt he could manage, and it hadn't even occurred to him to ask his God for help. He had done it all in his own strength.

He was happy to be going back to the scene of his father's victory. It was here Abraham had settled his dispute with Abimelech and had built an altar and worshiped and thanked his God, who had revealed Himself as El Shaddai, the almighty God.

Now Isaac not only intended to claim the well again but reestablish his relationship with the God of his father and to seek His help. He was not disappointed. That night as he slept the Lord appeared to him, saying, "I am the God of Abraham thy father. Don't be afraid for I am with you and will bless you and multiply your seed for My servant Abraham's sake."

The next morning he called his two sons and the servants and told them they were to build an altar. They would sacrifice the sheep they had brought with them as a thank offering. "We will have no more trouble. Our God, the God my father knew as El Shaddai, the Almighty, is coming to our aid."

When this had been done, and the last sounds of their chanting had died on the crisp morning air, he ordered his men to start digging another well. "This time we will succeed. No one will come against us," he assured them.

This was something Esau and Jacob would never forget. They had been skeptical because they had suffered so much disappointment in the digging of the wells. They talked with each other and wondered how he could be so sure they would succeed this time. What difference could the building of an altar and giving thanks make in their situation?

✳ ✳ ✳

Esau and Jacob were not to wait long. News came by a runner that Abimelech himself with Ahuzzath, one of his friends, and Phicol, the chief captain of his army, were coming up from Gerar to see their father. They speculated as to what his purpose might be. Was it because he had heard that Isaac was not only digging another well but was removing the stones and debris from the well his father had dug? To their surprise it was on quite another matter that they came.

Anatah, the king's sister, had been bitterly disappointed that after the great sacrifice of her son, there had still been no rain. The days went by and then the weeks, and she had spent them in growing disillusionment.

Gradually, she had begun to question her whole belief in the goddess. It was Isaac who was prospering. His God had given him a beautiful wife and two sons, and now it seemed to be his God who blessed him even in the midst of the famine.

On impulse she went to her brother's apartments and confronted him. "Who is this God that Isaac worships?" she demanded.

Her brother had at first looked startled and then puzzled. "Why are you interested?" he asked.

"It's evident that his God has blessed him. Even with my great sacrifice to the goddess, we have had no rain. She is either deaf or, worse yet, doesn't even exist."

Abimelech frowned and stood up. He tugged at his short beard as he began to walk back and forth across the floor. "Isaac and his father, Abraham," he said, "believed in Elohim, the creator God. A God not made with hands. There was a time when our people too believed in that God. We called Him El."

"It is that God, then, who has blessed Isaac."

"You are right. The God of Abraham has blessed Isaac even in the midst of the famine. However, Isaac did deceive me about his wife. I cannot forgive him for that."

"But he did it out of fear. You must admit, there have been times when husbands have been killed, even in Gerar, for their wives," Anatah reminded him. "We must not forget that when he had grain he shared it with us, and he was always generous with his animals."

Abimelech buried his face in his hands as he pondered what she said. It was all true. Isaac had been his friend. They had shared many good times together and he had to admit that while the goddess had miserably failed them, Isaac's God had continued to bless him. "It is evident that I must go to Isaac and tell him all of this. We can be friends again."

Abimelech was a man of action, and so the very next day he gathered his chief captain and some of his friends and started out up the Way of Shur to find Isaac's camp and make things right with him.

✳ ✳ ✳

Isaac had expected the worst as he prepared to greet the king and his men at the door of his tent. "Why have you come?" he challenged. "Everyone knows that you hate me and have caused me nothing but trouble."

The king motioned for his chief adviser to speak. Ahuzzath stepped forward with a bow of reverence and kissed the hem of Isaac's robe. "We have seen that the Lord is with you," he said, "and we have come to make a covenant with you. Let there be an oath between us, that you will do us no hurt as we have not touched you but have done good things for you and have only sent you away in peace."

Isaac was so astonished that he motioned for his servants to wash his guests' feet and serve them dried fruit while he went aside to take counsel with his men.

"They have spoken falsely," one old man said. "They have caused us nothing but heartache and trouble."

"They did not send us away in peace as they say," Esau said with a bitter tinge to his voice.

"They have seen that El Shaddai is blessing you and they are ready to make peace. This is the time to attack them and make them pay for all the trouble they have caused," one of the young well diggers said with great feeling.

"They want peace only because they see that you are stronger than they are," Jacob charged.

"Ah, but they are sincere in wanting peace," Isaac said. "That is all I need to know. Revenge is expensive while peace is all we have ever wanted."

"But . . . they deserve to be punished," his men chorused in a harsh whisper.

Isaac raised his hands for silence. "Who are we to turn our backs on the gift of peace? This is an answer to our prayers."

With that he turned and went back out to where the guests sat and welcomed them and urged them to rest for the night while he ordered a feast prepared in their honor.

Everything went well and the king was friendly as he had been in the past. In the morning they called witnesses together, not only of their men but of some men passing through with their caravans, and they swore an oath and made promises that they might have peace between them.

No sooner had they finished, and the king and his men were vanishing into the distance along the old caravan route leading back to Gerar, than Isaac's well diggers appeared. They were streaked with mud so that their white teeth flashed in brilliant smiles as they set a leather bucket before Isaac.

"We have found water. Plenty of water," they shouted as they dipped their hands in it up to the elbows and stood laughing and dripping, waiting for Isaac's approval.

Isaac reached out to his sons, and they in turn impulsively linked their arms with the men on each side of them until a great circle was formed of singing and dancing men. They stomped their feet to get the rhythm set and then were off pounding and whirling as they sang the age-old songs of their people. Such joy and excitement filled the air that everyone felt the troubles of the past were surely over and they were to have the very special blessing of Abraham's God.

Such was the joy and exuberance among the men that none of them noticed that Esau was missing. He had slipped away to hurry up the goat trail that led to Kirjath-arba, where he intended to meet Judith. He had impulsively decided to have her under any conditions. If he didn't act soon, someone else was likely to take her, and he didn't want that to happen.

As it turned out, Esau did not marry Judith right away because of the opposition of his parents. "You are the son of the promise," Isaac warned. "You must consider this before you decide to marry anyone."

Rebekah was even more emphatic. "Her ways are very different from ours," she said, "and there would be nothing but strife among our women."

Though it was a tradition, recognized by everyone, that the young wife must be totally submissive to the mother in her new family, this was often not attained without difficulty. The mother was the one who taught the new wife. She was responsible for seeing that the young bride knew the manners, customs and traditions, likes and dislikes of her new family. If she met any resistance, she was expected to use force and even severe punishment to bring about the desired result. It made for many unpleasant situations.

If the new bride was from a similar background, everything went much more smoothly. Esau understood this since he had seen the problems that arose when some of his friends brought home women with foreign ways. However, he was optimistic that once Judith belonged to him and was brought into his mother's tent, all would be well.

Rebekah tried to warn Isaac. "Esau is not one to give up easily, and you are the only one he will listen to."

However, Isaac was so preoccupied with the success of his wells and irrigation schemes that he hardly heard what she was saying. Even more pressing were the headaches and failing eyesight he was experiencing. He found that riding out into the bright sunlight of the desert morning or afternoon was more and more difficult. Even to leave his tent in the early evening when the sun was low caused severe strain. With these problems occupying his mind, the fact that Esau was courting a girl from among the Hittites didn't seem urgent.

At the same time that Isaac was being apathetic, Beeri, the father of Judith, encouraged Esau. "I was forced to give my daughter to be a priestess in the temple of Anat because of the famine. I couldn't feed my family and she was just a girl. She has done well there, but for a price you can buy her back," he said.

"What price would they ask?"

"You have herds of goats and sheep. The next new moon, give them five goats for their sacrifice."

"And I can have her for five goats?"

"And, of course, for myself there must be some small payment."

"Five goats too," Esau said eagerly.

"No, no, I am the father. It cost me much in food and clothes until she went to the temple."

"But the temple paid you . . ."

"A small bit of silver that was soon gone. No, I must have five sheep and three lambs."

Esau was surprised that the whole deal could be settled so simply. He didn't even take time to haggle and bargain as Beeri had expected. "I will have one of the shepherds deliver them just before the time of the new moon," he said with growing excitement.

Beeri was obviously elated that he had made such a good bargain. "You must be very rich," he said, as he followed Esau to the door. "You didn't even try to bring the price down. Perhaps I should have asked for more."

Esau paused. "And I would have probably paid it. When I want something I usually find a way of getting it."

This disturbed Beeri, but when he went to the temple and told the high priestess of his bargain and saw that she was favorably impressed, he was satisfied that he had done quite well.

Esau told Isaac and Rebekah very little. He didn't mention that Judith was one of the young priestesses in the temple of Anat. He simply told Isaac that he had met a young woman in the city of Kirjath-arba that he was attracted to and that he had already bargained for her. "I will need a few goats and some sheep," he said.

Esau insisted he could not live without this young woman, and so Isaac agreed to give him whatever was needed.

When Esau went to tell his mother, he had a harder time explaining. She wanted to know all the details, and she was not impressed with the few facts Esau gave. "Her hair is loose and thick and her eyes are like the eyes of one of the gazelles," he said. "She is slender like a rush growing up in the Besor."

"And can she cook and weave? Does she know how to take wool, dye it, and using the spindle make it into fine twined threads?"

"Mother," Esau smirked, "I would hope we could have servants to do such things."

"And what will she do with her time if she knows none of these things?"

Esau shrugged. "She'll play her stringed harp and charm us with her flute."

"I can see that I'll have to teach her everything. I don't understand. Where is the girl's mother?"

"She is from one of the prominent Hittite families. They have suffered much from the famine."

When he had gone, Rebekah ran to Isaac's tent and confronted him. "Have you given permission for this marriage?" she demanded.

Isaac reached out for her hand as he could no longer make out her features. "It seems to be all arranged. Esau did it himself. He probably realized I can't go up to Kirjath-arba to make the settlement."

"But she is a Hittite," Rebekah almost screamed, pulling her hand away.

"I wasn't told that. The Hittites are strangers here in this land much as we are."

"That isn't the point. Don't you remember Esau is the firstborn? You have said he is to have the birthright and the blessing. Can it be that he can marry a Hittite without your protesting?"

"Rebekah, you can see how difficult everything is since this trouble with my eyes. Perhaps I'll be better soon and then I can manage to find him a more suitable wife."

"And . . . for now, it doesn't matter that he marries a Hittite?"

"Esau is a creature of strong and lusty temperament. He needs a wife to help him settle down."

"But not just any wife."

"He can take other, more suitable, wives later. This is what he wants and he is determined. If we oppose him there'll be no peace."

"And if he brings a Hittite into our family, there'll be no peace."

Isaac took her two hands in his and leaning forward spoke confidently. "Oh my dear," he said, "you are clever, I'm sure you'll find a way. I have every confidence that you can teach this young girl all she needs to know to be a good wife to our son."

Rebekah pulled her hands away and turned to go. "Then you are not going to oppose him?"

"You know very well it's not my way to draw lines, make rules, and confront people. I prefer peaceful solutions. I want us all to live in peace."

Rebekah stood and looked at Isaac with tears in her eyes. She could see it was hopeless to press the point further. "It's obvious," she said finally, "that you have no idea of the trouble this will cause."

"Trouble comes and goes," he said. "We seldom have much control over it."

She poured some goat's milk and handed it to him. Without waiting to see that he drank it, she turned and hurried from his tent.

\* \* \*

By the time Esau informed his mother that he was bringing his bride home at the time of the new moon, she had become resigned to its inevitability. She reluctantly ordered the bridal tent erected. They would stay in the tent for a month, and during that time the girl could come to her during the day and receive instructions. She knew very little of the ways of the Hittites, so Rebekah called her nurse, Deborah, to come and help her make plans.

Deborah told her all that she had heard. "The girl has been in training in the temple of Anat," she said. "Because of the famine her family was forced to sell her to the temple priestess."

Rebekah was horrified. She immediately went to report this new bit of news to Isaac.

Isaac refused to be disturbed. "I trust the lad," he said. "He has been reminded of his responsibility and I'm sure he has thought this through."

"But she is not just a Hittite with Hittite ways but has also been in training in the temple. Who knows what that means!"

"Of course it is not good," Isaac said, frowning, "but we must make the best of it. I'm sure you can help the girl adjust to our ways. Perhaps she is unhappy there and Esau sees himself as rescuing her."

Rebekah buried her head in her hands; she could see it was hopeless to try to reason with him. He had always been a man who sought peace, and now with his growing blindness he seemed to have retreated into a corner where he refused to face any reality if it would cause conflict.

She went back to her tent and told Deborah, "He'll not confront Esau. It's hopeless. It's obvious I can no longer depend on him to make difficult decisions."

"He doesn't understand; he thinks you can manage everything," Deborah said. "He doesn't realize that if you are stern and harsh, most women will obey, but there will be a price to pay. They don't forget."

"Deborah, you must help me," Rebekah insisted. "Esau will have his way and we must deal with the problems as best we can."

\* \* \*

Esau went up to Kirjath-arba at the feast of the new moon and was gone for a week. When he returned he brought with him not only his new bride but also two young slaves. Her belongings were all packed into a few finely woven reed baskets.

It was Deborah who reported to Rebekah that Judith carefully carried one of these baskets herself and warned that no one must touch it. "Inside the basket," Deborah said, "is supposed to be a large, coiled snake."

Rebekah drew back in horror. "Do you suppose she means to keep it?"

"I'm sure she does. Esau has bragged to some of the men that she has tamed it. He is proud of her accomplishment."

Rebekah sank down among the cushions and pulled Deborah down beside her. "I can't tell Isaac. What shall I do?"

"There may be very little to do at first. She has a young boy who must catch small rodents to feed the snake and this, plus her new husband, will occupy her for at least a month. By the end of the month she'll undoubtedly be pregnant."

Rebekah let out a cry. "And this, this Hittite is to be the first of my grandchildren."

"And if it is a boy . . ." Deborah said.

"It will inherit the birthright and the blessing of Abraham!" Rebekah whispered the words in horror, and the two women looked at each other with tears in their eyes.

\* \* \*

It was indeed as Deborah had predicted; Judith was pregnant by the time the first month was up and Esau was elated. "She is strong. The child will undoubtedly be a boy."

Judith was soon nauseated and dizzy. She clung to the snake as a familiar creature that gave her comfort. "She even talks to the snake," one of Judith's women reported.

At first Rebekah refused to have her moved into her tent as long as the snake must come too. However, within a fortnight, a situation arose that forced Rebekah to take the girl even with the snake.

Since his new wife was pregnant and needed the care of his mother, Esau was again free to wander up to Kirjath-arba. He was now welcomed among the Hittites as one of them, and it was not long before a Hittite named Elon encouraged him to take his daughter as a second wife.

"She has been one of Judith's friends," her father said, "and the two can be company for each other. My Bashemath can cook the food we are used to and she can help when the baby comes."

Thus Esau brought home another new bride who stayed with him in the bridal tent while Rebekah took care of Judith. To her surprise Judith was not unhappy with the turn of events. She spent many of her days sitting with Bashemath at the tent door and eating the familiar food that Bashemath cooked. When she returned to Rebekah's tent for the night, she was sullen and demanding. "I'm not used to living like this," she said, motioning around the tent with a look of scorn. "I'm used to the city."

When Judith went into labor, Hittite women came down from the city and took over the birthing tent with their strange herbs, chants, and good luck charms. The birth was difficult, and when the child finally came, the women saw with dismay that it was only a girl. They rubbed her with salt and wrapped her in the prepared swaddling clothes and then brought her in for Judith to see. She thought the baby was ugly. She turned her face to the wall and insisted that she wanted nothing to do with the baby. "See," she said, "it's not strong. It was not meant to live." With that she refused to nurse the baby.

The midwife brought the child to Rebekah and thrust it into her arms. "It's just a girl and a poorly one at that," she said. "It's not worth saving."

Rebekah took the little bundle in her arms and rushed to Deborah's tent. "We must have some warm goat's milk," she said. "The foolish girl refuses to nurse the child."

"That's the way of many of the women of the city. If it were a boy and strong, they would be more than willing to care for it. To have a girl doesn't bring them gifts and praise from their husband, nor does it make other women envious."

Rebekah wept for the small, helpless little form. She couldn't speak but sat pulling the warm milk up into a small reed and letting it flow drop by drop into the little mouth. The child cried a weak, mewling cry that was more like that of a small animal. At the end of a week it was evident the child would not live and Rebekah was frantic. She had spent so many years wanting a child, any child, that she could not bear to see this little one die.

All this time Judith resented Rebekah's efforts. "The child is mine and I should be able to do with it as I please," she said with an angry toss of her head.

When the child finally died, Judith packed up her belongings, gathered her servants, and followed the midwives back to the city. Within a week she was back in the temple, refusing to see Esau or take any message sent from him.

It was not long until Bashemath disappeared, and when Esau went up to the city, he found that she had returned home. Her father, Elon, was embarrassed. "I can't give you back the lambs, but I do have another daughter who will be glad to come in her place. Her name is Adah and she has envied her sister. She will make you a good wife."

Esau shook his head. "This has been a painful experience. My mother is very upset and my father disappointed."

"Come, see if you are not impressed. Adah is not beautiful but she will be cheerful and is sure to give you sons."

They walked over to the edge of the parapet and looked down into the courtyard. They could see Adah and Bashemath baking bread. It was obvious that Adah was not beautiful but she moved quickly and only smiled when Bashemath snatched the first rounded loaf of bread and started to eat it instead of helping.

Esau liked what he saw. He wanted desperately to please his mother, and he could see that this girl would not be as offensive as either her sister or Judith. It also looked as though she knew how to bake bread and did it well. He was about to agree to the arrangement when Elon motioned him to come sit under the awning; he had something further to say.

When they were settled, Elon edged up on the subject cautiously. "My daughter Bashemath tells me that if the child recently born to Judith had been a boy, you would have had him cut. Is this true?"

It took Esau a few moments to understand and then he realized he was referring to their tradition of circumcising. "Yes," he said. "It is a covenant with our God."

Elon frowned and nervously pulled at a loose thread in the hem of his robe. "You know, this is not our custom and my daughter would be very disturbed to have this done to any child she might have. I will have to insist this not be done for any of the sons she might bear."

Esau frowned. "Then it is impossible. This is important to my people."

Elon coughed and adjusted his headpiece. "Well, well, I suppose Adah can get used to new ways. It just seems rather cruel to us."

Esau was about to challenge him on the idea of cruelty. It had seemed very cruel that Judith refused to nurse her child and yet that was completely accepted. He was about to turn away when he realized that Elon now owed him a wife, and he didn't want to go back home alone.

"I'll have to have three more lambs for Adah," Elon said, leaning back and studying Esau with half-closed eyes.

"I'm not about to pay three more lambs when she may very well run back home like her sister."

"No, no, don't be afraid," Elon said. "I'll tell her that if she tries to come home, I'll beat her. She won't come back. I can promise you that."

With this promise Esau took Adah back with him to the camp. He saw that she was not beautiful and he did not feel any great attraction to her, but he was satisfied when at the end of a year she had borne him a son. She said nothing when he was circumcised, and she let Isaac give him the name of Reuel, meaning "God's friend."

Esau was still restless, and while Adah was pregnant, he had made friends with a man named Zibeon, a Hivite who also lived in Kirjath-arba. They went hunting together, and it came about quite naturally that eventually Zibeon urged Esau to marry his daughter Aholibamah. She was young and seemed to be attracted to Esau.

Esau had noticed how she leaned over the parapet to watch him when he sat with her father or hurried to open the door to the courtyard when she knew he was coming. She had large, dark eyes and a slow, seductive smile. It wasn't long until Esau had cut a sharp bargain with her father and taken her home with him.

He had not realized that since she was of a Hivite background and tradition, she would be in constant conflict with Adah, whose family was Hittite. There was a steady round of bickering and hurt feelings, which only annoyed Esau. He would go off hunting and leave the problem for his mother to solve.

\* \* \*

As time passed, things did not get better. Esau's two wives were constantly fighting and their children were quarrelsome and ill-mannered. Rebekah was continually annoyed and irritated. The grandchildren she had hoped to enjoy were like a passel of wild cubs. They fought and screamed. Their little faces were always wet with sweat and streaked with dirt. They paid no attention to their mothers and hardly were aware of their grandmother. Only Esau could manage them, and this he did with a few good-natured cuffs to their ears.

Gradually Rebekah left the care of Esau's children to his wives and the servants while she retreated as often as possible to Isaac's tent. Here it was usually peaceful and quiet, since he was now almost totally blind and saw only those who came on urgent business. He was feeling old and useless. "Surely a man in my situation cannot live long," he kept saying.

As she had feared, he began to think about passing on his responsibilities and turning everything over to Esau as his firstborn. Rebekah now shamelessly listened whenever Esau visited his father, and it was on one such occasion that she heard the conversation she had been dreading.

"You see, my son," she heard Isaac say, "I have grown old and sightless. I will soon be feeble and could die at any time. I would like you to take your quiver and your bow and go out into the field and get a young deer. When you have made that savory dish I love, bring it to me and I will eat and then give you the blessing I have promised."

Rebekah's hand flew to her mouth to stifle a startled cry. It was evident that Isaac had paid no attention to her reports of Esau's many and irresponsible marriages. She shuddered to think that it would be Esau's sons who would have the blessing of father Abraham. If she and Isaac had not insisted, Eliphaz and Reuel would not have been circumcised. Esau was more like her brother Laban, who could worship many gods and saw little benefit in limiting one's chance of good luck to only one god.

She was behind the curtain that divided Isaac's tent, and she must at all costs be quiet. It was against their tradition and custom for a woman, even a wife and mother, to eavesdrop on her husband's private conversation. To appear uninvited on his side of the tent and interrupt a conversation was unthinkable. She quietly rose and nervously adjusted her headpiece and fingered the brass beads at her throat. Something must be done and quickly, but what? Isaac would not listen to her and Esau was determined to do as he pleased.

For a brief moment she toyed with the idea of trusting Elohim to work things out. It was so obvious that Jacob was the one to have the blessing. At the same time, she had to admit that even Jacob was not very interested in building altars or spending much time worshiping Elohim.

"At least he's not encumbered with pagan wives and quarrelsome children," she muttered as she impulsively decided to act. If Elohim had entrusted her with the message that it was Jacob who was to have the blessing, then surely He expected her to help bring it about.

Quickly she tiptoed out of the tent and sent a young boy to find Jacob. While she was waiting for him, she ordered a fire built and water brought. All the time she was gathering her spices, she was mulling over just what could be done.

By the time Jacob came, she was ready to explain everything. She first told him what she had heard. Then clutching his sleeve and searching his face with narrowed eyes, she said, "Now is the time to act. There's no time for discussion. It's obvious that you must pose as Esau. You will bring me two young kids from our herd, and I will quickly prepare the dish your father loves."

When he had gone she hurried back to the simmering pot and, squatting down beside it began to think of anything that might possibly go wrong. Esau was hairy and Jacob was smooth. If Isaac suspected anything, he was sure to reach out and touch Jacob. He would embrace him and would surely notice the smell of fresh fields and dried herbs was missing. She must have Deborah bring one of the rough, hairy garments belonging to Esau. That still left the problem of his arms and neck being smooth without the bushy feel of Esau.

When Jacob came, he told Rebekah that he too had been thinking of all the difficulties. He saw no solutions. "My father can tell by my voice I am not Esau," he said. "Now that he can't see, he depends on how things feel, and he will notice right away that I am not hairy like Esau. He will judge me as a deceiver of the worst kind and instead of a blessing I'll be cursed."

Now Rebekah stood up, holding the stirring stick in one hand and brushing the damp strands of hair back with the other. Her voice was low and urgent. "Upon me and me alone be your curse," she said. "Now go and prepare the goats and also bring me the skins. We must be quick about this business if we are to succeed."

With that Jacob stumbled out of the tent strengthened by his mother's fierce insistence. He captured the goats and prepared them in a trance. His mother would somehow come up with a plan, and he must go along or everything would be spoiled.

By the time the goats were simmering in the broth, Rebekah had formed a plan by which she could disguise Jacob. She sent Deborah to find one of Esau's cloaks while she busied herself over the skins. The short, soft underskin of each goat's belly was just right for her purpose. She scraped them clean and then told Jacob to hold out his arm. When he saw what she was going to do, he again objected. "This won't work," he said. "My father will know right away that we have tried to deceive him."

All the time that he was complaining, Rebekah was working to fit a strip snugly around his neck and then two others to cover his arms. When they were firmly in place, she leaned back and studied the effect, then reached out and felt of it. She smiled. "It will do," she said.

Jacob was still nervous. "People will see me," he said, holding out his arms awkwardly. "I can't go to my father's tent without being observed."

"Don't worry, Deborah has sent the children away and given everyone else orders to keep away from Isaac's tent so he can have quiet. There is nothing to fear, but you must hurry."

With that she felt of Jacob's arms once more and then, with a nod of satisfaction, handed him the bowl of fragrant stew and some bread and ushered him out of the tent.

The entrance flap to his father's tent was raised, which was a sign that his father was waiting for someone. Jacob felt a slight twinge of fear and guilt as he realized that it was Esau he was expecting. Then remembering all the hurts and slights he had received in Esau's shadow, he stiffened and entered the tent. In the dim light he could see Isaac sitting among the cushions; his legs were crossed and his hands on his knees. "My father," he said.

Isaac immediately became attentive. "Here I am," he said. "Who are you?"

"I am Esau, your firstborn." He paused a moment, fearing that his voice may have already betrayed him. "I have done as you commanded," he said, "and here is the venison."

Isaac seemed to hesitate and Jacob urged, "Come and eat, so that you can bless me."

Isaac still hesitated. "How have you found it so quickly?"

Jacob was temporarily paralyzed with fear. He frowned and then hurried to assure him. "Because," he said, "the Lord, your God, brought it to me."

Again Isaac hesitated, paying no attention to the fragrant stew Jacob had placed before him. "Come closer so that I can feel whether you are really Esau or not."

Sweat broke out on Jacob's brow. His anxiety mounted until he remembered his mother was standing just outside the tent listening. Quickly he put out his arm and guided Isaac's hand to feel the rough, hairy skin.

"The voice is Jacob's but the hands and arms are Esau's," Isaac said. "Are you truly my son Esau?" he asked directly.

"I am," Jacob said with as much conviction as he could muster.

"Bring me the venison that I may eat before I bless you," Isaac said, and Jacob knew this was going to be another test. If the dish his mother had prepared was not quite right, his father would immediately sense the deception and all would be lost. Jacob handed him the dish and then sat where he could watch as his father dipped the bread in the warm broth and ate. At first he was hesitant as though testing to see if it was really the dish he was waiting for, and then to Jacob's relief he ate hungrily. When the dish was finished, Jacob brought him wine and stood watching him drink. He had begun to feel more relaxed. Then just as he was sure the ordeal was almost over, his father stretched out his arms. "Come near now and kiss me, my son," he said. Jacob knew this was the final test. His father was still suspicious.

Jacob helped him to his feet and felt his arms around him, his fingers digging into Esau's cloak, his face buried in its rough folds. He kissed him, then held him at arm's length. "Yes," Isaac cried, with tears running down from the sightless eyes. "This is the smell of a field that the Lord has blessed. It is the smell of my son Esau."

Jacob knelt and Isaac placed his hands on his head and blessed him. "May the Lord give you of the dew of heaven and the fatness of the earth with plenty of corn and wine.

"Let the people serve you, and nations bow down to you, and cursed be everyone that curses you and blessed be everyone that blesses you."

Jacob rose and stumbled toward the door of the tent. He did not want to risk saying anything that might give his act away. He had the blessing and now he wanted only to escape.

\* \* \*

He did not want to wait where he would see Esau coming in with the venison and then patiently building the fire and boiling the water. He rushed to his mother's tent and let Deborah and his mother pull the skin from around his neck and his arms. He flung Esau's cloak from him and sneezed at the earthy odor. He plunged his arms, again and again, into the basin of water Deborah brought. He scrubbed them until they were red and raw trying to get the odor and the dried blood off. His mother was elated and kept praising him for managing everything so well.

He could feel none of the elation. He felt soiled and disappointed. It wasn't at all what he had thought it would be. What he had gotten was not something he had earned or deserved but something he had been forced to cheat to gain. He rushed out and sat under an overhanging projection of rock where he could think. It occurred to him that maybe he didn't really have the blessing at all. If it was Elohim who had to approve and agree, it was doubtful that He would approve such deceit.

He decided not to share these fears with his mother. She wouldn't understand. He loved her for wanting him to have the blessing. It would be a terrible blow to her if she ever thought that in spite of all her plans, Elohim had not approved of what they had done.

It was dark when he returned home and went directly to his mother's tent. He had expected to find his mother smiling and joyful; instead he found her pacing back and forth, now clutching the tent pole, then sinking her fingers into her flying hair, her eyes fierce and her jaw thrust out as though in defiance. "We must go immediately to your father's tent." The words sprang at him like sharp nettles. "Esau has come," she said, "and they are demanding an explanation."

*A*t the last moment Rebekah decided that she should go alone to face Isaac and Esau. "It may be dangerous for you to come while Esau is still with his father," she said.

"Perhaps I should agree to give him back the birthright and the blessing," Jacob said.

"No, no, it's impossible. That's why Esau's so angry. It can never be taken back."

"Then I must go and try to make it right."

Rebekah was hurriedly twisting her long hair into a knot and thrusting in a wooden pin to hold it in place. "There's nothing you can do that will make it right in his eyes," she said.

She snatched up her head cloth and going to the brass mirror on the tent pole quickly wound it into place covering her hair. She broke off a sprig of blossoming basil from a clay pot and thrust it into a fold. Leaning closer into the mirror to survey the effect, she moistened her lips, wet her finger, and nudged the hairs of her eyebrows into a curved line. Then smoothing down her robe with a swift, agitated movement, she looked long and pensively at Jacob.

With a stifled sob she reached out and grasped Jacob's arm. Her fingers dug into the soft folds of his robe as she whispered, "You saw how disturbed I was when you arrived," she said quietly. "Deborah had just told me she heard your brother means to kill you. If not now, then when your father dies."

Jacob staggered back with a look of horror on his face as the full meaning of her words sank in. "And . . . what am I to do?"

"You are to do nothing. I'll go and see what can be done."

With that she hurried out and down the path toward Isaac's tent. As she approached she could hear a terrible wailing. It rose and fell on the air like that of a wounded animal. She quickened her steps and rounding a corner came face-to-face with Esau. He seemed not to recognize her at first, but then with a sudden lunge and a face contorted with rage, he clawed at her. "You, you are the one. You have always favored my brother." He was quickly steadied by two friends who struggled to hold him back.

In spite of his friends' efforts, he again lunged forward and spat at her. With that and some wild curses, he turned and let his friends lead him off toward his own tents.

Rebekah was badly shaken as she lifted the tent flap and faced Isaac. She could see that he had heard everything. She saw the bowl of venison sitting to one side untouched and the bread strewn randomly beside it, and she was grieved for the pain of her elder son.

"Why, why did you let him do it?" Isaac asked, his face lifted and his sightless eyes glazed and cold.

Impulsively she knelt before him and bent to kiss the hem of his robe in respect, then leaning back on her heels, she spoke quietly and firmly. "You have forgotten the message given me by Elohim before the twins were born. You yourself told me to go and inquire of Him."

Isaac was suddenly quiet and thoughtful. "I do remember something like that, but it was so long ago," he said. "What happened?"

"The answer came to me quite clearly. 'You are to give birth to twins,' He said, 'and the younger will serve the elder and rule over him.'"

"And you told me this?"

"Of course, but you never paid any attention to the prediction. From the moment they were born, you assumed Esau was to have the blessing and the birthright."

Isaac buried his face in his hands and moaned. "You are right; what you say is right. I remember, I remember everything. Why didn't you remind me? Why did you think you had to trick me?"

"Men don't listen to women, especially if they are saying something that doesn't sound logical."

"Yes," he said, lifting his head and turning toward her. "Yes, that was the problem; it wasn't logical."

"So you didn't think Elohim would give a woman a message that wasn't logical."

"I should have known. That's the way it's always seemed. He isn't logical. His ways are mysterious."

"Esau blames me."

"It's my fault, all my fault," he groaned. "I encouraged him even when I knew he'd sold his birthright to his brother. I just assumed since he was the eldest..."

"He is the eldest, but he knows nothing of your father's God and has encumbered himself with the daughters of Heth. His wives and their children are obnoxious, a constant burden."

"Even I have sensed disruption and turmoil," Isaac said. "Why didn't you come and tell me?"

"You've not been well..."

Even though he could not see, Isaac was aware that she had settled herself on a cushion beside him.

"And what else have you been keeping from me?" he questioned.

"It's Jacob," she said, taking out the sprig of basil from her headpiece and running her fingers over the delicate leaves. "If he takes a wife, as Esau has done, from the daughters of Heth, it will be impossible to bear."

"So...?"

"Perhaps we should send him to my brother in Haran. He has many wives and must have some daughters."

They talked awhile longer, and when she rose to go, Isaac told her to send Jacob to him for a final blessing. "It's right that he not take a wife from our neighbors. I've let Esau do as he pleased and it's not been good. I must do better by Jacob."

\* \* \*

As Rebekah hurried from his tent, she realized that she had not told him of Esau's threat. Actually it didn't matter since he had given his permission for Jacob to leave.

Knowing how violent Esau could be when he was opposed, she hurried Jacob over to Isaac's tent. She didn't trust him to go alone lest something go wrong. She would wait just inside the tent where she could quickly see anyone approaching. If Esau had any idea of what was to happen, he would be dangerous.

She couldn't hear what Isaac said, but she saw that he embraced Jacob with real feeling. When she saw Jacob kneel and Isaac place his hands on his head, she knew that at last everything was right and as it should be. He was giving Jacob the blessing again, and this time knowing that it was Jacob whom he blessed. She didn't know what he said but that didn't matter; it was the blessing she wanted for Jacob.

Jacob would have to flee feeling his brother's hatred, but he would know that at last, after all these years, he had his father's love and blessing.

* * *

It was growing dark as Rebekah said a hurried goodbye to her son. "You will find plenty of relatives and there will be some young beauty for you to marry. I'll send for you when this trouble dies down. Esau can't be angry for long."

"He remembers slights and snubs," Jacob said. "I don't expect him to get over this quickly." All the time Jacob was adjusting the packs of dried figs and cheese and a blanket roll on the back of a donkey. Rebekah grasped his hands and looked at him with tears welling in her eyes. "How happy I'll be to see you coming with a bride from my own house."

"I am afraid for Father. He looks so old and worn."

Rebekah hugged him and kissed him on both cheeks. "Don't worry. You won't be gone that long. The time will pass quickly."

With a final hug she let him go, and was just watching him start to move down the path toward the two slaves who were going with him when she remembered something important. "Jacob," she called softly as she hurried to catch up with him, "be careful around my brother Laban. He is a hard bargainer and a real trickster. Don't let him get the best of you."

Jacob smiled and gave his mother a last quick hug. "So it will be one trickster against another. Isn't that what you named me?"

"I've sometimes regretted naming you Jacob."

"Maybe the name will stand me in good stead in your brother's house."

"Remember your father's blessing. May the God of your grandfather Abraham go with you and protect you." With that she let him go and watched him disappear into the darkness.

She went back to her tent and sank down among the cushions. She took the bowl of warm broth Deborah had prepared for her and set it to one side. She couldn't stand to eat anything. "I just want to be alone," she told Deborah.

When the crying children were finally carried off and the tent was quiet, Rebekah sat thinking over all that had happened. Isaac had been so understanding when she had explained everything to him. Why had she not done that from the beginning? What had she been afraid of? Now, because of her silence and deception, Jacob was gone and Esau was lost to her forever. She had worked so hard at manipulating things. What if she had just trusted Elohim to work out His own promise?

✳ ✳ ✳

Jacob slipped quietly out of the camp and was on his way up to the high plateau where he would skirt around Hebron and Bethlehem and get as far as possible on this first night. He must get so far that Esau could not easily catch up with him.

He had only his rough sheepskin cloak, and the night air was crisp and promised an early frost. From his satchel he pulled out some dried figs and ate as he hurried along. He dared not stop and light a fire for a proper meal. He didn't ride but walked beside the donkey because he wanted to think. He felt burdened, oppressed by some choking pain that seemed to tear at his insides until he wanted to cry out in anguish. The night was dark, but he felt as though he were walking through a darkness that was almost palpable. He tried to get at the cause of the pain.

At first he felt it was the memory of his old, blind father stretching out his hands to give him his final blessing. The words flew around in his head like black crows. "May El Shaddai, the almighty, all-powerful God, bless you and make you fruitful and multiply you" . . . and then the part that made him almost retch with the pain, "and give the blessing of Abraham to you and your seed that you may inherit the land that God gave to Abraham."

These were his father's last words. They were words said to him and not to his brother Esau. They were the words of the blessing he had craved and lied to achieve. The problem was that he still didn't feel that they belonged to him. Neither his grandfather Abraham nor El Shaddai would give blessings to a deceiver. He had thought, and his mother had thought, that to just wrest the words of the blessing from his father was all that was needed. Now he knew his father could say the words, but unless they were prompted by El Shaddai, they meant nothing.

The moon rose over the distant mountains of the Dead Sea and continued slowly into a high arch above him. The stars blossomed like small dove's dung flowers in the soft black of the sky. He was aware of nothing but the rough stones in the path and the frequent cry of an owl. He walked fast to keep time with his turbulent thoughts. It was late when at last he came to a hillside looking out on the village of Luz. The village was small and the gates were closed. There would be no chance of rousing someone so he could spend the night in their guesthouse.

He found a grassy knoll and spread out his cloak. He needed a headrest. He looked around and saw a stone that seemed just the right size. He pulled it over to the grass, set it in place, and lay down, and was soon fast asleep.

He was exhausted and his sleep was deep and troubled. He saw Esau in his dream and then his father and finally his grandfather Abraham. They all seemed to look at him with disapproval. One word hung in the air around him even in his sleep, "Supplanter, you are a supplanter. With deception you have supplanted your brother."

He was slightly aroused by an owl's cry. He looked up into the now moonless sky and felt the stars pressing down upon him. They seemed almost within reach. A thought began to form in a hazy, dreamlike state. If only he could go to the gate of heaven as he had gone to his father and have it settled once and for all. If he could know that it really was Elohim who had chosen him as his mother said, he would have peace.

He turned over and was again aware only of some small creature digging near his headrest. He heard the owl cry once more and then he drifted off into a strange dreamlike state. He was gradually aware of steps, large steps, that led upward invitingly. He could not see the top, as they seemed to disappear into a bright, glowing mist. He lay still, very still, and watched as from the midst of the mist, he saw, very faint and far away, feet begin to appear descending the stairs and coming toward him.

Within moments beings of great power and beauty were coming down the stairs and then, just as they reached the bottom, turning and ascending in the same way. There was the smell of sod wet with spring rain and the fragrance of white lilies. There was the atmosphere of joy, bright, cascading joy.

Suddenly the mist at the top of the stairs glowed with a brilliance that made Jacob cover his eyes, and the beings on the stairs fell to their knees. A warm and encouraging voice sounded from the head of the stairs. "I am the Lord God of Abraham your father, and the God of Isaac. The ground you are lying on belongs to you; I will give it to you and your descendants. You will have as many descendants as the dust. They will cover the land from east to west and from north to south. All the nations of the earth will be blessed

171

through you and your descendants. I am with you and will protect you wherever you go, and I will bring you back safely to this land. I will be with you constantly and will give you all I am promising."

Jacob awoke with a start. Though the stairs had disappeared, the atmosphere was still charged with vibrant life. The glow faded and the stars were again all that was visible. "God lives here," Jacob burst out in terror and awe. "I've somehow stumbled into His home! This has to be the very entrance to heaven!"

The next morning he awoke early before the sun had fully risen over the mountains in the distance. He impulsively set the stone that had been his headrest upright and poured olive oil from his pouch over it as he had seen his father and his grandfather do when they were consecrating an altar. "I shall not forget this place," he said. "It must have a name, a name separate from the village nearby. I'll call it Bethel, for it is indeed the house of God."

He paused beside the pillar and thought. It seemed important that he make some vow, some commitment in the place where the great El Shaddai of his father and grandfather had sworn such promises to him. "If," he began, not wanting to vow or promise something he could not manage. "If this God of my fathers will help and protect me on this journey and give me food and clothes and bring me back safely to my father . . . then," here he paused and thought. Here would be his part of the agreement and it must be something appropriate and not so difficult he couldn't do it. He continued slowly and thoughtfully, "then I will choose El Shaddai, Elohim as my God! This memorial pillar will become a true altar and place of worship."

He paused again and tried to think what sort of promise would his father make if he were dealing directly with his God. "I will give You back a tenth," he said at last, "of everything You give me."

As he turned and continued on his way, his mother's warning flashed through his mind: "Be careful around Laban." He wondered briefly what she meant. Then still glowing with the experience of the night before and the assurance that El Shaddai, the almighty God, was to be with him, he felt able to deal with whatever might arise.

* * *

It did not take Esau long to discover that Jacob had fled. His first impulse was to hurry after him and wreak his revenge. However, his friends soon convinced him that it was his mother he had to deal with, not Jacob. Jacob could be punished later. With his anger only slightly abated, he stormed over to confront his mother.

Rebekah had been expecting him. She had fixed honey cakes and poured out a cup of her best date wine. She saw him as he came up the path beside the brook Besor, swinging his riding prod viciously at the reeds along the bank. She rose to meet him with peaceful words, but before she could say anything, he burst out, "So . . . where is that heel-grabber, supplanter brother of mine?" He stood in the door of her tent, feet wide apart, his eyes blazing with hatred and his hands angrily twisting the prod.

"Come sit and I'll tell you," she offered.

"I'll not sit in this tent," he said with an ominous toss of his head.

"If you wish to hear anything from me, you'll come sit and have some of these honey cakes I baked for you."

Esau seldom had honey cakes as his wives were busy with children and gossiping and didn't take time to make such things.

He reluctantly came and sat on the cushion she offered and then took a fistful of the honey cakes and gulped down the wine before he again demanded, "Where has my brother gone? What mischief is he up to now?"

Rebekah motioned for the serving girls to take the screaming children out so they could talk, and then she turned to Esau. "When you sold your birthright, did you not realize what you had done? And when you married these quarrelsome idol worshipers, did you think to receive the blessing of your grandfather Abraham?"

Esau dropped the riding prod and ran his fingers through his unruly hair. He shifted uneasily on the cushion. "Women don't count," he said. "It's the man who must deal with his gods."

Rebekah sat looking at him and feeling a great sorrow for this willful, wild son. She didn't know how she could explain. "You want to know where your brother Jacob has gone?" she asked finally.

Esau's whole demeanor changed. His face took on a sullen sneer as he said, "Yes, I demand to know."

"He has left for my brother's family in Haran." She could see that Esau was visibly shaken. He had not even imagined such a thing.

"Why's he going there?"

"He's going to find a bride who is suitable."

"What do you mean . . . suitable?" Now he was hostile, ready to defend his own choice of wives.

"You don't understand, do you?"

"Do you mean he thinks he'll find someone more beautiful?"

"He's looking for someone who knows our ways and follows our customs, even understands why we worship a God who can't be seen."

"Every one of my wives is beautiful. He won't find anyone in Haran more beautiful."

"Esau," she said, reaching out to him in real compassion, "your wives are pretty but they don't fit and never will. They see nothing wrong with having idols and they think circumcision is cruel. They even at times take your children with them to their pagan festivals."

Esau fell back as though he had been slapped. The riding prod fell from his hand and his expression became pained. "I can get rid of my wives; I'll send them back to their fathers with apologies and gifts."

"It is too late for that," Rebekah said. "There are some things in life that cannot be changed. You have children. These are your children and the wives are your wives. These are the result of decisions you made freely. While wives can be sent back, children cannot be thrust back into the womb, no matter how much you pray or wish it to happen."

"You don't understand. I had no choice. The only women available, as you say, were not suitable."

"If you had asked me, I would have at least suggested that you go and visit Ishmael. He has daughters."

Esau got to his feet and, slapping the prod against his right leg, moved to the door of the tent. "I understand," he said thoughtfully. "My wives were only a whim of the moment. I didn't think about children or their fitting into our family. Now maybe I should go visit Ishmael and see if I can't find at least one suitable wife."

With that he ducked down and made his way out of the tent in a hurry before she could object. After he was gone Rebekah sat alone thinking. How hard it was to make things right when they had gone so wrong. Even her own best qualities had been used in the wrong way. The girl who joyfully watered the camels for Abraham's servant so long ago was also the one who, wanting to make things turn out right for her son, went to all the effort of disguising him to pass for his brother. Now her beloved son was fleeing for his life and her only other son was filled with hatred enough to kill.

And Isaac, who was so patient and kind, let Esau destroy himself with big expectations and bad marriages rather than discipline him.

What would have happened, she wondered, if she had trusted Elohim to work out His own plan for their lives? What would have been different if she had not felt it necessary to manipulate and manage everything?

If she had reminded Isaac of Elohim's words, perhaps he would have made the decision to bless Jacob. As it was, things could not have turned out worse. Esau had been badly hurt and her beloved Jacob would undoubtedly receive a rough welcome from Laban. She knew her brother well. When he realized Jacob had come with no gifts, only promises of birthright and blessing, he would not be pleased. She feared that Jacob would find only thorns in Laban's house.

As it happened Jacob did not go directly to the house of his uncle, nor did he meet Laban until he had first seen that his uncle did indeed have a beautiful daughter. It happened quite by chance. He was thirsty, his water cask was empty, and he turned aside to join some shepherds. "Where can I find a well?" he asked.

"You're in luck," one of them said. "We're waiting till all the shepherds arrive to lift the stone off the well and water our sheep."

"Where do you live?" Jacob asked.

"We live in Haran," they said.

"Do you know someone named Laban, the son of Nahor?"

"Certainly!"

"Is he well?"

"Not only well but prosperous. It's his daughter we're waiting for. She should be coming with his sheep."

"He has no sons or servants to care for the sheep?"

They rolled their eyes and looked at each other, nodding their amazement. "It's obvious you know nothing of Haran. Laban has sons and servants and slaves aplenty. He's very wealthy, but his daughter is young and likes to herd sheep better than staying at home."

"Look! Here she comes now," one of the men said.

Jacob looked in the direction the old man pointed and saw a young wisp of a girl standing first on one rock and then another as she counted her sheep. When she was satisfied that they were all there, she gave a shrill, piercing whistle and proceeded to lead them right to the group by the well.

Jacob stepped back so he could observe her before she noticed him. He saw that she wore no covering on her hair but a chain of daisies that she had obviously woven while she watched her sheep. Her hair was thick and curly, her mouth generous, and her eyes sparkled with good humor. Her gown, hiked up to make walking easier, displayed doeskin sandals whose laces crossed back and forth over slim ankles and up tanned legs. The long sleeves of her gown were folded back, leaving her hands exposed.

Something seemed to amuse her, for she did a quick, waltzing step and landed on the well cover with her hands on her hips and looked around at the rest of the shepherds with a saucy challenge. "I see that none of you were able to lift the stone," she said in a slow, confident voice.

Jacob saw this as an opportunity to get acquainted. He stepped out from the group of shepherds and with one swift movement lifted her from the stone. Then with a surge of strength that surprised even him, he rolled the huge stone aside. Without waiting for her reaction, he reached for a leather bucket he had noticed hanging from the limb of a nearby tree and lowered it again and again into the well as he drew water for her sheep.

When her sheep were all watered, he threw his head back and drank hungrily of the water before handing it to one of the other shepherds.

Rachel had been standing to one side observing everything with admiration but was totally taken aback when Jacob turned, pulled her into his arms, and kissed her. He held her at arm's length and studied her face with obvious approval. "There," he said. "I've set the record straight, evened things up I should say."

Rachel pulled away and pretended to straighten her gown, while all the time she was looking at him sideways, out of the corner of her eye. "Who are you?" she asked. "Surely we have no such impetuous men in Haran."

Jacob laughed. "Of course you don't. But I'm your cousin. The son of your aunt Rebekah."

Rachel gasped and then laughed. "I remember Aunt Rebekah drew the water and watered all your father's camels. There were ten of them."

"Exactly," Jacob said, smiling with pleasure that she understood.

Without another word, she blushed and pushed back her curls, toppling the wreath of daisies from her head. Then she turned and, forgetting her sheep, ran toward the village.

Jacob looked around at the shepherds and motioned for them to come water their animals. "Are all my uncle's daughters so lively?" he asked.

"He has only two unmarried daughters," one of the men volunteered.

"And you say he has many sons?"

"Yes. But then he has had many wives. His youngest and favorite wife gave birth to only the two girls."

"If he has sons, why should such a beauty be out here with the sheep?"

"You might say," one of the men leaned forward to whisper, "your uncle's hiding her out here with the sheep." Jacob looked around at the shepherds who were now clustered around him and noted that they were all old and weathered. No wonder it took them all together to lift the stone from the well.

By the time Laban appeared, Jacob had gleaned a brief history of his situation. "His first wife brought him great riches," they began, "but gave him only one son." She was still alive but was rarely seen. His other wives and concubines had given him many sons who were now engaged in the family business of trading, wine making, and producing wool cloth from the shearings of the sheep. The last wife was young and shapely but was ill-tempered because she had been able to produce only the two girls. However, everyone agreed that Laban loved her the most.

"Here comes your uncle now with several of his sons," one of the shepherds said.

Jacob turned and saw several men hurrying toward him. He knew the thin, important looking man who led the way must be his uncle Laban. He had a staff that helped him navigate the rocks and boulders of a shortcut he had chosen in his excitement. Jacob ran to meet him and was immediately swept into his uncle's strong embrace. He was aware of the wiry strength of this man and the faint odor of costly sandalwood, as well as the flash of large rings on the fingers that dug into his arms.

"Welcome! Welcome!" Laban exclaimed boisterously as he led Jacob back toward the village and the family home. Things happened so fast that it was only after they were settled in a dim, musty room off a large courtyard that Jacob got a good look at his uncle.

The shutters had been flung back so that light flooded in through two narrow windows and full upon the face of Laban. His head was shaved, his beard trimmed and fashioned to a point, making his face seem long and angular, but it was his eyes that Jacob noted with surprise. They seemed unusually large and slightly protruding. This gave him the look of an almost deceptive innocence and generosity.

Jacob noted that he was dressed in the same style of clothes his grandfather had worn on special occasions, who said it was the way they had all dressed in Ur before the trouble. It was a long fringed cloak pulled to one side, leaving one shoulder bare, and held in place on his other shoulder by a large, dull, silver toggle pin. His knee-length skirt was also fringed. Jacob remembered hearing that only the wealthy city dwellers could wear such things.

The reception room had obviously been opened just for this occasion. The cushions were of good quality but worn, and the room had a musty smell of spoiled fruit, rose water, and a mixture of dried thyme and basil. There was the constant buzzing of flies and from outside in the courtyard came the excited voices of women and the incessant crying of a baby.

From the moment he entered the courtyard and was ushered into this room, Jacob had been overwhelmed with the thought that this was where his mother had grown up. She would feel at home here and might recognize many of the relatives without difficulty. He was seeing everything through her eyes when he was nudged from his reverie by a question put very carefully by his uncle, "And you have come all this way with only a mule and two servants?"

"Yes, yes, I came away in quite a hurry." As he said it he realized by the look on his uncle's face that he suspected some dark, unsavory secret.

"And what was the cause of this hurry?"

Jacob hesitated only a moment and decided against telling him the whole truth. "My mother didn't want me to marry strangers as my brother had done. She hoped I would find a bride among my relatives."

Laban's eyes narrowed as he leaned forward and tugged at his short beard. "As I remember, there were ten camels loaded with gifts when your grandfather sent his servant here on the same mission. Has your family fallen on some bad luck? Is your father perhaps so poor he cannot send gifts?"

At first Jacob was taken aback by his uncle's frankness and then amused as he remembered his mother's description of her brother. "He's terribly greedy," she had said.

"No," he said, running his hand a bit nervously around the tasseled edge of the cushion he sat on. "My father is very wealthy. I just left in a hurry."

"And why such a hurry?" Laban asked, leaning forward. His eyes studied Jacob with a critical glint.

Jacob could see that he would have no peace until he admitted the whole seamy business of his conflict with Esau. "My brother and I are twins. He happened to be born a few minutes before I was and so claimed both the birthright and the blessing. Due to some amazing circumstances, I now have both the birthright and the blessing and my brother has threatened to kill me. My mother insisted I leave until he forgets the whole thing."

179

"And your mother thought it would be a good idea for you to marry one of my daughters while you were here." Laban smirked and leaned back among the cushions, giving Jacob even closer scrutiny.

"Yes, in fact that is exactly what she thought," Jacob said, totally missing his uncle's negative reaction.

"And . . ." said Laban, leaning forward with his face almost cruel in its deliberation, "what were you to use for a bridal price?"

Jacob fell back as though physically slapped. He struggled to find words to answer, but all he could say was that he was to receive the greater share of his father's wealth at his death.

"Promises cannot buy my daughters. They are the beauties of this area, and I will not give them even to my sister's son without proper recompense."

No more was said on the subject, but as they rose to join the rest of Laban's sons for the evening meal, Laban clutched Jacob's arm. "I hope there's no offense. You understand, I have only two daughters remaining to me. We'll discuss this all later, after I have thought about it. In the meantime you may join my sons. It's shearing time and we could use another hand."

* * *

Jacob went out every day to work with Laban's sons at shearing the sheep. It was long, hard work and they didn't spare him; instead they chided him for being slow and awkward. He finally had to admit that he had very little experience in shearing sheep. At home he had been spared such arduous tasks.

At the end of the shearing, when the wool was bundled and ready for carding, there was a great feast. It was the custom in Haran for all of the men to go to the bathhouse for the day to wash away the grime caked on them from their week with the sheep. For the first time Jacob experienced the delight of Haran's bathhouse. At home he had bathed in the stream, and only when they lived in the city of Gerar had he gone with the men of his family to the bathhouse. "We must rid ourselves of the stench of sweat and wool before we can enjoy the feast," one of Laban's sons explained.

Laban was also there, though he had not so much as ventured a visit to the shearing. He was lounging in the final room where it was clear he had just had a massage. He was drinking some of last year's wine and eating grapes that lay on a woven mat in front of him. When he saw Jacob, he motioned for him to come and relax and ordered another jug of wine. It was obvious he had some business to discuss with him.

"My son," he said hesitantly as he watched to see if Jacob recognized his change in status. He was evidently satisfied as he went on. "You have worked hard and have learned quickly the intricacies of shearing a sheep. I could use someone like you. What would you ask for wages?"

Jacob almost choked; he had not thought he had actually done that well. He had worked very hard but it was not as easy as it had at first appeared. Without hesitation he looked at Laban and answered, "If it's true that I have found favor in your eyes, then give me your daughter Rachel as my wages."

Laban drew back, set his jug down very deliberately, and looked at Jacob with hooded eyes and a tightness to his mouth that expressed his displeasure more than words. "How long do you suppose you would have to work to earn a treasure like my Rachel?"

Jacob realized he was not dealing with a man who made easy bargains. He again remembered his mother's words, "My brother is greedy." He also realized that Laban had no intention of making any bargain that involved his daughter. At the same time Jacob knew that the only thing Laban had that he wanted was his daughter Rachel.

"I'll work a year for her," he said, thinking that he was being generous, but knowing that Laban was going to ask double at least.

"Never, never," Laban almost shouted in a great frenzy that brought his sons over to see what was the matter. "This fellow, this cousin of yours thinks I'll give him Rachel for only one year of work," he said.

The sons laughed and nudged each other. "Jacob, you are asking for the moon," one of them said.

"She is the light of my father's life," another said.

"And it isn't as though you know how to do many of the things that have to be done around here," a third added.

Jacob had been well aware during the month that all of Laban's sons worked hard for their father and they all knew how to do many things. He began to see that to offer to work for a year when he didn't really know how to do anything wasn't, in Laban's eyes, acceptable.

Jacob had always been good at bargaining. "If you know what you want," he had often said, "then you don't give up." Now he knew that more than anything in his whole life he wanted Rachel. In fact as the bargaining heated up, he knew he would give any price for her.

The frightening thing was that it was very evident his uncle also prided himself on his bargaining ability. There was a fleeting moment when Jacob realized that it was not his own father, Isaac, he resembled but this wily uncle, and he wasn't pleased with what he saw.

Before the bargaining was over everyone in the bathhouse had gathered to see what the outcome would be. They all knew Laban and they knew when he had set his mind against making a deal that it was impossible to shake him. They could not believe this newcomer dared to challenge him.

At the last, when Laban was getting tired and Jacob was feeling he might be winning, Laban said, "I have another daughter, Leah; you may have her for working four years."

Jacob's mind was made up; he wanted no substitutes. It was Rachel he wanted and he would not settle for less.

Finally when Laban saw that his nephew really seemed to care for Rachel, he decided to ask the impossible, and if the lad agreed, he would give in to him. "All right," he said, "my final decision: If you will work for me for seven years, I'll give her to you."

There was a gasp as everyone estimated what could be gotten for seven years of work. The tension in the air was almost unendurable. They hated to see this feisty young man lose, since he had put up such a struggle, but they knew Jacob could not agree to such a bargain. Who knew what Laban would ask of someone under those conditions.

They watched Jacob carefully. He seemed to be toying with five grapes he had lined up. That seemed to be as far as he would go; five grapes must represent five years. Everyone's eyes were now on the grapes. What would he do? They had never seen anyone want a woman so badly, and they found that they wanted him to win.

To everyone's surprise they saw him look at Laban as though trying to make up his mind about something, and then they saw him deliberately tear off two more grapes and put them beside the other five.

A great shout went up as they realized that Jacob had won and in a way Laban had also won. Jacob would work seven years for this slip of a girl he had seen only briefly. What would happen to such a man? they all wondered. Would he really get the girl after the seven years, or would the uncle outmaneuver him? However it worked out, they went away liking this young man who had come up out of the deserts of Canaan to challenge his uncle and wrest his favorite daughter from him.

Laban had not expected his challenge to be accepted, but he was too exhausted to go one more round against this upstart of a nephew. He was actually so exhausted he had to have two of his sons help him out of the bathhouse, and he did not appear at the feast that evening.

Jacob toyed with having some written record made of the agreement, but he thought better of it when he realized that there had been so many witnesses that this would be more binding than anything recorded in clay.

Euphoria carried Jacob through the afternoon. He had won and he had won in fair combat—no tricks, just his wits—and he felt good about it. He dressed carefully for the feast, realizing by that time Rachel would have heard the news and would be taking a long interested look at him. He also determined to somehow get a glimpse of the other daughter Laban was so willing to give him.

Before going to the celebration, Jacob called for one of the slaves he had brought with him from home. "Tomorrow," he said, "you must leave for Beersheba. Tell my mother all that you have seen here and let her know that I have committed myself to work seven years for my uncle's daughter." The young man nodded and agreed that he would go as quickly as possible. He should be able to find a caravan with which to travel most of the way.

For the first time Jacob realized the full significance of the bargain he had made. He would not be able to go home for at least seven years. There could be many changes in that time. He could barely endure the thought that his mother and father would be older or that one of them might even have died. He determined to leave as soon as he had been given his bride. He would not let Laban trick him out of going home.

\* \* \*

The festivities of the evening were held in the large courtyard and involved Laban's whole family. His sons were there with their wives and children, along with some of the neighbors. As was the custom, the entertainment was provided by a village juggler, some dancers, and an old woman who sat in a corner with a large drum keeping time for the dancers and providing a background for several singers.

Before the evening was over, most of the women had stepped out into the circle of light and danced their village dance, and then the brothers had also done their traditional circle dance. Jacob, standing in the shadows, felt his heart quicken when it was Rachel's turn. She stepped out into the circle of light, smiled, and then motioned to someone in the midst of a clump of women. "Leah," she said, "we must do this one together."

Jacob was immediately interested. This must be the sister Laban was willing to give for a lesser price. He saw that the girl hung back and Rachel had to reach out and pull her out into the lighted open space. The girl stood awkwardly, shielding her eyes from the light. She was obviously embarrassed by Rachel's insistence.

"Leah," the women urged, "don't be shy. Dance with your sister."

Rachel laughed and refused to let her sister go back to her place with the women. "Come," she said, "give me your hand and we'll show them how well Laban's daughters can dance the shepherd's dance."

With a shrug of resignation, Leah let Rachel take her hand. The old woman beat out a lively, tantalizing rhythm while Rachel moved her feet slowly at first to catch the beat, and then whirled into the dance, pulling her sister along. Everyone began to clap and shout encouragement to Leah until she also began to enter into the spirit of the dance. It was obvious that she did not enjoy either the movement or the attention, but she went along almost as a shadow of her more animated sister.

Jacob felt sorry for Leah. She undoubtedly shone in other areas. He imagined she was a better cook and would be talented at weaving and basket making, but she had not the fire and spark of Rachel. Leah would make a good and competent wife and mother, but it was Rachel he loved.

\* \* \*

There was no getting around the bargain he had made. Laban extracted the seven years from Jacob down to the very day. During that whole time, he had made certain that Jacob could only see or speak to Rachel when there were large family gatherings. He also managed to have the two sisters always together so Jacob almost never had a chance to speak to Rachel alone.

Jacob was quite resourceful and took advantage of every opportunity to leave flowers where Rachel would find them or give her a carefully constructed cage of reeds to house a small songbird. He anticipated her needs and was rewarded by her look of surprise and delight. At times she even noticed him and smiled. With such small morsels of joy, he was able to endure the seven years and actually felt it had been a small price to pay for such a prize.

At the same time it was Leah who grew to love Jacob with a hopeless devotion. She was always seeing that he had the choicest bits of meat, the freshest fruit, or the best of Laban's wine. All of this went without any special notice from Jacob.

As the seven years came to a close and the time approached for Jacob to claim his bride, Leah grew so distressed she became ill. When Laban checked to see what was wrong, she told him that she no longer wanted to live. "I am the oldest and should be the one getting married. I am the one who loves Jacob the best. How can I endure seeing my sister married to the only man I will ever love?"

This bothered Laban. It was indeed true that it was an age-old custom that the oldest daughter should be married first. "But," he countered, "it's Rachel that he loves. It's Rachel he's been working for all this time. How can I tell him, he cannot have Rachel?"

"Father," Leah begged, "it's just that he hasn't noticed me. If I were married to him I could make him love me."

Laban began to mull about the possibilities. Maybe everyone could get what they wanted. More than anything he wanted to keep Jacob from leaving with Rachel. He knew that this was exactly what Jacob had in mind. *What if I marry Leah to him and then promise him Rachel within the week if he'll agree to work seven more years?*

To do this he would have to manage many things secretly. He could tell Leah only part of his plan, but he must keep it all from Jacob and Rachel. He would definitely need the help of the old idols in the space under the stairs. The old goat-man could be depended upon to help further any scheme that involved secrets and careful manipulation.

\* \* \*

When the day of his wedding feast actually came, Jacob could hardly endure the slow, dragging necessities. He went as in a trance with the sons of Laban to the bath and endured their crude jokes and lively banter. He sat at the feast without noticing the food or that it was Laban who sat beside him instead of his veiled bride. "You are one of us," Laban said, "my own sister's son. We do not need such formalities."

Laban was so jovial and complimentary that Jacob relaxed. He knew that the best wine had been brought out for the occasion, and he didn't question his uncle's motive when he filled his goblet again and again. He also didn't notice that Laban was nervous and kept having whispered conversations with several servants.

At last when the moon had disappeared and the torches gave off only a dim glow, Laban himself escorted Jacob to the marriage chamber. "These old women have seen that the chamber is ready," Laban said. "You'll find my daughter already inside waiting for you." Laban opened the door and nudged Jacob into the dark room, then closed the door.

Laban stood listening for a few moments, and when he heard no unusual outcry, he went out into the courtyard and up to the roof. He sat alone in his usual seat under the grape arbor. He could not help remembering his own marriage to the daughter of Nazzim so long ago. He had not seen her, but he knew very well what he was getting. It was Nazzim's influence and money he cared about, so it didn't matter what she looked like in the morning when the veil was removed. The bargain had been a good one. She had given him one son and eventually Nazzim's wealth.

In the bright light of day, Jacob would also know the truth, if not before then. Laban had to admit that Jacob was being badly tricked. Laban shuddered to think of facing him in the morning. He would, of course, have the goat-man to blame. He would insist it was the old goat-man idol that gave him the idea. "You have to marry the eldest first," he would insist the idol had advised. "Then if he still wants the other sister, you can give her to him after a week, but only after making sure that he agrees to work another seven years."

The cunning of the goat-man was unequaled. Laban knew these thoughts came from him because they were so brilliant. "I have never been that clever," he muttered to himself.

He sighed as he rose and headed for the stairs. In the morning he would not only have to face Jacob but also Rachel. Since his first wife was now living in her own rooms apart from the rest of the family, he had taken Rachel to her for safekeeping. With Barida's consent he had locked them both in her rooms and wouldn't let them out until morning.

Barida was now old and bitter since Laban had taken many other wives. She especially hated the mother of Rachel and was ready to do anything that would cause her or her daughters distress. Her eyes glinted with an evil, crafty look as Laban left Rachel with her to be dressed for her wedding night. She winked at him as she handed him the key, and he felt twinges of guilt that he should please her so at Rachel's expense.

* * *

The next morning it was even worse than Laban had anticipated. To his surprise Jacob blamed Leah for deceiving him and hurting her sister. As Laban found out later, Jacob had discovered the trick with the first light of day. Instantly he had yanked Leah's arms from around his neck and flung her from him in disgust. "How could you do this!" he demanded.

Leah pulled the covering from the bed and fled, wrapping it around her in big clumsy bunches. She was so distraught that she ran to Laban's room and wept bitterly. "I don't understand," she cried. "He did love me, and passionately, until he saw that it was me and not Rachel."

"Don't worry. He'll have to understand," he said. "The eldest must marry before the younger; everyone knows that."

"But I thought Jacob had agreed that it should be that way," she cried.

"No, no," he said, "we didn't need to tell him something everyone knows."

"You tricked him into marrying me," she charged bitterly.

"You wanted to marry him, and there was no other way. Now you've had your wish and you must work out the difficulties."

The look she gave him was hard, cold, and sorrowful all at once.

"You must understand," Laban said, "this was not my idea at all. It was the old goat-man under the stairs that hatched this plot." Without waiting she pulled away from him and ran to the door under the stairs. Flinging the door open, she stared at the ugly little idol. "So," she said, "it's you who've worked this out. Now you must make him love me." Somehow she felt this would not be so easy.

* * *

Laban found Jacob pacing the floor of the small bridal chamber. Unbeknownst to Laban, Jacob's wild anger and frustration were tempered only by the guilty thought that this was how Esau must have felt when he had tricked him out of the blessing. *So,* Jacob reasoned, *I deserve this, but how can I live without Rachel?*

"Now I see that you think I have played a cruel trick on you," Laban said. "Actually I should have told you from the start that we must always marry the eldest daughter before the younger. There was nothing else I could do."

He waited for Jacob to give some angry response, but when he simply sat and stared at the wall and said nothing, Laban went on. "I'm not as cruel as you might think," he continued, studying Jacob's strange lack of response. "You can have Rachel at the end of the week if you'll promise to work seven more years for her."

Jacob wanted to cry out at the unfairness of it all. He wanted to shout at his crafty uncle, telling him that he had already worked seven years for Rachel. He wanted to say that he would never, never have worked one day to marry Leah. However, he was so overwhelmed with the feeling that he was somehow being paid back for cheating his brother that he said nothing.

Laban took his silence as acceptance and promptly went and told Rachel all that had happened. Rachel had been crying and suspected that Leah had somehow planned all of this. "No, no," Laban told her, "don't blame your sister. Blame the old goat-man idol. He's the one that put the idea in my head. Actually, you will find it is for the best. I've arranged for Jacob to have you at the end of this week, but he'll have to stay and work seven more years."

Rebekah said sulkily, "You always blame the old goat-man for any crafty thing you want to do. I know that Leah has wanted Jacob. She thinks he'll love her but he won't. He loves me and she'll live to regret this trick she's been a part of."

For the first time Laban began to worry about what he had done. He loved his daughters. What if, he wondered, by trying to manage things, he had actually made it very difficult for them to ever find happiness?

At the end of the week of feasting, Laban kept his word and gave Rachel to Jacob. When it came time for Jacob to claim his bride, he found himself in the same bridal chamber, only this time everything was different. A small oil lamp cast shadows on the whitewashed walls. As was the custom, Rachel sat on the colorful, straw-filled mat among many cushions. He could hardly recognize her. The gleam of a golden headpiece nested squarely in her dark curls, and a dancing waterfall of gold cascaded from each ear. Around her neck was a spiral of gold latticework interspersed with carnelian beads.

She sat with her eyes cast down and her hands, lying on her knees, were upturned. Jacob realized at once that while Leah had been forced by the circumstance to come to him very much as one of the local harlots, Rachel came as a true bride. It was unnerving. Somewhere in all the bridal array was his little shepherdess, and it was his duty to coax her out of hiding.

Here was the crux of the mystery that women spent endless time whispering about and men grew silent remembering. It had obviously been designed from ancient times as a challenge to the groom's ingenuity. He must win her or she had every right to reject him and flee back to the safety of her family. The wise, confident bride did not give in too easily. Their whole future relationship depended on this moment's going well. The bride must feel totally accepted and adored, while the groom must take pride in having won, with difficulty, a worthy prize.

Jacob sat on the mat beside Rachel and took her hand in both of his. His heart was bursting with the joy of finally getting to sit beside her and actually hold her hand. It was small and soft, and the perfume of her garments was subtle and hypnotic. There was the hint of spring flowers and he realized her wedding dress had undoubtedly been packed in sprigs of lavender.

He struggled to find words that suited the occasion and expressed his feelings. He had worked so hard and waited so long for this moment; he must not spoil it in any way.

He glanced at her and found to his surprise that she was looking at him. He was relieved to see that her face and lips hadn't been painted in the customary masklike rigidity. Her eyes were rimmed with dark kohl and her lips were touched with crimson, but it was still the dear, familiar face he'd grown to love. She smiled at him, then giggled, and finally fell back among the cushions laughing. Her cap of silver fell off and her bracelets jangled as she tried to fit it back in place. "I have frightened you," she said as she dabbed at her eyes lest the black kohl streak down her face.

"Of course you frightened me," Jacob said, laughing.

"I love the fuss and bother of being a bride," she said, holding out her arms and admiring the jingle of her bracelets and the sparkle of her rings. "Don't you find me much more interesting this way?"

Jacob reached for the small, jeweled hand and slowly began to remove the ornate rings. "There," he said when they were lying in a pile beside her, "it's you I have loved from the moment I first saw you. Whether you are dressed in worn homespun wool out with your sheep or in the elegance befitting a princess makes no difference."

"Are you angry that you have already worked seven years for me and now have to work seven more?" She was serious now. Her eyes studied his face to catch any hint of unhappiness.

Jacob took both her hands in his and smiled. "I am a man who knows real value, and I assure you that I am the one who has won the prize in this bargain."

* * *

The next afternoon Jacob called his second servant to him. "Go back to my family in Beersheba and tell my parents I must work seven more years. Tell my mother she was right about her brother, but in this bargain I have won. He has given me both Leah and Rachel, and with Rachel I will be unbelievably happy."

## 19

*R*ebekah was delighted when the first seven years were up and she knew Jacob would at last be coming home. She had been terribly upset that her brother had made him work seven years to pay for his daughter. She was glad she had warned Jacob to watch out for her brother's greed and craftiness. She should have known that going to get a bride without the bridal price gave Laban too tempting an opportunity to cut a sharp bargain.

She blamed herself for his having to leave home so quickly and going so unprepared. He should have gone to her brother loaded with gifts, but there had been no time. Esau was probably still angry. She would have to test the situation carefully, even now, to be sure Esau would not harm Jacob.

The opportunity came the next evening when she saw Esau near the tents. "Your brother will be home soon," she told him.

Esau's body tensed and his face clouded. "What does he want from us?"

"He doesn't want anything," she said. "He's just soon to be married. The seven years are up and he'll be coming home with his bride."

"I suppose he's expecting to benefit from all my hard work."

"I don't understand."

"He's been gone seven years," he said, "while I've been here tending the sheep and building up a big flock."

"And you think he'll come and claim the two-thirds as his birthright."

"Of course, I can see it all now. It's just like him to come and reap the benefit while I've had to do the work." He paced angrily back and forth, then with a great curse strode out of the tent. Once outside, he turned abruptly, and clutching the tent flap, leaned in to confront his mother. His face was red and distorted with hatred. "I said I'd kill him before and my threat still stands," he said, biting off the words in sharp, forceful thrusts.

With that he was gone, leaving Rebekah in tears. "My poor, poor boys," she cried. "Esau's whole life is colored by this anger. He hates me as much as he hates his brother. And Jacob, what will become of him, armed only with his wits and muscle to get a bride?"

As she sat alone in her tent trying to face the ugly facts and find a way to welcome Jacob in spite of Esau's threat, Deborah arrived. "Rebekah," she said. "There's bad news from Haran."

"Not more bad news." Rebekah's hand went to her trembling lips. "I can't imagine more bad news than I have already received, but tell me. What's happened?"

"There's a caravan that's just arrived."

"Is Jacob on his way home as he told us?"

"No, there's been a second caravan with more recent news from Jacob."

"Oh, pray God he's not dead."

"No, no," Deborah said. "He's not dead, but neither can he come home."

It took awhile for Rebekah to understand all that the young messenger had to say. When she finally understood that her brother had actually tricked Jacob into marrying his elder daughter and only agreed for him to marry the younger after Jacob had promised to work seven more years, she burst into hysterics. "When will we ever be through with cheating and tricks, cruel tricks?" she said at last.

It was far into the night before she realized that all was not lost. Things had evened out. This was not the time for Jacob to come home when he would have to face Esau's anger and hatred. "But seven years," she kept saying. "Even in seven years, will Esau be ready to accept his brother?"

"We won't know until the time is up," Deborah said.

"Then it'll be fourteen years since I last saw my favorite son," Rebekah said. "He'll have children I've not seen and wives I won't know. Isaac may not even be alive in seven years."

"But," Deborah said, "he's at last married to the one he loves and she is of your own family. One must be thankful for whatever good one can find."

Rebekah choked back the tears. "You're right. Jacob's still alive and Esau has not been guilty of murder."

\* \* \*

In Haran things were not going well with Jacob's wives. Despite the fact that Jacob, by custom, had to spend equal time with each wife, he could not bring himself to spend the required time with Leah. She was so eager to please him and wept so bitterly whenever she realized he preferred to be with Rachel. He tried to tell her that he couldn't help loving Rachel. He didn't intend any slight to her, but she wept all the more.

No matter how often he tried to explain that her sulking and demanding attention only made matters worse, she could not change. "You have to love me; I'm your wife and I love you."

Finally he confronted her with her part in the deception. "You knew I loved Rachel and you went along with your father to trick me. How can you expect me to love you?"

"I didn't really understand . . ." she started to explain.

"When in the night I called you Rachel, you didn't correct me," he argued.

"But I did it because I loved you. I love you more than Rachel does. I am always thinking of things to please you. How can you not love me?"

Then there was the matter of the children. Right away Leah became pregnant and produced a son she named Reuben, meaning "God has noticed my trouble."

"Don't bring God into this," Jacob roared in real frustration. He resented the fact that she didn't follow the custom of letting the father name the son. She was too intent on making a point she could constantly dangle before his face.

When she saw that this got his attention, she could not resist naming her next son Simeon, meaning "God heard."

Again Jacob complained. "Why have you not waited for me to name my son?" he demanded.

"You were too busy. You didn't come until after he was rubbed with salt water and wrapped in his swaddling clothes, so I named him."

"And what are you trying to tell me by this name?"

"It's quite simple. It seems that even your God has heard that I am unloved and has given me another son."

* * *

Now it became a source of great irritation to Rachel that Leah should get pregnant so easily while she herself had no children. To make matters worse, Leah had started to provoke her sister with snide remarks. "Jacob loves me the best," she would say. "I wouldn't be having all these children if it weren't true." Then just to torment her sister, she named her next son Levi, meaning "attachment." "It's children that bind a man to a woman," she said with a bitter twist to her mouth.

This sounded logical to Rachel. Surely if Jacob loved her as he said, he would also give her the children she wanted so badly. "Give me children or I'll die," she began to plead.

Jacob felt so trapped and frustrated that he finally lashed out. "Am I God?" he roared. "It's Elohim who gives children. He's the one responsible for your problem."

Leah, of course, heard of the encounter and rejoiced. Now she felt that she was surely triumphing over her sister. This certainly meant that she had found favor with the God of Jacob. To her great delight, she again became pregnant and this time she called the little boy Judah, meaning "praise." She had now attained a new status. She was the mother of four sons, and more than that, it was obvious she had found favor with Jacob's God.

When the sisters married, Laban had given each of them a serving girl. To Leah he had given Zilpah and to Rachel, Bilhah. Now in desperation Rachel begged Jacob to sleep with her serving girl. "Bilhah will give me any child that is born," she told Jacob. When he saw how eager she was, he reluctantly agreed.

To Rachel's delight the girl became pregnant two times and both times produced sons.

When the first little boy was placed in her arms, Rachel wept for joy. "I'm going to name him Dan," she said. When Jacob asked what the name meant to her, she said, "Dan means justice. God has heard my plea for a son and at last He has given me justice."

The second son born to her, through Bilhah, she named Naphtali, or wrestling. When asked why she named him this, she quickly answered, "I am in a fierce contest with my sister and I am winning."

Jacob felt that with these two births the conflict would be finally settled. Leah had four sons and now Rachel had two that she had adopted as her own. He was content when Leah no longer became pregnant.

It was well into the tenth year of Jacob's work to pay for Rachel that he decided to move. There were too many children to fit comfortably into Laban's house. There was too much noise and confusion. Laban himself facilitated the move by giving him a house nearby that had belonged to Nazzim.

It had been a long time since anyone had lived there, and though it was of sturdy stone, built around a generous courtyard, it was badly in need of repair. The beams of the roof were still strong but the reed mats, thorny wood covering, and clay mortar had all given way during the rainy seasons. The roof would have to be completely redone.

Inside, the rooms were knee-deep in debris that had fallen from the roof. There were cobwebs and field mice, and the courtyard was cluttered with odd bits of broken yokes, plows, bows, and several clay ovens that were cracked and useless. Since it was Leah who had the children who needed more space, and since she was the one who wanted everything clean and orderly, it became her lot to see that the house was made livable.

Leah and her children were to have the two rooms on the left of the courtyard and Rachel, though she had only the two sons by Bilhah, insisted on the same number of rooms on the right. In the middle was a long room that was used for any formal entertaining and sometimes eating when it was raining outside. Most of the time everyone would spend their days outside in the courtyard or on the roof, where Leah planned to keep her loom.

When the roof was finished, Jacob chose to have a room built for himself up there, where he could have peace and quiet. From time to time, he would call one of the women to join him or entertain his close friends, leaving the rest of the house to his wives and children. "Men don't need to be bothered with the children and the household activities" was the thinking of most people in Haran.

*  *  *

In the new house things went along much as usual, except that Leah found that she was no longer able to get pregnant. In the midst of great frustration, she determined to do as her sister had done and give her maid, Zilpah, to Jacob. Zilpah readily agreed and it was not long before she was pregnant. When Leah heard the news, she was delirious with joy. She insisted that Zilpah be given the freshest fruit, the choice bits of meat, and be relieved of all work. "It's important that you have a son," she said. "Even my sister, Rachel, is taunting me."

"Taunting you?" Zilpah asked.

"Yes, she says my lucky days are over. I'll have no more children. I must prove her wrong."

Zilpah didn't take her seriously, but when the child was born, she understood. Leah named him Gad, meaning "my luck has turned." When Jacob heard of the turn his wives' rivalry had taken, he was in despair.

It seemed to him that one could not put a foot down anyplace inside the courtyard without stumbling over a child. He had not imagined that he, coming from a family of few children, could possibly produce so many children. After years of earnest prayer, his grandfather Abraham had only been able to have Isaac with Sarah. His own father had produced only twins. He was not prepared for this blossoming. He remembered Elohim's promise to his grandfather that his seed would be as the sand or as the stars, and he began to fear that he alone was about to fulfill that prophecy.

He could not understand Leah's obsession. She never stopped planning how she could get more children. "Sleep with Zilpah again," she urged Jacob. "Let's see if my luck has truly taken a turn for the better."

Jacob found Zilpah a pleasant change from Leah. She was young and eager to please. Most of all she was quiet and never came with some hidden motive. So it was easy for him to let Zilpah take Leah's turn. To his surprise once again she became pregnant. Leah was overjoyed. She named the child Asher, meaning "happy." "What amazing luck is mine," she said. "How the other women will envy me. I am truly happy."

Now there was constant tension intensified by Rachel's decision to make their courtyard more attractive. "I want it to be both pleasant and restful," she said.

For a whole month she worked planting herbs and flowers in the narrow plot against the far wall. She brought in servants to chop up the hard-packed earth and dig pits for a grapevine and finally a fig tree. Last of all she bought reed cages for pigeons and small songbirds. It took time and a great deal of work, but it totally transformed the humble courtyard.

It was not to last long. Leah's rowdy sons tumbled and tussled, roughly breaking off the tender twigs of the fig tree to swat at each other, then wrestled in the flower plot totally crushing the small plants. Finally, they climbed up and opened the cages just to see the birds fly out.

Rachel was at first crushed and then furious. "If Bilhah and I can manage our boys, surely you can do as well," she chided Leah.

"They meant no harm," Leah said. "There are just so many of them." She seemed almost proud that her sons were so boisterous and unruly.

Relief finally came when it was decided that the older sons of Leah could help with the wheat harvest. They were young, but many tasks could be easily done by the boys. Jacob was proud to have sons who could help him in the field. They could not wield the heavy flint sickle, but they could follow the reapers and gather the stray stalks.

The boys had watched with interest as Jacob had taken an old sickle loaned to him by Laban and repaired it. He had found some of the matched pieces of flint missing around the edge and had carefully reshaped new bits of flint to take their place. He then had melted the pitch and glued them in place. When he was finished he had a sickle that was better than the new ones that he had seen in the market.

Every part of the harvest was of interest to the boys. They had energy enough not only to glean every stray stalk of wheat but also to explore and make discoveries that were quite unrelated to the harvest. They found old bird nests, strangely shaped stones, hedgehogs, and small mice to collect and take home.

It was Leah's oldest son, Reuben, who made the choicest discovery. He was running after one of his brothers when suddenly, right at his feet, he saw a strange plant with ovate green leaves and whitish flowers. He stopped abruptly and bent down to look at it more closely. He was sure it was the plant his mother prized above all others. He took a stick and dug around the base until he had totally loosened it. Then, with a tug, the plant came free in his hand. He saw the strange human shape and knew it was indeed a mandrake.

He didn't stop to tell anyone where he was going but ran as fast as he could back to the house. He sprang into the courtyard with a bound and came face-to-face with Rachel. "What have you there?" she said.

"I think it's one of those plants my mother treasures. They give a woman the children she wants."

Rachel looked at it more closely and saw that it was a mandrake and immediately wanted it. "Where are you going with it?" she asked.

"I'm taking it to my mother." He held it behind his back and edged toward the door to his mother's room.

Rachel followed him. "Your son has found these mandrakes," she announced to Leah. "Of course you have no need of them."

Leah quickly snatched the mandrakes from her son and turned to Rachel. "So," she said, "it's not enough that you have stolen my husband, but now you are about to steal my son's mandrakes."

"No, no," Rachel said. "I am ready to bargain. Give me the mandrakes and you can sleep with Jacob tonight."

Leah hesitated only a moment, and then she thrust the mandrakes into Rachel's hands. "I accept the bargain. I get Jacob tonight and you get the mandrakes."

* * *

Leah wasted no time. As soon as the door was shut, she hurried to change her clothes, twine gold threads through her hair, and outline her eyes with dark kohl. She snatched up a head covering and was soon hurrying across the courtyard and out the gate. She wanted to meet Jacob and make sure he knew that he was to spend the night with her.

To everyone's surprise she became pregnant, and when another son was born, she named him Issachar, or "wages." She wanted to remember that she had bargained for Jacob and had been given this son.

She was to have one more son, and this one she named Zebulun, or "gifts." "God has given me many gifts for my husband. Now he will surely love me, for I have given him six sons." By this time Leah was sure that Rachel could never catch up with her. "She will never have a child of her own," Leah said. "Surely I have won in the conflict with my sister."

When a baby girl was born to Leah, she decided to relax in the knowledge that she had given Jacob a whole quiver full of children. "What can my sister do to equal what I have already done?" Leah reasoned to herself. "Surely he will love me now more than he loves her."

* * *

When the mandrakes failed to produce the desired result, Rachel gave up all hope of ever having her own child. She had done everything possible, even trusting the small fertility goddess tucked into the fold of her waistband. "Year after year I have gone to consult the women of magic and spells and have done all that they have advised," she told Jacob at last. "There is nothing more to be done."

Jacob was surprised. He knew that women had, from the beginning of time, resorted to various methods to get what they wanted, but it seemed obvious to him that only Elohim could give children. "Has your sister, Leah, gone to all this effort?" he asked, taking the small image she handed him and studying its harsh features.

"No, she was so angry at the old goat-man for not making you love her that she's refused to have anything to do with any of them," Rachel said.

"Have you asked Elohim for a child?" Jacob questioned.

"Not really. I thought you would deal with Him. How can you ask anything of someone you can't see?"

Jacob didn't answer right away. He was deep in thought. It had been at Bethel he had first experienced the reality of his God. "Rachel," he said finally, "put all these charms and potions away. Forget everything you have been told by the old women who deal in magic. When you have done all these things, sit down by yourself and just talk to Elohim as you are talking to me. Tell Him you want a child and see what happens."

"The charms work for others," Rachel said. "Why won't they work for me? I know many friends who have gotten pregnant after eating a mandrake root."

This puzzled Jacob. There were mysteries he didn't understand. However, he was beginning to see a vague pattern in situations his father would call "the ways of Elohim."

"Perhaps," he said at last, "this child is to be a very special child and you must know that he is a gift to you from Elohim."

That surprised Rachel. "You sound as though you already know I will have a child."

Jacob laughed. "I'm not sure of anything. However, from what you yourself have told me, I can see that you bargained to get the mandrake from Leah. You ate the mandrake and she didn't, but she got pregnant."

Rachel looked at him in amazement. "That's right," she said. "Perhaps it really is Elohim who gives children."

"I can see how it seems logical that a little fertility goddess would be the one to give a woman a child. But don't you see, this is only made of clay."

"I know the clay itself has no strength, but there seems to be some magical power that works through this little idol."

"It may be that power is from the evil jinn. In our family we trust in Elohim, the supreme, creator God. Ask Him for a child and see what happens."

Rachel didn't answer, but when he handed the small idol back to her, she took it and held it for a few moments. "Here," she said. "You keep it and I'll do as you say. If I become pregnant, you can destroy the little image."

To Rachel's great surprise and joy, within the fortnight she was actually pregnant. She did not dare tell Leah until she felt the child moving when she placed her hand on the growing mound of her belly. "I'm pregnant," she said. "I really am going to have a child." She cried and laughed and hugged Leah and Bilhah and Zilpah in her excitement. They could not believe her at first.

"Don't celebrate too soon," they warned. "It could be just a knot or a stone."

"A stone that kicks and jumps?" she countered. "No, it's a child and I'm going to enjoy every moment."

"Enjoy!" they exclaimed. "There's nothing to enjoy until the child is safely here."

"You don't understand," Rachel said. "For you this is all so easy. It isn't wonderful and exciting, but for me it's a miracle."

Leah was annoyed. A woman wasn't supposed to enjoy the process of being pregnant and giving birth. It was a time when most of them complained and called attention to their aches and pains. "Well," she sputtered finally, "if you really are pregnant, you'll soon find it isn't as pleasant as you're thinking."

It was on a sunny day in early spring when Rachel went into labor. Outside the storks were flying north and several dropped down into the courtyard to peck at some grain. "It is a good omen," some of the old midwives announced. "This child will be a special child. He'll do amazing things and go places we can't even imagine."

Leah heard them and scoffed. "It's the business of old women to please new mothers with such predictions." Nevertheless she could not hide a bit of compassion for her sister when she saw her sweat-streaked face, her hair hanging in damp curls around her cheeks, and her joy.

Rachel had insisted on bathing the baby and rubbing him with salt, and she was struggling to wrap him in the swaddling clothes. "See how perfect he is," she said and beamed.

Leah only saw that he was small and very red with an astonishing shock of black hair. He was not as plump and pretty as her babies had been, but impulsively she squatted beside Rachel to help her. "Here, let me show you," Leah said.

She took the long strip of cloth and starting at the neck neatly wound the cloth so the child's arms and then little legs were held firmly in place. As she wrapped she instructed her sister. "It's important to keep the wrapping on until the tender bones become strong enough to move about." She then placed the baby in a leather cradle suspended from one of the rafters.

Rachel reached out to take the child from the cradle but Leah stopped her. "It's best to leave the child in its bed and gently move the cradle with this cord." She demonstrated by tugging on a hempen cord. "Both night and day you have to hold on to the cord," she said.

"There," she said, as she tied a few shells for good luck to the hempen cord. "I hope you're giving proper credit to the mandrake I let you have."

Rachel looked up at her sister in amazement. "No, that was a long time ago. It didn't work. It's Elohim of my husband who at last saw my plight. He's the One who has removed the dark slur against my name and has given me this child."

"So," Leah said, "what have you named him?" She hoped in this way to find just what her sister's plans were for the child.

"I've named him Joseph, for I want Elohim to give me another son."

"Joseph," Leah repeated. "'May I also have another.' What a strange name for a child. If the old midwives are right, this child is special and there'll never be another quite like him."

"I know he's special," Rachel said without looking up to see her sister's amusement.

Word spread quickly among Leah's sons that the midwives had pronounced great things for this child and that Jacob, their father, was delighted with him. They crowded in to see him while grimacing and winking to each other as they covenanted to stick together. "It's all of us against him. We'll see how special he can be," they said and smirked. From that moment on, they were determined to see that this new brother would get no special treatment from them.

\* \* \*

The fourteen years were soon up, and Jacob was eager to return home. He had mentioned this several times to Laban when they were out in the fields and had gotten no response. A great fear began to take possession of him. He could see that Laban was mulling over the situation and hatching some plot to keep him and his family in Haran.

At last, when they were sitting together under the grape arbor on Laban's roof watching for the new moon, Laban spoke. "You must agree that these have been good years. My daughters have blessed you with sons and I have seen that you have had a house and food."

"And you have grown rich with my labor. Now the fourteen years we agreed on are up. It's time for me to take my wives and children back to my own family and home."

Laban shifted uneasily. It was obvious that he had been expecting this very thing. He knew he must handle it carefully. "Of course I don't want you to leave."

Jacob quickly interrupted. "When I came I did not expect to remain here such a long time. I've stayed the fourteen years you asked of me, and now my wives and my children belong to me."

Laban frowned and coughed nervously. "I admit all that you say is true. I'll even admit that since you have been here, I've prospered beyond anything I could have imagined. I checked with a fortune-teller in the market and she agrees, the blessings I've received are because of you. You are like a lucky stone. You bring people luck who have none in themselves."

Jacob grew impatient. He ignored Laban's fine words and interrupted him to say, "I must return home. Surely you can understand; I've not seen my mother or father for all these years."

Here Laban fumbled with his walking stick and glanced nervously at Jacob. "If you leave now, you'll go with only the clothes on your back, your wives and children. You'll go home in poverty to meet your brother, Esau."

At the mention of Esau, Jacob flinched. "The last word from my mother was that he has not forgotten his anger. He intends to kill me."

"And you still want to go? You would expose my daughters and grand-children to such danger?" Laban was beginning to feel confident that he would win in this struggle.

"I would have to rely on my God to protect me and my children."

"Look," Laban said, leaning over and clutching Jacob's arm, "I'm ready to pay well for your services. What do you want? Just state your price."

Jacob had already considered the weak position he would be in if he re-turned home as poor as he had been when he left. He was also alarmed that Esau was still carrying his grudge. "If you'll do one thing, I'll go back to work for you," he said finally.

"And what would that be?" Laban asked, expecting something costly.

"Let me have any speckled, striped, or black sheep or goats from your flock and any lambs that are born speckled, striped, or black. These will be mine. I'll ask nothing more for wages."

Laban could hardly believe his ears. In the market it was the pure white wool that was prized. "How do you propose for our flocks to be kept apart?" Laban said.

Jacob thought quickly. "I'll send my sons with a few older shepherds three days distance away with the flock you separate out for me."

Laban was pleased. "And you will stay and tend my flocks."

"Of course. I'll claim only the spotted or striped animals," Jacob assured him.

When Jacob got up to go, he could tell that Laban thought he had made an excellent bargain. How could he possibly lose? With a flock of all white sheep, how could there be any speckled or black lambs appearing?

At the same time Jacob felt he had just the chance he needed to become wealthy. Since he would be in charge of Laban's flock of white sheep, he felt sure he could, with a few clever tricks, get some speckled and streaked lambs for himself.

He had been tricked in so many ways by Laban that he didn't hesitate to make a few questionable plans. If they succeeded, he would be richly rewarded for his time.

Not all of his schemes worked, but within five years, Jacob had become very wealthy. He had not only managed to increase his flock, but by clever trading on the side, had become the owner of camels, donkeys, and many servants. This caused Laban's sons to complain, "How can this cousin have prospered so quickly at our father's expense?" Laban himself grew hostile.

At this same time Jacob received word that his mother was ill and perhaps even dying. He was terribly upset. It seemed to him that Laban and his schemes had robbed him of precious years with his own family. If his mother should die before he returned home, he would not be able to bear the pain.

For the first time he pictured his mother always waiting and listening for the message that he was at last coming home. Isaac was blind and could be no comfort to her and he knew that Esau, with his many pagan wives, was a constant frustration.

"I must go home." The words kept drumming in his mind night and day, but he did not know how to manage it. Laban would certainly think up new ways to detain him, and his wives might refuse to leave the only home they had known.

In a most astonishing way, at this moment of real crisis, Elohim spoke to Jacob. "Return," He said, "to the land of your fathers and to your own relatives, and I will be with you."

Jacob felt encouraged though he was aware of many problems. Would his wives support him, or would they side with their father against him? And Laban, what would he try to do just to keep his daughters, grandchildren, and a good worker from leaving? He was not one to easily release someone who worked long hours and did disagreeable things for very little real wage.

He decided to send word to his mother that he was coming home. He could not say how soon, but at least the decision to go would have been made.

*R*ebekah received the word that Jacob was coming home with great joy. "He has two wives, two concubines, and eleven children," she told Isaac. "Imagine so many children when I was barely able to have the twins." Every afternoon she came to sit with Isaac and brought him some savory stew or ash cakes with honey. She tried to tell him what was happening around them, the changing of the seasons, the birthing of new lambs, and the news that came with the caravans. They were now living just outside of Kiriath-arba by the oaks of Mamre. Esau was taking care of their flocks with his own, and there was no need for them to live in the barren desert of the Negev.

Since Isaac couldn't see, he was unaware that Rebekah had grown thin and ill. The winter cold and rains had left her with a cough and then fever that she had not been able to shake. To Isaac she was always the young, vibrant beauty he had fallen in love with. He would not believe it when she tried to tell him differently. "You are the most beautiful woman in the world," he would say when he was especially pleased with something she had baked.

She would laugh and pat his hand. "I have no intention of spoiling your illusion," she would say.

When Esau came that evening, she told him that Jacob was coming home and then watched to see his reaction. His face clouded, his eyes became thin slits, his teeth clenched, and the tic in his cheek muscle twitched. "Why are you telling me this?" he snapped. "Do you think I'll call for a celebration?"

Rebekah stifled a sob, but she could not stop the tears from rolling down her wrinkled cheeks. "He has been gone so long. We must welcome him properly," she managed to whisper.

"Of course, he must be welcomed and praised, and we must all celebrate as though we are glad to have him back." Esau's words were sharp with a cruel bite. "I'll welcome him with my army of bowmen. He may as well know right from the start how I feel."

Rebekah sobbed and coughed, becoming so weak that Esau was frightened and Isaac grew nervous wondering what was happening.

"Please, Esau," Rebekah said, "can't you forget the past and be glad that your brother is coming?"

"It's always been Jacob you've loved. You never loved me. The blessing meant nothing to me, but for you to love him so . . . sticks in my throat like a thorn."

"Oh, Esau," she cried, "I loved you both . . . but your father loved you so much that Jacob seemed left out."

She noticed that Esau looked surprised and then without a word turned and disappeared into the night. She sat for a long time pondering all that had happened. Why had it taken all these years for her to explain things to Esau? She had taken for granted that he understood the way things were in their family. It had been so obvious to her.

She quickly picked up the empty bowls and handed Isaac the linen square scented with rose water to wipe his hands. She could see that he was lost in his own thoughts and seemed not to have even been aware of Esau's visit. She helped him stretch out on his straw mat and waited until she was sure he was asleep before tiptoeing out of the tent.

Back in her own tent she sank down among the cushions and for the first time admitted to herself that she was not feeling well. "I must get well. Jacob is coming home at last, and I must be well and strong when he comes." She said the words but hoped that Jacob would come soon.

\* \* \*

Back in Haran Jacob was wondering how he was going to manage such a big move. It was encouraging that his wives had agreed and were already making plans.

However, as the days passed, his situation grew steadily worse. Laban no longer bragged about having made such a brilliant bargain with Jacob, and Laban's sons openly began to accuse Jacob of some treachery. "How can it be," they questioned, "that so many of the sheep are suddenly speckled?" They confronted Jacob at every opportunity and were not satisfied with his answers.

They even complained to Leah and Rachel. "This fine husband of yours has to be cheating. He's getting only the speckled animals, but there are now more of them, and they are the stronger, healthier ewes and rams."

Finally Jacob sensed a growing hostility when he joined Laban's sons or sat with Laban in the evenings. Leah had even told him that their complaint seemed to be logical. "They say that you are becoming wealthy at our father's expense."

He knew that with such feelings it would not be long before there would be a carefully constructed plot to get rid of him. At first he merely shrugged off the growing fear and anxiety. He rationalized but finally had to admit the situation was serious. He felt alone and vulnerable and soon began to feel trapped.

One day while he was out in the field, he sent for Leah and Rachel so he could talk to them privately. The day was crisp and cool with a few scattered clouds. They joined him under a hastily constructed brush arbor. He waited until one of the old shepherds had served them some fresh pomegranate juice before explaining.

"I hear that your father has turned against me," he said. "You know how hard I've worked for him while he has never dealt fairly with me. He's cheated me and tricked me over and over again. However, in spite of all his cunning plans, my God has not permitted him to really harm me."

"It's true," Leah interjected, "that when he said all the speckled and streaked young goats and sheep should be yours, then all of them seemed to be speckled and streaked. Your flocks have grown while his are much smaller."

Jacob toyed with a blade of grass as he hesitated. He wondered if he could trust his wives, the daughters of Laban, with the secret of his success. Finally, he made up his mind. He had nothing to hide. He must be open and frank with them if they were to understand.

"This cunning is not from me," he said finally. "It was at the mating season that I had a dream. One of God's messengers appeared to me and told me that my God, the God who appeared to me at Bethel, had seen all that Laban had done to me. He then showed me how to manage so that I would prosper in spite of Laban's plans."

Both Leah and Rachel were listening intently. They understood how unfair their father had been, how he had constantly taken advantage of their husband. They had watched with amazement as Jacob had prospered in spite of their father's plans. "What did the angel show you?" Rachel said, leaning forward with an expression of intense interest.

"In the dream the angel called to me and told me that if I brought the striped and mottled he goats to mate with Laban's white nanny goats, most of the young goats would be mottled. You see the result. I did what the angel told me, and I have been blessed beyond anything I could have imagined. That's why your father and brothers are angry."

"We know they are angry," Leah said. "What will you do?"

"The angel must have known this would happen, for he instructed me to return to the land of my birth. I have also received word that my mother is not well." He looked at them to see what their response was to such a radical solution.

He was relieved to find that Leah and Rachel were both tired of their father's tricks and told Jacob they were ready to leave. "We can wait a few days until the time of the sheepshearing. Everyone will be so busy they won't miss us right away. That'll give us time to gather our things," they said.

Elaborate plans were being made for the shearing. Laban and the brothers had decided this would be the time for a final showdown with Jacob. They would count his flock and then their flock and demand an explanation. "He will have to confess to whatever trick he has used to get so many speckled or streaked animals," they said.

✴ ✴ ✴

Since Laban and his sons were so occupied with their plots and plans, no one noticed that Jacob's wives were busy packing all of their important belongings. Leah had so many children that she had to choose very carefully what each would carry. They now had slaves and servants to manage the larger, more cumbersome things such as grindstones, kneading troughs, wineskins, tripods for making the goat cheese, and woven material for shelter from the sun or rain.

Rachel took very few practical necessities. Bilhah, her faithful maid, carried her cosmetics, medicinal herbs, and perfumes. She herself carried only her jewelry and two of the birdcages.

At the very last moment, after Laban's family had left for the shearing sheds, Rachel made her way stealthily to her father's courtyard. She went straight to the door that opened into the space under the stairs where Laban kept his household gods. Then, swiftly and silently, she picked out all of the small teraphim that were supposed to deal with women's problems. They were stone or clay figures with legs stiff and rigid, heads small with prominent noses, and arms held straight and close to their sides. They were not at all beautiful but were considered to be very powerful in matters that might concern a woman.

The collection was greatly prized by Laban. Many of them had been made by his grandfather in Ur, and others had been traded by desperate landowners in time of drought. A small fertility goddess could even be bartered for food.

Rachel especially wanted the ones that were to help a woman become pregnant and protect her in childbirth. She desperately wanted to become pregnant again. She had prayed to Jacob's God to give her a child but had had no results. "What harm would it do," she reasoned, "to try asking the clay images for help?"

Also she was terrified to think of setting out on such a long journey with no household gods. She had seen her father consulting them and then throwing the colored stones when he had difficult decisions to make. She could not imagine how anyone could have a moment of peace with no household gods to protect them.

She quickly bundled them into a basket and covered it with some loaves of bread. She set the basket on her head and started to hurry out the door. She paused for a moment before leaving, to look around the familiar courtyard for the last time. It held no happy memories. Instead she could remember vividly the night she was to have been married to Jacob. She had been dressed and ready with all the love and pent-up excitement that had been building since the day she had met him at the well. She was the pretty one he obviously loved. How cruel of her father to keep her locked away while Leah took her place.

She steadied the basket on her head as she thought how glad she would be to leave all these sad memories behind. In the doorway she stopped and looked at the good luck charm fastened to the lintel. She remembered her father putting great store by touching it as he left for the market or field. He gave it credit for many of the good things that came his way.

She reached up and tugged at it until it came free, then quickly slid it into the basket under the bread. Laban had stolen her wedding night, and she would rob him of his good fortune. She did not want the old goat-man god or the ugly horned images of Sin, the local god. They were too big to carry or to conceal. But she had just the place for her collection of small images, in a pocket she had devised in the straw filling of her riding saddle. The images would fit in it nicely, and no one would be the wiser until they were miles from Haran.

*　*　*

As it turned out they had been gone three days before the revelers at the shearing missed them. Jokes and sly remarks had been made about Jacob and his sons, who they assumed must be late in rounding up their extensive flock. They could hardly wait to confront him and divide his flock among themselves.

When three days had passed and Jacob had not come with his family and flocks, Laban grew suspicious. He sent several of his sons back to Jacob's house in the city to question his daughters. The sons found the courtyard empty with only a few tools leaning against the far wall. The house itself was dark and silent.

"They left just before the shearing festival," an old woman told them.

It took a few more days to determine just what had happened. Laban came hurrying home and consulted with his sons. They all speculated as to where Jacob would take such a large, unwieldy family.

Finally when Laban discovered the small fertility teraphim and the good luck image from his door gone, he realized this was no short trip. "They have obviously left to go back to Jacob's family in Canaan," he said.

"What can we do?" his sons asked.

"We'll go after them. Jacob can't sneak off like this with my daughters and their children. And what an insult for him to steal my good luck images."

"They can't have gotten far," one of his sons said. "They have children and large flocks."

In less than a day they were mounted and ready to ride.

By asking questions as they went, they were able to follow the trail exactly, with few mistakes. They rode down along the Balikh River, crossed the Euphrates, and when they reached the Gilead mountains, they knew that within a day or two they would catch up with Jacob's more cumbersome band.

As they traveled, Laban spent most of his time gloating over the way he would punish Jacob. His eyes glistened and his mouth twisted into an ugly grimace as he swore to deal out severe punishments to him. His whole entourage began to fear the worst. They knew Laban as a man who had a fine-tuned temper and would tolerate no insubordination.

How surprised they were when they finally caught up with Jacob to find Laban strangely ready to make peace. "I had a dream last night," he told Jacob. "The God of your father appeared to me and warned me not to harm you. However, why did you have to steal my lucky idols?"

Jacob's face grew red, and he clenched his fists in frustration. He had never had any dealings with Laban's idols, and he resented being accused of stealing them. Without hesitation he pronounced a great curse on anyone who might have taken the idols, saying, "Whoever has taken them, let him die."

Then he gave permission for Laban to search everyone and every place. "Search the camp," he said, "and if you find them with anyone, they will surely die."

Laban sent his men in every direction while he himself checked his daughters and their children. When he came to Rachel, she very cleverly insisted she could not rise from the camel's saddle because it was that time of the month.

Laban dared not challenge her for proof. She looked pale and fragile and he did not want to do anything that would upset her. Laban immediately called off the search. His whole attitude changed. Though he cited all of his grievances and listened to Jacob's complaints, he finally agreed to make a peace pact with Jacob.

At that, Jacob took a huge rock and placed it upright between them, then calling his men, he told them to pile a great heap of stones around it. They called the pile of stones "the witness pile." In Laban's language it was "Jegar-sahadutha," but in Jacob's "Galeed."

This was to be a barrier across which neither one would go to attack the other. "This pile of stones will stand as our witness if either one crosses this line," Jacob said.

"This will be our watchtower (mizpah)," Laban said. "The Lord may be the only one who will know if we keep this bargain when we are parted from each other. If you are cruel to my daughters or take other wives, I won't know, but the God of your father will see it."

Jacob took a great oath in the name of his great-grandfather Terah, grandfather Abraham, and his own father, Isaac, that he would respect the boundary line. Then he made a sacrifice to God and ordered a feast prepared for everyone.

In the morning, Laban arose early, kissed his daughters and his grandchildren, then with tears in his eyes blessed them and departed for home.

After Laban had gone, Jacob pondered briefly over the missing idols. Was it possible, he wondered, that someone in his company could have taken them? He had questioned Rachel, and she had laughed her silvery laugh and admitted it wasn't really that time of the month but insisted that she knew nothing of the idols. "I thought he was being too pompous and it would be nice to get even with him for all the times he has tricked you."

* * *

As Jacob traveled on southward, he became more anxious about meeting Esau and more concerned about his mother's illness. He prayed that he might have guidance and the assurance of God's presence. He received no definite answer but instead had a strangely reassuring encounter with what appeared to be a host of heavenly beings.

It happened at dusk one evening. Just ahead of him on the path where two cliffs seemed to bar his way, he saw an army of light. Two camps of ethereal beings were dressed in full armor. As he slowly and cautiously advanced, they parted and let him pass. With sudden understanding, he exclaimed, "This is God's host; they have come in two camps to protect us." He promptly named the place Mahanaim, or two camps, so he would not forget the place where this miracle happened.

With this to encourage him, he determined he must immediately send a message to notify his brother, Esau, that he was on his way home. He must deal with the problem of Esau first before he could return to his mother and father. It was very possible that Esau still harbored such a grudge that he would threaten to kill him.

Time was running out. He had been procrastinating, putting it off long enough. The time had come to act. He didn't know just what to do, but it was obvious he must settle that relationship before he could return home.

He finally singled out five young men to go as his messengers. "You must tell my brother that all this time I have been living with our uncle Laban. Tell him also that I have prospered so that I own oxen, donkeys, sheep, and many servants. I'm not coming back as a failure, and I hope he will be friendly to us."

In what seemed a very short time, his messengers returned with the frightening news that Esau was coming to meet him with an army of four hundred men.

Jacob was wild with fear. He didn't know what to do. Finally he went alone back up into the hills to pray. "Oh, Jehovah," he prayed, "You told me to return to the land of my birth and that You would do me good. I am not worthy of all Your loving-kindness. I remember how I left home with only a walking stick, and now I am two large camps. Please protect me from my brother, Esau. I am frightened, terribly frightened. I know he's coming to kill me. Please remember Your promise to make my descendants as the sands along the shore or the stars in the sky."

After he had prayed he felt better and could think more clearly. "I must send him presents," he said as he ordered his shepherds to single out from his flock,

200 nanny goats

20 billy goats

200 ewes

20 rams

30 milk camels with their young

40 cows

10 bulls

20 female donkeys

10 male donkeys.

Jacob gave the men who were to take these gifts to Esau instructions that they should arrive one after the other, with enough space in between to be impressive. As each arrived, they were to announce that the animals were a gift to Esau from his servant Jacob. In this way he hoped to soften Esau's heart.

Jacob moved down to the brook Jabbok and camped there while he waited. He had done all he could to placate his brother. The waiting was nerve-wracking. He paced back and forth, trying to imagine the worst that might happen. With four hundred men, Esau could quickly wipe out his whole family. He struggled to think of some preparation he could make that would lessen the blow.

He finally reasoned that Esau would be looking for him, not his family. He must somehow separate himself from his family. He walked around thinking and planning, and finally he came to a decision. He would divide his family into two camps. Leah and her children would be in the first camp that Esau would meet, and Rachel and her children in the second.

It took the whole day to accomplish, but when night fell Jacob was still not satisfied. He tried to sleep but was too disturbed. It seemed to him that there must be something more that he could do. He finally rose and woke his wives and their children. "I have decided," he said, "that it will be safer if we put the river between us. It's me he will be looking for, and he will not harm you until he first finds me."

213

They quickly passed over the Jabbok and settled down for the rest of the night, leaving Jacob alone on the opposite bank. The moon rose over the Gilead mountains behind him, touching the rocks and shrubs with a soft light but leaving the gorge of the Jabbok dark and shadowed. He could hear nothing but the rushing water crashing against the rocks and gurgling in its hurried descent.

A cold, damp, chilling mist rose along the rocky banks of the river. Jacob shuddered and hurried to wrap himself in his sheepskin cloak. He found a level space with soft tufts of grass and lay down, making sure he could keep watch over his family on the far bank.

Now that he was quiet, he could hear the sound of a child crying faintly and far away. One of his shepherds was playing his flute. Everything was calm and peaceful. It seemed hard to imagine that disaster could be coming toward them up the Jordan valley.

No sooner had he settled himself to sleep than he was suddenly aroused by the soft crunching sound of sandaled feet walking somewhere nearby. Then a shower of stones was dislodged above him. He jumped up and was immediately wrestled to the ground by a large man who seemed to have sprung at him out of the darkness. He assumed it was Esau come to take his revenge. Fear drove him to desperate measures. He wrestled, exerting every bit of strength at his command. The moon came out from behind a cloud and shone for just a moment on the man's face, and Jacob saw that it was not Esau. It made no difference. The man had attacked him and he must prevail at all costs.

The man was stronger and bigger than Jacob, but Jacob tussled and wrestled him to the ground again and again. Sheer terror enflamed him. When Jacob would not give up, the stranger lightly touched the hollow of his thigh, putting it out of joint. Jacob was in excruciating pain but even then he would not give up.

"Let me go," the man said. "The day is breaking."

Exhausted, dripping with sweat and caked with mud, Jacob clung to him. "I will not let you go unless you bless me," he gasped.

"What is your name?" the man asked, still trying to pull away.

"Jacob! My name is Jacob," he almost sobbed.

There was a pause and then looking down at Jacob, the man said, "Your name is no longer Jacob but Israel, for as a prince you have prevailed. You have power with both God and man."

Jacob stumbled to his feet and peered through strands of matted hair at the man. "What is your name?" he questioned softly.

"Why must you know my name?" the man asked. "It is enough that I have blessed you." With that he was gone as mysteriously as he had appeared.

Jacob lay back exhausted. He must have dozed, because in what seemed just moments, the sun was up over the distant mountains, birds were singing, and the terror of the night was completely gone. Jacob felt oddly refreshed. He roused and looked around, remembering the struggle with the stranger of the night before. *Surely it was just a dream.*

Then he rose and found his hip was painful where the stranger had touched him. He took a few steps and found that he limped. With difficulty he made his way down to the river and knelt to wash his face. Stooping was painful. He saw his image in the water waver and break. "This is no longer Jacob," he said with amazement. "I am no longer the trickster, the supplanter; I am Israel, God's prince."

He laughed a joyful, excited, gut-shaking laugh. "All my life I have had to plot and scheme to get ahead. I never dared to face a man or a problem head-on. Last night I wrestled with no tricks and won. I am Israel!"

The word sounded beautiful, even musical. He said it softly, then chanted it, then shouted the word so it echoed against the rocky heights behind him. He wanted to leap and run and dance, but his hip was too painful.

He stood and pondered the strangeness of it all. He would have been sure it was a dream but for the pain in his hip and the limp that didn't go away. "It was all real," he concluded. "I wrestled with God and won a blessing from Him and a new name."

He gathered up his sheepskin cloak and started for the river. *I must give this place a name.* "Peniel," he said. "I'll call it Peniel, for surely I have seen God face-to-face."

With that he went down and waded across the turbulent, bubbling water of the Jabbok and stood on the opposite shore, eager and ready to meet Esau. "I am not afraid," he shouted. "I am Israel, God's prince."

＊　＊　＊

The next day Esau came riding a white mule with his four hundred men strung out behind him. Behind his men came the animals that Jacob had sent to him as gifts. Jacob stood watching him come, no longer hiding behind his large family but out in front ready to deal with his brother.

While Esau was still a considerable distance away, Jacob bowed himself to the ground, and as Esau came closer he bowed himself seven times to the ground. As he rose he was surprised to see Esau running toward him with his arms outspread and tears running down his cheeks. They hugged and laughed with the joy of reunion.

Finally Esau stood back and looked around with amazement. "Who are all these people with you?" he asked.

"They are my wives and my children." At a nod from Jacob the concubines, Zilpah and Bilhah, came forward with their children and bowed before him, then Leah came with her children, and finally Rachel with Joseph. They all bowed and they could see that Esau was impressed.

Jacob took him aside to a large tent where they could sit while Esau's men were served refreshments. "Tell me," Esau asked, "where did all these animals come from that met me on the way?"

Jacob laughed. "They are my gift to you. I will admit it was an attempt to gain your favor."

Esau laughed. "You must keep them," he said. "I have plenty."

"No," Jacob said, "you must keep them. You have no idea what a relief it is to see you smiling and friendly. I was so frightened. Please take my gifts; God has been very generous with me."

Esau could see that it was important for him to accept Jacob's gift. "You have been more than generous," he said.

They sat for a time in silence marveling at the strangeness of it all. "You are my only brother," Jacob said at last. "No one will ever be closer to me. We are not just brothers, but we are twins."

"We are closer even than wives," Esau said. "Never mind that we have never gotten along. We were fighting, our mother says, even before we were born." They laughed now as they realized how unique their relationship really was.

"How are my mother and my father?" Jacob asked suddenly and rather abruptly.

Esau fidgeted and looked away. "Our mother is not well. She suffered greatly with the cold this year, but our father is much the same as when you left."

Jacob didn't ask further as he sensed that Esau was reluctant to tell him anything that would spoil their reunion.

They spent the day getting acquainted. In the early afternoon, Esau said he would have to go but offered to take Jacob and his family with him.

"No, no," Jacob said. "I have such a large family and so many animals we would slow you down."

"Then let me leave one of my men with you to guide you to my home in Mount Seir."

Again Jacob desisted. "We will manage just fine, so you must not be worried about us."

With that Esau left and Jacob relaxed in his tent and thought of the strangeness of it all. For years he had been alone without his family. He had been at the mercy of his wily uncle and felt so weak he could not confront him openly. Now everything was different; he had wives and sons and a brother who cared about him.

Just as Jacob was feeling that everything was going to be all right and his homecoming would be wonderful, a messenger arrived from Esau's band. "I have a message for my master's brother. I am to give it to him in the privacy of his own tent," the messenger said.

Jacob was puzzled but he led the young man into his tent. For a moment they looked at each other as Jacob tried to read in the young man's countenance the nature of the message. He could tell it was not good news. The young man looked as though he could hardly bear to say what he had come to tell.

"Come, tell me what is it my brother wants me to know. If it is bad news, it is not the first time I have ever heard bad news," Jacob said.

"My lord," the young man said, "my master could not bear to tell you in person, but your mother is dead and has been buried in the cave purchased by your grandfather." With that the young man turned and left, and Jacob fell back among the cushions almost unconscious with wave after wave of grief and despair.

*J*acob lost all interest in returning home. He could not endure the thought of seeing his mother's tent and his mother's belongings without her. A great lethargy came over him. He could take no pleasure in anything. Each day seemed like a burden that must be endured. How could it be possible that his vibrant, alive little mother had died just as he was coming home? He had been afraid that his father would die before he got home, but it never occurred to him that his mother might die.

When he had thought about going home, it had always been to fit himself, his wives, and his children back into his own family as he had known it. Now he realized that his mother had been his family. Isaac had been a shadowy figure who had preferred Esau. Esau would be managing the family flocks and herds. Esau would be taking care of his father. And Jacob's homecoming would be an intrusion.

If he went back, everything would become complicated. The old conflict over the birthright would flare up. Esau would again resent him. The truth was that he had all the sheep and goats and servants he needed, but Esau would not see it that way.

The more he thought about it, the more he determined to take more time and test things out before going back. Temporarily it would be best if they could stay right where they were until things became clear. He crossed back over the Jabbok and went down to the Jordan. It would be difficult to cross the Jordan with his family and his flocks at any time, but at this time of year with the spring flooding, it would be almost impossible.

He tramped around and found a level expanse that would make an acceptable place for them to camp. They would cross the Jordan when they were better prepared. They would have to make temporary shelters for the animals, but his servants and sons could do that easily. Jacob called the place Succoth because of the booths they built, and he stayed there for several years.

Once the family was settled, Jacob hiked in all directions looking for a permanent home for them that would not conflict with Esau. The land was large and the desert of the Negev was not the choicest land for cattle or for raising a family. He crossed the Jordan, and found that by going up the Wadi Fara, he came out onto a fertile valley.

He learned from shepherds that the two mountains facing him across the valley were called Gerizim and Ebal, with a sizable city lying between them called Shechem. He remembered his grandfather telling him that it was from the top of Mount Ebal that Elohim had shown him the land He was to give him and his descendants. He was excited. This large, fertile valley seemed the ideal place to settle.

He went back to the camp across the Jordan and began to seriously consider moving to an area near Shechem. He would have to go about it carefully. He would make friends of the important men in the city and then offer to buy land. Water would be a problem. He would have to set his men to digging a well as he had seen his father do in the Negev.

By the time he was ready to leave the safe environment of Succoth, his sons had become handsome young men and his daughter Dinah was as beautiful and charming as Rachel. People often thought she must be Rachel's daughter, as she looked nothing like her own mother, Leah. Joacob had no way of knowing that her beauty would upset all of his plans of a happy new home.

He did everything properly. With several of his sons, he went to visit Hamor, the king of Shechem, and bought land from him for one hundred pieces of silver. He explained to the king that they had extensive herds and would not choose to live in the city but would dig a well in the valley so they would not be a burden to anyone.

"We will be so happy to have you settle here," the king said. "We are a hospitable people, and your sons will be welcome to come and visit my son Shechem, and your wives, the women of my family."

Jacob was elated with the arrangement. He walked over his land and noticed every detail. There was a huge old tree that Hamor had explained was considered sacred by the shepherds and villagers. He had asked that they let them continue to celebrate some of their festivals in its shade. This did not seem to be a problem to Jacob. He was more interested in digging a well that would supply them with water.

When the well was finally dug, Jacob went back over the Jordan to Succoth and brought his whole family to settle in the valley. They were all surprised at its wide green pastureland, and the well, so convenient for everyone. *Surely this is the blessing the God of my father, Isaac, meant me to have. The difficult times are past and we will be happy here.*

The first thing he did was to erect an altar and gather his family to worship and thank their God for bringing them to this fruitful valley. "We will call this altar El-Elohe-Israel, the altar to the God of Israel," he said.

Some noticed that he did not say, as in the past, "the God of Abraham and Isaac," but he now said "the God of Israel." They had heard of his struggle in the night and the new name, but they had not realized how profound the change had been. He was actually claiming a new name, Israel. They pondered the meaning of it all.

* * *

When the invitation came for the women of Jacob's family to visit the wives of the king of Shechem, their excitement knew no bounds. They had been traveling and camping out for such a long time that they had not had a chance to wear their festive clothes. Now they spent hours assembling the makeup they would wear, the headpieces that would look the best, and the gowns and jewelry that gave the right impression.

When the day came, they rode to the city on donkeys decked out in fancy trappings with tasseled headpieces and decorated saddles. "You do honor to our family," Jacob said as he stood with his sons and watched them go. There was no warning, no sense of foreboding that this innocent trip to the city of Shechem would turn out disastrously.

The party that had been planned for them was a great success. They liked the women of Shechem and were impressed with their easy elegance. They had large, fringed hangings on the wall, fancy brass braziers giving off not only heat but also a subtle fragrance from the incense that was periodically sprinkled on the coals. They served wine from decorated clay jars, and the nuts, dried fruit, and small honey cakes were served on woven mats painted with intricate designs.

One of the women sang a poem composed in their honor, then village dancers came and danced their traditional dance. Small children entered into the excitement. They shyly hid behind their mothers' skirts and peeped out from time to time with soft brown eyes filled with curiosity. The happy, joking women had few worries. They asked questions and looked at Leah with admiration when they heard how many sons she had given her husband.

Rachel dreaded it when they turned to her and asked how many sons she had. When she told them only one, their faces fell in immediate sympathy. One of them jumped up and gave her more sweet cakes and an extra portion of wine. "Poor one," she said, "and so beautiful."

They all admired Dinah. One of the women seemed to be especially attracted to her. "I have a son," she whispered, "a handsome young man who'll be king when his father dies. He would like you. Come, it won't take but a moment. I want him to see you."

Leah realized that it was the queen of Shechem who was so interested in her daughter and she was flattered. She had heard the conversation and was immediately excited. *How wonderful if my daughter should find favor in the eyes of this young man and his mother. Where would we ever find anyone more appropriate for Dinah?*

She nodded her permission for Dinah to go with the queen and then settled back to enjoy the attention of the women, who were all wanting to hear more about Dinah.

Within a short time the queen returned, smiling, without Dinah. She told the women, "My son is charmed with this delightful girl." Then whispering to Leah, she asked, "Would you mind if she stays here with me for the rest of the day? I will see that she gets home safely."

Leah was flattered and could see no harm in leaving Dinah. She hoped that this elegant woman and her son would like Dinah and would ask for her in marriage.

When Leah arrived home and told Jacob what had happened, he also thought it would be a wonderful bit of good fortune if Dinah could marry the prince. It was not their custom to leave a young girl in someone else's house, but Leah assured him the queen was going to look after Dinah and see that she was brought home safely.

It was evening, just as Jacob's sons were bringing their flocks home to water, that Hamor the Hivite, king of Shechem, rode up with his son Shechem. They asked to see Jacob. When they were comfortably seated, the king broached the subject he had come to discuss. "My son Shechem has fallen madly in love with your daughter and wants to marry her. She has been with him this afternoon and he does not want to part with her."

Jacob was astounded at the turn of events. He saw no problem in Dinah's marrying the young prince, though it disturbed him that she had not come home as had been promised. Hamor saw his hesitation and so he hastened to add, "Please let him marry her. He is a wonderful son and is truly in love with her. Furthermore this would make a bond between us. Your young men can marry our daughters and your daughters marry our sons. We will let you live wherever you like, and you can grow rich with our blessing."

Then Shechem spoke. "Please let me have her as my wife. I will give whatever you ask. No matter how much dowry, or what gifts you demand, I will pay it . . . only let me have her as my wife."

Dinah's brothers had come into the tent and had heard all that was said. They saw that the young prince was handsome. His eyes were hazel, his hair clean and shaped to his head with a slight curl that at times hid the gold headband that showed he was the prince. His hands were covered with rings; they had no callouses from well digging and shearing sheep. Immediately they hated him. "Where is our sister now?" they demanded.

"She is at my home in the city," the prince said, looking at them for the first time.

The brothers whispered together and then Levi spoke. "I suppose you have had your way with her."

"She loves me and gave herself to me freely. I want to make her my wife and will pay any price."

This made the brothers furious. They again whispered together and Simeon said, "It's obvious he has raped our sister and is forcefully holding her prisoner in his rooms. He has disgraced the skirt of our father and the head of our mother, but we must move carefully. They are obviously a powerful family."

They came back and sat beside their father, facing Hamor and Shechem. "We can't possibly give you our sister since you are not circumcised. It would be a great disgrace for our sister to marry such a man."

Shechem's face fell. "What can we do?"

Hamor looked at Jacob. "My son really loves your daughter. She has given herself to him willingly."

There was a moment of silence. Jacob could tell his sons were barely hiding their hostility under smiles that were too polite and gestures that were deceptively casual. "Of course," Simeon said, "if you would consent as a people to be circumcised . . ."

"Then we could intermarry with you and become one family," Levi added.

"If not," Simeon continued, "we will take our sister by force and be on our way." The last words were said with such hostility Jacob was afraid that Hamor and Shechem would be turned away. To his surprise, they seemed not to have noticed.

"My son is very popular with our people," the king said. "I'm sure if he goes before the council and presents such a plan, they will all be willing to do whatever is necessary."

\* \* \*

Shechem and Hamor convinced the council. "These people have flocks and herds," Shechem said. "They have already dug a well with fresh, clear water. If we can get them to stay, and we intermarry, it won't be long until all that they have will be ours."

The men agreed. Jacob's sons came and went through the city, circumcising every man, including Hamor and Shechem.

Jacob felt the matter was settled. He had not expected the grown men of the city to agree so readily to being circumcised. He did feel a bit uneasy that the young prince had gone about things in such a high-handed way. Granted he had said she loved him and had given herself to him willingly. But that was not the way such things should be done. The joining of families and producing children was a matter of greater importance than the chance attraction of two young people. He wished he could see Dinah and be sure she had not been forcefully raped.

\* \* \*

All seemed to have gone well. The men of Shechem had been circumcised, and plans for a marriage feast were being made. It was only necessary for them to wait until the men of Shechem were healed. Three days had passed when all of Jacob's bright hopes came to a tragic and sudden end. In the midst of what had been a sunny, quiet day, shocking news reached Jacob.

It was Joseph who came with the news. He was breathless from running and his eyes were wide with the horror of what he had seen. At first Jacob could not make sense of what he was being told. "Levi and Simeon," Joseph said, "have killed all the men of Shechem."

"What do you mean 'killed all the men of Shechem'?" Jacob tried to appear calm while his heart was pounding and his knees felt weak. At mention of Levi and Simeon, he feared the worst. For some time he had noticed a brash cruelty exhibited by these sons of Leah, and it had disturbed him. He had felt that sooner or later some tragedy would take place, and they would be at the center of it.

"They have been over in Shechem all morning wielding their swords and killing every man they could find," Joseph said.

Jacob struggled to comprehend what he was hearing. "Why would they do such a thing? How could they even manage it?"

"This is the third day since the men have been circumcised," Joseph said, "and they are so sore they can't fight. They went to rescue Dinah but they became so angry . . ."

"How do you know all this?"

"I heard them planning. Then they strapped on their swords and started out for Shechem. They are coming now all bloodied, but they have Dinah."

Jacob was frantic with alarm. How could his sons do such a thing when it was so important to build good relationships with the local people? He stood and, with a show of calm he didn't feel, walked to the tent door.

"There, see." Joseph pointed to a crowd of women advancing from the city gates of Shechem all screaming, beating their breasts, and throwing stones at two tall young men Jacob recognized as Simeon and Levi.

Even from this distance, Jacob could see that they were streaked and matted with blood. As they came closer it was obvious that they were hustling Dinah along between them. "Go get Leah," he told Joseph, and then braced himself to confront his sons.

Simeon and Levi seemed drunk with the power they had wielded. They flung Dinah down on the ground before Jacob. "There," they said, "we have brought our sister home where she belongs. She is defiled, ruined; no man will have her now, and it is all the fault of that evil prince."

When they said this, Dinah let out a cry and covered her face with her hands. Her garments were soaked with blood and her hair loose and caked with dirt and blood. "He loved me," she wailed and again sank down covering her face.

"She has disgraced us," they said. "We came to rescue her and she clung to him shamelessly so that we had to tear her from him. That's why she's all bloody."

Leah arrived, her eyes pinched and questioning, her mouth gaping until she covered it with trembling hands. She looked first at one and then the other of her sons and finally down at Dinah. "I thought you had been killed!" she screamed as she rushed forward and clung to Simeon.

"It were better if they had been killed before they brought us to this evil day," Jacob said as he glared at their grinning, blood-streaked faces.

"What happened? Where have you been?" Leah begged.

"You told us to go to Shechem and get our sister and we did," Levi said proudly.

Dinah jumped up screaming and beating her fists on her brothers. "You pulled him from my arms and killed him. You killed the prince and he loved me."

Simeon drew back his hand and slapped her across the face. "Slut, whore, you encouraged him," he shouted.

Leah grabbed his upraised hand and pled with him to be patient. "Your sister is in shock; she is grieving."

Jacob had seen enough. He had grasped the whole picture of what had happened and he was horrified. "Leah," he said with a catch in his voice, "take your daughter and comfort her." He then turned to Levi and Simeon. "You have fouled our camp. You have sullied our good name. From now on we will be despised and hated among the people of this land. We are just a small band of men with our flocks and herds, and we can't stand against the hostility of all these people."

For the first time Levi and Simeon realized what they had done. They hung their heads and Levi threw up his arm to cover his eyes so he would not have to see the anger of his father. "Punish us any way you like," Simeon said boldly. "We have saved the women and children of Shechem to be our slaves and we have rounded up their cattle."

"Where are the other sons of Leah?" Jacob asked. "Have they taken part in this slaughter also?"

"Right now they are looting and gathering up the treasures of Shechem."

Jacob groaned and pulled at his beard in frustration. He walked back and forth trying to determine what punishment to mete out against these murderous sons. "You should be killed," he said. "An eye for an eye, a life for a life."

"No, no, not my sons." Leah had come back just in time to hear Jacob's statement. She clung to both of the young men, shielding them from Jacob's wrath. "They are the sons of promise, Elohim's gift to father Abraham," she screamed.

Jacob groaned again and ran his fingers down his cheeks. "Go from my sight. I can't trust myself to mete out justice."

"Punishment," Leah said. "What is their punishment to be?"

Jacob paused a moment and studied his two sons. "The greatest punishment will come in the future when they will find they are no longer the leaders. Reuben will be first and then Judah, and Levi and Simeon will be placed at the end. Wherever they are mentioned in the annals of our family, this terrible deed will cling to their names like a plague and they can never erase it."

He had barely gotten the words out when he heard a great chorus of weeping and wailing and shrieking that seemed to come from the region of the great tree. It was the women and children of Shechem who had followed Levi and Simeon. They were in a veritable orgy of grief. They were terrified. Their men had all been killed and their homes vandalized. They had no place to go.

Jacob covered his eyes and fervently wished it would all vanish. Who would feed these women? What would they do with them? "Slaves," Levi and Simeon had said. "We are the ones who will be the slaves," he muttered. "They are helpless. Their old women and children will be nothing but a burden."

\* \* \*

Jacob went inside his tent and knelt with his face to the ground and prayed, "What shall I do? My own flesh and blood have done this evil thing. We will be hated and feared. How can we ever settle here?" There was silence. He felt all alone. The skies were shut against him. Elohim of Abraham and Isaac could not bear to look on any of them. They were all evil and flawed. Not worthy of the blessing. *I am no longer Israel, God's glorious prince, as I had thought, but just Jacob.* Sons born of a Jacob can never be anything but a disappointment.

He straightened up and sat back on his heels while he thought about all that had happened and wondered if Elohim would ever speak to him again.

All that night he struggled with the terrible realization that his sons were hopelessly evil. The sons he hoped to present to Isaac as the sons of Elohim's promise were not worthy of his attention or blessing. He couldn't see how they would ever be any different, and there were so many of them.

In the stillness of the early morning, after the moon had set and the stars were fading, a wonderful thing happened. A cool spring breeze sprang up and Jacob became aware of the now familiar voice of Elohim speaking to him. "Move on to Bethel now and settle there," Jacob was told. "Build an altar and worship the God who appeared to you when you fled from your brother Esau."

As the sun came up, Jacob was no longer confused. It was clear that they must destroy the idols, cleanse themselves, put on fresh clothing, and prepare to journey to Bethel. He must take them all to Bethel, where he had first encountered the God of Abraham and Isaac. At Bethel they would build an altar and repent of the evil each one had harbored openly or secretly.

He thought of all the things that he had ignored just to have peace in his family. He had not disciplined his sons. He had left that to his wives. Worse yet, he had known for some time that Rachel had been the one who had stolen Laban's idols and then lied about it. She desperately wanted another child, and when his prayers had been of no avail, she had brazenly brought out her little idols and set them up where everyone coming into her tent could see them.

He felt no better, but he knew what they must do. They would go back to Bethel and start over again, this time with Elohim and only Elohim as their God.

The camp was strangely quiet. No one had come to disturb him. He went to the tent door and lifted the flap to let in the morning sun. To his utter amazement, he saw a huge pile of jewelry, trinkets, chests of gold, ornate belts, jeweled swords, and garments of fine Egyptian linen all piled in a heap. It was the loot his sons had gathered from the houses of Shechem.

He knew immediately what must be done. His sons would have to divide up the treasure among the women and send them back to their homes in Shechem. They must not keep one bead or wedge of gold. There must be no benefit from the massacre. How the women would manage in the city without their husbands and fathers, he could not imagine.

He found his sons were too ashamed to face him. Neither did they want to go back to the village and see the devastation they had brought about, but Jacob made them go. They saw the broken wine jugs, the scattered grain, broken grindstones, and torn cushions and mats. Worst of all were the bodies of the men lying just where they had fallen. "You must dig graves for them," Jacob commanded.

When these things were accomplished, Jacob called them all together. "We can never go back to the innocence of yesterday. We must go on. We must somehow go up to Bethel where I first encountered the God of Abraham and Isaac, but we cannot go as we are. We have found that each of us has failed. Elohim has seen all the evil we have done, even the thoughts that are hidden, and He is not pleased."

Suddenly there was a shrill cry as Leah covered her face and wept bitterly. Dinah hurried to her mother and tried to comfort her, while her sons one after the other found their eyes stinging with tears. "It is me and my sons, my sons that I was so proud of, and my beautiful daughter who have brought this disgrace to our family. I cannot bear it. It is too much," Leah wailed, rocking back and forth in her grief.

Jacob was moved as he saw the pride of Leah crumble. She had never thought of herself and her children as being anything but perfect. What a blow it was to her. How difficult to see her dreams of glory crushed by her own children.

He glanced at Rachel and saw that she was astonished to see her sister so humbled. His dear, beautiful Rachel with her one son was the only untarnished part of his family. Joseph would never be guilty of such unbridled cruelty. "Could it be," he wondered, "that after all I am the guilty one? I have never loved Leah or her children."

\* \* \*

"What can we do with these?" Jacob had been so engrossed in his own thoughts that he had not realized Rachel had left the group. Now here she stood with the hated idols gathered up in her mantle. She was holding them out and pleading with him to rid her of them. "I have not trusted in Elohim," she said. "I can't go to your Bethel and face Him with these."

"Father," Joseph said, "we must bury them under the great tree and then we will be ready to go to Bethel."

That was what they finally did. Each person brought out the strange gods, charms, stones of divination, and even the earrings and jewelry they had purchased at fairs from temple craftsmen. They piled them all up in a heap and then stood back and watched as Leah's sons dug a pit and shoveled them in. Some of them had precious jewels, and Rachel's idols had been crafted by Terah in Ur and were family treasures. Once the ground was level and the grass again placed over the spot, they felt somehow lighter, less burdened. They had done all they could think to do and were now ready to go up to Bethel.

That night Rachel wept, thinking that now she would never have another son. The fertility idols were gone and Elohim never seemed to listen to her prayers. When Jacob came, he found her crying. "I had so hoped to have another child," she said.

Jacob had been deeply touched by her sacrifice of the idols. He knew what it had cost her to give them up. She had never heard the voice of Elohim and she had wanted only one thing, to have children, and that had been denied her except for Joseph.

With a great feeling of tenderness for her, he stayed with her, and it was from that night she counted her pregnancy.

* * *

They could not leave immediately. There were too many decisions to make, too much to do. The flocks were not ready to travel with the young lambs, and the barley they had planted must be harvested. However, the day finally came when they were ready to go. Each one looked around at the valley that had seemed so peaceful until they had arrived, and they regretted having to leave.

Jacob stopped by the well and lowered a jar for water. "We will never find sweeter water," he said reluctantly. As he drank he thought of the great mystery of a well. They would leave the valley and never return, but the well would be here giving water to multitudes of people he would never see. To dig a well was a great and good thing. Perhaps it was the only bit of lasting good they had done during their stay.

He watched as the women watered the animals for the last time, then filled their water jars and skins in preparation for the journey to Bethel. They were silent with bitter memories of all that had happened here. Sadly, each one turned and joined the column that was already headed out on the southern trail that would lead them to Bethel. They hoped to find peace at Bethel, but they would never again think of themselves as deserving Abraham's blessing.

## 22

*f*rom Shechem to Bethel is not a great distance, but Jacob's company was large and cumbersome. To add to the many other complications, Rachel was nauseated because of her pregnancy. She would often be faint and dizzy, begging them to stop for a few days so she could rest. Others insisted on moving slowly because they were fearful of what they might encounter in the cities they had to pass along the ridge. To their dismay, the news of Shechem's tragedy had gone on before them, and the people in the villages were afraid of them.

When they had to stop near a well for water, they found the women and children backing away, then running from them shrieking in terror. When Jacob and his sons approached men sitting at the town gate, the men would stand up, push back their stools, and hurry inside. The gates would be forcefully closed and locked. No more friendly advances were made to them, as had been made at Shechem. It was obvious that everyone wanted them to pass by as quickly as possible.

When they finally came near the city of Luz, Jacob sent gifts to their king and finally messengers explaining that they wished only to camp close by and to worship their God.

It was evening when he received word from the elders in the city of Luz that he and his family would be welcome. They could use the well and graze their herds on the open hillside.

He did not know whether the welcome was extended because of the gifts or out of fear, but he was determined not to let anything spoil his return.

"Tomorrow we will come to Bethel," he announced with great excitement. "It is the very doorway to the house of our God." He seemed not to notice that most of them were frightened.

"How are we to come to this place?" one of them asked. "Is it with tears and weeping?"

"No, no," Jacob said. "We will come with singing and dancing and celebration, for all the promises made to me when I fled from home have been abundantly kept. Most of all, we will come with thanksgiving and praise to the God who has been faithful."

While the men and boys were setting up the tents, Jacob walked off by himself. He wanted to ponder all that had happened to him so long ago. It was here he had stopped for the night as he fled from home, and it was here that he had seen the steps with the angels ascending and descending. Most important, it was in this place Elohim, God of his father and of his grandfather, had given him encouragement and a promise of protection. Then he had not imagined it would be so many years before he would return.

Now he could see the hillside was barren and windswept. If one looked to the east, it was almost possible to see the deep depression of the Jordan and to the west vineyards and olive trees clinging to their terraced plots. The open area where he had stopped was still covered with stones. Some were outcroppings from the ground, but others lay scattered aimlessly about. It would be easy to build an altar. He remembered the stone he had used as a pillow and how he had set it upright and anointed it with olive oil. To his surprise the stone was still there, only it had been tipped on its side as though it was used for some shepherd's seat.

"We'll build the altar here," he said to himself. "We'll offer sacrifices unto our God and seek forgiveness for all the wrong we have done. We have cast out the false gods and have put on clean clothes; now we must cleanse our minds and our hearts so we can be worthy of the blessing."

Everything worked out as he had planned. The altar was built and the sacrifices made. He could tell by the expressions on their faces that each one had entered into the spirit of the occasion. He was pleased to see that Simeon and Levi were especially moved by the whole experience. He felt greatly encouraged. In fact, as his sons gathered around him, he reached out to them with tears in his eyes and said, "You are indeed becoming the sons of blessing and promise."

At that moment he felt that each one had been cleansed of the evil impulse that had so often controlled them in the past. Now he hoped they could move on to see his father, Isaac, with no dark secrets.

Only one thing bothered him. He was not sure that he still merited the new name given him by the secret wrestler at the Jabbok. He did not feel that he deserved to be called "God's Prince." Maybe, after all, he was still Jacob, the manipulator, the grabber.

Since Rachel was having more difficulty, he found that reason enough to stay right where they were for a while. They were in no hurry. He remembered that when he had been instructed to return to Bethel, he had also been told to settle there. This suited him well for the present. His sons found plenty of game in the thickets of the Jordan, and their herds grazed freely along the barren hillsides.

He knew at some time he would have to go see his father and settle things with Esau. There were many things he didn't know and didn't understand. It seemed best if, for the present, he camped right where he was.

Often he would go out in the evening and look down the road that led past the small towns on the way to Kirjath-arba where his father was living. It wasn't far, for he knew the road went straight as a hawk might fly. He could picture himself going down the road and coming to his father's tent, but there the whole dream came to an end. What did his father think of him now? Would his father only remember him as Jacob the cheater, the manipulator? For a brief time after his experience at the Jabbok, he had felt that the old Jacob no longer existed. He was a new creature; he was Israel. But after Shechem he was no longer so sure.

On this special night he walked out from the camp alone and sat under an olive tree. He felt exhausted with the struggle to deem himself worthy of meeting his father. The problem had been ticking relentlessly at the back of his mind ever since he had decided to leave Haran. He had gone over and over every bit of the deception he had engaged in. He cringed remembering his blind father's questioning and finally accepting that he was indeed Esau.

Then he also had to think of how he had cheated his brother. He had felt so justified at the time. There had been his mother's assurance that she had heard it from Elohim. That made it seem right. Now he must also face the crushing news that his mother was no longer alive. He must go home and face his father and his brother without his mother's support.

In the end he came to the conclusion that if he could be sure it was Elohim that had chosen him for the birthright and the blessing, then he would be free of this torment. Since living in Haran, he had become acutely aware of the Laban-like craftiness in his own nature. His father, Isaac, and even his brother, Esau, had never resorted to such underhanded deceptions. Since he had seen himself in this light, he could not believe that he could possibly be chosen by the God of his father for the blessing.

Gradually, in the midst of these dark admissions, a strange and wonderful thought began to emerge. First at the edges of his mind and then in a sunburst of revelation. If he could ever be sure it was Elohim's choice for him to have the birthright and the blessing, could he not also believe there was also a good plan for Esau? Esau was very different. He wanted different things, had different goals. He was a man who judged his success in physical terms: his land, his wives, his herds, and the chance to amass a fortune.

Jacob was so excited he jumped up and paced back and forth. All these years he had felt such guilt. Of course he had been wrong to go about it in such an unscrupulous way. But what if Elohim knew that the blessing wouldn't fit Esau? Esau was not a man who would ponder the ways of his God or bother to build altars. He plunged into life with full assurance that he would succeed. If he made mistakes, he didn't mull over them; he just altered his course.

It was late but Jacob could hardly contain his excitement. He sat down on an outcropping of rock and leaned back on his elbows so he could look at the stars. His father, Isaac, had set great store by the stars. With only the two sons, he still believed his descendants would be as the stars in number and as the grains of sand. Of course both Abraham and Isaac had envisioned these descendants being perfect. What would they have thought of Dinah's willingness to give herself to a man who wasn't her husband, his sons' ugly slaughter at Shechem, and the many idols he had found among his own family? Esau too had disappointed his father with his idol-worshiping wives.

Jacob felt a great stillness settle over him. It was beyond remorse or guilt. He no longer excused himself, nor did he try to hide from ugly truths. He had nothing to offer Elohim but himself, and now he had to admit that if he were Elohim, he would not place even one bet on him. At the Jabbok when the stranger had wrestled with him and then called him Israel, the full extent of his unworthiness had not become evident. Now he was sure the wrestler would never call him Israel.

Jacob realized it was late and that he should return to his tent, but he was strangely hesitant. He was vaguely aware that all their campfires had been extinguished; the pinprick of light from clay lamps no longer glistened through the rough camel hair of the tents stretched out below him. The distant, muffled murmur of voices had died down and even the bleating of the lambs had ceased. The full moon rode high over the distant mountains above the Jordan.

A slight breeze began to blow. The sand at his feet rose in small clouds;

the olive tree at his back came alive at the wind's movement. Clouds scudded across the sky and covered the moon. He tried to stand but felt the growing tug of the wind pulling at his cloak, dislodging his headpiece, and pushing him back onto the stone seat. There was something almost human about the wind's attack. He felt a powerful presence hovering over and around him. He cringed, covered his face with his hands.

Just as suddenly as it had begun, the wind ceased and a strange calm surrounded him. Then out of the midst of the silence, he heard the familiar voice. "You shall no longer be called Jacob the grabber," the voice said, "but you shall be called Israel, one who prevails with God." Jacob began to weep. He could hardly believe what he was hearing. "I am El Shaddai, the Almighty God," the voice continued. "I will cause you to become a great nation, even many nations. Kings will be among your descendants. I will give to you and your descendants the land I gave to Abraham and Isaac."

Jacob had fallen on his face at the first sound of the voice. He was aware of a great and blazing light and was not surprised that the being identified Himself as El Shaddai. This was the glorious God of Abraham and Isaac his father. The same God who had spoken to them was speaking to him. He knew he would never forget one word that had been spoken, but most of all he would remember he was to be called Israel, meaning God's Prince. He really was to have a new name and the name was a wonderful name. "Israel," he repeated over and over, with a great joy welling up in his heart.

He was awake the rest of the night, trying to grasp the meaning of what had happened to him. With the first streaks of dawn rising over the mountains of the Jordan, he woke the whole camp to tell them what had happened. He led them back to the hallowed spot and challenged them to build a pillar of the stones to make a memorial. "Such a wonderful happening must never be forgotten," he said.

✷ ✷ ✷

While they were busy constructing the pillar, someone shouted that a strange caravan was approaching from the south. The lead camel bore a litter on its back that was plain but well made and suggested the passenger inside might be a lady who was not well. To everyone's surprise the small caravan did not go on past. Instead it paused while the curtains of the litter were drawn back, and a very old lady leaned out and looked around. "Is this the camp of a prince called Jacob? I was told I could find him here," she said.

The small children ran giggling and laughing to tell Jacob that someone wanted to see him.

Jacob approached the caravan with great suspicion. He could not imagine who would know to look for him here. "Can I help you?" he asked hesitantly.

The old lady leaned out farther and stared at him and then past him as though searching for a familiar face. She frowned and ordered the boy to have the camel kneel so she could alight. With amazing agility for one so obviously old, she clambered down from the nest of skins she had been lying in. "I must see Jacob," she said.

Jacob had stood puzzling over the strange sight. The woman was vaguely familiar. She clung to the young camel boy as though she was in pain, but her head was held high and her eyes, kind and gentle, moved over the small gathering as though she was looking for someone. "I must see Jacob," she said. "I have an important message for him."

At that Jacob recognized her and ran forward. "Deborah," he said, choking back the tears. "You are Deborah, my mother's nurse."

✳ ✳ ✳

It was indeed the Deborah who had not only been his mother's nurse but had also taken care of him when he was a baby. He wanted to take her to his tent and see that she had all the attention and special care she might need. He could see that she was not well.

"No, no," she said gently smiling. "I'm tired of being closed in with the odor of unguents and ointments and goatskins. Let me sit under that lovely oak tree and get a look at your family, and then I must talk to you. I have much to tell you."

The oak tree turned out to be a very good choice. A rug was thrown down and quickly a mat with back piece and armrests was placed under the tree, and she was led to this shaded bower by Jacob himself. When she was settled and had been plied with cool melons, fresh figs, and some pomegranate wine, Jacob suggested that she rest.

"No," she said leaning forward and clutching his sleeve with her thin fingers. "I must see your wives and your children and then I must talk with you. My time may be short and I have much to tell you."

Jacob could see that she was serious, so he had Leah and Rachel come and sit with them. He then told Bilhah and Zilpah to bring his children so she could meet them. To each one she had something special to say, some unique blessing in the name of Rebekah their grandmother and Isaac their grandfather. It was obvious that she saw the sons as wonderfully handsome young men and Dinah as lovely as her grandmother. Jacob could see the surprise in his sons' eyes as they realized that she saw only the potential and knew nothing of the reality.

When the children had gone, Deborah turned to Rachel who was sitting next to her. "My dear," she said, "I can see you aren't well. It's not easy to carry a child under these circumstances."

Rachel smiled. "To one who has been childless for so long, it is no trouble." Deborah gave her a strange, sad look and patted her hand.

"The young boy with the curling hair and the questioning, intelligent look who brought me the pomegranate wine was your son?" she asked.

"Yes, he is Joseph," Rachel said proudly. Then a bit shyly she added, "I have only the one, while my sister, Leah, has so many."

Deborah seemed to notice Leah for the first time. "Her blessing is obvious," she said smiling, "while yours is all contained in one special lad."

Leah beamed and Rachel felt comforted.

It was only after they had left that Deborah turned to Jacob. "I know you think I should rest, but I have much to tell you and I must do that first."

Jacob protested but he could see that she was determined. He found himself fearing what she might have to tell him. He dreaded hearing of his mother's disappointment when he didn't get home before she died, and he was sure Esau had been critical of him. What his father was thinking he could not imagine. He almost expected her to tell him that he was no longer welcome in his father's tent.

Somehow, being a wise old woman, she was able to see all these conflicting emotions and thoughts without Jacob's telling her anything. "Don't be afraid, Jacob," she said, laying her hand on his arm and looking at him with a sharp intensity. "I am bringing you good news."

"How can it be good news when my mother has died?" he asked with a catch in his voice, turning away so she could not see the tears that welled in his eyes.

"Your mother was concerned about that, and she made me promise that I would come and help you understand."

"Understand what? It's quite obvious that I broke her heart and wasn't there when she needed me."

"No, no, you don't understand. She had peace about her going because she could see that everything was working out. It was almost as though she had to go for you to come home and work things out with your father and Esau."

This surprised Jacob. He couldn't even imagine what she meant. "My mother was at peace about her going?" he asked.

"I know it must be hard to believe but it's true. While you have been gone, Esau has had time to discover that he does not find enough challenge and excitement in managing sheep and shepherds. He has often wished you would come home and free him from the burden of his father's wells and herds."

"What does he want to do?"

"Well, you remember just as you left he went off to marry one of Ishmael's daughters. It was Ishmael who first gave him the idea of becoming a partner with him."

"A partner?"

"Yes, you see Ishmael is not only a clever trader but also has bands of men and outposts manned by his sons to protect the pharaoh's trade routes. He has wanted Esau to control Mount Seir and make the trade route safe in that whole area."

"I understand. That is the shortest route north to Damascus and Carchemish. The King's Highway, it's been called."

"Esau has been impatiently riding over to this area. He has driven out the Horites who had terrorized the caravans, and now he wants to move there with his family."

Jacob could hardly believe what he was hearing. "Then you think he really wants me to come home?"

"He wants to move to a natural fortress in the mountain of Seir; Petra, it's called. He would still keep some herds but only for his own use."

"And my mother wanted you to come and tell me this?"

"Yes, and more than that, she wanted you to know that everything had worked out for the best. Esau never did want the burden of the birthright or the blessing."

Jacob ran his hands through his hair, tugged at his short beard and smiled, then laughed. "Then I really can go home and find a welcome."

Deborah smiled. "Esau will feel relieved. He can then leave his father and his father's herds in your hands. At the same time, your father will feel greatly blessed to have so many strong young men to take care of his burdensome wealth."

"It'll take awhile to get everything ready to leave. As you saw, my wife, my dear and beloved Rachel, is great with child and not at all well."

Once more Deborah reached out and touched his arm. "There are many hard things that must be endured, but that is the only way we become strong. Your own mother learned that. It was not easy losing you and dealing every day with Isaac's blindness and the willful wives Esau married."

"But she died without ever seeing me again or my children."

"That was another heartache, but she had come to see that in some ways it was her own fault."

"Her own fault?"

"She often told me that if she had trusted Isaac's God to work things out and not tried to manage everything, you probably would never have had to leave."

"She must have suffered terribly."

"She felt guilty that you had to leave and that Esau harbored such hatred. She blamed herself for everything."

"She shouldn't have. Without Esau's threat I probably would never have gone to Haran. I would never have married Rachel. How poor my life would have been without my children and my wives."

"Perhaps she did have a hint of this. Just before she died, she called me to her side and said, 'I have to trust that things have not gone too badly for my Jacob.'"

Deborah studied his face to see his response.

He smiled. "I wish I could have come in time to reassure her."

"What would you have told her?" Deborah pressed on relentlessly.

"I would have told her," Jacob said, "that from the very first night I spent alone, here in this very place, the God of my father and grandfather made Himself known to me and directed my path. I went out with only a walking stick and have come back with wives, children, and servants. My wealth exceeds that of either my father or my grandfather. But most important, Elohim Himself has given me a new name. A wonderful name."

"And what is the new name?"

238

"Israel, he called me Israel."

"Then you have found blessing even in the difficult way you were forced to take."

"That is true."

They sat silently watching a hawk dip and soar over the valley before them as they contemplated all that had happened to both of them. Finally Deborah spoke, "As you may have noticed, I am not well. I have prayed only that I might have strength to come and give you the message your dear mother entrusted to me. Now that I have done that, I can depart in peace."

Jacob gave her a startled glance. "No, you mustn't think that . . ."

Deborah patted his arm. "When I am gone," she said, "I would like to be buried under this tree."

Jacob could not bring himself to speak. He was too emotionally moved, but he nodded and reached out to press her fragile, long fingers.

During the weeks that followed, Jacob, his wives, and his children became better acquainted with this wise old woman. She told them many stories of their grandmother Rebekah. Their favorite was always the story of how she came from Haran to marry Abraham's son Isaac. "Isaac loved her the moment he saw her," she would say, "and she thought he was more handsome than she had even imagined."

She would usually end her stories by telling them, "Isaac was the son chosen by Elohim and his father for the birthright and the blessing. Isaac always thought Rebekah was his blessing, and he never fretted over the providence that gave them only two sons, your father and his twin brother, Esau. He has lived longer than his father, and in all this time he has had only the one wife and the two sons."

It never failed that one of Jacob's sons would look around at his brothers and then ask, "And who has the blessing now?"

Deborah would lean back and study them with a piercing, searching gaze as though she were trying to search out which one of them might inherit the blessing. "Now your father has both the birthright and the blessing," she would say.

\* \* \*

Some weeks passed as Jacob prepared his family to ride down the ridge to meet his father, who was camped under the great oaks of Mamre. This period of preparation was a happy time of expectation and celebration. Jacob and Rachel were looking forward to the birth of the new baby; Leah was once again busy seeing that all the practical matters of their family went smoothly. Dinah was silent and withdrawn but found some sense of peace in helping her mother. All was going so well, and then once again tragedy struck and the happy times came to an abrupt halt.

The first of the hardships was the death of Deborah. Even though they had expected it, they were all surprised at how much she meant to them. As was the custom, they wrapped her in a covering of woven reeds and buried her that evening beneath the oak tree she had grown to love.

Jacob grieved openly with his wives and their children joining him. Until this time no one in their family had died, and so they wept not only for their loss but in the sudden realization of life's frailty. "We will call this the oak of weeping," Jacob said as they were all packed and ready to move on.

With the death of Deborah, a nagging fear settled over Jacob. Rachel's pregnancy was not going smoothly. She was in a great deal of pain. *What would I do, how could I live if Rachel should be taken from me? She never complains. She wants this child so badly.*

It hurt him to think that part of her wanting was tangled with her constant need to compete with her sister for his love and approval. It was all so nebulous. So unreachable. He had loved her and only her from the moment he first saw her.

He watched her closely now and saw how pale and weak she was. At times she clung to him as though she were afraid of something. Often at night she would wake up in a cold sweat and cling to him. "Jacob, you must promise me," she would say, "when I am gone you must protect my son. Leah's sons are jealous of him. They are capable of great cruelty."

Jacob was startled by her choice of words, not "if" but "when," she had said. Jacob would hold her and reassure her that he would watch out for Joseph. "But nothing can harm our son," he would tell her. "Elohim will watch over him and preserve him from evil."

"But sometimes even if we pray, things go wrong," she said.

Jacob had often had the same thought. However, his own experience had taught him that though at times everything seemed to be going wrong, if one just waited and withheld judgment, things eventually would come out right again. What had seemed so hopelessly tangled could even become a blessing when left in Elohim's care.

He tried to find words to comfort her, but there seemed to be nothing that would ease her pain or bring her peace. *If we could just get to the town of Ephrath where there would be proper houses and midwives who could help her,* he kept thinking as the camels plodded on and no village was in sight.

## 23

The road leading around the small city of Jerusalem was rough and stony. It bordered a brook called the Kidron. Jacob, with his large family, came along this road and, seeing a pleasant grove of olive and myrtle trees, decided to stop so Rachel could rest. He was troubled by her obvious discomfort and, at times, real pain.

"I will be stronger in the morning," Rachel said as Bilhah helped her down from the litter and led her to a cushioned seat in the shade of a large olive tree.

"Reuben," Jacob said, "come with me. We must go up to the city and tell them of our plight. We will need their permission to camp here."

When the elders of the city heard their story and determined that Jacob was indeed the grandson of Abraham, Melchizedek's old friend, they gladly gave their permission. The story of Melchizedek's meeting with Abraham and Abraham's generosity in paying him a tenth of the spoils taken in battle had been told over and over until they knew it well.

They not only gave their permission but ordered supplies of cool wine and big round loaves of freshly baked bread to be given them for their evening meal. Because Jacob feared that the elders may have heard of the massacre at Shechem, he hastened to assure them that they would stay only for the night. He could tell by their quick glances back and forth among themselves that they were relieved. "Stay," they chorused, "stay as long as you like."

When Jacob returned to the camp with the news that they could rest there for the night, everyone was relieved. Bilhah almost wept with gratitude. "My lord," she said, "Rachel has only this moment fallen into a deep and troubled sleep. I bathed her poor, swollen hands and feet in cool water from the brook and made her an herbal drink."

"I must see her," Jacob said.

"She's sleeping," Bilhah warned him. "Go and eat. There's nothing you can do."

Jacob moved past her as though he had not heard. Determined not to wake Rachel, he quietly sank down on the mat beside her. To his surprise she reached for his hand, breathed a sigh of relief, and went back to sleep. He sat without moving, studying the dear, loved face and pondering the strangeness of things. It was obvious that no one came into the world in any other way and no one, no matter how elegant or important, could leave without dying and being buried.

He shifted uneasily. He did not want to carry those thoughts to their conclusion. He preferred to think that with a bit of rest Rachel would be all right.

It was late afternoon and from a distance came the rhythmic, swinging chant of harvesters. Looking up he could see men driving their animals around the threshing floor on a great rock that rose above the city to the north. Nearby he could hear his wives giving orders in whispers and his sons guiding the sheep down to the brook with soft cooing sounds. In the darkening sky above the olive trees, small sparrows dipped and swooped, then settled on the lower branches to rest.

Evening came quickly. It was announced first by the call of watchmen on the city walls above them. Then the hollow, strident tones of a ram's horn signaled the end of day and the closing of the city gates. In their camp, fires were lit and the tempting odor of roasting game filled the night air. Later, much later, there was singing. On this night it was the lonesome, haunting songs they sang, with no exchange of the usual jokes or dancing.

Joseph came from the fire to where Jacob still sat holding Rachel's limp hand. He didn't say anything but crept close to his father and was soon asleep. Jacob dozed off hearing only the periodic, eerie call of the night watchmen on the city wall announcing the progression of the night. When Rachel stirred he gave her sips of hot broth brought to her by Leah. Then finally, even he drifted off into a sound and dreamless sleep.

In the morning, before dawn, Jacob roused and noticed that Rachel was having periods of contracting, wrenching pain. She would be in real labor soon, and they must try to reach his father's camp near the Oaks of Mamre. With growing alarm, he ordered everyone to quickly gather up their things. "We must be on our way out of this valley before sunrise," he said.

Just as the sky was lightening in the east, they headed down the road that led around the city to the Hebron road. They stopped briefly at a cave that contained a spring to fill their water skins. "It's called Gihon," a shepherd standing nearby told them. "Gihon means 'bursting forth,' because it flows out in bursts," he said. The water was cool and refreshing and they felt encouraged.

It was the end of summer and almost time for the early rains. The brief light at dawn quickly faded and soon dark clouds rolled in, covering the sky. There was an unwelcome chill in the air, a barren look to everything. Instead of the bright flowers that carpeted the ground in spring and summer, there were now only the thickets of thorns and leafless vines hanging over the stone terraces. Most of the olives had been harvested, and only rarely did they see women out beating the branches to gather the last green nub. These trees still had their leaves though they were now a gray-green, dusty and tattered.

Fear clutched at Jacob's heart as he nudged the pack animals along. He knew they must hurry, but to get to his father's camp began to seem impossible. It could be that in the very act of hurrying, they would bring on some disaster. He struggled to remember how far it was to the Oaks of Mamre from the fortress of Jerusalem. *Perhaps, if we cannot get that far, then dear God, let us at least make it to Ephrath.*

They passed a cluster of small, stone houses and were told the place was called Giloh. The women stood in their doorways staring at them with wide, troubled eyes. They had heard that the wife of the wealthy prince was already in labor. No one threw stones at them, and even the dogs didn't bark as they passed by onto the high plane above the village.

They were encouraged when at last they began to catch glimpses of Ephrath in the distance. "If we can just get to the city and find proper lodging," Jacob urged, "there is a well on the north side and many caves where we could find shelter if there is no room in the inn."

They had not gone much farther before Jacob ordered them to stop. "We must let Rachel get down and rest a bit," he said, mopping his brow. There was a small cave nearby, and he decided this was the only suitable place for her to rest.

Leah came forward and took charge. She first checked Rachel to determine her condition, and then quickly ordered the men to go to the well and get as much water as possible.

Jacob didn't move. He looked at her with alarm and then frustration as he said, "You sound as though you think the child will be born here."

Leah didn't even look at him but kept helping Rachel get as comfortable as possible. "That's right," she said. "This child is on its way and it is not going to be easy."

Rachel didn't seem to hear her, but Jacob did. He grabbed Leah's arm and pulled her away, demanding, "What do you mean? She can't have a child out here by the road."

Leah impatiently tried to pull away. "We can't control that," she sputtered. "We can only make the best of things."

Jacob pulled her around so he could look at her directly. "Is she . . . is she in any trouble?" he asked, cringing as Rachel gave a piercing cry.

Leah whirled to look at her sister and pulled away from Jacob. "The child's not positioned right, and that means plenty of trouble."

Jacob lunged forward in a desperate effort to help Rachel, but Leah pushed him back. "There's nothing you can do but pray and see that the boys get water and build a fire. Now, go! We'll do the best we can."

As Leah turned away, Jacob saw red blood spurting like a fountain and he fled a short distance away and sank down on an outcropping of rock. He was far enough away that he could barely see what was happening and could not hear what was being said. "Oh, God of my fathers, take pity on Rachel," he cried over and over again. Then burying his head in his hands, he pled, "Don't be angry that she carried off the idols. She doesn't understand. She wants a child, that's all she wants. She just wants a child."

Time passed and he grew more anxious. Something was wrong. In desperation he cried, "Why Rachel? You can have Leah or Bilhah or Zilpah, but not Rachel, not my only love Rachel. Don't take Rachel. Rachel's my joy, my life. Take anything I have, but not Rachel," he pled desperately.

It seemed that hours had passed when Leah motioned for him to come. He hurried down and knelt beside Rachel. He tried to hide the shock of seeing her so pale and weak. He searched her face and then looked at Leah and the women, seeking reassurance that she was all right.

He felt a gentle tug on his sleeve and saw that Rachel wanted him to see the child. For the first time he looked at the bundle she held. He had seen so many round, red faces with tufts of curling, black hair; he didn't expect to feel anything unusual. "I'm calling him Ben-oni, son of my sorrow," she whispered with difficulty as she studied his face to see if he understood.

"Ben-oni," he repeated puzzled.

"I'll not be here to enjoy him," she said with a catch in her voice. She bent her head and with a terrible tenderness kissed the dark curls.

Seeing how much she treasured this tiny token of their love, Jacob looked again and was surprised at the surge of emotion that choked him so he couldn't speak.

They called Joseph and he came and knelt beside his mother, all the time struggling to keep from crying. Rachel was now too weak to speak, but she moved Jacob's hand so that it covered Joseph's, then with tears dropping onto the dark curls of the sleeping child, her head fell forward, her hand loosened, and they knew she was gone.

Even though they had been aware of her weakness, none of them had imagined she could leave them so quickly. Jacob's other wives had all survived having children and no one had thought such disaster could strike so suddenly and at such an unlikely time and place.

Only Leah had the presence of mind to lift the baby from Rachel's arms. She handed him to Jacob. He was already in swaddling clothes and wrapped in Rachel's mantle. Jacob buried his head in the folds of the white homespun, and smelling the lavender of Rachel's garments, he wept.

Everyone knew she must be buried before sundown and they wondered how it could be managed. To their surprise Jacob handed the new arrival to Leah and then took charge. He first took the cloak Rachel had woven for him and, removing it from his own shoulders, gently wrapped her in it. Joseph brought a wreath of sand lilies and black iris to place on her head. This reminded Jacob of the floral wreath she had worn when he had first seen her at the well in Haran. It moved him so deeply he had to turn away until he could regain his composure.

With a heartrending sob, Jacob placed her in the cave. Then with feverish activity, he encouraged his sons to join him in gathering stones to build a monument to mark the site.

When it was finished, he sought out Leah. Taking the baby from her, he announced, "I intend to call him Benjamin, son of my right hand."

* * *

The next day they pressed on to camp beyond the tower of Eber. The plan was to stay there briefly while preparing themselves for their arrival at Isaac's camp beside the Oaks of Mamre.

Jacob was so consumed with his grief and pity for his two motherless sons that he was totally unaware of the growing resentment of his other wives and their sons. Reuben, the eldest, was the most affected. He saw the love his father had for Joseph and this new child, and a great fear and resentment rose within him.

It was as though Jacob suddenly had no children but these two children of Rachel. Reuben had been able to endure his preference of Rachel over his own mother, but now his obvious favoritism of Rachel's sons was too painful.

When he tried to talk to his father, it was as though Jacob didn't even hear what he was saying. When Reuben thoughtfully and patiently waited on him, Jacob took it for granted. Finally, when Reuben sought his father out to discuss his future, Jacob didn't have enough time. Reuben had been led to believe that he, as the eldest, was the one to receive the birthright and the blessing. Now he strongly suspected that his father would choose Joseph. Then there was the matter of his marriage. If he, Reuben, was to receive the birthright, some thought should be given to his marriage.

All these concerns had been pushed aside for the greater matter of Rachel and her children. Jacob seemed consumed with their welfare. He had for some time openly favored Joseph, and now they had all seen him rename this new child "son of my right hand." What could that mean but that he was thinking of giving Benjamin the birthright or the blessing?

Others felt equally left out. Bilhah had always depended on Rachel's friendship to make her feel needed and loved. Now that was gone. Leah had found a wet nurse for the new baby, and Bilhah was left to grieve and mull over her new situation. She had always shared Rachel's tent, and now that tent had temporarily become her own. It was filled with Rachel's belongings; in the future, when Joseph married, it would become his wife's tent.

Bilhah was still young. She had borne two sons with little or no attention from Jacob. Gradually as she had seen the love and concern he had lavished on Rachel and Rachel's sons, she had become resentful. She felt cheated. She had at last become resigned to the fact that no matter what she did, Jacob would never love her.

With these feelings it was quite natural that she should also be very aware of Reuben's frustration. He was a proud and sensitive young man and would never think of complaining to any of his brothers or even his father. It didn't seem as threatening to come to Bilhah's tent, where he could talk over his situation and find a sympathetic ear.

"My father has never come out and said that I am the one to receive the birthright and the blessing, but I am the oldest," he confided one evening as he sat eating the honey cakes she had baked.

"But this need not concern you now," she said.

"But don't you see, I should have taken a wife long ago."

"I don't understand."

"If I am to have the blessing of my father, I can't marry just anyone."

"And . . ."

"When I mention this to my father, he never answers. He is only concerned with his two favorites." He said this with such an air of bitterness that Bilhah was immediately pleased.

"And if you talk to your mother . . ."

"She can only warn me to wait. 'If you marry the wrong person,' she says, 'you could lose the blessing.'"

"Then you want this blessing that much?"

"It means everything to me."

In this way an understanding grew between Reuben and Bilhah. She who had been given to Jacob to bear him sons had no claim on his affections. Now suddenly, she was flattered to find this young, handsome man interested in her. It was not long until the exchange of mutual grievances grew into a bond, and then into a forbidden sexual intimacy.

Joseph was the one to discover their secret. One evening, coming to his mother's tent looking for Bilhah, he discovered the two together. They were so engrossed in each other that they neither heard nor saw him. He staggered back, letting the tent flap fall quietly in place. He was careful not to make any noise. Then, while struggling to control the choking, tearing waves of shock, he hurried to a secluded place under the wide limbs of an ancient fig tree.

Dark clouds of loneliness engulfed him. Reuben had been his friend and Bilhah an important part of his world. Now to the grief over his mother's death was added the burden of this terrible revelation. He saw it as an affront to his father. Young as he was, he knew that to lie with the wife of a tribal leader was to lay claim to his position. Reuben, his friend and big brother, was not just committing a great sin but was challenging his father's leadership.

He was also aware of his father's continuing grief. Jacob, now called Israel, moved among them in a daze. He didn't eat and there were dark circles under his eyes from lack of sleep. What would the knowledge of this treachery do to his beloved father?

At first he determined to shield his father from the knowledge. Then he changed his mind. If Reuben, by this action, was trying to displace his father, then his father must be warned.

That night, when Jacob was alone, Joseph crept into his tent and as gently as possible told him what he had seen. It was dark, with just a small oil lamp burning, so Joseph could not see his father's face but heard the groan. He felt his father's hand stiffen then withdraw from his shoulder. He heard him mutter, "It is too much. First Simeon, then Levi, and now Reuben. Where will it all end? Who will be worthy of my father's blessing?"

Joseph was surprised that his father made no move against Reuben. The subject was never mentioned, but Reuben, who must have felt his father's displeasure, made no more trips to Bilhah's tent. Instead Joseph noticed that his father set his face, now hard as flint, toward the Oaks of Mamre and Isaac's camp.

\* \* \*

Though Jacob was numb with grief and disturbed by the actions of his sons, he managed to observe the expected niceties of one coming home. He sent runners with rich gifts and shepherds with some of his prize goats. Remembering his father was blind and could not read, he singled out a young boy who had the talent of chanting poetry suited to the occasion. The boy was quick to size up the situation and weave gracious, rhyming phrases in honor of the dignitary chosen.

As Jacob approached the oak grove, he had to stiffen his resolve to return to his father. He was not at all sure of his reception. So much had gone wrong and he felt he could not endure one more disappointment.

He had thought everything would be easy after wrestling with the stranger at the Jabbok and getting the new name. He had bought the land at Shechem, dug the well, and was ready to build a new life for himself and his family. He had been so sure that nothing but blessing was about to be heaped upon him.

Then there had been the tragedy of Shechem, their burying the idols, and then going up to Bethel. Once again at Bethel, everything had felt so right. The dark stain of Shechem could never be wiped away, but they had settled things with Elohim. Building the altar and making the sacrifice had made it possible for them to make a fresh start and try to forget their dark and devious mistakes. They had feasted and sung the old songs, put on the new garments; they were all ready to start over again. Everything was going to be right from that time on.

As he left Bethel with his new name firmly in place and a glow of excitement for the expected blessings he now felt worthy to receive, he was suddenly confronted with the greatest trial of his life. In one terrible blow Rachel was taken from him and his firstborn son had committed the terrible, unthinkable sin that would forever cut him off from the blessing.

Now he fully expected some terrible disaster to await him at the Oaks of Mamre. Perhaps Esau would regret their reconciliation. Maybe his father would renounce him for the old deception, turn him out, take away the birthright and the blessing.

To come home and find it was no longer the home he had imagined could be devastating. What could home possibly be like without his mother? There would be a sting in remembering her loving touch and fond acceptance of her sons. He did not know how he could endure it. So much had happened, so many disappointments, such tricks played on him. He was a different Jacob coming home than the young man who had left. Who was left to understand him now that both Rachel and his mother were gone?

As it turned out, Jacob-Israel's homecoming was far more wonderful than he could ever have imagined. Since his father had been told that he was coming, Jacob found him sitting on cushions brought to the door of his tent. The seat of honor was reserved for him on his father's right hand, while Esau sat on the left. Isaac was too feeble to rise, but he reached out and pulled Jacob down to him with a great sob. "My son, my long-lost son," he kept repeating over and over.

Jacob was so overcome with emotion someone had to nudge and remind him to introduce his wives and his children. As Jacob did this he realized how astonishing it must seem to his father, who with great difficulty produced only two children. "I have been greatly blessed," he said. "I have wives and children, sheep and goats, servants, and stores of precious metals."

When he finished showing his father his entire family, he hurried on to recount all that had befallen him since he had left home. He did not hesitate to tell his story truthfully, recounting both the good and the bad. When he told of Rachel's death, his father wept, saying, "I know, I know my son. I lost your mother not too long ago. Now I have only waited for your coming before joining her."

Jacob realized how welcome he was when Esau pointed out that his father had ordered ten sheep slaughtered and roasted, one hundred loaves of bread baked, and the best wine brought out and served.

After they had all finished eating, there was singing and dancing and recounting various stories of their family's past. Esau's family viewed their new cousins with interest and were not pleased when Esau told them they would be staying only until his brother was comfortably settled.

The next morning Esau took Jacob aside and explained. "I have only waited for your coming to join our uncle Ishmael in a new trading venture. We have driven the Horite giants out of Mount Seir and their stronghold called Petra. I, with my sons and servants, will protect the pharaoh's trade route going north to Damascus. Of course I will extract payment for this protection. It is much more to my liking than herding sheep and digging wells."

"And Ishmael? How did this come about with our uncle?"

"You forget I'm married to his daughter."

"And he can trust you."

"I suppose."

"When will you leave?"

"I will stay only long enough to help you get adjusted. It may be that our father will not live much longer. He has said he only wanted to live long enough to see your safe return."

Jacob was deeply moved by this bit of information. He had not imagined his coming or going meant that much to his father. "You think he will not live much longer?"

"He's very weak. He talks more and more about his death. It seems to comfort him that he will be buried in the cave with Rebekah. He moved to the Oaks of Mamre so he could be closer to the cave where she was buried."

"I would appreciate your staying until he goes," Jacob said. "Mount Seir is a long way off."

* * *

It so happened that Isaac died a short time after Jacob's return. He had lived long enough to take joy in Jacob's recounting of his many encounters with Elohim. Most of all he loved to hear how Elohim had given him the new name. "Israel, He called you Israel," he said with a slight smile. "What a splendid name it is."

He died with both his sons at his side and his many grandchildren gathered around. There was a great look of contentment about him as they wrapped him in the finely woven shroud. He had lived long and well and had loved with none of the complications of either his father or his sons.

As Jacob-Israel stood waiting for the great stone to be rolled in place over the tomb's opening, he pondered all the times the family had gathered here in their sorrow to bury someone they loved. He briefly wondered if he himself would be buried here, and would it be Leah who would be placed here beside him? He wondered about Esau and all their children. He wondered if they would all be gathered here in this final resting place or would they, like Rachel, be buried along some lonely road on their way home.

He said goodbye to Esau, knowing he would not see him often but knowing that they were both at peace. Esau had his kind of blessing with his large family and his chance for wealth and position. Jacob, on the other hand, treasured above all else the excitement of getting to know Elohim, even in a limited sense, and being a part of His purposes.

# Epilogue

$J$acob's troubles were not over. Jealousy and hatred led the brothers to sell Joseph to some traders going down to Egypt. Jacob was told he had been killed. This was the final cruel trick that was played on Jacob.

In an amazing turnaround, Joseph was richly blessed in Egypt and saved his whole family from starvation. We read that he brought his father down to Egypt, where he was presented to the pharaoh and where he actually pronounced a blessing on the pharaoh.

Jacob gave each of his sons a word of blessing before he died, and as Joseph requested, gave a special blessing to Joseph's two sons, Ephraim and Manasseh. Ephraim was the younger, and when Jacob placed his right hand on his head, Joseph thought he was mistaken. "No," Jacob said, "I know what I am doing. Manasseh too shall become a great nation but Ephraim, the younger, shall become greater."

Jacob then instructed his sons to take his body back to Canaan and bury it in the cave with his ancestors. Joseph had his father's body embalmed, and then with a great number of Pharaoh's counselors and senior officers of the land, a great number of chariots and cavalry as well as all of Joseph's family went to Atad—meaning the place of brambles—beyond the Jordan. Here they held a great and splendid funeral. Then his family went the rest of the way to the cave of Mach-pelah and buried him beside Leah and his ancestors.

At Joseph's death he predicted that at some time in the future the family would return to Canaan. "When you return," he said, "you must take my body back with you so that I may be buried in Canaan."

This was done. In Joshua 24:32 we read that Joseph was buried in the parcel of land that Jacob had purchased so long before from the sons of Hamor at Shechem.

At this same place, on the West Bank near the site of the ancient city of Shechem, and on this same parcel of land, is the well that Jacob dug. Today many tourists come here to drink of the clear, cool water of this well. At one time a large church was built over this spot, but now there is only a small edifice protecting the well.

Tourists can still see the tomb of Rachel on the road to Bethlehem. It has had many exterior changes over the years, but the place has always been noted.

Then there is the site of the Oaks of Mamre, which until recently had a few ancient oak trees that were reported to be, if not the original oaks, at least oaks that grew from seedlings of those oaks. Not far from this place, a mosque has been built over the cave of Mach-pelah, where all the patriarchs are buried with their wives.

If you are wondering who received the birthright, you will have to turn to 1 Chronicles 5:1, which tells us that though Israel's firstborn son was Reuben, he dishonored his father by sleeping with one of his wives, and his birthright went to his half brother Joseph by being given to Joseph's sons.

# Character List

Nahor: Brother to Abraham, father to Bethuel, grandfather to Rebekah and Laban

Rebekah: Nahor's granddaughter, Laban's sister, youngest daughter to Bethuel and Milcah

Laban: Nahor and Milcah's grandson, Rebekah's brother, youngest son to Bethuel and Milcah

Bethuel: Rebekah and Laban's father, Nahor's son, Milcah's husband

Terah: An ancestor (Abraham and Nahor's father)

Deborah: Rebekah's nurse

Abraham: Rebekah and Laban's great-uncle, Sarah's husband

Milcah: Nahor's wife

Reumah: Nahor's concubine

Barida: Laban's wife

Nazzim: Barida's father

Isaac: Abraham and Sarah's son

Keturah: Abraham's concubine

Eleazar: Abraham's old friend and chief steward

Ishmael: Abraham's son by Hagar

Zimran: Abraham and Keturah's son

Anatah: One of the king's daughters, attracted to Isaac

Zeb: A young goatherd from the family of Urim

Judith: Esau's first wife who eventually returns to her family

Bashemath: Esau's second wife who also returns

Adah: Esau's third wife, sister to Bashemath

Elon: Adah and Bashemath's father

Beeri: Judith's father

Zibeon: Esau's friend

Ahoolibama: Zibeon's daughter, Esau's fourth wife

Reuel: Esau's first son with Adah

Eliphaz: Another son of Esau

Rachel: Laban's younger daughter
Leah: Laban's older daughter
Reuben: Leah's first son with Jacob
Simeon: Leah's second son with Jacob
Levi: Leah's third son with Jacob
Judah: Leah's fourth son with Jacob
Zilpah: Leah's serving girl
Bilhah: Rachel's serving girl
Dan: Bilhah's first son that she gave to Rachel
Naphtali: Bilhah's second son that she gave to Rachel
Gad: Zilpah's first son given to Leah
Asher: Zilpah's second son given to Leah
Issachar: Leah's fifth son with Jacob
Zebulun: Leah's sixth son with Jacob
Joseph: Rachel's firstborn with Jacob
Dinah: Leah's daughter with Jacob
Benjamin: Rachel's second born with Jacob
Manasseh: Joseph's older son
Ephraim: Joseph's younger son

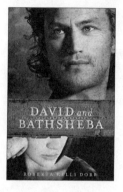 

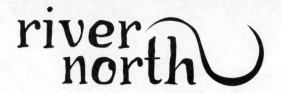

*Thank you! We are honored that you took the time out of your busy schedule to read this book. If you enjoyed what you read, would you consider sharing the message with others?*

- Write a review online at amazon.com, bn.com, goodreads.com, cbd.com.

- Recommend this book to friends in your book club, workplace, church, school, classes, or small group.

- Go to facebook.com/RiverNorthFiction, "like" the page and post a comment as to what you enjoyed the most.

- Mention this book in a Facebook post, Twitter update, Pinterest pin, or a blog post.

- Pick up a copy for someone you know who would be encouraged by this message.

- Subscribe to our newsletter for information on upcoming titles, inside information on discounts and promotions, and learn more about your favorite authors at RiverNorthFiction.com.

# midday connection

Discover a safe place to authentically process life's journey on **Midday Connection**, hosted by Anita Lustrea and Melinda Schmidt. This live radio program is designed to encourage women with a focus on growing the whole person: body, mind, and soul. You'll grow toward spiritual freedom and personal transformation as you learn who God is and who He created us to be.

**www.middayconnection.org**

MOODYRADIO

*Where you turn. For life.*

# the LAND and the BOOK
## with Dr. Charlie Dyer

Dr. Charlie Dyer provides biblical insight into the complex tapestry of people and events that make up Israel and the Middle East. Each week he presents an in-depth look at biblical, historical, archeological, and prophetic events and their relevance for today.

**www.thelandandthebook.org**

**MOODYRADIO**
*Where you turn. For life.*